THE
BUILDERS

Jeanne Sommers

D0937782

A Dell/Bryans Book

Published by
Dell Publishing Co., Inc.
1 Dag Hammarskjold Plaza
New York, New York 10017

Dell ® TM 681510, Dell Publishing Co., Inc.

ISBN: 0-440-01389-5

Printed in the United States of America

First printing—October 1979

THE
BUILDERS

1

Liberty Wells O'Lee. Not Liberty Wells but Liberty Wells O'Lee!

Even after two months of marriage Liberty liked repeating the name, for it excited her, filled her with a kind of rapture she'd never known before. Dan O'Lee was hers forevermore. They could put the past and the horrors of war out of their minds. It was to be a new beginning, a second birth.

"Thunderation! What damn fool devised this stupidity?"

The complaint, in a booming-baritone voice came from their hotel bathroom. A moment later Dan's rugged, worried face appeared in the doorway. He frowned when he saw his wife lost in thought at the window rather than sitting at the dressing table.

"Liberty?" Hiding his annoyance, Dan took a few hesitant steps into the room. "The Judah's carriage will call for us soon . . ." Try as he might, Dan couldn't mask the slight limp he'd had since being wounded at the Battle of Shiloh the April before. Then, as he peered over Liberty's back, his tone softened: "Come on, Lib, let's get moving. You'll have a long time to study this new town."

7

Liberty turned to him quickly. Her green eyes danced with excitement.

"Oh, Dan," she cried. "I still can hardly believe we're here."

He grinned at her. "Well, as for me, Sacramento doesn't strike me much different from when I was in these parts as a boy, taking gold out of the ground. And I'm not that much different. Couldn't stand collars and ties then and still can't."

Liberty rose, laughing. "Because you won't admit that a simple little thing like a bow can defeat you. Here, let me."

Deftly, she fixed the black silk tie around his white starched collar and tied it. She patted his shoulders when she was done.

"Now you look handsome, you old bear."

He grumbled. "Don't feel old. Feel like an idiot. Look at these damn tight pants. My legs feel like they had corsets around them."

Liberty smiled. She eyed him speculatively.

"Tonight, Dan O'Lee, you are to be a gentleman. You are not a prospector, a Union soldier, or even a self-taught engineer. Mr. Huntington said this was proper attire for the affair and I'll not have you looking any different from the other gentlemen present."

Dan pulled her close, tilted her chin and rewarded her interest with a long, lingering kiss.

"Oh, Dan," she whispered, "I love you so very much."

"And I . . ." Dan did not finish. Words of love often embarrassed him. He let the touch of his lips to her forehead finish the statement for him. "Libby, best get your dress on now."

"And now, you can help me. Just wait until you see the gown Anna Judah helped me select at Crocker's."

"Is that where she took you? You certainly know

how to spend a man's money before he even earns it."

Liberty made a wry face. "Crockers, my dear," she cooed, perfectly imitating the tones of New England-educated Anna Judah, "is the only place in town for wonderful new patterns in calico and dimity—to say nothing of crepe."

Liberty took the crepe up from the four-poster bed, where she'd laid it. As Dan came to her, she dropped her robe and raised her bare arms so that he could lift the filmy skirts up, then down over her. In the long mirror against the wall she saw how the soft green gown almost perfectly matched her eyes. Anna had good taste. But then, Anna also had had eight years experience with the people they were to meet and knew how highly they rated first impressions.

As Liberty continued her appraisal of the gown, which was rather revealing, she heard Dan's querulous gasp:

"Your shoulders and bust, Libby! They're hardly covered!"

"Nonsense!" She touched the lace that extended from her throat to her bosom; she thought her breasts quite amply covered. "Mr. Huntington didn't seem to think so." That, she reflected at once, was not quite true. Huntington had commented at length about her ability to make the gown seem "extra special," and she'd known instantly what he'd meant.

"Huntington?" Dan said. "Why was he along on your shopping trip?"

"He wasn't silly. He came into the store to see Charles Crocker just after I had tried the dress on. That's all."

Dan had no intention of dropping the subject.

"Not quite. Is Huntington the one who arranged the line of credit for that dress and my suit?"

"He made it simpler, yes. What's the problem?"

Dan frowned. "Damn it, Liberty, Huntington and Crocker are only two of the four men who will be paying my salary. Ted Judah warned me back in Washington that there's plenty of contention in the group. I don't want to get caught in the middle and have Huntington expect me to side with him because he paid our way to California."

Seeing his worriment, Liberty squeezed his arm. "Don't look a gift horse in the mouth, Dan. Didn't Mr. Huntington make it quite clear that the trip on Commodore Vanderbilt's clipper ship was our wedding present? If we're in debt to anyone, it's to that Colonel Seymour for recommending you to Ted Judah and Collis Huntington in the first place."

Dan wasn't appeased. What he was getting into was big business, the railroad business, and he just didn't know his way around in it. For instance, he knew Colonel Silas Seymour by reputation only; he'd never met the man. He was aware of little more than that Robinson, Seymour & Company had built the 22-mile Sacramento Line for Ted Judah up to Placerville, Grass Valley and other mining centers. But according to Judah and Huntington, Colonel Seymour was well-acquainted with the engineering work he, Dan, had done while a Union army officer and had recommended him so highly that Judah wanted him as a consulting engineer on the Central Pacific Railroad project.

Dan's thoughts went back to the time Judah had visited him in the army hospital in Missouri. He'd thought the Yankee humorless and opinionated, but it turned out that they had an obsession in common: to build things other men said couldn't be built. Dan guessed he could understand why Judah was called "Crazy" Judah, for he'd dreamed up a transcontinental railroad that would have to go through the almost impassable barrier of the Sierra Nevada range. But Dan had once seen the railroad Judah had built over the Niagara Gorge, another so-called impossible project of his, and he welcomed the opportunity to work with him.

Trouble was, Ted Judah, like Dan, was only a hireling.

Things got complicated when, on their second meeting, Judah brought Collis P. Huntington along to the hospital. Almost the first thing Huntington did was make a play for Liberty; it was as if he were there interviewing her for the job rather than Dan. The man had powerful connections. He was so sure he had Dan in his pocket that he had used his influence to get him an immediate medical discharge from the army. The order bore the signature of A. Lincoln. It was granted on the President's belief that Dan O'Lee could best serve the cause of the Union by helping to build the railroad, rather than by going back into battle.

That first display of Collis Huntington's power had stunned Dan. The second had left him wary. The man had taken it upon himself to arrange for Liberty and Dan's wedding, imposing himself upon the service to give the bride away. He made their wedding reception a kind of double ceremony, for on that muggy first of July, 1862, President Lincoln signed the Pacific Railroad Act.

A jubilant Collis Huntington left the next day for California. In his wake he left instructions for Judah and, for Dan, a three months salary advance and a somewhat too large wedding gift.

All in all, Dan was suspicious of his good fortune. While Ted Judah lobbied in Washington for the money to buy rail ties, spikes, locomotives and cars, all badly needed for the war effort but essential at that moment if they were to make the long voyage down around Cape Horn and back up to California, Dan observed the action from a distance, let his wounds heal—and Liberty carefully hoarded his money. Mistrusting Huntington, he feared the enterprise might blow up at any moment.

They'd sailed from New York in mid-November, shortly after Dan left the hospital. The five weeks' voyage around the Cape might have made for a wonderful shipboard honeymoon, except that Ted Judah was along, wanting to acquaint Dan seemingly with every detail of the project.

Consequently, Liberty and Anna Judah had a chance to cement their own relationship. Liberty also met a young girl traveling with the Judahs, and was intrigued by her. The girl, who was about 18, was Lydia Mae Tedder. She was quite mysterious. Through the influence of Anna Judah, she had gone to New England schools for seven years. She was both well-bred and witty. But her origins were obscure, and she refused to clarify them, except by referring to her mixed "pioneer" and "royal" family background. Liberty had not liked the sound of either side of her family, but she did like the girl herself. She felt warm at the prospect of having two friends like Anna and Lydia when she got to California.

So Liberty was relatively content the night of the party in Sacramento. It was Dan who had these "business problems" on his mind. He still felt himself at the mercy of a man he felt he couldn't really trust.

A roll of wheels on gravel drew Liberty to the window. "It's their carriage," she said, "we'd best go on down."

Wordlessly, Dan helped Liberty into the wrap that was designed to go with her gown, drew on the frock coat that went with his suit and stubbornly plopped a stove pipe hat onto his head.

"Libby?" he asked. "Are you scared?"

It was the moment of truth she had been praying he wouldn't ask her to face.

"Terribly," she answered truthfully. "It's odd, but all I can think about is what Lydia May told me about her mother and grandmother. They're hosting the party, after all. And Lydia made them sound so . . . so . . ."

"High and mighty?" he chided. "Well, you've got some background of your own to fall back upon, remember. Your father owned a passel of land and he was an army officer, to boot."

Liberty smiled weakly. "That hardly seems adequate at this moment. Oh, Dan, I only want to do what is best for you and this job."

"Us," he corrected gently. "What is best for us. And what is best for us is to be just that—ourselves. You look so grand, I really hate to share you with them."

Liberty smiled knowingly. "You might have said sharing two of us with them, Dan. And I wouldn't worry about me looking too seductive. This dress may have to go into sachet bags for several months after tonight."

He blinked. "Spell that out for me, Lib. You can't mean . . ."

She grinned. "I do. I—I think you'd best prepare yourself for becoming a father, Dan."

He stared at her. *"Now* you tell me? Oh my God, Lib, that's wonderful! But oh, my God, now what do I do? I've got to make this job work—it makes no difference what price Collis Huntington puts on my head!"

"Oh!" Liberty gasped, as the Judahs' carriage pulled up in front of the brick castle-like structure. The house seemed huge and cold and forbidding.

Anna Judah took her hand to comfort her. She laughed. "That, my dear, was my first reaction when I saw it in May of 1854. "I said, 'oh!' I expected all of the west to be quite primitive, you see. But Selena Tedder's house simply isn't, except when Grandpa Tedder comes to call. As Lydia may have told you, he is a Tennessee pioneer prone to speak his own mind, and when he's there, everything gets turned upside down." She frowned. "Selena's quite different. She's of English peerage stock. She's—well, you'll see." Anna's mouth set grimly.

Liberty looked at Anna Judah as they stepped from the carriage, and perhaps saw her clearly for the first time. The small regal-looking woman, with her bunned hair and neck-high dress was loathing this Christmas Eve dinner party as much as Liberty was fearing it. It was as if she had been through this course many times before and knew it for what it was—not so much a party as just another evening centered around the building of the railroad.

The fact was that had this annual social affair been started by any other than Selena Tedder the Judahs would not have found themselves on the guest list. They were not members of California society. They were among the used.

Theodore Judah had all but sold his soul to the devil to get the Sacramento Valley Railroad completed. Afterwards, though he could have returned east to work on the railroads there, he chose not to. He had remained in California, stubbornly keeping his eyes on the Sierra Nevadas.

Nazareth Tedder, Selena's husband, had shrewdly seen to it that Ted Judah got every surveying job that came along. As a result of his efforts, the Judahs' living costs had been more than paid.

It was not through altruism that the Tedders, Nazareth and Selena both, had done this. The friendship they'd established with the Judahs was based on deeper considerations. Other Californians might call Ted Judah crazy. For one thing, the isolated gold-based society simply didn't want a railroad cutting into its stage lines, steamboats and the like, so they laughed about the crazy engineer who wanted to build one. But the Tedders, knowing of the respect Judah commanded from rich railroad families in the east, all but supported him and watched his movements intently.

Ted Judah would not give up. Though his enemies had been able to pass a new California law that called for stock subscriptions of $1,000 per mile before a railroad could be incorporated, he went ahead determinedly and wheedled stock pledges out of anyone who would listen. But he found no enthusiasm among the financiers of San Francisco, whose thoughts were on the Civil War and talk of a California secession.

The turning point had been reached on a June night in 1861, when Anna, seeing Ted's misery, took his hand.

"Darling," she said gently, "I have an idea. But first, why not rest for a few days?"

"Rest," he scoffed. "If I were a bird, Anna, I could fly the seventy-five miles to San Francisco. But those damn men who own the steamboats want to keep me twisting up the estuary and dodging sand bars in the river channel for twelve hours and 150 miles. Damn short-sighted fools. I can't rest. I've got to keep getting to those bankers."

"You missed the opening of Crocker's new store on K Street," Anna said, as though purposely changing the subject. She hesitated. "It's really quite a handsome brick edifice. Nazareth Tedder built it. It struck me, as I looked at it, that a great deal of the gold that's come out of the ground in the last six years has found its way back into Nazareth Tedder's pocket. Why, Ted, this year alone he has built a new grocery for the Stanford brothers and a hardware warehouse for Hopkins and Huntington. And if Mr. Stanford is elected governor, you know he will get the contract to build the new capitol building and governor's mansion."

"I'm very happy for him," Judah answered drily.

"Yes," Anna mused. "He seems to have money and know the right men who spend their earnings for the future. I think you have been looking in the wrong place for your backers. You might look to Nazareth for support. We are on friendly terms with him, you know. We do look after Lydia May on our various trips east."

Ted Judah said nothing, but studied the thought all night long. Nazareth thought it an excellent idea for Ted to make use of his influence. He arranged for a small public meeting to be held in the loft of the hardware store.

Of the twelve men Nazareth assembled only four remained to the end of his discussion. Nazareth had left shortly after making the necessary introductions. Selena was not about to let him invest one red cent in the project. She had dreams of another new home, grander than the one Nazareth had built for Jane Stanford.

Judah sized the remaining men up as rich storekeepers of limited imagination and dwelt mainly on how the railroad would make them merchant princes of northern California.

It was what the four, already given a vote of confidence in Judah by Nazareth, wanted to hear.

As Judah sat stunned they agreed to advance the cash to incorporate, with certain public figures to head the firm; namely, Leland Stanford as president, Collis Huntington vice-president, Mark Hopkins secretary-treasurer, and Charles Crocker member of the board. Ted Judah was to be chief engineer and the lobbiest who would go to Washington and push the Railroad Act through Congress.

While he was away, the four men quickly saw that a railroad would depend upon access to the state and national treasuries. Fearing that Judah was not a powerful enough voice in Washington, Collis Huntington was dispatched to back him up and the other three made sure that Leland Stanford was swept into the governorship.

Things should have been looking very bright for Ted Judah, but Anna could read his every mood. He had been overly quiet that Christmas Eve day and now stalked toward the Tedder mansion as though ready to do it battle.

Anna Judah shivered, but not from the cold.

2

"Really, Nazareth," Selena said icily, straightening the white ostrich tips and aigrettes in her pale golden hair, "the guests are starting to arrive and I've said all I am about to say on the matter."

"It's Christmas Eve," he insisted. "The first Christmas Eve paw has been able to spend with Lydia May in six years."

"Enough!" Though Selena Tedder's temper was increasing, she tried to be reasonable. "I have already bent over backwards to appease Lydia May and squeeze in her shipboard friends. I just don't have a place to put your father."

"He can eat in the study with Lydia May, Nathan and the other children." He frowned, watching the effect of his pleading words.

"Lydia May is eighteen, Nazareth. I shall never forget the torture you inflicted on me when you told me she was dead. But no matter. She will sit with the adults tonight. I so command. Now, I'm going downstairs. You may do with your father what you wish, but just keep him away from me."

"I usually do." Nazareth winced. He often did when

his wife brought up the darkest incident of their dark past.

What had he done, Nazareth wondered, to be so tricked by life—to have a father who had rarely spoken to him in the past eighteen years, to have a wife now who all but hated him. But inwardly he knew what he'd done. He could blame neither his father, Howard, nor his wife, Selena, for their feelings towards him.

No one outside the family knew that the very respectable Tedders' had so many skeletons in their closets that they fought for space.

Nazareth had been a boy of sixteen, Selena only fifteen, when they had first met on a wagon train West. Their childish dalliance in a wagon one night had produced Lydia May. At the time Selena did not want Nazareth or the baby. Nor did her mother, Lady Pamela Buttle-Jones. So the widowed Howard Tedder had taken the child briefly while a sullen Nazareth had struck off on his own for the California goldfields. But the feelings he had taken with him—feelings he hadn't known himself capable of! He remembered his loneliness in San Francisco, his yearning to have his baby daughter with him. He remembered the hatred growing in him towards the child's mother, who had rejected her and himself both. He'd acted on both feelings. He'd returned and taken Lydia May from his father, thereby hurting him, something he had not wished to do. Then, back in San Francisco, a strange set of circumstances had allowed him to wreak his vengeance on Selena.

Nazareth still felt guilty about what he'd done. Lydia May, just a tot, had taken ill with cholera. He'd brought her to a hospital where a nurse told him she was sorry but that the child was dying—nothing could be done for her. He'd looked through his tears at the nurse and recognized her as she did him—it was Lady Pamela, Selena's mother! Nazareth remembered his rage at the mere mention of Selena's name. He'd rushed from the hospital, carrying Lydia May to a private doctor, expecting her to die in a week's time or less. But he couldn't wait for his revenge. How twisted his mind had been! Lady Pamela had shown sympathy for his plight—more than sympathy, grief. Perhaps if he put a burial notice in the paper and held a mock funeral, burying an empty wooden box, she'd get her hateful, self-absorbed daughter to attend it. Maybe he could make Selena suffer as she had him!

It's what he'd done.

Selena had indeed attended the funeral. He remembered how, his eyes narrowed with hatred and feeling a sadistic surge of joy, he watched her collapse to the ground—in guilt, grief, sorrow, in every miserable feeling that was coursing through him. Except that he had a shred of hope left, that Lydia May might miraculously recover.

She had.

God knows how he and Selena had gotten together again. Perhaps his making a fortune in gold had helped. Perhaps hatred was only a stone's throw from love, as people said. He didn't know, didn't trust his ideas on the subject. All he knew was that three years later, after Selena had had her affairs with men and he'd had his with women, he'd sought her out, taking Lydia May with him by the hand, and told her what he'd done. She'd gone into a screaming fury; he thought she was insane; he feared she'd kill him. Then—after this tantrum of magnificent proportions—she'd fallen into his arms, sobbing.

Maybe it was the shared sin of Lydia May's birth, recalled after all their other sins, that brought them together again. Who knew? More likely it was his gold, Nazareth thought sourly.

It was a loveless, bloodless contract, their marriage. With the birth of Nathan, Nazareth felt that Selena would soften and start loving him again. He didn't know, or didn't want to know, that Selena had used up her love and desire for men she'd known in the mining camps. The mere thought of a man ever touching her again turned her cold. But no one could deny that she provided a good home for her husband and children. And in eleven years she had become the undisputed doyenne of the nascent society of Sacramento. An invitation to her Christmas Eve affair was a coveted prize.

"Anna!" Selena called joyously from the top of the sweeping staircase. "Welcome home and a Merry Christmas."

Poised there, less to view than to be viewed, Selena figured to take her arriving guests in at a glance.

There was Anna, going to extra pains, it seemed, to look like a frump. There was Ted Judah in his everyday brown suit, as expected. Selena suddenly stopped, her heart beating rapidly. Was that Dan O'Lee? Danny O'Lee? It couldn't be—yet it was. She hadn't seen Dan in a dozen years, not since the gold rush days of '49— but my God, he'd been in love with her! And she'd had a deep affection for him. She'd recognize him anywhere, older though he was, no longer the raw Irish lad she'd known. The woman he was with—his wife. Silently Selena prayed that if Dan recognized her—and surely he did—he would act the gentleman and not expose either of them to embarrassment.

As for Liberty, she stared up at Selena with frank envy. Her hostess's royal-blue gown, her heavy diamond necklace and matching earrings, her house, as much of it as Liberty could assess by looking at the banister draped with red velvet bows—all gave her the sense of having been transported to royal England. She was both enraptured and intimidated.

Selena swept down the stairs. Not an inch of her hooped skirt fluttered. Then, halfway down, she abruptly stopped. Liberty looked and saw a boy huddled on the stairs close to the darkened wall.

"Nathan," Selena demanded sharply, "why are you sitting here?"

"I'm watchin' " he answered in a surly manner.

"Watching," Selena corrected. "Lord, I let you spend one afternoon with that grandfather of yours and you come back sounding just like him. Now, on your feet and follow me down."

Reluctantly, Selena's son did as ordered. Watching him descend the staircase lagging far behind his mother, Liberty's heart went out to him immediately. He was about ten or eleven, she saw now, tall for his age and, with flaming red hair, almost angelically beautiful. This was the sort of son she'd like to have with Dan. This was Nathan. She remembered Lydia May speaking of her brother aboard ship.

Then Liberty's attention was distracted by Lydia May herself, as she too came down the stairs to greet them—but at a bounce. In pink tulle she was nearly a copy of her mother, except for her auburn hair and radiant youth.

The introductions were noisy and confusing. Others began arriving and Selena started to shoo them all into the main parlor. Liberty started to follow. Feeling eyes upon her, she turned to catch Nathan Tedder regarding her with open admiration. Then her eyes were diverted upward. Two men were coming down the stairwell that made her look back and forth from them to

Nathan. One was his father Nazareth, in somber black. The other was Grandpa Howard Tedder, a man with large, red, laborer's hands dangling from the cuffs of his newly purchased formal tailcoat. What struck Liberty was the close similarity of the Tedder faces; all three could have been one man at different stages of his life.

Before the two older men could reach them, Nathan sailed over and bowed to Liberty.

"I am Nathan Alexander Tedder," he announced. "And I think you are the most beautiful woman in the world."

"Why, I—I thank you," Liberty smiled. Then she blushed and put her hand to her neckline. In response to her warm greeting, the precocious Nathan was standing on tiptoes to peer into her clevage. "Nathan," she said nervously, "please . . . introduce me to your folks."

The men, who had heard much about Liberty from Lydia May, chatted with her genially once the initial amenities were over. They behaved exactly as Lydia May had said they would, "as comfortably as old bedroom slippers," discussing the voyage with Liberty as though they'd all been friends for years. Howard almost immediately thereafter insisted that she call him "Grandpap."

"All right. Grandpap. Though you certainly don't look your age," Liberty said. "Nor do you act . . ." She stopped what was to be a heartfelt compliment at the sight of still another family member coming down the stairs—this one a majestically beautiful woman in her fifties who looked at them all with haughty disdain. Liberty stared at her, feeling suddenly cold.

Nazareth took a quick look over his shoulder. "My mother-in-law," he said. "The Lady Pamela Buttle-Jones." His voice was not without sarcasm. He looked

back at Liberty and pretended to study her intently as
Lady Pamela swept by them without speaking and went
into the parlor.

"A mean one she turned out to be," Howard Tedder
said flatly.

"Yes," Liberty said absently. "I mean—" She
flushed. "I mean, I guessed it was Lady Pamela. Lydia
May said that she—" She could say no more. With her
imperial features, with her strong dowager figure, with
her neck and fingers covered with far more diamonds
than her daughter Selena had on, Lady Pamela was the
most imposing woman Liberty had ever seen in her life.

"It's not that my mother-in-law doesn't like me,"
Nazareth said mildly, eyeing her. "It's that she hates me.
She hates Selma, she hates Nathan, she hates—" He
shrugged. "Don't let me bore you, Mrs. O'Lee. Shall
we join the party?"

Liberty needn't have worried about committing a
faux pas at Selena Tedder's high-society fete. Most of
those assembled were too taken up with gold-fever
schemes to notice her.

After dinner, Governor Leland Stanford began ma-
neuvering the evening in his best political manner.

"Excellent meal, Selena," he beamed. "Now cigar
and brandy for the men and tea for the ladies, what?
Separate rooms, of course. Shouldn't wish to foul your
pretty faces with smoke."

Selena held his gaze with icy disdain, if only for a
moment. Stanford had all but usurped her husband's
role as host, he'd monopolized the dinner conversation,
and his condescending attitude toward her was flagrant-
ly obvious. But there was little she could do to stop him
having his way; he was like a railroad engine under a
full head of steam.

"Thank you," she answered simply. At least she wouldn't call him "Governor." She wouldn't call him anything. And she wouldn't make a move—either to leave with the ladies or invite the men to go.

Mark Hopkins cleared his throat and rose. This thin, bent, prematurely aging man thought himself able to smoothe over any matter that might get out of hand. Hopkins raised his wine glass in a toast.

"To Selena," he wheezed. "A perfect hostess and the first lady of Sacramento."

Hopkins had accomplished what Stanford had not. He'd gotten twenty-three people on their feet. In the position of having been flattered, Selena felt she had no choice but to take the standing ladies away. Still she hesitated. She simply did not enjoy being manipulated. It was Jane Stanford, Leland's wife, who did the deed for her. Noticing the look of consternation that appeared on her husband's face at the mention of Selena as "first lady"—rather than herself—Jane said gaily, "Come, ladies. Our company is no longer required."

So the ladies departed.

"That man Stanford," Selma muttered to another woman in the foyer, "has the ambition of an emperor and the spite of a peanut vendor."

Alone with the men, Governor Stanford took on his mantle as president of Pacific Associates.

"It's good to see you back, Judah," he said. "Now we can begin to get something done around here. Although I don't mind telling you I am less than pleased with many of the provisions of the Pacific Railroad Act."

Judah shrugged. "Then you're in the same boat as Tom Durant of the Union Pacific Railroad, governor. He's just as unhappy as you are over the control clauses."

Collis Huntington injected, "Durant's fear is the

same as ours Leland. The Federal Government, if it survives, is granting us vacant lands with ten miles on either side of the lines reserved for homesteads in five alternate sections per mile. The Homestead Act supercedes us by a month. If we don't start acquiring all the land, we're going to find it chopped up by 160-acre plots with sod houses and shacks on them."

"That's a future worry," Mark Hopkins said drily. "I'm concerned that we are not moving fast enough to take advantage of the five percent bond issue. As I understand it, in the next fiscal year, those 30-year bonds will go to six percent."

Collis rose to pour himself more brandy. The solidly built young man moved with assurance. At forty-one he was already considered a millionaire.

"Really, Mark," he sniffed. "On a fifty million dollar loan we are only talking about an additional $16,000 per year over thirty years. That's exactly what they will allocate per mile on construction to the base of the mountains. I think Judah did well to gain us $48,000 per mile on a hundred fifty miles of mountain construction and $32,000 per mile for trackage across the desert high plain of Nevada and Utah."

"Now wait a minute," Judah growled. "That last you can't count on. We've only been granted the right to build up to the California and Nevada border."

"Gentlemen, gentlemen," Nazareth chuckled, "you get deeper and deeper into a subject matter that leaves the rest of us baffled."

"Hardly a time to be baffled," Stanford said. "There is not a man here who will not benefit in some way from my railroad—and that includes you, Tedder. Now, Judah, do you see any problems with the board granting us the Nevada-Utah contract?"

Nazareth sat in strained silence, his hands clenched

in his lap. But his anger was no greater than that of Ted Judah. Judah's railroad had just become Leland Stanford's railroad.

"Plenty of problems," Ted mumbled. "For God knows why they've got men like Ben Holladay from Overland Stage and Louis McLane from Wells, Fargo on the commission. They're gonna throw all manner of monkey wrenches into the works."

"Then," Huntington mused, a little acidly, "I think it's about time that our chief engineer should focus his time on right-of-way, construction of shops, and assembly of locomotives and cars. Leave the commission and lobbying to others."

Judah mentally scoffed. There was nothing that he would like better than to get on with the job—but the right way. He realized that the scowling, hawk-nosed merchant spoke the truth. He was bone-tired of the labyrinths of wrangling things out of Congress and the commission.

"Excellent point," Stanford enthused. "And the first thing he must do is bring Dan O'Lee up to date on his survey and estimated construction costs."

Dan felt the attention swing to him and he felt uncomfortable. "We've already done that, sir," he said hesitantly, "on board ship. Seems right to me that it will average about $90,000 a mile for the hundred forty miles to the Nevada line."

Listless through the meal, Charles Crocker punched a clenched fist down onto the table.

"Horseshit!" Crocker growled. "Those costs have got to be brought down, and I aim to see that they are. They have got to be brought more in line with the government loan figures."

"Well," Judah sighed, as though preparing to lecture a child, "we have known all along that the government

loans would only cover a third of our needs. We aren't
selling dress goods by the yard. We're building a railroad by the mile. There is quite a difference."

Crocker started to retort, but Stanford stopped him
with a hand signal. Now they were getting into areas
that were best left for private discussion.

"Now, now," Stanford soothed, "we all agree that we
will pay as we go and never run a dollar in debt. Isn't
that the way you put it, Collis?"

"More or less. If we can't pay a hundred workermen,
we will pay fifty; if not fifty, then ten; if not ten, one.
We will employ no more than we can pay."

"And that," Crocker declared vehemently, "is the
exact way I plan to hire and run the construction company."

Ted Judah sat back and tented his fingers together.
He had waited all evening to find out if a certain rumor
he had heard was correct. Crocker had just floated the
tip of an iceberg to the surface.

"Interesting," he mused. "Would you care to elaborate?"

"Ted," Mark Hopkins jumped in quickly, "there are
many things that we have to bring you up to date on.
This is hardly the time or the place."

"I hardly see the need for secrecy," Judah intoned
flatly. "Did you know you have a new competitor in
town, Nazareth? The Charles Crocker Construction
Company. Now, I find that most interesting."

"Ain't nothing illegal about it," Crocker flared. "I
volunteered to resign from the board if my contract is
approved."

There was an embarrassed silence. The engineer
Judah kept staring in wonderment at Crocker the dress
merchant. What did he know about building a railroad?
Huntington anticipated a scene. For a moment he did
not care if it developed. He personally thought the

group would be much better off without Judah in it. Fortunately Nazareth had the good sense at that moment to announce that it was time to rejoin the ladies.

For the rest of the evening everyone shunned the more explosive topic of railroads, by unanimous consent. But it was clear that the hollow-eyed Ted Judah was a man who faced more problems than just building a railroad.

As the ladies had daintily sipped their coffee, Liberty began to sense the same unease as Dan was feeling with the men. She and Anna Judah were all but relegated to a private corner of their own, until Lydia May joined them.

"Look at them," Lydia May hissed, "a bunch of pea-hens choosing up sides for a battle. It disgusts me, Auntie Anna. I wish I were back east where people are at least civilized."

Anna smiled. "What does that sound like to you, Liberty?"

"After five weeks of hearing about nothing else, I would call it homesickness for a certain young gentleman."

Lydia May flushed. "Oh, please, I haven't even dared mention Randy to my mother yet."

"And why not?" Anna scolded. "The Porters are a very fine family."

"Yes, by your family's standards, which means something in the east, but you know mother. She doesn't even think I know what boys are. Could you kind of soften her up, Auntie Anna?"

Anna frowned. She did have a certain way with Selena, but sensed what a stormy conversation it would be. "Let's let it rest until after the holidays, dear. Then I'll find the right moment to chat with her."

"Thank you," Lydia May beamed, and kissed the woman on the cheek. "Now I must fly. I promised to walk Grandpap home so I can see Uncle Theo."

"Theo?" Liberty mused, after the girl had left. "That would be Nazareth Tedder's twin brother, right?"

Anna laughed. "Twins, but hardly alike. I've never seen such a shy and reserved man. Quite a handsome devil. I'm told that he came near to marrying Elizabeth Stoddard, but Collis Huntington stole her away."

"Which is she again? I'm so confused."

"In the wing-back chair by the fireplace."

Liberty was surprised, almost shocked, by the woman's appearance. All evening she had taken her to be the wife of one of the older men. She looked far older than her years, and tired and ill. Hardly the mate for the dashing, flowery-tongued Collis Huntington, Liberty thought.

"It's funny," she said, "how much like their husbands the others are."

"In more ways than one," Anna said sourly.

Mary Deming Crocker was as bull-like in frame as Charles, with the same insensitive face, sharp nose and extremely high cheekbones.

Jane Stanford was much younger than her husband, Liberty surmised. Her large flashing dark eyes and handsome features made her appear quite friendly, but she could sense in her the same hard-driving ambition and determination she'd observed in the governor.

"Isn't there a Mrs. Mark Hopkins?" Liberty asked.

Before she could answer, Ted Judah came storming into the room, whispered to his wife and bid Liberty a curt goodnight.

Anna kissed Liberty on the cheek and whispered. "Dan is still with Collis and will see you home. Let me get my firebrand out of here."

Liberty was left standing alone and a little embarrassed. The majestic Lady Pamela rose and came to her as though granting a royal audience.

"Look at those former housewives," Lady Pamela commented. "Money can't change everything."

Liberty stared. She didn't know quite how to answer.

"The only real aristocrat just left the room," Lady Pamela went on. "Oh, don't look so puzzled. When my daughter deemed it necessary to send Lydia May off to school, I had the Judahs checked out quite carefully. As a Pierce, Anna Judah's family could probably buy up everyone in this room—except for me. But that's not why I came over. You seem to have made quite an impression on my granddaughter, Mrs. O'Lee."

Liberty flushed. "Lydia May is a charming and beautiful girl." She hesitated. "Lady Pamela, after five weeks with her aboard ship I arrived here tonight feeling as though I knew each and every one of you. Of course that was through Lydia May's eyes."

Pamela grinned, wickedly. "And now you have been able to use your own. Well, I suspect you'll use your own judgment about us all. I take you for a shrewd young woman. I sat and watched you totally evaluate every wife of the men your husband will be working for here."

"My husband will be working only for Mr. Judah," Liberty insisted.

"My dear, let me inform you that Collis Huntington hired your husband so that he could more easily get rid of 'Crazy' Judah."

"That can't be possible," Liberty gasped.

"Possible?" Lady Pamela snorted. "Anything is possible around these vultures and their petty egos."

"But why are you telling me?"

Pamela sighed. "Mrs. O'Lee—Liberty, if I may— I have come to love my granddaughter very much—although I didn't at first. Lydia May has great admiration for the Judahs, and I don't blame her. I don't want her hurt when these money grubbers hurt Ted Judah. Be there, as a friend, to help her. And in the meantime, for your own good, learn the rules that these people play by. Most of them came up out of the gold rush days and will continue to play by those hard and fast rules."

Just then Dan came in looking for Liberty. He was tired and his limp was more pronounced. Liberty had never seen him look so worried, and thought it best that she get her own firebrand away as well.

Thanking Lady Pamela and Selena, she had the odd sensation that Selena was not the least bit sorry to see them leave.

Huntington ordered his carriage to take them to the hotel, and on the way she spoke fiercely. "I'd like to know what kind of a vultures' den we've landed in, Dan O'Lee."

"The worst kind, Libby," he said with quiet disgust.

Despite herself Liberty laughed. "I bet we could compare notes on tonight and they would be about the same."

"Hardly," he said darkly, "I have a feeling that four men are out to slit a fifth's neck."

"Namely, Ted Judah?"

His breath caught. "What made you say that so quickly?"

"Women's talk."

"In front of Anna Judah?"

"Oh, no," Liberty scoffed, "the wives of the big four kept Anna and me at arms length."

"That's good, Lib," he laughed, "for that's exactly how they act—as if they were the four biggest men on God's green earth. The Big Four. I've got to remember and tell that to Ted tomorrow."

"No, you will not," Liberty cried fiercely. "I will not

have Anna's Christmas dinner spoiled by what might prove to be a rumor. Let's not be choosing sides, Dan O'Lee, until we get a better lay of this land."

"Whatever you say, Lib."

Liberty was quiet for the rest of the ride. She was thinking. Suppose Ted Judah was fired? She didn't want him to be, but suppose he was? Dan would then obtain a post she had dared not dream he would reach. He was prepared and qualified for it, of that she had no doubt. She was the one who would have to learn what all of this railroad business was about.

Dan was thankful for her quietness. From the moment Selena Tedder had arrived at the top of the stairs the evening had become a nervous strain for him. Thirteen years and all the finery in the world could not change her. Nor could it change Lady Pamela—Pamela, really, for so he had known her in their own moments of intimacy. But when they had been introduced it was like meeting a stranger—there was no recognition in Selena's eyes, in her voice, in their touch at shaking hands. At the time he had been grateful, for the explanations to Liberty would have been lengthy and a little embarrassing. To say nothing of the explanations Selena might have to make to her husband.

But during dinner, when she seemed purposely to ignore him, his male ego and vanity began to feel pangs of pain. He had been a boy—she had been his youthful love—how could she so easily forget him? How?

Lady Pamela Buttle-Jones carefully and methodically removed her clothing and make-up. She, too, had started out the evening on a note of strain. Never one to forget a name, she had prayed that Lydia May had erred, or that there might be two Dan O'Lees abroad the land. But there was no mistake. She had watched her daughter carefully, her tensions easing when Selena appeared not to recognize the man he had become. Then, in studying Liberty O'Lee, she could see that this wife of Dan's wasn't aware of the past alliance either.

In her constantly calculating mind, Lady Pamela was grateful for this. Using a bit of overheard gossip about Ted Judah, she had momentarily put Liberty in her debt. She would collect that debt, with Lydia May as the pawn. She might lose Liberty a husband, but she would gain full control of her granddaughter's destiny.

Selena Tedder removed her clothing and make-up in furious rage. Governor Stanford had dominated her dinner party with never-ending stories centered around himself; his wife had added all the amendments over the ladies' tea. Then her mother had the gall to walk away and hold a long conversation with Dan O'Lee's wife—and leave her trying to vie with Jane Stanford. But her ire reached its zenith when Nazareth had calmly told her that he had allowed Lydia May to walk Grandpap Tedder home.

Selena glared at the mantel clock. She would give Lydia May fifteen more minutes and then she would dress and go after her. She would not have her daughter lowering herself by hanging around Howard Tedder.

Wrapping a robe about her still willowy figure, she slumped into a chair and considered the worth of putting another log on the fire.

Staring into the dying flames she tried to picture young men who might be suitable for Lydia May. Locally, she could think of none that measured up to her strict standards. She began to tick off what she called the characteristics—financial worth and the like —of many of Lydia May's young suitors so as to form her own composite picture of the perfect mate for her. She, of course, had to call upon her own background for the majority of the pieces. Part way through her thinking process, she began to shudder. Her back grew rigid, her hands clammy; her head began to throb.

"Oh, my God!" she wailed. "Danny! Please don't give me away!"

As though the room was suddenly possessed with evil spirits, she ran to her bed and covered her head with the covers. She was no longer worried about Lydia May; she was worried about herself. Had her mother recognized Dan? Had he recognized her? What game was he playing with her?

A thousand unanswered questions later she calmed. She thought out the situation very seriously and smiled.

"Idiot," she told herself, "he's just a nobody. I think it's time for me to take an interest in this railroad to make sure that he remains a nobody and a very, very quiet one."

"I thought Grandpap would never go to bed," Mimi said, sighing. "I just had to talk with someone in the family, Uncle Theo."

Theodis Tedder was struck with the humor of the situation. He was the last member of the family that anyone ever held a discussion with.

"All right," he smiled, "but it is getting late."

"It may already be too late—for me. There is this boy, you see." She flushed, realizing how badly she was putting her case. "Oh, not too late in the sense you might think—you must believe me!"

"I do believe you," Theo said gently. "Why don't you start over?"

She nodded. "First, he is not a boy but a twenty-one-year-old man. His name is Randolph Porter and he is the most wonderful person of mind and spirit . . . and I'm afraid I've fallen hopelessly in love with him."

Theo chuckled. "And you're afraid your mother will say that he is not good enough for you."

Lydia May sat very still, looking at him.

"Worse," she said sadly. "The Porter family doesn't think I'm good enough for Randy."

Theo stared at her incredulously.

"Now, really," he began, "you can't be serious."

"Mrs. Porter is very serious," she said, almost angrily. "Oh, she is very nice and sweet to my face and told Auntie Anna what a lovely child I was, but she didn't mince words with Randy."

"Does he love you?"

"Desperately."

"Then why didn't you stay in the east and elope with him? Would that have been so impossible?"

"Impossible? Hardly that. Let us say, difficult. He has just graduated as an engineer and works for his father. He was afraid that our marriage would cost him the job and his family."

Theo scowled. "There are other jobs, if he is really serious about you."

"Please," Lydia May pleaded, "please don't say what I couldn't bring myself to say. His is an old family and he would do nothing to bring it harm or dishonor."

"Then I don't know what to tell you," he said sadly.

"Please," she whispered, near tears, "help me think of a way to make the Porters see that I am suitable for Randy."

She began to cry, and Theo drew her against him. As they clung together in the dim room, all Theo could think of was that it was Randolph Porter's responsibility to prove himself worthy of his niece.

3

Jove-like Oliver Ames presided over his own brandy-and-cigar session that Christmas Eve of 1862. Although the assembled men had heard the story many times before none dared remind the fifty-five-year-old eccentric of the fact.

"Shovels, gentlemen," Ames exclaimed. "That is the key word. My brother Oakes and I made practically every shovel that dug the gold out of California. Those shovels paid for our building of the Easton Branch Railroad in eighteen and fifty-five. Shovels will do it again. It's going to take a heap of shovels to fight Mr. Lincoln's war for him—a heap of shovels. And those shovels are going to help pay for our building of the Union Pacific, by damn!"

One would have thought that Ames was talking to the newly elected officials charged with the creation of the Union Pacific organization. But not a single one of those gentlemen sat at his fashionable table. Ames surrounded himself with men he could trust. And he liked to remind them that they had his trust.

"Grenville," he snapped, "Tom tells me you're thinking of getting out of Mr. Lincoln's army. Don't like that. Don't like that at all, for the present. I knew you were a smart one when you engineered the Easton Branch for Oakes and I. But I didn't realize you were ambitious till you came to me after your little talk with Mr. Lincoln. He seems to like you, my boy, and you'll serve Oliver Ames best by staying his friend—for it's no secret that I don't get along at all with the rail-splitter."

General Grenville Mellon Dodge nodded his curly head. His surveys for the western expansion of the railroad had been the deciding factor that convinced the President to sign the Railroad Act. He had arrived at the Ames mansion jubilant at the thought that he might be named the chief engineer. Now he sat momentarily crushed and defeated. He knew there was no way to change Oliver Ames's mind—not at that moment, anyway.

"Yes," Ames continued, "I need a strong set of ears and eyes for me in Washington. You all realize, of course, how beneficial it will be for me to stay in the background. For the time being we will let Stanford beat his gums in the west and let Ogden parade himself around as the Union Pacific President. Tom will be able to keep his sensitive surgeon's finger on the pulse of matters as vice-president and general manager."

Dr. Thomas Durant had found that there was more money to be made in the stock market than from patients' pockets. With a jaundiced view of investors' money he had escaped the financial disaster of 1857-58 and had also been helpful in keeping the Ames brothers from ruin. Oliver Ames had a long memory for friends and enemies. Now Durant, thinly handsome with a walrus mustache, puffed up with importance, much to the chagrin of another in the room.

"Which reminds me," he intoned, "I talked with George Train today and he will take the position."

Robert Porter's head came snapping up. "Train? Why have we use for that promoter?"

A nephew of Ames's by marriage, Porter had purposely directed his comment toward his uncle. Ames
was not about to answer him. The family was already
in a stew because Robert had not been named general
manager. Ames just wished that the short-sighted inept
man would wither into obscurity.

Because of Ames's silence, Porter was forced to look
to Durant.

"It's very simple," Durant said. "When they open
the books for the hundred million in capital stock to
the public we will need a drum-beater to sell them.
You must admit that Train is a promotional genius."

"I disagree," Robert Porter insisted. "Uncle Oliver,
the Pacific Railroad Act limits the holdings of any one
person to two hundred shares of stock. The promotion
would seem a waste of money."

Ames glowered. "Robert, use your head. In the next
year I want every man, jackass and prehensile financier,
to think of nothing but railroads, railroads and more
railroads. I want them to puff up the commission's
dreams and buy that damn government stock for its ten
percent down. George Train is going to create such a
smokescreen with his ballyhoo that no one will be
aware that Durant is quietly gaining that stock back in
the name of a few. Then, when I am ready, Durant will
see that the stockholders vote the Union Pacific into
an independent company without any direct supervision
from the government's commissioners."

It was the first that any but Durant had heard of
Ames's scheme and the audacity of it left them speechless.

"But," Oliver said with heavy emphasis, "that is in
the future. At the present my concern is the Central
Pacific Railroad—if it ever gets built. Colonel Seymour,
are you sure there is no way that we can hide Ted
Judah away from Stanford and his thugs?"

Colonel Silas Seymour rose. Aristocratic in bearing, Seymour had the manner of a man who knew the worth of his extreme handsomeness in attracting the ladies and making lesser men stand in jealous awe of him. But his tastes were costly and he was capable of any assignment that would line his pockets with more than just his military pay as a liaison between the army and the railroad commission. He had sought out Oliver Ames, been given one assignment and had been successful. He too wished to operate behind the scenes.

"There is no way, sir," he snapped. "But I am sure that our placing of Dan O'Lee in Judah's hands will help trigger Huntington to move. Dr. Durant can tell you how the two wrangled and quarreled during our meetings in Washington."

"Quite true," Durant agreed. "But it's plain to see that Stanford likes Judah. What if he insists upon keeping him?"

"Yes," Ames mused, "I've been considering the same point and will come back to it in a moment. Now, let's just suppose that Judah is fired and this O'Lee man replaces him. Who is to say that he won't be able to get the job done?"

General Dodge laughed. "Mr. Ames, O'Lee is a fine man and officer—but he has few credentials as an engineer. I know the High Sierras. It will take a highly educated engineer to put rails through them. A minor mistake up there could cost months and millions."

Ames chuckled. "And each month and million they lose can come right back to us. Randy, my boy, the brandy decanter is nearly empty. Be a lad and go get it refilled for your Gee-you."

As a child, Robert Porter's son, Randolph, had been unable to say "Great Uncle Oliver" and it had come out Gee-you. He and Ames still shared the term after twenty-one years.

Obedient to a fault, Randy did as requested. Oliver Ames followed him from the room with his eyes. Not an overly affectionate family man, he loathed his niece and merely tolerated Robert's ineptness. But he held a special warm place in his heart for Randy.

"Gentlemen," he said, "it is usually not my custom to discuss family matters at a business session, but they do seem to go hand in hand. My great-nephew Randolph has been smitten by the love bug."

"Uncle Oliver," Robert protested, "what has that to do with these gentlemen?"

"Shut up," Ames said, "and you shall learn. Now, the young lady in question is one Lydia May Tedder. Robert and my niece Alisa are dead set against their marriage—and for once I have to agree with them. The girl's background is a little unique, to say the least. Her grandmother is a titled Englishwoman—or so she claims. Her father, from pioneer Tennessee stock, does impress me from the Pinkerton reports I've received. The man is a building genius in my opinion. I believe he worked for you and Judah on the Sacramento, Seymour. Nazareth Tedder, his name is."

Seymour frowned. "Yes, now I recall. A relatively young chap, but quite astute."

Ames grinned. "Quite astute, indeed. What better man and construction firm for Stanford to call upon? Seymour, in time it is going to be your responsibility to keep me informed of every spike, every rail, every mile they cover. In the meantime I want someone there who will have enough sense of family obligation to answer any questions I might wish to ask."

"But that is spying!" Robert protested.

"Exactly!" Ames shot back. "When you prepare for war you make damn sure you know what the enemy is about. At the moment, on the surface, we are not rivals of Governor Stanford, but are both doing the bidding of Mr. Lincoln to connect up with the Pacific for the war effort. But when Stanford begins to see, as I already see, the monumental fortunes to be gained in this venture, then it will be all-out war. Before that happens, I want a telegraph message sent to Ted Judah to see if he has room on his staff for a very capable young civil engineer."

Robert Porter jumped up from his chair. "Not Randolph! You will be placing him right back in that viperous girl's clutches. I refuse to let him go!"

"Refuse?" Ames bellowed. "I wish a union with the Pacific, not one for my great-nephew. I shall make his family obligation quite clear to him, Robert, since you apparently won't. This opportunity is too great not to act on. Who can question two young lovers for wanting to be near each other? As another reason for Randy's departure, you might even suggest, Seymour, that the commission might not look too kindly on two members of the same family working on the same line."

"Two?" he puzzled.

Oliver Ames walked over and put a bear-like paw on Robert Porter's shoulder. The man nearly cringed away.

"Two," Ames echoed. "After tonight, Seymour, Robert, here, will be my liaison. Neither you nor Durant are to associate with me publicly. In a way I am giving Robert more responsibility than any of the rest of you and I know I can put my full trust and faith in him."

Robert Porter slowly relaxed. He had dreamed of hearing words like that from his uncle, but never thought the day would ever arrive. He cast a smug, victorious glare at Dr. Durant.

Durant, in turn, painted his face with a pained look of defeat. He was no fool. He had read Oliver Ames's intent quite correctly. Robert Porter could no longer refuse to let his son go west—if Judah approved of him.

He had been neatly boxed into a position where he could do the least amount of harm.

Ames smiled. "Now, gentlemen, as this might be the last time I shall see Colonel Seymour for awhile, I would like a few private moments with him in my study. Then, Robert, you may send Randy to me. Good night, Grenville. Keep Mr. Lincoln's fires burning for him. Good night, Thomas. I expect interesting reports from you and Train, shortly."

In the foyer Ames stopped short and indicated the coat-rack. "You may get your wrap, colonel, for what I have to say is quite short and simple. When I deem it time to take over this railroad, I will be ready to go all the way—even if it means to California. At the moment I can't give you a direct order, just a piece of gristle to gnaw on. Shall we say one percent a mile for every mile taken away from Leland Stanford? Oh, Randy, take the brandy into my study please, Gee-you would like a private word with you. Goodnight, colonel."

Not until Colonel Seymour settled back in the hansom cab seat did Oliver Ames's words strike him with full impact. He went back to his hotel, checked out and took the last train for Washington. He was quite alone Christmas day in the Railroad Commission offices, pouring over the charts and maps that Ted Judah had filed for the hearings. When he was finished he sat back and began to doodle dollar signs and zeros on a fresh sheet of paper. He wanted to see exactly what a million dollars really looked like. Then he sent the telegram.

"Oh, Anna, you are a romantic," Ted Judah laughed.

It was so nice hearing that sentiment coming from him for a change that Anna cherished it for a moment. She took up the telegram and read it again.

"Perhaps I am being a little romantic, Ted, but it sounds to me like Randy developed a bit of backbone and has stood up to his mother and father."

Judah frowned. "I like the boy, no question of that. He was the sharpest student at Norwich University when I lectured there last year. But something still puzzles me about Seymour's telegram." He paused, frowning. "If Robert Porter is involved with the Union Pacific, as Silas implies, then Oliver Ames is in the woodwork somewhere. Look how hard he tried to get me back east. You may look at it romantically, Anna, but I bet that old shovel-maker is sending Randy here to pull on my ear."

"And what will you do about it?"

Judah grinned. "Let him come and work and learn that Crazy Judah listens only to the wind whistling down off the Sierras. I'll stop and send the telegram on my way to that damn stupid board meeting. I don't even know why I waste my time attending. I'm always out voted four to one."

Toward dusk she heard the familiar sound of his returning footsteps. Standing at the door, his hands loose at his sides, Judah told her, "Anna, it's hard to believe, but they've given Crocker the contract for the first eighteen miles. Edwin Crocker has replaced his brother on the board and Stanford has brought his own brother onto it as well." He seemed to struggle for breath, and quietly he went upstairs.

Anna did not move. This was a time her husband had to be quite alone. Above her Ted walked back and forth across the chamber. She heard a thump, and realized that he had dropped to his knees beside the bed. The minister's son was turning to his strongest source of aid and comfort.

After a long silence Judah came downstairs, his step

quicker, firmer. He had a calm that Anna had not seen in him in weeks.

"Dan and I will leave at dawn," he said quietly. "I want to introduce him to the mountains."

"How long will you be gone?"

"About two weeks."

She had known that would be his answer. The ground-breaking ceremony was set for January 8th. He was purposely going to miss it.

4

Governor Stanford, five state senators and numerous city assemblymen orated everyone into a state of stupefied boredom. To Anna's chagrin, her husband's name did not even appear in the official program. If she had not had Liberty with her, she would have been tempted to leave and let the reporters know the reason why.

"Anna," Liberty whispered, "who is that stern-looking man lecturing Collis Huntington?"

Anna snickered. "Next to the governor, probably the most important man in northern California. His name is Kai Soong."

Liberty was fascinated. The man was much taller than the Chinese houseboys and cooks in their uniform-like white linen jackets and baggy blue pants. He was immaculate in a mandarin gown of peacock blue with matching cap, from the center of which his neatly braided queue hung halfway down his back. His two-inch-long fingernails had been painted to match the gown.

But her real fascination lay in the man's face and bearing. Deep-set eyes as black as midnight seemed to pierce out of the shadow created by his bushy eyebrows.

46

The drooping mustache and long-pointed beard gave his face an elongated sternness.

As though sensing he was being stared at, he turned and stared back. Embarrassed, Liberty started to pull her eyes away. The oddest sensation trickled up her spine. It were as though she was being commanded to stare into his eyes so that he could enter her soul and learn what manner of person resided therein. She saw his thin lips move, but couldn't hear the words. A moment later Collis Huntington joined the women and Kai Soong broke the stare.

"Good afternoon," Huntington said politely, "sorry your husbands couldn't be in attendance. Liberty, I've presumed to make a few arrangements for you. Kai Soong's daughter will remain in Sacramento for a few days and help you find a house and servants."

"Oh, no," she protested, "I'd best wait for Dan."

"Not another word, young lady. Mai Ling will present herself to you at the hotel. Good afternoon."

The smile vanished from Huntington's face the moment he turned and looked at Kai Soong. Liberty wondered immediately if the suggestion had originated with the latter. Regardless, she'd have preferred to spend most of her time with Anna.

"They certainly didn't leave me much choice in the matter, did they?" she said.

Anna laughed, and took Liberty's arm as they started to walk away. "That is very typical of Kai Soong. He controls his people like an ancient emperor. I have never seen it, but Ted tells me that his house in San Francisco is like a palace in China."

"Controls people? How do you mean, Anna?"

"During the gold rush days Chinese trading companies—they call them 'tongs'—brought over indentured servants to work in the mines. When the mines went to heavy equipment there was no longer any need

for this 'coolie' labor, but the gold was being transformed into mansions here and in San Francisco. So
the tongs got smart and turned the laborers into houseboys, cooks, gardeners and coachmen—and I must say
they work for very little."

"I will hardly know what to pay them."

"You will be told, my dear. You might recall the man
who came to the house the other afternoon while you
were visiting. He was a tong agent. He will call on you
monthly and you will pay him directly, not your servants."

"Why, that's almost medieval, Anna."

Anna sighed. "My very words eight years ago. But,
you see, these coolies cannot become American citizens.
The law forbids it. They are servants who will be sent
back home when their passage has been worked off. In
the meantime, the tongs collect the four to eight dollars
a month that they earn and act as their bankers, in-
surance men, marriage brokers and concubine purveyors. Each tong handles a certain aspect of their lives.
Not even the Chinese merchants who operate the porridge restaurants, teahouses, food and herb shops can
hire a coolie without going through a tong agent."

"Then, from the look of his dress, this Kai Soong
must run a very big tong."

"Big," Ana laughed, "hardly describes it. He is of
the House of Soong in Canton, which is a very old and
powerful Chinese trading company. The House of
Soong controls every other tong in California. That's
why I said he was almost as powerful as Governor
Stanford."

Liberty stopped, puzzled. "Anna, you mentioned Chinese concubines, but I have not seen a single one since
I've been here."

"You won't, here in Sacramento. And in San Francisco they are illegal, but the tongs have enough power

to make the authorities look the other way. Oh, not to change the subject, but we got a wire from Randy Porter today. He's on his way west and will be here in a couple of weeks. I'm dying to tell Lydia May, but I think I'll save it as a surprise. What do you think?"

"What? Oh, yes, I think you are right."

Liberty's attention had been distracted by a figure standing on the hotel verandah. The girl was young and exotically beautiful, dressed in a tight, light-blue gown of moire that revealed a stunningly seductive slim figure. Her skin was like an unripe peach in tint, making her raven black hair and eyes seem even darker.

"It's Mai Ling," Anna whispered. "She speaks many Chinese dialects, as well as excellent English. Come, I'll introduce you. You'll have to watch your step with her—she's as sharp as a needle."

They went up on the porch. Anna said cheerfully in the Mandarin she had learned from her houseboy, "Greetings to the daughter of Kai Soong."

The girl turned. Mai Ling stared at them and suddenly her face brightened. "Oh," she said in musical English, bowing her head and shoulders gracefully to the right, "you are Madam Judah of the engineer man!"

Anna introduced them. Mai Ling looked at Liberty for so long that Liberty almost blushed. "Madam O'Lee," she said, her large dark eyes fluttering, "I was not told of your youth and beauty. It shall honor me to serve you with kowtows."

"Kowtows," Anna laughed, "are more serious than bows, Liberty. They are the little unasked-for favors that show respect and admiration."

The simplicity of the explanation made Mai Ling smile. "Madam Judah puts it very well, but then she is a woman of great learning."

A diminutive houseboy came shuffling up, bowing

low, mumbling fearfully and thrusting a sheet of paper at Mai Ling.

"How fortunate!" Mai Ling said excitedly. "This, dear madams, is one Wang Wu, houseboy to the honorable Master Huntington. The good master has supplied us with three addresses of houses that might be for hire. My three bows to heaven and three bows to earth are already being heard. I shall go at once and make a decision on which would be most suitable for Madam O'Lee."

"It is still early," Liberty said. "I shall go with you."

"It is most improper," Mai Ling said politely. "It is the work of a man or his agent to select a house."

"But this is America," Anna said, chuckling. "You had best take Liberty along with you and I'll just run along home."

Mai Ling bowed in submission. Not that accustomed to Sacramento she commanded Wang Wu to escort them to the various addresses.

Liberty soon learned that she might as well have stayed in the hotel. Mai Ling was a forceful business woman, gaining most of her information from the respective houseboys before talking with the house owner.

The O'Donnell house was available only on a six months lease while the former prospector and his wife made a trip to Europe. Liberty had to agree with Mai Ling that the house was far too large for her needs and the rental price staggering. The Bucknell house was ill-equipped and the furniture badly abused.

The Flanders house was a two-story colonial that Nazareth Tedder had constructed. There were no servants and the house was immaculate. The foyer was crowded with steamer trunks and baled wooden crates. Cloris Flanders was attired for immediate departure.

"I am a recent widow," she said with formality, her

voice trembling slightly, "and am returning east where I have family. The carriage should be here shortly to take me to the steamboat to San Francisco. It was kind of Collis to send you, but . . ."

"The house is not for rent?" Mai Ling asked.

Cloris Flanders inhaled deeply and sighed. "All I asked Collis to do was send out workmen to board it up after I left. A house should be lived in and loved. Only my husband would know what to charge as a rental."

Mai Ling quickly suggested a monthly figure, based on a year's lease and paid in advance.

The figure stunned Liberty. After Mrs. Flanders's nodded consent and Mai Ling's quick whispered instructions to Wang Wu, the Chinese girl had to practically drag her on an inspection tour.

"We can't afford it," Liberty said heatedly. "The monthly rate seems reasonable, but we do not have the capital to put out a full year in advance, Mai Ling."

Mai Ling smiled secretly. "Such things you leave in the hands of Tin How—the Goddess of Heaven."

"It is silly to go on, Mai Ling. I said I can't afford it."

"*Aiyoo,* my kowtow madam," said Mai Ling despairingly, "you must put your faith in the orders my father directed me to carry out."

In the foyer a beaming Wang Wu and Cloris Flanders awaited them. With nervous fingers the old widow signed the lease document that Collis Huntington had quickly prepared, and accepted his check drawn on a San Francisco bank.

In her heart, Liberty knew that Dan would react unfavorably to being put that much into Huntington's debt. But things were happening very quickly. Soon a carriage arrived to cart off Cloris Flanders and her possessions.

With the house keys deposited in her hand, Liberty still felt as though it were a flash dream that would momentarily evaporate.

"You rest, Madam O'Lee," Mai Ling said gently. Wang Wu and I shall go and collect your things from the hotel."

"But I shall stay there tonight."

"For what reason? This is now your home and tomorrow Mai Ling will staff it. Besides, my father tells me you are with child and should rest. The first baby is always difficult."

Liberty's eyes nearly popped. No one, not even Anna Judah, had been told of her condition. Again a strange sensation crawled up her spine. It was as if Kai Soong had indeed looked into her very soul. Speechless, she let Mai Ling go about her business.

Within an hour Mai Ling was back with Liberty and Dan's luggage. Then she disappeared into the house. Just after sunset she called Liberty into the dining room and placed on the table steaming bowls. She picked up a large white bun and placed it on Liberty's plate. "This is *char sil bow,* Madam O'Lee. The barbecued pork filling is made from a secret recipe of my honorable father. And here we have chicken fried noodles, which make very good bones for new babies."

"But where is your plate?" Liberty protested.

"I eat in the kitchen, madam."

"Nonsense! You are not a servant! Now you get a plate and sit down with me, or I won't go along with the kowtow business, Mai Ling."

The girl filled the room with flute-like musical laughter, quickly setting a place for herself. Her transformation from oriental to occidental was quicker than a snake shedding its skin.

"I love your pronunciation of my name. In Chinese

it is My and you make it May—like your spring month."

Liberty laughed. "I shall do my best to get it right. But you must stop calling me madam. In our country a madam is like your concubine purveyors."

Mai Ling blinked her black lashes and then started to giggle. "I am most aware of that and delight in calling some of these occidental women by the title. You I wish not to embarrass and ask permission to call you Liberty."

"Permission granted."

Like two girls getting acquainted over their first meal at boarding school the very dissimilar women chatted away.

"You embarrass me," Liberty gasped. "Really, you do. Here you have far more education than any woman I have ever known in my life and you are cooking and running errands like Wang Wu."

"It is part of my filial duty," she replied sternly. "You forget the words I said about my education. Girl children are nothing; they are often sold off by even the best of families. When my mother died at my birth, that should have been my fate. But my honorable father was wise to the future and saw no new wife for himself on the horizon. He had no son, but he had a child. Now you might understand why I say I was dressed as a boy for my early years of tutoring. The tutors were impressed by my agile mind and encouraged my father to give me every advantage. He would have lost face by educating a mere girl, and he would have been looked on as foolish to deny further education to such a talent. So my hair was queued and my breasts strapped flat while I attended the all male universities. My age kept them from questioning my high voice and my father made sure that my roommates were his respected agents to keep me from learning of life."

"But how long did this go on?"

"I am twenty years old, Liberty. When I was ten my father's people sent him here to represent the House of Soong. At that time my grandfather lived and saw reason in my father's education of me. This year, with the death of my grandfather, my Uncle Chang became the Master of the House of Soong. Chang Soong does not believe in education for his son or his daughters or his niece. His interest is only in the money my father sends from America to keep his fat belly full of pork and wine. He took me from the university, still clad as a boy, and freighted me off to my father. But I was lucky."

"Lucky?" Liberty flared. "You might be just as well off back in China without your education. You are being used as little more than a servant."

"By your standards," Mai Ling said, chuckling. "I do my father's bidding, because I'm well aware he had a purpose in directing me so. You do not force the future, Liberty, or you face a stone wall. I am content in my mission, because it has brought me to you." Then she looked at the clock and gasped. "Look at the hour. I must be up early to select the finest of the servants my father will send down on the early steamer."

"Will they speak English? I don't speak Chinese. Oh, Mai Ling, I'm suddenly so confused."

"Naturally," the girl said, giving Liberty's cheek an affectionate pat. "Because of the child, mainly. Have you had the sickness of the morning?"

"It has been getting worse. I haven't told anyone."

"Then I have a tea that will help you. I fix now and then you go to bed."

Liberty didn't sleep well that night. She tossed in bed dreaming and thinking about Dan. She hoped that he would return soon, and yet was afraid of what he

would say about the house and their debt to Collis
Huntington.

Dan didn't sleep well that night. He tossed in his bedroll dreaming and thinking about Judah's mountains,
alternately loving and hating them. He awoke in the
mountain air and rolled over to stare at the vast stands
of redwood and fir. Ted Judah had the coffee started
already.

"Ted," Dan ventured, "in view of the millions of feet
of timber that will be needed for ties, stations, warehouses, water tanks, engine fuel, bridges and tunnel
linings, why in the hell doesn't it all come from here?"

Judah smiled jubilantly. "Boy, that is why I brought
you to my mountains. You're beginning to see them as
I do. What do you propose?"

"Carve a wagon route up the Donner Pass to get
all the timber out of here. Later, the deadhead trains
can take some back down to sell as surplus lumber."

A glitter came into Judah's eye. "I told the same to
Huntington in Washington. He scoffed. Think you can
sell him?"

"Damn right. Construction costs shouldn't run over
a thousand a mile, if the bridge builder knows what he
is doing."

"Oh," Judah mused, "the man I have in mind for
that knows what he is doing, if Crocker doesn't get in
his way."

Dan grinned. "Nazareth Tedder?"

"None better."

"What of Crocker?"

"He can't lay track without rails and those I ordered
are waiting payment for shipment. Give it a go, lad,
give it a go."

* * *

Over the strong objections of Charles Crocker, who still tried to act as though he were a member of the board, the wagon route was immediately authorized with Nazareth Tedder as a sub-contractor and consulting engineer. A small advance was made to Crocker Construction to begin preparing the first eight miles of roadbed out of Sacramento.

The meeting had run past midnight and all Dan desired was to get out of his travel clothes, bathe, and see Liberty. Collis Huntington walked along with him and finally broke the news of Liberty's move when he had Dan in front of the new home.

"I can't accept it," Dan said darkly.

"Look, Dan," Collis said sternly, "you gave us something tonight that makes a year's rent seem like a small favor in return. The construction of the Donner Pass wagon road has nothing to do with the Central Pacific. That will be a separate corporation altogether. I intend to see that you get a piece of it."

"And Ted Judah?"

"Now look, Dan, the board has already been generous in agreeing to award Ted stock without payment in appreciation for his seven-year struggle to create the Central Pacific, and the lobbying through of the Pacific Railroad Act. That is only fair to him, as this is only fair to you."

Dan stood quietly staring at the dark house. Collis stood staring at Dan. Kai Soong had advised him to divorce himself from Ted Judah and place his trust in the young engineer.

"Dan, I leave this week for the east again. I have a scheme that I have discussed with no one, but I think I can wangle the first rail shipment out of the Pennsylvania companies by pledging the personal fortunes of the men who were in that house tonight. If that works, then we can start buying up the stock of the more timid shareholders and really get this project moving this summer and fall. What do you think?"

Dan felt uncomfortable. It was a discussion he felt Collis should have been having with Judah.

"Sounds fine. That might give you time to get the rails to the Sierras and Dutch Flat before next winter."

"Hardly," Collis laughed. "It will take more than the government subsidy of $16,000 per mile to get that far along."

"But that's only for the first seven miles, Collis. The Sierras start at Arcade Creek."

"That's impossible," he chuckled. "The terrain is pancake flat for fifteen miles after Arcade."

"I know," Dan frowned, "and I've been having the same argument with Ted. He says the base of the Sierras is where the Lord placed the first granite outcroppings—twenty-two miles east of Rocklin. Now, I'm no geologist, but learned a piece from the ones who worked with me in the army. If they taught me anything it is that the base of a mountain begins where the brown earth of a valley's flood plain ends and the red soil of a range begins. I say that is seven miles east of Sacramento."

Huntington beamed. If that could be proven those fifteen miles meant an additional $480,000 worth of Federal subsidy bonds. It also pleased him to hear that a crack in the Judah-O'Lee friendship had developed. He intended to use the issue to make the crack a chasm.

"That's most interesting, Dan. I'm going to have the state geologist quietly check it out. If Ted is taking issue with you over this, maybe it's best not to let him know of our discussion."

"On that," Dan grinned, "I can fully agree. He nearly chewed me up and spit me out over it. I thought sure he was going to fire me on the spot."

"Fire you? Dan, you forget, that it was I who hired you and not Ted Judah. Goodnight, now."

Dan had the strangest sensation that Collis Huntington had wished to add several other things he didn't want Dan to forget. He was beginning to see that he might have to take sides on several issues, and wasn't sure he wanted to be on Huntington's side.

Bone weary, he went onto the porch and tried the door. He was amazed to find it bolted. He had never had cause to live in a locked house in his life and gently started a steady knock to arouse Liberty.

More quickly than he anticipated a light shone through the window and the door came flying open. A moon-faced houseboy gave him a silent, toothy greeting and bowed him in.

"Where is my wife?" Dan asked.

He didn't answer but nodded his head toward the stairs.

Mai Ling appeared on the landing, holding a lamp high.

"He has no English, as yet, Master O'Lee," she whispered, and then in Chinese told the boy he could go to bed. "We were informed of your arrival, but when the hour grew late Madam O'Lee retired. I am Mai Ling. Please come."

Dan trudged up the stairs, appraising the fineness of the house. Then, near the top, he stopped and gaped. Mai Ling's gown fit nearly skin tight. It was so filmy that the nipples of her perfectly rounded breasts seemed ready to rend the fabric for escape. Her pose made the fabric cling to her waist and legs, revealing her every curve.

Dan gulped. He couldn't help himself. His pulse was racing, and his face and neck were hot. He had never

seen a more exciting body in his life. Almost in a
trance he ascended the last steps and peered down into
her dark eyes and ruby lips. He could feel the dream-
like sensation of kissing the rosebud mouth, the thrill
as his tongue darted inside, tasting the heat and moisture
of her.

Mai Ling smiled broadly and lowered her lashes. She
shivered queerly inside. She was aware that Dan was
older than Liberty and had expected a much older man.
It pleased her to sense his silent approval of her and
the strain of his manhood against the taut material of
his Levi's told her the true measure of her effect on
him. Having been raised as a boy, she was well aware of
what men carried between their legs but it never dawned
on her until that moment that occidental men might be
quite different in size and length. Then an odd sensation
overcame her: whatever this man wished of her, she
would gladly do.

"Madam is fast asleep," she whispered.

Dan almost succumbed to the tantalizing suggestion
that he could have Mai Ling without Liberty hearing
or knowing. He was instantly ashamed that his thoughts
of the girl had brought his passion to a point of danger
beneath his new roof.

"Where is she?"

"I show." Mai Ling turned and started down the hall,
holding the light to guide Dan. Try as he might, Dan
could not take his eyes off the seductive sway of her
rear. He didn't know what position she had in the
house, but she was going to have to go or drive him
mad.

Liberty was so beautiful in sleep, that he felt ashamed
all over again. He bent and kissed her gently on the
cheek and she didn't move a muscle.

"The baby has given her much illness, Master Dan,"
Mai Ling whispered. "I have given her a herb tea to

make her relax and rest. Tau Ti, your houseboy, has put a tub of water in the alcove for you. I wish you a welcome home and a goodnight."

He nodded and watched her bow her way out of the bedroom. He looked at the tub of water, wondering if he had enough strength to bathe before going to bed. He sat down on his side of the bed and struggled to get his boots and socks off. It felt so good to have his feet free that he sat wiggling his toes. Off came three layers of flannel shirts, before he unbuttoned the top of his long johns and squirmed out of them down to his waist. Then, with his feet still on the floor, he sank back against the pillow, telling himself he would rest for a moment and then take off his trousers and bathe. As he drifted off, he couldn't get Mai Ling out of his mind.

At first he thought that Liberty had come awake, removed his clothing and was sponging off his body with warm cloths. It was so soothing and relaxing that he automatically stretched, and as his head turned he caught sight of the back of Liberty's head on the next pillow. He stared at Liberty dumbly. He could still feel the cloth and hands resting just above his groin.

He raised on his elbows and stared at the beautiful face of the kneeling Mai Ling. Her black eyes were transfixed in awe on his groin.

"We'd better not go any further." Dan put his head back on the pillow as he whispered.

She remained silent. Still she did not remove her hand. She was captivated by the daring of the moment.

"Does it grow even larger?"

Dan felt like laughing tremulously. He was caught in that hesitating moment of temptation. "Aw, come on, girl, we're in big trouble if Liberty wakes up."

"She no wake. Herb tea make her sleep soundly for eight hours. She hear, see nothing."

"Well, then—" He audibly gulped, but couldn't go

on. The excitement of doing something this dangerous was beginning to filter into his brain. He was beginning to feel like he always felt when confronted by danger. For the first time he realized that the feeling had always been sensual. And his last words tumbled out quickly. "You'll have to see for yourself if it grows more."

He could feel her hand begin to tremble.

Mai Ling's desire had been to see his flesh and little more. Now she saw sprawled before her a long-limbed man with a stubble-bearded face. His black hair was rumpled in devilish curls. The massive chest was trembling in anticipation.

She sat in awe of the sensual feel of warm flesh pressing hard against the back of her hand. It had tripled in size since she had begun to bathe him. She turned her hand around. It trembled to such a degree that she moved her lithe fingers all along the hardness to still it.

Dan stretched his head and chest upward and backward, thus forcing more of himself into the soft palm of her hand.

Shaking all over, she let her hand encircle the shaft and felt its final growth.

"Mai Ling, kiss it," Dan said with meaning emphasis.

Her black eyes widened.

"No one will know."

But Mai Ling no longer heard Dan. She had heard of Chinese boys being dismissed from school because they had put their mouths down on each other. But she was a girl, and there was no school to be dismissed from, and the words kept echoing in her brain: "Kiss it . . . no one will know . . . kiss it . . . no one will know . . ."

Dan gasped like he'd been doused with icewater when her moist lips made their first contact. But the sensation was hot, not cold. Enjoying the feeling of her hot lips on him, enjoying the sensations of newness that flowed from her body to his, he forgot the length of time that he had been without and erupted like a volcano.

"Damn," he gasped. "Next time will be different.

A sharp cry came from her throat. "No!" There was no mistaking the tinge of fright in her voice. She leapt to her feet and started running from the room.

"Mai Ling! What's the matter?"

"No more!"

"Mai Ling, come back!" Dan could hardly get the words from his throat, he was so constricted with panic. He was sure that she would tell all to Liberty in the morning. Angrily wiping his belly clean, he cursed his own stupidity for going as far with her as he had. But through his panic came a moment of self-satisfaction: not since he had been a boy had mere arousal been able to make him fly off the handle that fast. Lying back, closing his eyes, he tried to imagine what the next step would have been had Mai Ling remained.

But all that would come was the memory of the other women who had been a part of his life and so he tried to think of nothing. That didn't work either, and he turned and tossed as the worry of the next day returned.

To his utter relief the Chinese girl ignored him the next morning. A superior feeling returned and he smiled. In time she would come to him.

5

As Liberty's pregnancy increased, so did her illness and Dan's frustration in not being able to have her or Mai Ling. He grew short-tempered and ill-mannered, and Liberty silently blamed it on the tensions at work.

Dan tried everything in his power to get the Chinese girl to notice him again, desire him again, but she carefully avoided him and gave Liberty only weak solutions of the herb tea to ease her pain and make her sleep lightly.

Dan grew so enraged that he wanted her fired, inventing an excuse to place before Liberty. Liberty was dumbfounded.

"Dan, how can you be so cruel as to accuse Mai Ling of stealing? I'll have her question the houseboy and cook."

"Can't you question them yourself?" he snapped back.

"No," Liberty sighed, "as yet I can't. Dan, Mai Ling is not being paid. Out of friendship to me she stayed to train these two because they don't speak English. And what thanks does she get? Your carping and snarling. I don't know what's come over you, Daniel O'Lee, but I'm not liking it."

As was becoming his custom, he stormed from the
room without answering.

Mai Ling overheard the conversation, as she overheard every conversation in that house, and smiled. Her
father had instructed her well. It was not by accident
that the servants knew no English, or that she was holding her favors back from Dan. She would obey the
wishes of her father, as he was obeying the wishes of
Collis Huntington.

But she felt as though she were walking the sharp
edge of a knife. On one side was the respect she felt for
her father's orders and the loving friendship she had for
Liberty; but growing stronger each day were her own
frustrations. She only felt alive when Dan was around,
even when he was screaming at her. She understood the
reasons for his screams and wanted to scream right back
that her desire for him was also driving her to near-
panic. Many times she wanted to drug Liberty's tea so
heavily that she could spend the entire night with Dan.
But she was conditioned to do nothing that would go
against her father's wishes.

Liberty did not see Dan's problem as frustration;
she only recognized it in two others.

The arrival of Randy Porter, and his lodging with
the Judahs, gave Lydia May the courage to confront
her parents with the fact of her love. Selena flew into
such a tirade that Nazareth had to send for Anna Judah
to help calm her down. It was, perhaps, a fatal mistake
on his part.

When Anna tried calmly to explain who Randy was,
Selena cut her short.

"I am not interested," she snapped. "I do not care
who he is or where he comes from. Lydia May is not to
see him!"

"But, Selena . . ."

"Don't you 'Selena' me, Anna Judah," she hissed.

"I don't believe you could do this to me, after all that I have done for you."

Anna blinked. What had Selena Tedder ever done for her?

"I am unaware," Anna said calmly, "what it is you think I have done to you."

Selena eyed her narrowly. "Done? Don't crawl behind that mousy mask of yours. You have known of this romance for two years and never said a word to me. Lydia May tells me that you were the one who talked Ted into hiring this Lothario and bringing him west to keep their dalliance alive. Can you deny that?"

Anna sighed. "I can't deny that I thought it a good opportunity for Randy. And a good opportunity for you to get to meet him and know him."

"That is an opportunity I can forego," Selena said icily. "He is never to set foot in my house, and as long as he is under your roof that shall go for you as well."

"Selena, you are upset and don't know what you are saying."

With cold dignity Selena rose and went to pull the bell cord, challenging Anna with her eyes until a houseboy shuffled in.

"Get Mrs. Judah's wrap, Liu Ma," she commanded regally. "She is leaving."

Anna rose slowly, her mind seething. When she had married Ted Judah, she had accepted her new life and left the old one behind. She had never felt that it was important to inform anyone that she had been Anna Pierce, of the Pierce-Arrow Wagon and Foundry family. She didn't think that was important now. She did think it important to inform Selena of Randolph Porter's family background—one that she considered far more worthwhile to the advancement of America than a jaded English title that was worthless in Sacramento. But Anna held her silence. She suddenly saw that

Randy could have been the great-nephew of Abraham Lincoln and it would not have impressed Selena Tedder. She wasn't quite sure what Selena's problem was, but she set her mind at that moment to help Lydia May and Randy in any way that she could.

Liberty had listened to Anna and felt compassion. While Dan, Nazareth and Ted Judah were out on their final survey of Donner Pass, she extended an invitation to Selena and Lydia May to attend a dinner party for the "widows." Selena declined, because Anna would be in attendance, but allowed Lydia May to attend because she thought Randy was with the other men. This was exactly as Anna had planned and she and Liberty took their dinner in the upstairs parlor.

Because Lydia May and Randy were allowed to dine unchaperoned it embarrassed Tau Ti to serve them and he mentioned the fact to Wang Wu who made sure the news reached the ears of Liu Ma. Liu Ma's respect for his mistress was such that he reported the incident to Selena.

As inscrutable as the boy reporting to her, Selena took the news quite calmly. For the moment she did not want to strike out at Liberty, fearing the backlash Dan could bring about by revealing her past. Fully blaming Anna, she decided to hold her peace and wait for the proper moment to make the Judahs the focal point of her vengeance.

Collis Huntington came home jubilant and mysterious. He would reveal nothing until he had the board gathered together for a private dinner party. It was rather an odd gathering. Ted Judah, sensing what Huntington had to report, flatly refused to attend. A few days before the event people began taking to their beds with the flu and Selena and Elizabeth Huntington found themselves to be the only women in attendance. Aside from the "big four," Dan was the only male present. He made Liberty's excuses for her, and everyone understood.

Because the gathering was so intimate, Collis took command of the conversation from the first course, rather than waiting for the brandy and cigars.

"It was amusing," he laughed. "I found myself shopping for rails and locomotives in the same manner that Elizabeth goes after a silk dress. But the locomotives they are building are better suited to sit in a parlor— shimmers of brass trim, gold scrollwork, and hand-painted scenes on their sides. I told them all I wanted was a plain locomotive that would climb the Sierras without blowing up and you would have thought that I had broken all ten of the commandments in that single breath."

"Doesn't that confounded foofaraw raise the cost?" Mark Hopkins asked.

Huntington explained, "The railroads, they say, need the approval of the ladies. Hence, the locomotives are being made stylish from headlight to cab. Here, I've brought back drawings of the six locomotives I agreed to purchase. These two, grossing fifty and forty-seven tons, we will call the Atlantic and Pacific. This one will be called the Governor Stanford. Look at the blaze of brass that begins on the headlight stand and dazzles back through the bell to the valves in the cab. They have some of the finest artists in the east to paint the sides of the headlights with these pastoral and mountain scenes."

"Real foofaraw," Hopkins grumbled, "look at that vivid scarlet paint for the drive wheels and gold-leaf scrollwork on the spokes."

"I think it is quite handsome and appropriate," Stanford beamed.

"Why not?" Hopkins grumbled, "look at the size of your name on the damn thing."

Charles Crocker had been studying the renderings of the two eighteen-ton work-train engines, his face growing darker as he squinted at the lettering on the cabs.

"I don't mind you boosting your own vanity, Collis, by naming one of these the 'C.P. Huntington,' but why in thunderation is this one called the 'T.D. Judah'?"

Huntington grinned broadly. "Simple logic, Charles. When I left here our tiny cash reserve was already overpledged. We are unknown in the east, whereas Baldwin, Norris and Danforth Cook have worked with Ted Judah for years. With Ted being a member of this board of directors they agreed to only a twenty percent down payment, instead of their customary fifty percent. I saw it as politically wise to have an engine bear his name."

"That is scrupulously dishonest," Stanford chuckled. "I love it."

The hawk nose twitched. The thin lips arched into a smile. Time to drop his next bombshell. "Well," Huntington admitted, "you may not love me for the deal I made at the steel mills. I guaranteed our personal fortunes for the mills to ship the rails, pre-pay the freight costs and deliver in San Francisco C.O.D."

Hopkins paled, Stanford pursed his lips, and Crocker exploded.

"Not with my money you don't," he roared. "Not unless I go back on the board!"

"Now, Charles," Huntington soothed, "get your fat head out of the sand. Everyone knows that you control Edwin's vote on the board. And how are you going to make money out of your construction firm if you don't have the supplies to build a railroad? I had to do the same with the toolmakers, bridge designers and the blasting-powder chemists. Do I seem worried? No! First, because the wagon road is going to bring in cash while the railroad is being built. That route from Dutch Flats to the Nevada line is going to wean toll money away from those Downiesville and Placerville routes."

"You're talking peanuts," Crocker scowled, "and Judah is an engineer, not a grade-gang boss. He's more interested in the parallel route for the railroad, and the work is going damn slow."

"Is that right, Dan?"

Dan toyed with the food on his plate. He had thought the same, but never thought he would have to publicly admit it. "That's not the only reason, Collis. There has been a lot of illness and bad weather, and we just don't have the kind of hard-backed Irish labor force to draw on as back east. It takes a certain type of man to pick and shovel for ten straight hours each day."

"Because you spoil them," Crocker insisted. "Nazareth Tedder may pay his house builders $1.25 a day, but I still maintain road crewmen shouldn't be getting more than a dollar a day."

"It's too late to reduce their wage," Hopkins quickly started to arbitrate, "but Charles and Dan have each made some good points. As I see it, Charles won't be able to start laying rails till late summer or fall. Why don't we let Charles supervise the grade gangs until that time?"

"Excellent! Excellent!" Stanford agreed. "Mark, you've done it again!"

Dan sat silent, glad that he would not have to be the one to break the news to Ted Judah.

Throughout the main course Collis Huntington sat back and enjoyed his meal. He had yet to come up with his biggest surprise.

As dessert was being served, he took a document

from his breast pocket and laid it on the table as though it were the first gold found at Sutter's Mill. "We owe this document to an idea presented to me by our talented associate, Dan O'Lee. Dan, the Department of the Interior fully agrees with your theory. Here, my friends, is Abraham Lincoln's signed order moving the base of the Sierras to Arcade Creek. That was a half-million dollar idea you had, Dan."

"And it will make Judah choke," Crocker chortled. Then he immediately turned dour again. "But the subsidy bonds you need won't be issued in time to meet your C.O.D., Huntington."

Huntington lit up a cigar, watching the smoke waft upward as though he had just been made the emperor of the whole world.

"Won't need to be," he said simply. "Before Durant could get wind of this, I took President Lincoln's order to Boston and New York. I was able to borrow $400,-000 against it at the standard wartime rate of three per cent interest a month. I went right back to Washington and bought Federal bonds, which pay five per cent interest a month. To run the war, the government is being very generous. C.O.D., to me, means Collis Outdid Durant!"

Stanford was immediately upon his feet. "My friends, a toast. Collis!"

Stanford's sudden gleeful rise, her additional sip of wine, made Elizabeth Huntington feel lightheaded. She quickly asked that the ladies be excused. Selena followed her.

When they were gone, Collis turned to Dan.

"Words are not enough to thank you. Would you mind excusing us for a few minutes so that I can talk my associates into a more fitting reward?"

Dan had no choice but to leave as well. He didn't see Huntington take an envelope from his pocket and whisper instructions for its delivery to a houseboy. He would personally give Dan a reward that would put Dan even tighter under his thumb.

Dan started into the parlor and stopped. Selena was alone; out of the corner of his eye he saw Elizabeth ascending the stairs. He shrugged, knowing he couldn't avoid the issue any longer.

Selena saw him coming. She stood still, her eyes somber and questioning.

"Selena, I—" Dan began.

"Yes?" she said quietly. "Yes, Danny?"

"I wanted to tell you why I've avoided you and pretended we'd never met before."

Selena's brows rose sharply.

"I'm listening."

"I greatly admire your husband. He could probably build this railroad alone, if something happened to Ted and me. I would never do anything to hurt that man."

She stood looking at him, her eyes widening and darkening in her fine face.

"You kept silent for Nazareth's sake? That is interesting. A wife's past is saved by the virtue of her husband. My, my, the hungry little boy has grown himself into manly hero boots."

"Don't give me a halo," Dan laughed. "You know I wouldn't have said anything, anyway."

"And how am I to know such a thing?"

"You've got a good thing going for you. Why should I ruin it for you?"

She did not move. Her face was still and white as though it had been carved from alabaster. She couldn't be sure if he was being sincere or playing cat and mouse. Astutely, she thought it best to arch over the topic.

"Thank you," she said. "It's also nice to hear good things about one's husband."

"Good!" he enthused. "He's great! The bad part is that Ted overrules us on a lot of things Nazareth and I think would work better."

A glimmer came in Selena's eyes. Her fear of Dan gave way to the thought of what an excellent ally he could become.

"From the dinner conversation I gather that Ted Judah is starting to get on several peoples' nerves. Perhaps you and my husband will be sharing the laurels sooner than expected."

"I hate to see that," Dan said darkly, "but damn, he can be an obstinate man. This new man, Porter, is excellent, but Ted treats him like a schoolboy still."

"Isn't he?" she asked snidely.

"Hardly! But I get your point, Selena. Liberty explained it to me before we had Lydia May and Randy over for dinner last night."

"Last night?" she roared. "Lydia May went to Beth Caldwell's for dinner last night!"

"Then she has a very beautiful twin who sat across the table from me. But what difference does it make?"

"Difference?" Selena said coldly. "My daughter has gone against my word and lied to me. I overlooked your wife's first involvement, because I blame that solely on Anna Judah and her attempt to steal my daughter away because she has none of her own. But now, I would kindly ask your wife to honor my wishes and not make her home a trysting place for those alleged lovers!"

"Aw, come on, Selena! Hell, they're both so lovesick and naive they don't know what more to do than hold hands. They think that kissing is what makes babies. They aren't like we were that age. Hot damn, I remember the time that you . . ."

"Enough," she said so low, so acidly, that he started. "I knew your true colors would surface sooner or later. I have not been with a man, including my

husband, since the birth of Nathan. I want you to forbid your wife to play cupid between Lydia May and
that jackass. In exchange I will be to you what you
once wanted and I denied!"

Dan studied her, his brow furrowed in a frown. Then
he grinned, wickedly.

"Look, Selena," he said quietly, "I don't see what
you have against those two being together. But I can't
accept your offer. I'm sorry, but I just don't desire you
any more."

Wang Wu came to call Dan back in with the men.
Selena stood there a long time after he had gone. He
doesn't want me! she told herself, he doesn't want me!
To save her daughter she had offered the greatest sacrifice of all and he had not understood. She began to
seethe with rage. She found her own wrap and stormed
the block home, her mind coldly plotting. Make one
false step, Dan O'Lee, she thought, and I'll bring you
down faster than I plan on bringing down Ted Judah.
And don't think I'll overlook Liberty!

Then she stopped short, ignoring the snowflakes
gathering on her hair and eyelashes. Remembering the
whole evening, she examined every statement intended
for the ears of the directors. When she came to one particular discussion, she went over it again and again
until her mind was made up.

She would take Lydia May to San Francisco on a
shopping spree. She would spend her own time on a
different kind of shopping spree: dropping a few rumors
and picking up some Central Pacific stock after the
rumors had spread.

Dan went home, his head swimming. The directors
had doubled his salary. Elated, he ran up the stairs to
share their good fortune with Liberty and found her

soundly asleep. Thinking the news would keep until morning, he undressed, blew out the lamp and got into bed.

With his arms behind his head, he lay thinking of his annual salary in terms of the years it might take to build the line. Opinions varied from ten to fifty years. Dan's own estimate was seven—and seven times the salary he had heard that night was a pleasing sum.

When the door opened, he raised his head to whisper out, but it was too dark to see anyone. He started to rise, to find out what was going on, when Mai Ling, in the room now, suddenly lit a candle she was holding. Dan gasped. Stark naked, she stretched to her tiptoes in the candlelight, so that he could view the full bloom of her lemony full breasts, the subtle slimness of her delicate waist.

Dan stared for a second. She had shaved her body hairless. He got up from the bed and went swiftly to her.

She giggled. "I use your razor to make Mai Ling as smooth as your face."

"My goodness," he said slowly. "Is that so we can be closer together?"

"I no understand," she answered innocently.

"Then perhaps I'd better show you." He grinned.

"Mai Ling always good student. Is Master Dan good teacher?"

"We'll go to your room and you can judge for yourself."

In China it is said that a teacher gains no wisdom unless taught by the students. It is hard to say if Dan grew wiser. But Mai Ling did learn to use more than her fingers and lips.

The rest of Sacramento may have thought the remaining winter nights harsh and damp and bitterly cold. For Dan and Mai Ling, they were torrid. Whatever Dan suggested, she was eager to try and enjoy. Caught up by their sensual needs, they became more and more daring. Mai Ling caressed Dan's leg and groin under the table while she dined with him and Liberty. She fondled him in the hall while Liberty dressed for the day. She crawled into his bed with Liberty drugged with herb tea and asleep beside them.

There was nothing Dan could do about his passion except enjoy it. As for Mai Ling, she obediently obeyed his every whim not only because she too was thoroughly enjoying it, but because the note from Collis Huntington had informed her that her father commanded her to draw Dan into an "unforgettable" affair.

Yet the deeper Dan became involved, the more his shame increased each morning. Where had his will power gone? He did not know. Around Liberty he was curt and irritable; around Mai Ling loving and tender.

He began to take his ill temper to work, which made Ted Judah frown and Collis Huntington gleefully smile. And the Chinese houseboys began to grapevine messages which were tittered over, gasped at, or mulled over carefully—depending upon whose ears they reached.

Selena Tedder listened only half-heartedly to her servant's reports. Though she had enough evidence to bring Dan swiftly down in the eyes of his wife, she was not quite ready to strike in that direction. She had bigger fish to fry.

"Ah, Mark," she gaily called, sailing into Hopkins & Huntington Hardware at an hour when she knew she would not run into Collis Huntington. "You are just the man I hoped to find. Please, I have a very womanly admission to make and dread going to Nazareth for counsel. Can you help me?"

"Selena," Hopkins said graciously, "I am always at your service."

"Mark, this is difficult." Theatrically, Selena paused before resuming. "When I was in San Francisco recently I secured Central Pacific stock at the going ten percent down. Now, as I understand the rumor going around"—a rumor that she herself had started among San Francisco bankers—"the Central Pacific never intends to build across the Sierras, but will end at Dutch Flats and serve as no more than a feeder line for this wagon road proposed by Ted Judah."

"Selena," he soothed, "do you really believe such poppycock?"

"Frankly, Mark," she said intently, "I do!"

Mark Hopkins's ulcer began to burn fiercely. It was not the first time he had heard the rumor. San Francisco bankers were helping it gain credence, because they stood to gain little from the railroad. The Central Pacific was losing the millions Collis Huntington had gained for them faster than he had acquired them.

"All right," he openly admitted, "the rumor is nearly killing us, but it is only a rumor. Damn, I can hardly keep my books straight with the buys and sells at lower and lower figures. I would love to get my hands on the person responsible for this slide."

"Mark Hopkins," Selena said indignantly, "I gave you more credit than that. Are you not aware of who benefits the most? Those who made pledges of ten per cent but have yet to put up their first dollar on the stock. The lower it falls, the less their initial investment becomes. I recommend you go back and study that set of books and start making them pay up or else release their stock so that honest people can buy it up."

Selena was interested only in the stock being held by one certain party. She sat back and waited while Hopkins methodically reviewed his books.

When pressures were subsequently exerted on the stockholders by Hopkins, some forfeited through non-payment and others—those who did put up the money —sold out quickly as the rumors continued. It was a close race between Selena and the Associates who gained the most. But the largest block of stocks were withheld until Selena's patience grew thin. She all but demanded action from Mark Hopkins.

Hopkins finally called Ted Judah to his office.

"Ted," he smiled in a dry, formal manner, "good of you to come on such short notice. I have been reviewing the books and find that you are remiss on your ten percent down payment on the stocks you were offered. You may be aware that I have been calling in all of those options and cancelling them for non-payment."

Ted Judah blinked several times. "Hopkins, you know those stocks were to be put in my name with no payment due."

Hopkins nervously shuffled the papers about on his desk. "Strange, I find no mention of that in any of the official minutes of the meeting."

"Nonsense! You were there! It was a verbal agreement between all of you the night we formed."

Hopkins shrugged. "It is not here in writing. Ted, I am responsible for the company records. You, an engineer, should recognize the importance of records and factual data. Before this stock can be listed in your name, you will have to make the ten percent cash payment on it or get a written record into the directors' meeting."

Word by word, Ted Judah informed Anna of the meeting. At last he exploded: "We have no meetings of the board nowadays. And I have not been invited to sit or vote in their private conferences. They have me, Anna. We don't have the money for the down payment."

"There is always my family."

"No! They cannot go back on their verbal agreement, Anna. My hands now seemed tied, but if they continue on this course, they will rue the day they started this railroad."

But the scheme to drive Judah out was continued devilishly. The man's engineering genius was regarded by his partners as of paltry value compared to the bond-issue prize glittering atop the government's money tree. When it took months to drive pilings across the American River outside of Sacramento, Judah was blamed. When a survey report came up missing, ten miles of the wagon road had to be resurveyed.

The quarrels didn't remain just between Ted and the quartet. He fought with Dan, found fault with Nazareth's work and blamed Randy Porter for the loss of the survey.

As spring melted into summer tempers rose as fast as the temperature.

Liberty's gaze rested briefly upon the face of her husband. Then she looked down at the size of her belly. Miserable both day and night, she wasn't sure that she could last another month. More important was her belief that Dan might not last another month.

What's happened to us? she thought miserably. I've become nothing but his whipping boy. She had an impulse to lean across the lunch table and take Dan's hand. But one glance at his face was enough to stifle that impulse completely.

In less than a year, Dan O'Lee had aged visibly. There was no light in his eyes now, no challenge, no youth. He was a man with three loves, each demanding supremacy. Liberty's constant illness irritated him; as much as he loved his work, the constant squabbles were loathsome; and Mai Ling had become like a terrible incurable disease. He was almost powerless to stay away from her, yet felt eternal damnation when he returned to his own bed. But by the next night he would reason it out that it was a secret matter between Mai Ling and himself and what Liberty didn't know, didn't hurt her.

Liberty looked at the food untouched upon his plate.

"Dan, please," she whispered.

"Eh—what? Oh, I'm not hungry. I have to get to a meeting with Charles Crocker."

"But this is the first meal we've had together in ages."

"Hardly my fault," Dan said honestly. "You're always asleep by the time I come home for supper."

"I know," Liberty said miserably. "But not today. I have to go out this afternoon and I'll force myself to stay up, pain or no pain."

He stood up and she came to him, but he did not kiss her.

"Don't make rash promises," he said meanly. "You act as though you were the first woman in the world ever to have a baby."

"Oh, Dan," she whispered. "It's not my . . ."

"And don't cry! God damn, I'm sick and tired of your crying."

Liberty blinked back her tears and watched him leave. The baby gave a violent kick that nearly doubled her over in pain. She gulped for air but refused to call out for Mai Ling or Tau Ti. As soothing as the herb tea was, it always made her so drowsy and she wanted to be quite alert that afternoon.

Walking slowly, she went into the foyer, put on a poke bonnet and left the house. It was far too early for her appointment, but she thought a slow walk in the July sun might soothe her and give her legs some badly needed exercise. After two blocks her legs were like jelly, her forehead was damp with cold sweat and her heart was thumping wildly. Grabbing hold of a tree she thought, Oh Lord, I'm going to have the baby right here. The shade was cooling and for a moment she closed her eyes and rested her head against the tree bark.

"Liberty! Are you alright, child?"

She opened her eyes to peer into the frightened face of Anna Judah.

"Yes," she smiled weakly. "I just needed a moment's rest."

"You must be crazy, coming out on a hot afternoon like this. Where in the world are you off to?"

"You will never believe this, Anna," she laughed. "But I am off to see Selena Tedder."

Anna's brows arched in wonderment.

"Yes," she went on, "she sent me a note yesterday. She wants to discuss with me the problem of Lydia May and Randy."

"Damn woman," Anna huffed. "She knows your condition and should have come to you. Just like her to make her subjects come crawling before her throne."

"I don't mind, Anna. I thought the outing might do me some good. Besides, the note made it sound as though she is ready to buckle under."

That, Anna thought suspiciously, didn't sound right. Just that morning at breakfast Randy had told her he had been unable to see Lydia May for the past two weeks; he had been told by Nazareth to stay away from his daughter. No, she reasoned, Selena was winning that fight. She had another fish to fry and Anna thought she knew what it was.

"Well, Libby, from the looks of you, I don't think the outing is doing you that much good. Let me see you back home."

"But Selena!" Liberty protested.

"We'll send her a note with your excuses."

"You're right, of course. But I am feeling much better and hate to take you out of your way."

"Well," Anna said slowly, "I do have a slew of errands to run. If you're sure you'll be all right, I can stop by Selena's and leave word with Liu Ma at the door."

"I'll take it slow, I promise you. I think I'll go back by way of the park. It's shadier and I can sit and rest a minute if I have to."

"Very good. Now, you send word to me if you need anything."

"Thanks, Anna. Goodbye."

Anna Judah had no great amount of errands to run and had no intention of just leaving word with the Tedder houseboy. She brushed Liu Ma aside and marched right into the sun parlor.

"You!" Selena said.

"Yes," Anna said coolly. "I found Liberty nearly collapsed on the street and sent her back home. She informed me of your note and I am here to make her excuses."

"You have, so goodbye!"

"Awfully mysterious note, if you ask me," Anna declared, with no intention of leaving just yet. "Funny that it is just opposite to what Randolph Porter was telling me at breakfast this morning. What is your game, Selena? What was the real reason you wanted to get Liberty over here?"

Selena looked at her with some astonishment.

"Now, really," she began. "You are all but calling me a liar. What I wish to discuss with Liberty O'Lee is no concern of yours."

Anna walked closer, her cheeks flushed. But one look at Selena's cool face, and she stilled the hot words on the tip of her tongue: it was quite apparent that she had judged Selena's motive correctly and angry words would solve nothing.

"In the nearly eight years that I have been here," she said quietly, "I have thought it, with my pinch penny New England upbringing, a very wise move to learn enough of my servants' language so that they would be unable to cheat me. They are not aware of how much I have learned and jabber quite freely when I am around. To gossip with one another about the people they work for is for them an amusing sport. Some, like your Liu Ma, even boast about the rewards they receive from their mistresses for passing along tasty bits of gossip. They call it 'No-tong-go-home-money.' Am I making myself quite clear, Selena?"

"Hardly."

"Then let me put it squarely to you. I'm not sure of your reason, which is usually devious to begin with, but if you intended to inform Liberty about the affair her husband is having right under her nose, then I would advise you to keep your mouth shut."

Selena exploded, "She needs to know for her own good!"

"No, Selena, if that were the case I would have informed her long before this. You were going to do it because you have a curious desire to hurt people you think have done you wrong. Blame me for Liberty entertaining Lydia May and Randy, but don't blame Liberty."

"I blame you all," Selena sneered, "and it's not going to stop me from showing that bitch the manner of husband she is married to."

I should do it now, Anna thought. In her world, a secret gained was a secret held forever. But sometimes a secret exposed could keep many others from being unmasked.

"I see," Anna said steadily. "Then what is to stop me from informing Nazareth of the manner of woman he is married to?"

The silence stretched thinly between them.

At last, Selena tried to bluff. "I don't know what you are talking about."

"Then I'll put it simply," Anna said ominously. "Lydia May has always been quite frank with me. She is well aware of her birth, your years of desertion and what you were about during those years."

Selena growled, "Damn Howard Tedder for telling her! Damn her for telling you! I'll never forgive her for this, never!"

"That's odd," Anna murmured, "because she forgave you and loves you in spite of the past. It is a forgotten memory, as far as she is concerned. It should be forgotten as far as anyone is concerned. I feel ashamed having to use it as a weapon against you, but I can see no earthly reason for Liberty to be hurt unnecessarily."

Slowly, quietly, Selena rose.

"I'm not going to argue with you, Anna. I argued with you before . . . it still hasn't solved my problem with Lydia May. I don't know the answer; I know only I am dead set against her marrying Randolph Porter. But you knew you had me beat when you brought Nazareth into the picture. I have not been a loving wife, because I don't think I was ever taught how to really love. But Nazareth has been faithful. I will say that for him. I wouldn't hurt Nazareth for anything in the world."

Without another word she turned and fled from the room. Only when she was on the staircase did it dawn on her that she had used practically the same words as Dan O'Lee. What irony, she thought. Dan had turned her down because of Nazareth and now Nazareth stood in the way of her exposing Dan's affair with the Chinese girl. Well, she mused, there was more than one way to take honey from a hive without getting stung. If she hurried, she might be able to catch Charles Crocker in his store. Now, more than ever, she wanted to rid her life of the Judahs.

Liberty was glad she took the short cut through the small park. It was quiet and peaceful, the trees masking off most of the sun's rays and the street noises. Even though her strength had returned, she sat down on a bench and stretched out her legs. It felt so good to be free from the prison of her bed and room that she contemplated just sitting there for the rest of the afternoon.

She was quite alone, with an excellent view of the sun-drenched street. A carriage pulled up before the great Huntington mansion, but she was unable to see who it deposited. From around the corner of the house she saw the houseboy, Wang Wu, shuffle across the street with his funny little trotting gait. He cut diagonally across the park without seeing her, his thin shoulders hunched over as though on an urgent mission.

Liberty folded her arms across her breast and let her head fall forward. Blessedly, she was experiencing a few moments without pain and she wanted to relish every moment of it.

She was unaware of how long she sat silently before the sound of running feet made her drowsily open her eyes. At first she thought it was just a couple of rag-tag Irish boys playing tag with each other. Then she saw two others, and the boy who was "it."

Liberty sat up straight. The fifth boy was Wang Wu. His short legs were no match against the others, and they were slowly boxing him in, breaking the semi-silence with their jeering comments. A dark suspicion began forming in Liberty's mind as she rose, but she wanted to get closer before making a mistake.

Then she knew it was no game. The thugs seized Wang Wu and were throwing him to the ground. Their fists pumped down on him. Wang Wu wiggled away, staggered to his feet, and was felled again. Stoically, he did not call out for help.

Liberty tried to run, but could only manage a fast waddle. When she saw the flash of a knife and the thugs holding Wang Wu by the head and queue, she screamed out at them.

The thugs turned in astonishment.

"Mind your own goddamn business, lady," one of them called out in a heavy brogue.

"Leave him alone," Liberty cried, waddling closer.

"Hurry!" the lone speaker barked at his mates. "Cut off his hair and then slit his yellow throat."

Liberty stopped, aghast. She had heard much about this from Mai Ling—the bitter struggle going on between the Chinese and the poorer Irish emigrants. But she had no idea it was happening here in Sacramento—and in broad daylight.

"I said stop!" she said sternly.

"And I told you to mess out, lady. These chinks gotta be taught to go back home and leave work for honest men."

Liberty was weaponless and took a desperate gamble. She opened her purse and stuck in her hand. The action suggested to the thugs that she might be willing to pay for the chink's life and they began to grin and nod at each other.

"My husband doesn't believe in a woman walking around defenseless," she said coolly, "and I assure you I am an excellent shot. I will give you one second to get out of here before I start firing."

She stuck a finger against the inside of the purse to

make it look like a revolver barrel—and prayed. To her relief the men turned and scurried away.

Wang Wu's face was gradually returning from a pasty gray to its natural yellow-brown.

"Madam O'Lee," he said in a high-pitched voice, "I am forever in your debt."

"Are you all right? Did they hurt you?"

Wang Wu felt his queue and grinned. "Wang Wu okay-dokay, he did not lose dishonor by losing his queue. My life is now yours to command, gracious lady."

"Nonsense! Come, I'll see you out of the park in case they're lurking behind some of these trees."

Obediently, Wang Wu rose and followed Liberty out of the park, across the street and up to the steps of the Huntington mansion.

"Now, Madam O'Lee," he said very seriously, "it is Chinese custom for Wang Wu to pay his debt or be in great dishonor."

Seeing the earnest expression on his face, Liberty said: "But there is nothing I wish from you, Wang Wu."

Wang Wu nodded as though puzzling over that problem himself. Then he smiled. "Old Master Kai is with us this day. We shall speak to him on this matter. Wang Wu will ask to become servant of number one wife of Master O'Lee for one year without pay, but not servant of Master O'Lee's concubine."

Liberty reeled. She did not believe she'd heard what she did. Perhaps the boy was confused.

"Oh, please, Madam O'Lee," he quavered, "do not repeat those unfortunate words from Wang Wu's mouth. Mai Ling has threatened to chop off Tau Ti's ears and tongue if he breathes one word about the happenings in the house of your husband."

Liberty remained stunned. She was unaware of the

opening of the front door and the approach of two figures until Wang Wu began to jabber rapidly in Chinese.

To her ears the jabber seemed to go on forever. Like a mortally wounded animal she was unsure of what to do, except crawl off to some dark place and lick her wounds. The voice that translated Wang Wu's words for Collis Huntington drew her attention back. She found herself staring into the deep reaches of Kai Soong's black eyes. They were warning her to say nothing that would be unnecessary.

"Liberty!" Collis gasped, "how heroic of you! I will see to it that the police patrol that park from now on. You look pale, my dear. Here, let me help you inside the house."

Kai Soong had been whispering to Wang Wu.

"My carriage is here," he said gently. "For the life of Wang Wu, I shall see Madam O'Lee safely home."

Liberty did not protest. She didn't think her quaking legs would take her a single step inside Huntington's house. When she turned Wang Wu had vanished and she mumbled something or other to Collis. Kai Soong helped her into the carriage and whispered his goodbye to Huntington. Liberty could not help but note the respectful, almost subservient manner in which Huntington treated the Chinaman.

Liberty was only a block away from home, but Kai directed the coachman to circle the park and then return.

"The delay," he said, in his deep soothing voice, "is to give you a quiet moment, Madam O'Lee. A troubled heart should not act in haste or it could cause itself even greater hurt."

Liberty turned in her seat and studied the man. He regarded her as a father would a troubled daughter.

"Did Wang Wu tell you everything?" she asked.

The barest grin broke around his thin lips. "With proper respect Wang Wu told me of his fortune in having you cross his path this day. He said no more. Kai Soong speaks of what he reads in your heart."

Liberty didn't quite believe him.

"At the moment," he went on gently, "words of comfort are quite meaningless. But in time you shall see that this is really a very minor matter and one you should not trouble yourself over."

Liberty's temper came boiling up. "Minor matter? I hardly call my husband having an affair with your daughter a minor matter!"

"Aha!" he mused. "The lady has as much fire and spark as a New Year's celebration. But, would the lady ask herself calmly if she speaks from wisdom, or from wagging tongues? It has been my experience that houseboys without women of their own tend to fabricate stories about those around them to make their rather humdrum lives a little more interesting."

"Are you suggesting that," Liberty demanded hotly, "because your daughter is involved?"

Kai Soong tented his long fingernails together. He was silent for a long moment.

"I am saying, Madam O'Lee, that regardless of the woman, she would be incapable of fully stealing your husband away from you. Likewise, there shall be no other man for you until your husband has left this life."

"Word, words," she protested. "You are being very masculine to protect my husband, if he has done me wrong."

"Your husband means no more to me than a grain of sand on the beach," he said indifferently. "Granted, in my land, it is custom to take more than one wife. But the number one wife remains as such."

"If it's your custom," Liberty snapped, "then why didn't you take another wife?"

Kai Soong nodded, and smiled. "My daughter's tongue also wags, I see. But there is no great mystery. I believe in following the destiny that was charted for me at birth. It did not reveal a second marriage for Kai Soong."

Liberty frowned, thinking. Mai Ling had told her almost the same thing about her father. Odd, but not once since she had learned the truth from Wang Wu had she felt any hatred toward Mai Ling. She'd felt that all women felt hatred toward another woman who took their husbands from their bed. But she did not.

She sat quite still beside Kai Soong, her eyes widening in her white face. Then, very softly, she began to laugh.

"You are quite mystical," she said. "Do you know my destiny, as well?"

Kai Soong turned to face her, the yellow oval of his face filled with maddening serenity.

"Entirely," he said coolly. "Your male child shall come forth on the tenth day of your August month. As that is the sign of the lion, and this is the Chinese year of the ox, he shall be named after his father, Daniel, and he shall one day become most powerful in the world of business and finance. He shall be the first of three children for you, the last being a troublesome female—for aren't all females troublesome?"

His deep black eyes glinted so merrily that Liberty found herself laughing in agreement and relaxing in his company.

"But that is of the future," he went on, "and still masked in some clouds of doubt, although there is no doubt that the future of Liberty Wells O'Lee shall be most brilliant."

She gasped. "How did you know my maiden name?"

Kai Soong's chuckle was deep and booming. "It is my main business to see much, know everything, and reveal very little."

"You've been revealing quite a bit to me."

Kai Soong bowed his head slightly and turned his gaze away. "Kai Soong shall reveal one more thing to you, Chu-chee. Oh, that means free one—or liberty—in my tongue. Before the year of the ox becomes the year of the tiger you shall see the depth of bitter gloom and then be raised to great glory from an unexpected trip of great meaning. Ah, this is your house. My steamboat leaves for San Francisco within the hour, so I shall humbly ask forgiveness for not accepting the hospitality within your abode that custom demands you offer me. I ask of you only that you follow the wisdom of a generous heart and not the impulse of your mind."

Speechless, Liberty descended and watched the carriage drive away. She had never felt so calm and peaceful and serene in her life. As though fully believing that Mai Ling could have had no involvement with Dan, she rushed into the house to share with her the strange meeting with the Chinese girl's father. But Mai Ling didn't answer her calls and Tau Ti only shrugged at her rapid questions that he didn't understand.

Liberty laboriously pulled herself up the stairs and down the hall to Mai Ling's room. It was neat as a pin and vacant of any of the girl's personal possessions.

Despite herself, Liberty could not keep from laughing. It had been true. The clever Chinaman had hoodwinked her with his fables to gain time and get his errant daughter out of harm's way. He had left her to handle Dan with the wisdom of her heart and not the impulse of her mind.

From the downstairs hall she heard Dan's voice. She waited by the open door until he bounded up the stairs and joined her.

"Where's Mai Ling?" he demanded.

"Her father took her back to San Francisco."

"Damn!" he growled. "This is a hell of a time for her to go off . . . what with you being so close and all."

"I'll be all right, really I will."

"Hell, without Mai Ling you can't even make that houseboy understand you. And who will make your herb tea for you?"

"I suddenly don't think I will need it any more. It makes me very sleepy."

As though they had violently argued over Mai Ling, and then lovingly made up, Dan was made to understand that there was no longer a reason for her to take the drugging tea.

"Well," he grinned, "do you think we can make somebody understand that I would like a drink before dinner?"

"If I get a kiss first," she said.

Liberty's face was very pale after that kiss. It took all of her courage not to pull away and confront Dan with the truth. But she fought to follow the wisdom of her heart and keep Dan from learning what she knew.

Good bye, Mai Ling! Liberty exulted. Then prayed that she was correct.

6

The summons had been so rapidly issued that it left Grenville Dodge apprehensive. His lips were dry and his hands trembled when the orderly at the White House waiting room called his name and opened the door to President Lincoln's office.

A brigadier, Dodge stood at attention and saluted his Commander in Chief. It had been several months since he had seen the president. He was aghast to see that the man seemed to have aged twenty years. The new beard made his face longer and gaunter. His eyes were tired and pouched. But his teeth flared white in a grin as his gangly frame lurched up and swung across the room, hand outstretched.

"Need you," he said. "Need you real bad, Dodge. I want you to help me decide the commencement point for the Union Pacific Railroad."

Dodge, surprised at the request, stood stiffly at attention until the president was back behind his desk and seated.

"General, there is not a town or village in the Missouri Valley area of Nebraska and Iowa that hasn't sent a lobbyist to try to smoke me out on the issue. How far along are they?"

Dodge fished a letter out of his pocket. "I heard from Peter Dey. They have finished the Mississippi & Missouri Railroad as far as Brooklyn, Iowa, and are slowly laying track toward Grinnell. But, frankly, Mr. President, whether or not they reach Grinnell depends a great deal on the sale of the Union Pacific bonds."

"Not going too well?"

"Another three months like the last six and we won't have a railroad, sir—hopelessly bad sales."

"Can't say I blame the people," the sad, even voice stated. "A war costing two million dollars a day would make any man wary of buying government bonds from a nation that could go bankrupt before we see the end of the tunnel. But, that's not why I had the War Department track you down and hurry you over here."

Dodge nodded and settled back in his chair. All of his worst fears flew away. But he had an odd sensation that the president wanted to continue talking about the finances of the railroad, and was hedging.

Lincoln reached into a desk drawer, pulled out a roll of maps, then—with droll asides—reviewed the arguments presented by the lobbyists for each community, giving Dodge an opportunity to counter each of their claims.

"Sioux City is too far north and Plattesmouth too dangerous during the spring floods."

"Where then?" the president asked sharply.

A smile flickered across the general's stern, fine face. "I would put it where an engineer would put it and not a politician, although it could have strong political overtones. Here, sir, is the Council Bluffs-Platte Valley throughway, which goes flat out across the prairie and plains to the base of the Rockies. If the terminal is Council Bluffs-Omaha, then you please both the Iowa and Nebraska delegations."

"Interesting," Lincoln said, a twinkle in his eye, as

though he had already covered that point in his own mind. "I shall give your points very serious thought."

Dodge started to roll up the maps and saw that the last ones were Ted Judah's Central Pacific proposals.

"I'm sorry to say this, sir, but I fear they have given you outdated maps."

"No!" the president groaned. "How can that be?"

"Well, this map shows the Central Pacific using a five-foot rail gauge."

"That is what was agreed upon," was the firm response.

"But the Union Pacific plans are based on a four-foot eight-inch gauge!" the general warned. "That would mean adjustable wheel tracks on every through car, or ruinous realignment of roadbeds and enlargement of every bridge and tunnel between Iowa and the Atlantic Coast. Furthermore——"

"And what of the Sacramento Valley tracks that are already down?" the president interrupted.

Dodge grinned to himself. He had an opportunity to throw a monkey wrench that would chew off a lot of teeth in the Central Pacific's gears.

"Sir, the Missouri Pacific, between St. Louis and Kansas City, is also a broad gauge line. Need I remind you of the transportation and supply bottleneck that it has caused in St. Louis? Everything must be off-loaded and reloaded onto their cars, and being a small line they have damn few freight cars. Had they been on a standard gauge, troops could have been moved faster to help at Shiloh."

"Standard? Are you saying that four-eight is standard, General Dodge?"

"It must be. If I may be so bold as to paraphrase, sir, 'A house divided cannot stand'—nor a national railroad."

Lincoln tilted back his head and roared with laughter.

"My enemies say that I am an inflexible baboon, General Dodge. Wait until I tell them that my own words were used against me. I will sign an order today making the official gauge of the railroads four feet eight inches." Then he swung his chair around and stared out across the White House lawn. "Tell me, quite frankly, what would you personally do about the disappointing sale of the Union Pacific bonds?"

"I think the vastness of the project frightens people, sir. The Pacific Railroad is too big for private enterprise. If we were not a democracy the government would build the whole thing. But the government subsidy seems too little and private enterprises contribute little at all, because of the war."

"That hardly answers my question," the president drawled. "Are you saying that the government should do everything in its power to encourage private industry?"

The question was so carefully couched that Dodge instinctively leaned forward. Something told him that this was the real reason for his trip to the White House.

"Yes, sir," he barely got out.

"Perhaps," Lincoln said slowly, "Congress might be willing to shift the federal loans on the Pacific Railroad from a first mortgage to a second mortgage category."

Dodge was stunned. Such a revision of the Act would enable Union Pacific and Central Pacific to issue first mortgage bonds without limit. Lincoln stared at him expectantly.

Dodge jumped to his feet and blurted out: "May I take the news to New York that the White House would consider such a revision of the Pacific Railroad Act?"

Lincoln rose and nodded. His two big rugged hands grasped the one outstretched. "And tell Mr. Ames that the baboon who sends the news thinks he makes a right good shovel."

The general left and Lincoln gazed dreamily over the river toward Virginia. After twenty-seven desperate months, the Union was grinding from defense to offense. Gettysburg and Vicksburg had turned the tide. The war might rage on in the South, but now the New West belonged solely to the Union.

For a moment the president forgot the present and thought of the past and future. War and depression, he mused, were the real cornerstones of the American dream. Upstate New York, the Ohio Country, Kentucky and Tennessee were areas that grew after the Revolution. The economic slack after the War of 1812 was taken up by a massive trek into Michigan, Indiana, Illinois, Alabama, Mississippi and Louisiana.

With Santa Anna's defeat and surrender of California, Texas, Western Missouri and Kansas Territory, the landless emigrants marched in with plow and oxen.

Now, he thought proudly, the New West will be there to attract the unemployed wanderers from this horrible war. And because of his actions that day he knew he would be giving them a throughway—a coast-to-coast railroad.

He chuckled softly as he paraphrased himself—he was tendering a ribbon of iron rails to help "bind up the nation's wounds."

As Kai Soong foretold, Daniel Patrick O'Lee was born on the 10th day of August 1863. By a strange quirk of fate it had taken that long for word of President Lincoln's decisions to reach Sacramento. Unfortunately, the only director who had not escaped the city's humid heat was Charles Crocker.

Crocker puzzled over the letter from the Railroad Commission for some little time and then went in search of Randolph Porter, whom he had taken a strong liking to because of the young man's natural respect for his elders.

"Son," he drawled, "this letter says the president is making the Central and Union Pacific railroads come in line with a standard four-foot-eight gauge. All summer long, the timber we've been getting out for the mills from the wagon road have been cut and stacked to cure, based on a five-foot gauge. How is this going to affect us?"

Randy wasn't sure, but didn't want to appear to be stupid. "Two inches on each side? It shouldn't matter that much at all, Mr. Crocker."

Then Randy thought it best that he check it out with Ted Judah. Judah just closed his eyes in pain, shook his head and motioned for Dan and Nazareth to follow him. All three got back to Crocker.

"It's *four inches,* Crocker—can't you understand that? Every damn tie that has been cut will be too long. It will give too much play on each end and it can cause spikes to pop out in just a couple of years time."

"Judah," Crocker said sourly, "do you know how much it is going to cost to haul all those ties back to the mill and have them recut? I'll just go along with Porter that it won't matter that much at all." Then he added, as though to cap off the argument, "Besides, we don't have the time to re-cut the ties."

"Time?" Judah exploded, the pain in his stomach slow-smouldering like a fire in a grate. "We're going to have plenty of time. If Huntington's locomotives and cars are on their way, they will have to be sent back. Their wheel bases were designed for five feet, unless you forgot. And every damn piece of equipment and rolling stock of the Sacramento Line is useless to us."

"No!" Crocker said hoarsely. "No!"

"That's the size of it, Crocker. You'd best call your playmates back from their vacations so we can do

some damn serious planning. This is also going to throw
the surveys off, you know."

"No!" Crocker got out, the word strangling in his
throat. He was filled with rage. He was a man of huge
appetites, of gigantic lust for power, but at that moment he only wanted to place blame.

"When they return," he said, "not before. We will
just continue on, as is."

Judah bent and picked up his coat.

"Then I will go to them."

Crocker pounced. "To cover up this gross error of
yours? You are the one costing us time and money.
Why didn't you see that your gauge was out of line
with the eastern railroads? You are crazy and we were
crazy to go along with you!"

Suddenly, convulsively, Ted brought up his big fist
and smashed it into Crocker's jaw. The short man
reeled from his chair, rolled on the floor and was instantly on his feet. But he would fight with words and
not fists.

"You crazy lunatic," he bellowed, "you're fired! Get
out! And take your motley crew with you! They're
fired, as well!"

Dan stepped in front of Ted Judah before he could
attack again, and deftly lifted Charles Crocker off his
feet by his shirt front.

"Huntington hired me, mister," he hissed, "and he's
the only one who can fire me. But that don't mean I
can't quit—which I do! Come on, Ted and Nazareth,
let's get out of here—it smells like skunk!"

Anna Judah was not surprised. She had been expecting something like this ever since Mark Hopkins
started pressing Ted for a down payment on the stock.

"What now?" she asked wearily.

Ted laughed. He felt quite relieved now that the bubble had finally burst. The ulcer in his stomach had ceased to burn.

"Now?" He shrugged. "Now, Ted Judah begins to fight back, my dear. Get me paper and telegraph forms. The east has wanted Ted Judah back for some time, and now Ted Judah wants something from the east. To get me they are going to have to buy out those who oppose me here and make sure that we build a real railroad."

"Can you do it, Ted?"

He grinned. "With one man alone, if need be. Commodore Vanderbilt refuses to invest in the Union Pacific, because it smells of Oliver Ames. They would make lovely rivals, don't you think?"

"Don't worry," Liberty said to her husband, cuddling the baby in her arms, "you'll find another job."

Dan took his eyes from the baby and looked at her.

"I want you to get this thing straight, Libby," he said. "I wasn't fired. I quit. Damn, what a way to remember the day of my son's birth."

"Now, Dan O'Lee," Liberty said, "don't fret on about it! There isn't a person in Sacramento who wouldn't have done the same. But I think you'd be better off not discussing it with anyone until Collis Huntington returns."

"I am not about to crawl on my knees to any man," Dan growled.

Liberty chuckled. "I picture it just in reverse, my darling. On his knees, Collis will have to come to you, because who else does he have?"

The question was, in part, Ted Judah's to answer. An old friend, Samuel Montague, had come overland seeking a job. A competent and forceful engineer who had worked with Judah on the building of the Sacramento Line, he was just the man Ted needed to mind his store while he prepared to go east. Montague was to apply for a job from Crocker, but play dumb about his former friendship with Judah.

Fearing that Randy Porter just might be wrong, Crocker was pleased to have someone like Montague to question. When Montague restated every argument that Judah had put forth, Crocker was perplexed. He hired Montague, at the same salary as Randy Porter, and still refrained from passing all of his news on to his associates.

Mark Hopkins was the first to return, toward the end of August. He listened solely to Crocker, wordlessly rose and departed. By noon the next day, worried and distraught, Huntington and Stanford were back.

Stanford was overly subdued and kept letting the meeting get out of hand. His ego had been sorely trod upon in San Francisco. His enthusiasms over the railroad had become downright embarrassing to the Republican leaders of the state. The Crocker Brothers bill before the California senate for the state to give the Central Pacific $500,000 outright had had as its chief lobbyist the governor.

The San Francisco enemies of the railroad were already rumbling about scandal, and the Republican leaders moved swiftly. They were ready to oppose Stanford's renomination by running Frederick F. Low against him. Stanford scoffed, until shown the tally sheets of Low's delegate strength at the forthcoming state convention. He knew he didn't stand a chance. His political career had been derailed.

Then, to make matters worse, he was called back to a debacle.

"What—oh, yes, Charley, I guess Judah should have been fired."

"And what do we do in the meantime?" Huntington demanded.

"I have it under control," Crocker boasted. "Porter is a fine young man and now has the help of Montague."

"A boy and an unknown quantity," Huntington sneered. "I could care less about Ted Judah, but I want Dan O'Lee back on the job."

"Over my dead body!" Crocker flared.

"Oh, if that were only possible," Huntington sighed.

"Leland! . . . Leland!" Mark Hopkins called.

"What—oh, yes, Mark, what is it?"

"I would like the floor to find out if we are conducting a meeting or another one of our four-ring circuses."

Stanford said, "What was it you wished?"

"To get away from senseless petty differences over personalities and grapple with reality . . . the reality of the revision of the Railroad Act. Look at this," Hopkins stormed, throwing a stack of yellow sheets down on the table. "It cost me a handsome bribe to get my hands on it. You all thought you were so smart getting me to force Judah to buy up the stock we offered him for nothing. Well, the worm has turned. If a man has money—big money—in the east, Judah has wired him and gotten many answers back. Lord only knows what he's gotten back in the mail, because the Pony Express office had a pouch only for him. But I will bet the answers are all about the same. They are more than happy to meet with the Railroad Prophet and discuss the purchase of his stock and the buying out of the other shareholders."

Stanford was instantly alert. "When is this planned?"

"I've learned that he sails on the *St. Louis* on October third."

"A month away," the Governor mused, "and another month for him to reach Washington, New York and Boston. Collis, this revision can help us more than hurt us, can't it?"

"In certain financial quarters, yes. But with the gauge change, we might face a great loss if those locomotives have been shipped yet."

"Yes," Stanford said sternly, regaining his feel for the management of affairs. "That was a serious blunder on your part, Charley. Wires have got to be sent to-night. Next, to stop-gap Judah, the chair would like someone to propose a motion that we pay Theodore Judah $100,000 for his stock and interests in the line."

"So moved," Huntington said quickly. "But, of course, we'll have to scrape the barrel to make the payment."

"No," Charles Crocker insisted. "Not one damn red cent."

Stanford ignored him. "Edwin, I think we are awaiting your vote."

Charles Crocker shot his brother a mean glare. It, too, was ignored. "Well," the deep-thinking lawyer scowled, "it sure would keep him from having anything to sell back east. But I'd like to amend the motion to read that his money be paid out of the first profits from the line."

"Excellent," Stanford chuckled. "That could be years hence. I won't even ask for a vote and shall call it unanimous." When no one spoke up, not even Charles Crocker, Stanford grinned. "Isn't it odd, gentlemen, that for the first time Ted Judah has a unanimous vote from this board? Now, Collis, I see it as most important that you get back east, by the fastest route, and make sure that we are not short-changed on this revision. Obviously, we will not have Ted Judah there to open doors for us."

Huntington grinned. "We have the next best thing.

O'Lee worked closely with Ted in Washington after I hired him; he's worked closely with him here."

"Which ruins your case," Crocker growled. "Birds of a feather."

But for once it was not Mark Hopkins who had to step in to avert a fight. The mediocre Leland Stanford was coming to grips with the fact that he would soon not have a state to run and possibly not a railroad, either.

"Charles," he warned, "one more word and I'll ask you to leave the room. Collis, refresh my memory. Wasn't it Colonel Silas Seymour who recommended O'Lee to us?"

"Yes."

"Interesting. His brother Horatio has the nomination for governor of New York and is a shoo-in. I think we should get very close to the Seymour brothers, because they seem very close to Durant. Charles, before you leave tonight, I wish for you to write a letter of apology to Dan O'Lee."

"Never!"

"As you wish," Stanford shrugged. "Gentlemen, as we seem to be forced into a delay beyond our control, I strongly recommend that we cancel all construction contracts forthwith and reopen them for bidding when the time is appropriate."

Crocker couldn't believe his ears. But, looking around the table, he saw that he now stood quite alone in his low regard for Dan O'Lee.

"Excuse me," he said gruffly. "I'm going into your den to borrow paper and pen."

"Of all the black-hearted dirty ways of making an apology to a man," Dan exploded, after reading the letter Collis Huntington had brought. "Read this, Lib!"

Liberty read the sheet swiftly—then looked up, her eyes bright with amusement.

"It would seem no one is actually crawling," she said, "but Charles Crocker is having a very difficult time walking backward toward you."

"Crocker is not important," Huntington said. "Small men never are. The important thing right now is the future of this railroad, and ourselves. The fastest way east is a horrible two-weeks bumpy ride on Holladay's Overland Stage and war-weary railroads that never seem to run on time. But if the three of us get there by mid-September it will give us time to lobby Congress before it convenes on the Railroad Act and before Judah can get there to talk to his money men."

Dan looked up, meeting Liberty's eyes, and they both said it at the same time: "The three of us?"

Then Dan protested. "Libby just had the baby two weeks ago, Collis."

"I'm well aware of that," Huntington said grimly. "But I'm also aware of Washington. Just think back. When Anna Judah was with us, she was able to shift away the chaff and leave us free to talk to the wheat. When she went to Greenfield to check on Lydia May Tedder, everything fell apart. We won't have Anna Judah with us, and I must admit that Elizabeth's drinking problem would do us more harm than good."

"But my baby," Liberty gasped.

"I know, I know," Collis said impatiently. "It's a matter I can discuss with Kai Soong. He will find a very competent wet nurse and 'amah' to care for the child while we are gone."

The mention of Kai Soong's name brought his words back to Liberty as though he were present in the room and speaking them: 'You shall see the depth of bitter gloom and then be raised to great glory from an unexpected trip of great meaning.'

The two weeks since Dan had quit the Associates had been the gloomiest she had ever known, even worse than the moments when she had learned about Mai Ling. That was a womanly thing, which she felt capable of fighting had Mai Ling stayed upon the scene. But a man, grousing about the house without work, is an animal that even the gods have been unable to name or classify. Mean, self-centered, vindictive, morose, fearful, caged, put-upon, demanding, hateful—and little-boyish in his need for understanding.

Dan had received the letter from Charles Crocker gravely, but with a merry twinkle in his eyes. She didn't need to be told that he had been bitten by the railroad bug and that he was itching to get back to work.

"I see," Liberty said slowly. Then she stood up. "Dan," she said, "would I be a help to you?"

"Dear Mother of God," he whispered, "you are my help and strength. But are you up to it?"

Liberty stilled the wild beating of her heart. She was scared stiff, with Kai Soong's echoed words making her even more frightened.

"I shall be ready," she said evenly, "when Collis tells us we should be ready."

7

Liberty had remembered Washington as an old-fashioned southern town of sixty thousand inhabitants. Now it was an armed camp with accommodations hard to come by and food and service poor. Building fronts were sand-bagged, and riflemen were a common sight on the roofs of most important government buildings. The city was no longer asleep. It had become aristocratic, skeptical, sneering in its attitude toward the administration and desirous of replacing it the next election.

It took Liberty a week to recover from the overland trip. It was just as well. There was little for Liberty to do and she felt such a tyro. There was little for Collis and Dan to do, as well. Everyone, who thought he was anyone, seemed to be in Washington to lobby for one thing or another. The lines seemed endless at every government agency, and a five-minute meeting with a congressman or senator could take up to two weeks to arrange.

With little else to do, Liberty began to read every newspaper available and cut out articles about the various officials that Collis and Dan wanted to corner.

"We may be gone all day," Dan said, as he dressed one morning. "We're having lunch with Senator Mc-Dougall. Collis hopes he will wrangle us an invitation to a reception at the British Embassy. That seems to be the only way to do business in this town. What will you do with your day?"

"About the same," she answered dully. "Read the newspapers and think up nasty letters to write to the editors."

"Why don't you put it on paper and dispatch a few?" he laughed.

Liberty shook her head. She didn't want to admit that she had become so incensed over one loathsome editorial cartoon that she had dashed off a note about it and had then grown embarrassed over her audacity.

"Well, in case we get the invitation, you'd best be dressed and ready by about five. I'll go get Collis now. Bye."

She waved her hand and pulled a newspaper open. She skimmed the depressing war news, and concentrated on the Congressional and social happenings. Laconically, a few minutes later, she rose to answer a knock on the door. It was becoming Dan's habit to forget his hotel room key and she automatically picked one up off the dresser and took it with her.

A young soldier stood with an envelope in his hand. "Message, ma'am," he said indifferently and turned away.

Liberty started to throw the envelope and key on the dresser and then noticed that it was not for Dan. It was addressed to "Mrs. D. O'Lee." Puzzled, she broke the flap and pulled out a white card. Then she began to tremble.

"My dear Mrs. O'Lee:

"You are hereby summoned to immediately appear in my office to clarify your recent letter.

A. Lincoln."

Perplexed, she scurried down the hall to catch Collis and Dan, but there was no answer at Collis' room. Now, beginning to fret, she wished she had never written the letter. Could she ignore it until she had a chance to discuss it with Dan and Collis? The words 'summoned' and 'immediately' weighed against it. Her mind rattled, she quickly dressed and went down to have the porter summon her a hansom cab.

When the card was sent into him fifteen minutes later, a smile lighted the somber face of the president. He waved his long arms impulsively to his secretaries and the waiting crowd of congressmen:

"Clear everybody out for a few minutes, boys; I've an appointment at this hour."

Because of her astute words, he had been expecting an older, more matronly caller. The tall figure bowed with courtly deference to Liberty's ravishing beauty and his voice was touched with deep feeling:

"I want to thank you personally, Mrs. O'Lee, for your kind words about my administration . . . and myself."

"I'm glad," was her nervous, smiling answer.

"Now, child, there is no need to be nervous around this old farm boy. Have a seat and tell me who you are and what prompted your ire."

Still nervous, Liberty blurted out her sentiments with candor.

"Neatly put," he chuckled when she was through. "I wish some of my long-winded cabinet members could put their reports as straightforwardly. So. You really think I'm being mistreated, do you? You don't think the newspapers should be calling me a baboon. . . ." His eyes twinkled mischievously.

Liberty said hotly, "I think it is very mean what the 'radical' editors in Washington write. Not only about you, but about the war. It's almost as if they want the North to lose."

He was still for a moment, looking at her gravely. "That may well be true, my dear. It is certainly true that they want to put me out of this house next election."

"They would never be able to do it if women had the vote!"

The president laughed. "And that too may very well be true—at least, I would surely hope so." He grew serious then, looking at Liberty with a frank, open expression. "I appreciate your sentiments, Mrs. O'Lee. I know they are honest feelings. You see, I know of your husband's contributions to our Union cause. That is one reason I felt warmly about inviting you here. Now, in return for your kindness, is there a favor I can do for you or your railroad friends?" Once more his eyes twinkled.

Liberty bit her lip.

"Please don't be embarrassed, Mrs. O'Lee," the president said gently. "Politics is often a game in which we exchange favors. I know that whatever it is you wish of me has been well-considered by you. And I shall do my best to grant your request."

Liberty hesitated. "I'm afraid, sir, that what I would ask of you would get you into too much hot water."

"Please let me be the judge of that. Some baboons, you know, float in hot water as well as in cold."

Liberty looked at the grinning president, grinned herself, then plunged right on. "Mr. Lincoln, my husband now sees the wisdom of your ordering the standard gauge, but it will cause the Central Pacific delay and financial loss."

He paused before commenting and looked at her steadily. "Are you qualified to give me sound reasons for that statement?"

Liberty suddenly stiffened. No, she did not feel qualified. But she had heard Dan and Collis discuss the matter at length. Slowly, dredging their arguments from her mind, she informed him of the change in ties, the added cost of having to rework the locomotives and cars that had already been manufactured, and the additional surveys that would be required.

Lincoln's big jaws clamped shut and his huge fist struck the table: "I am the most advised man and the worst advised man in history. Never once was this brought to my attention. Daily, it becomes necessary for me to think for myself or cease to think at all. It was not my intention to make the Central Pacific suffer because of those four inches. Please tell your husband that I want a report—for my eyes only—as soon as possible. You can assure him that I shall sign an order, if his report so justifies, to increase the Central Pacific's subsidy to compensate for the change. Come now and see mother and the children. I want you to know them and like them."

He rifled through his desk for a moment, then led her quickly into the family apartment and introduced her to Mrs. Lincoln. He found her in the midst of a grave discussion with Lizzie Garland, her colored dressmaker.

"This is the letter writer, Mrs. Liberty O'Lee, mother. After the railroad information I just got from her, I'm thinking of placing her on the diplomatic corps—for tonight, at least. I'm giving her Lord Lyons's invitation, which means you can stop fretting over your desire not to attend. I think she will ably represent the White House. And don't forget to invite her back again."

With a wave of his big hand he was gone.

Mrs. Lincoln's greeting was simple and hearty. Within an hour Liberty had found a place in her heart for life, the boys were claiming her as their own, and a train of influences were set in motion that would serve Liberty well.

Liberty's appearance at the British minister's party that night caused a sensation, not all of it flattering to her.

Lord Lyons seethed with rage as he discussed her presence with U.S. Secretary of State William H. Seward.

"We were led to believe that the president himself would be in attendance. This representative of his is only a woman!" the minister spluttered.

Seward said drily, "I am pleased to hear from Your Lordship that he has not lost his eyesight. Mrs. O'Lee is quite a woman."

Lord Lyons's lips tightened. "I had, however, some personal words to discuss with Lincoln. I can hardly do that with *her*."

"And why not?" Seward asked politely. "I speak to her Royal Highness, as representative of your government, milord."

"Surely, you are not comparing the Queen of England with this woman?"

Seward looked across the ballroom. At the moment, Liberty was chatting with a group that included Congressman Thaddeus Stevens, chairman of the House Ways and Means committee. "She certainly seems to be holding court," he observed. "There isn't a man present who hasn't tried to get near to her and find out Ole Abe's reason for sending her."

Lord Lyons sniffed. "Her husband and his companion make that reason quite obvious, Seward. If it wouldn't cause a scandal, I would put them both out. All they can talk about are railroads."

"Yes," Seward chuckled, "and quite a refreshing change from all this war talk. Well, well, look who's barging in on her now, Hannibal Hamlin, the vice president himself. He must really be curious."

In spite of her nervousness, Liberty was having fun— or was, until Vice President Hamlin interrupted her talk with Stevens. She had met so many people that she could hardly recall a name, though her head swam with impressions of the great and the near great she had met. Dan and Collis were ecstatic. At this party she'd gotten them into, they had been able to corner and speak to more legislators in an hour than they had in the two weeks they had been in town.

Liberty was listening to the anti-slavery Stevens's comments on Mr. Lincoln's recent Proclamation of Emancipation when Hamlin rushed up. He wasn't interested in railroads at all. She blinked as he grew furious with Stevens.

"I heard that last, Thaddeus. What you just said proves that you're not the radical you pretend. You know as well as I do that that proclamation is a worthless piece of paper."

"Hardly worthless, Hannibal. It just doesn't go as far as I would like."

"It goes nowhere," Hamlin said, his voice rising. "It will have no effect in freeing the slaves. As long as that southerner stays in the White House we will have some form of slavery."

"Really," Stevens said testily. Without looking at

Liberty, Hamlin said narrowly, "Can't help but wonder what the old baboon is up to by sending over a lady spy."

He suddenly turned on her. "I believe you were born in the south, weren't you, Mrs. O'Lee?"

"I was," Liberty said coolly, "but my sympathies have never been with slavery."

"Sympathies?" he sneered. "That proves my point. You've got to be either for or against. Just like Lincoln to pick someone who would ape his empty-headed policy for him."

"Sir?" Liberty snapped, "are you aware of whom you speak?"

"Damn aware," he growled. "Lincoln's a liar, a cheat, a rascally devil who don't give the real thinkers in his cabinet a chance to be heard."

Heads were turning, necks craning.

Liberty kept her voice deathly calm.

"Sir, you are a coward! If I were a man I would call you out. Not to defend the man, but to defend the office of the president of the United States. Please excuse me, Mr. Stevens."

Congressman Stevens put out his hand to hold her back, glowering at Hamlin, who glowered back, then turned and stomped away.

Dan came up, escorted by a dapperly dressed man.

"Everything all right?" he asked.

"Quite!" Liberty said, her cheeks beginning to burn with embarrassment.

Stevens laughed. "I don't think Mrs. Wells was aware of whom she was tangling with."

"I was well aware," Liberty insisted. "That man is just a heartbeat away from the office he must covet. He should show it more respect."

A low mischievous laugh was her answer as Dan brought his escort forward.

"Darling, this is Senator Andrew Johnson, who also serves as the military governor of Tennessee. Senator, my wife, Liberty."

There was just a touch of irony in Johnson's smile, and a sparkle in the brown eyes that took her in from head to foot. He was a strikingly good-looking middle-aged man, with no trace of self-consciousness or conceit about him. A self-made man, he had not spoken a dozen words before Liberty felt the charm of his singular and powerful personality.

"I know three score senators," he began, with a friendly smile, "who would love to put the vice president in his place as you have just done. Had you been a man he might have called you out."

Liberty looked into his eyes with mischievous challenge. She had recovered her poise.

"Isn't dueling one of the Old South institutions that this war wishes to do away with?"

"Yes, of course—" Johnson paused and the faintest suggestion of a smile flickered about the corners of his eyes. "Dan tells me you have had a most enjoyable day with the president and Mrs. Lincoln. Watch out, Thaddeus, or she'll have her hands into the pocketbook of your committee."

"Oh?"

Liberty laughed, "Don't make me sound as sinister as that, senator. The report will have to be prepared for the president first."

Stevens blinked. "Report? Pocketbook? You have pricked my interest, Mrs. O'Lee."

"Then I best turn you over to my husband. Senator Johnson, I think Mrs. Stevens and I would be desirous of some refreshments, if you would be so kind as to escort us."

Mrs. Stevens was grateful. The stout woman loathed politics. She had starved herself all day long so as to be able to sample all the culinary treats on the buffet table. She left them hastily when they reached the dining room door.

"You needn't bother, senator," Liberty said, smiling as she watched Mrs. Stevens hustle off. "I am not really hungry. It was just an excuse to leave my husband alone with Congressman Stevens.

"Honest to a fault, aren't you?"

"Why shouldn't I be? It is no big secret why we are here in Washington. I am at this party only because I was lucky enough to meet the president today."

"You know," he said strangely, "I have a strong hunch that things just don't happen to you by luck, Mrs. O'Lee. I'm just a simple man, but have always felt that we choose out destinies, however unknowingly, character is fate, as it were." He smiled. "How did you find him?" he asked then, a worried frown creasing his forehead.

"It's hard to say, never having met the president before. At one moment he seemed tired. The next he wanted to laugh away his woes. What a horrible job that must be." She shivered.

"Are you all right?"

"Yes. But I just had the most frightening thought. What a disaster it would be if Hannibal Hamlin were to become president."

"There are those," Johnson said tentatively, for it was the first time he had mentioned it in public, "who would like to see Hannibal's renomination denied him."

Liberty experienced another odd sensation. As if Kai Soong were commanding her she looked deep into Johnson's dark brown eyes and spoke right out.

"And you would like it for yourself."

"Why," Johnson said, surprised. "I have not even uttered such a thought to my wife."

"Do you like Mr. Lincoln?" she asked unexpectedly.

"Frankly, sometimes I do and other times I don't. But as far as I can see, he is the only man around bullheaded enough to see us through."

Liberty was silent for a moment and spoke in a low tone:

"Would you like him to learn of your vice presidential ambitions—subtly?"

"You've mistaken your calling, Mrs. O'Lee," Johnson said with emotion. "I think your statesmanship could just pull it off."

Throughout the rest of the evening Johnson watched her with interest. She had a manner about her that made men lose their hearts to her without making their wives jealous, and he sensed himself as one of those men. As they were leaving, he took Collis aside.

"Mr. Huntington, as a great deal of my time of late has been spent in Tennessee, I am not quite up to date on all of the aspects of this railroad revision. I would deem it an honor if you and your party would dine with me at the Willard Wednesday next."

"Our pleasure, Senator," Collis beamed.

Two days later Liberty received word that the negro dressmaker, Lizzie Garland, would be pleased to give her a fitting. Thinking that Dan or Collis had made the arrangements, she went to the address in the note. She was stunned when the president's wife opened the door at Lizzie's little white frame house.

"Mrs. Lincoln," she gasped, "this is a surprise."

Mary Todd Lincoln smiled conspiratorially. "My child, every animal has to have a quiet lair to crawl to once in awhile. Lizzie's house affords me such. Come, I think you will like the fabric I have selected for you."

"You?"

"Ah! Ah!" Mrs. Lincoln ventured cheerfully. "This

shall be our state secret. Father might call it a bribe, you know. Here she is, Lizzie; and here is the fabric."

Liberty exclaimed, "It's gorgeous. But I can't accept it or a dress."

"Nonsense!" Mrs. Lincoln eyed her speculatively. "Father has been whistling ever since news reached him of your triumph at the British reception. I'm dying to hear all the juicy details, but did not want to make you out the spy by calling you to the White House. Hence, my secret lair. Now, you just climb onto Lizzie's platform and you can tell me all while she takes down your measurements."

With a shrug, Liberty stepped onto the wooden platform, and Lizzie quickly and expertly went to work with her tape, pencil and pad.

She was hesitant at first, having trouble remembering all the names. But her apt description got Mrs. Lincoln to chuckling and supplying them. The president's wife roared with laughter at the story about her upbraiding Hannibal Hamlin. Lizzie joined in.

"Oh, Lizzie, isn't that just priceless?"

"'Bout time, Miss Ma'y, after all de bad things he say ag'in yore kin."

Mrs. Lincoln threw herself on the lounge and gave way to a moment of despair.

"Liberty probably doesn't know that, Lizzie. Both of my brothers are in the Confederate army, my child, and one of them is the commandant of Libby Prison in Richmond. I feel sometimes as if I've deserted them, and yet I never hear the end of it from Hamlin and others."

"Don't think that way," Liberty pleaded. "My father, Colonel A.G. Wells, was killed at Shiloh, Mrs. Lincoln. Being from Mississippi I was not in too great a favor because of my abolitionist feelings. Like you, I have been accused of being a spy and have kin who may never speak to me again because I married a Yankee. But I followed my heart and my husband, just as you have done."

"Thank you, Liberty," she said tenderly. "You are the first person to see and understand what I had to do. But enough of this. Tell me exactly what you thought of that snake in the grass, Hamlin."

"I don't think he should be re-elected vice-president."

The First Lady sprang up with flashing eyes:

"Did you mention that fact aloud?"

"In a way. I told Senator Johnson I thought it would be awful if the man should somehow become president. Senator Johnson says there are many who would like to see Hamlin denied the renomination."

"O my yes, and I am one of them. But my husband is a babe in the woods with wolves prowling after him. He won't drop Hamlin, because it might rock the Union. It is rocking anyway. There is another candidate against my husband for the presidency, you know."

"Mr. Chase?"

Mrs. Lincoln was surprised. "How were you aware of that?"

"I heard his name mentioned at the reception. He's the secretary of the treasury, isn't he? Well, and I don't fully understand all of this, they said he was too radical and too sectional a candidate; that if the Democrats go ahead and nominate General McClellan the Republicans will have to have a national ticket to take away Democratic votes."

"Well," she sighed, "the speakers must have been friendly to the president, for that is almost as he sees the picture."

"Very friendly, I would say, Mrs. Lincoln. One was Senator Johnson, and he asked me how I found the president."

"How very kind of Andy. Most would ask out of malicious intent, but he is one of the most sincere men I know. He sent me the most compassionate note when my Willie died last year."

"Sincere and compassionate," Liberty mused. "Yes, I felt that about him . . . and loyal. Too bad he isn't Mr. Lincoln's vice president."

Mary Todd looked at her with a twinkle playing around the corner of her eyes. She slowly paced the room.

"Liberty," she said at last, "you're a very astute young woman. You have given me the very name I have been racking my brain to come up with. Now to worm that name into Father's head and quietly let Andy know that Mary Todd Lincoln wants him to fight for the post."

"He's having dinner with us Wednesday next," Liberty said simply.

Mrs. Lincoln smiled delightedly. "My dear, it's a shame they don't allow the First Lady to have a staff of her own. You and I would make a team that would set this town on its ear."

The dinner party pleased Johnson enormously. For one thing, Collis Huntington had had to absent himself in New York and so Liberty ordered a more intimate dinner to be served in the O'Lee's suite.

Andrew Johnson hated to eat in public. He enjoyed savoring his food, chewing every last drop of flavor out of each bite before swallowing it. And he enjoyed simple table talk, of the sort he rarely had on formal occasions.

They did not discuss railroads or the war. They spoke instead of home—of farms and plantations and days they wished to recall before they were gone forever.

Nor did anyone reach for brandy and cigars at the meal's end. With Liberty's permission, Senator Johnson puffed on an old corncob pipe while he and Dan sipped on pure Tennessee bourbon.

"Would you be looking at that," he started, in amazement. "We've talked ourselves past midnight. I'm wearing my welcome out on my first stay."

"And would you be looking at what's been going on while we've been enjoying ourselves," Dan declared. "That snowstorm has turned into a real blizzard. There's not a cab on the street. You'll be staying the night with us, I fear."

"No need to put you to such bother."

"It's not a bother at all, senator. I'll fetch some things out of the hotel linen closet and we'll make you a bed there on the couch."

"I'll accept your hospitality, Dan, on one condition. That we're able to have another bowl of tobacco and a finger of whiskey before retiring."

Dan grinned. This was the first night he had thoroughly enjoyed since arriving in Washington. "I had a couple of bowls and several fingers in mind, senator."

"Then we've struck a bargain, if the fair lady has no objections."

There was no way Liberty would have objected. She was delighted to see Dan so animated.

In the morning Washington was still blanketed in a mantle of white, although transportation was beginning to crawl to life. Johnson thanked his hosts graciously and departed.

In the hall he did not see a man hesitate before stepping from a room—waiting just long enough for him to pass.

Harvey Crewes took note of the room Johnson had left and found the nearest floor maid to ask her who occupied it.

"Mr. and Mrs. O'Lee, suh. Dey here wid dat Mistah Huntington."

Harvey Crewes, private secretary to Senator D.T. Patterson of Tennessee, was well aware of the O'Lee and Collis Huntington railroad faction, but curious as to what purpose Governor Johnson would have with them at that hour of the morning.

"I see," he said to the maid, taking a coin from his purse. "Can you tell me when he arrived?"

"Last night fur supper, suh. I see'd him come and I jest see'd him go. Course, ain't none ah my business, but ah done hear dat Mistah Huntington and Mistah O'Lee am in New Yawk on business."

A second coin was added with thanks.

Piously Crewes reported the incident to Senator Patterson. Remarkably, Patterson never once thought to question his secretary on what he had been doing at the Willard that night. A rather cold, asexual person, Patterson considered his secretary to be of similar cut.

With something near glee he sat down and wrote the whole incident to his wife in Greenville, Tennessee. He had never liked Johnson, thought him too "earthy" and a thorn to his family pride. Now he had proof. Oddly enough, his wife was Martha Johnson Patterson, Andrew Johnson's eldest daughter.

Throughout September and early October Liberty continued to make her mark in Washington, with or without Mary Todd Lincoln. Concessions were made to the Central Pacific that Collis Huntington never dreamed possible. Thomas Durant, frantic to learn Collis's game, pushed Union Pacific President Ogden into going to Washington. The dignified and solemn Ogden could gain nothing and stalked back to New

York. George Train was sent next and was almost hired away.

"Get them up here!" Oliver Ames bellowed. "They seem to be the only people in Washington who can keep a secret and they are making monkeys out of us."

Collis Huntington read the carefully couched words of the letter with relish.

"Now we have them running scared," he chortled. "They want to discuss a meeting site for the lines. They don't mention Liberty, Dan, just you and me. What do you know about her?"

"Nothing, that I know of."

"Good," Collis grinned. "Liberty, I think we should pay a visit to Lizzie Garland tomorrow. You're coming along. A lady of your position needs a proper wardrobe for New York—at Central Pacific expense, of course."

As Lizzie Garland slaved over fabrics that even Mrs. Lincoln couldn't afford, the S.S. *St. Louis* was heading into Panama. A dingy Cape Horn schooner sloshed past on a course for San Francisco.

"Anna," Ted Judah said gloomily, "it's the S.S. *Herald of the Morning*."

"I don't understand."

"She's carrying the first hundred tons of rail for the Central Pacific."

"It will wait for you," she chided, then shivered. "Oh, how I wish we could have crossed in Nicaragua. I loathe this train ride across the isthmus. All this country seems to have is foul weather and mosquitoes."

The rains were torrential all the way to the Caribbean side. By the time the Judahs were aboard the ship for New York, Ted was ranging between clammy chills and burning fever. At first Anna thought he had just a bad cold and kept him to his bunk. But when his condition worsened, she sent for the ship's doctor.

As he examined Judah the doctor asked pointed questions, then shook his head sadly.

"The man has nearly worn himself out. Now he's been bitten by one of those heathenish mosquitoes. It's yellow fever. All we can do is try to break the fever."

"How long to New York, doctor?"

"Today is the twenty-sixth and we should dock on the twenty-ninth, Mrs. Judah."

He left hurriedly, not wishing to tell her that she might be disembarking alone.

Lizzie Garland delivered the six gowns to the Willard, wrapped in tissue paper, with an outer layer of old newspapers she got from the White House. They were stunning creations and she lovingly helped Liberty pack them into a trunk.

"You'all sure look fine in dem, Miss Lib'ty," she beamed. "Now, Lizzie'll just take her trash papers away."

"Wait," Liberty said, picking up one of the newspapers. "Why, this paper is from Missouri."

"Could be from most anywhere, Miss Lib'ty. Dey send free ones to Mistah Abe if they want him to read what nasty things they've said about him."

"Then, I'm going to fold them up and read them, Lizzie. Newspaper reading has become as much a passion with me as a needle and thread with you. I'd like to find out what has been happening outside of Washington."

Not expecting Dan and Collis until late in the evening, she wiled away the afternoon with the old newspapers, chuckling over social-gossip columns, fuming at pieces attacking the president. She was almost ready to write Colonel McCormack and his Chicago *Tribune* a nasty letter when an article caught her eye under the headline of THE PACIFIC RAILROAD. It was date-lined Omaha, Nebraska, Oct. 6th.

She re-read the article several times, puzzled that some things were apparently not as she understood them to be. She had just cut it from the sheet when Dan and Collis came in jubilantly toting a champagne bottle and glasses.

"Celebration time!" Collis cheered. "Today, the twenty-sixth of October, 1863, the first rails of the Central Pacific have been laid along Front Street in Sacramento. Let Ted Judah explain that to his fancy meeting when he arrives."

Liberty took the offered glass, but didn't drink. "Collis, didn't you say the commencement point for the Union Pacific hadn't been anounced yet?"

"Yes, Lincoln has it up his sleeve and won't release it until the stock requirement for charter is gained."

"$2,000,000?"

"Yes, two million. Why?"

She read them the Omaha article which announced that the money had been raised and turned over to the treasurer, that Omaha would be the eastern terminal and that a stockholders' meeting had been called to convene in New York City on October twenty-ninth.

"Durant!" Collis fumed. "We are being set up. He wants to win concessions out of us on the twenty-eighth and be a big hero before the directors' meeting the next day."

"But the meeting will be held under false pretenses," Liberty protested. "There is no way they could have raised that much money since George Train was here."

Collis and Dan blinked at her in amazement.

"Would you care to explain?"

"Well, I know Gladys Stevens wouldn't lie. She happens to know just about as much of the ins and outs of government financing as her husband, and that's why she got so upset. Train approached her when he was down here, because of her own personal wealth, and his offer really upset her. I only learned because I was having lunch with her that day."

"Damn it, Liberty," Collis stormed, "would you get to the point?"

"If I can remember correctly," she answered coolly. "I gather that he offered to underwrite the ten per cent down payment if she would accept the bonds in her name. Later, if she decided it was a sound investment, she could reimburse him."

"Whew. I'm sorry I blew up," Collis said sincerely. "Well, this is something. How do you see it, Dan?"

"Collis, I'm no money man, but it seems intriguingly simple. When we got here the Union Pacific had less than $400,000 worth of bonds pledged. A down payment of ten per cent on the rest of the stock needed to call an election of a board of directors would take only $160,000. That's three-fourths of all the outstanding stock."

"Yes, and I'll bet all of it is controlled one way or another by Durant. I think we had better leave tomorrow for New York."

"Oh," Liberty said, "I was having lunch with Gladys Stevens and Mary Lincoln tomorrow."

Collis thought a moment. Liberty seemed to be gaining more information from her luncheons than they were. Besides, he wanted to celebrate.

"What the hell," he chuckled, "we're laying track and they're a good three years away. What's another day?"

Collis Huntington was to learn that it was a day well worth giving over to Liberty's luncheon.

* * *

Their arrival on the New York Central was a noisy affair. Though Durant and Ogden were determined to give them a cool reception, the Washington Bureau of the New York *Tribune* had sent up full particulars on Liberty's social activities in the capitol and reporters were there clamoring for interviews.

"Mrs. O'Lee! Mrs. O'Lee!" a moon-faced man in a bowler hat called out. "Is it true that you have become intimate with the president?"

Liberty stopped, turned slowly and cocked her lavishly hatted head at a jaunty angle. "Sir, I am only intimate with my husband!"

Laughter rippled among the reporters and the man blushed.

"Perhaps," he stammered, "I phrased the question wrong."

Liberty rewarded him with a winning smile. "For that you are forgiven. In answer to your question, I hardly see how a person can become an intimate of another when they have only met once in their lifetimes."

"What of Mrs. Lincoln?" another reporter shot out quickly. "We are told that you have met secretly with her."

Liberty laughed gaily. "Secretly? Gentleman, you have found us out and I am forced to confess." Liberty paused at their murmurs of anticipation; pads and pencils were readied for a headline exclusive. "Mrs. Lincoln, who is a friend I shall cherish for life, did meet me privately at the home of one Lizzie Garland. It was a secret, in a way. Lizzie is a fabulous dressmaker and I did not wish the design of the gowns I would be wearing here to be revealed in advance."

With their headline evaporated the reporters were

momentarily without further questions. One did ask: "And how did you find your trip from Washington?"

"Ghastly!" Liberty said honestly. "I can now see why Commodore Vanderbilt is trying to gain full control of the New York Central. It certainly needs to be put in the same first-class condition as his steamship line."

Now the reporters had indeed latched onto a newsworthy item. It was common knowledge that Cornelius Vanderbilt would not invest his money in the Union Pacific because of his distrust of Thomas Durant. The canny Durant, who was remaining in the background with Ogden, moved forward quickly to curtail any further questions on railroad subjects that might embarrass him. But he did not move fast enough.

"You mention the commodore, Mrs. O'Lee. Are you aware that the Judahs arrive by ship today and that it is consistently reported that it is the Vanderbilt money he seeks to refinance the Central Pacific?"

Collis opened his mouth to deny vehemently that the Central Pacific needed refinancing, but Liberty cheerily gushed on:

"Anna and Hed in New York? How utterly delightful. I really must look them up when we have finished our business here."

"We?" one of the sharper reporters picked up.

Durant, also interested in her answer, listened intently.

"Gentlemen," Liberty laughed, "you certainly love to pick a turkey clean. Naturally, I personally have no business here—other than to act as hostess for the reception the Central Pacific is giving tomorrow evening."

Ogden's mouth flew open. So did Durant's. Durant fumed at a reception, news to him, that would infringe on his own meeting. Dan and Collis remained stonily quiet. Liberty's announcement was also news to them, but they were thoroughly enjoying the consternation it was giving Thomas Durant.

"Well," the reporter chuckled, "you sure know how to side-step questions with dignity."

"Thank you," Liberty said graciously. "The dignity of a woman depends on how she conducts herself. If I do indeed project dignity then it is intended. It was inculcated in me by my parents. Good day, gentlemen. I believe our carriage awaits us."

As if she were the head of the welcoming delegation, Liberty sailed along the platform, her bustles not moving an inch.

"Wow!" the bowler-hatted reporter sighed. "She sort of leaves you breathless."

"I think I'd better let our society page people know about that reception."

"Society, hell," someone scoffed. "The only person capable of covering her, in my opinion, is our business editor."

The trio was left unceremoniously at the Manhattan Hotel.

"Who in the hell is she?" Ogden demanded.

"How should I know?" Durant snapped. "Other than that she's O'Lee's wife."

"Humph! Engineers don't make money to dress a wife like that!"

"No," Durant mused, "and I know for a fact that Collis Huntington wouldn't spend that kind of money, either. Let me off here! I've got a lot of checking to do before tonight."

Durant caught a hansom cab back to the train depot and sent an urgent wire to Randy Porter.

* * *

Liberty yanked off her hat, thoroughly angry with herself.

"I really opened my mouth at the wrong time, didn't I?"

Dan had thought the same, but Collis was grinning broadly. "You were utterly unbelievable. There isn't a newspaper in this town that won't want to report on your every move and word. This reception thing may have just popped out of your mouth, but it is brilliant."

"In what way?" Dan queried.

"Well, Dan, you and I are to meet with Durant this afternoon to open discussions on a meeting site, right?"

Dan nodded.

Collis chuckled. "Think about it. To guarantee that his little bond scheme will be successful in winning a majority vote on the board elections, he must have already hand picked fifteen to twenty of the nominees himself. Their election, if we believe the Omaha paper, is tomorrow afternoon. Now, it would be most impolite for us to have a reception and not invite the new board members, don't you think?"

"My God!" Dan gasped. "You intend to ask him for that list today?"

"Subtly! Subtly!" Collis grinned. "He thinks he has us in the dark, so I will merely ask him for a list of people he thinks we should invite who are sympathetic to our two railroads. I think we should include some of the more prominent newspaper publishers and editors; several financiers who have already helped me; and some socially prominent people to drool over Liberty's regalia."

"And whose magic wand," Liberty laughed, "are you going to use to bring this about in a day's time?"

"My dear, you are now residing in a world all its own. The Manhattan, for the proper price, can serve a dinner party of a hundred on an hour's notice. We are giving them over twenty-four hours for a reception of, say, two to three hundred. I have used their services several times and they are quite remarkable. They have their own printing shop for quick invitations and even see to their addressing and hand delivery. If you are not too tired, Liberty, I can have Maurice call on you while Dan and I are with Durant."

"Me?"

Collis grinned wickedly. He had created his own Pygmalion and was enjoying the game. "After all, it was your idea. You announced to the press that you were to be the hostess. Besides, after those hungry-eyed reporters describe your arrival in their afternoon newspapers, there will not be a woman in town who will not claw for an invitation to attend with their husbands. Oh, I've got to run for the meeting with J.P. Morgan. Dan, the Balfour Steel offices are two blocks over, next to the Metropolitan Hotel. I think they'll like the order you worked out. I'll meet you in front of the Metropolitan at a quarter to one and we'll walk to Durant's office. Oh, Liberty, Maurice is a stuffy chap. To impress him that you are somebody with *real* money, make sure to question him closely on every dollar spent. Have fun!"

"Brother," Dan sighed, when Huntington was out the door, "doesn't he ever run down? Do this! Do that! Run here! Get your butt over there!"

"Are you complaining, Dan O'Lee?"

"Yes," he growled, scooping her into his arms and kissing her long and passionately, "because I'm having to share you with so many, my darling." Then he laughed. "Other than that, I have never felt so young and excited in my life. When was the last time you saw me limp, Lib? I think I've licked it for good. I hate to say it, but Collis is responsible. Funny, how you can start by disliking a person and then you learn so much from them that you can't help but feel respect. Lib, he is the Central Pacific, and we both know it."

"Not Ted Judah?"

"Lib, my pa always said that those who dream are bound to die, but God keeps those dreams alive in others if He wants them fulfilled. Collis can make that dream a reality more than Judah was able to; that I now believe."

Liberty frowned. "I never realized how large a city this was, Dan. How in the world would I ever go about finding Anna?"

"We'll worry about that later, darling. I've got to run now. Have fun with Maurice."

Unknown to either, at a quarter to one that day, their ship having docked sooner than expected, Dr. F.N. Otis and Anna Judah helped the near delirious Ted from a carriage and into the Metropolitan Hotel. There his ailment was passed off as "seasickness."

Liberty had no cause to worry about this development. Not a half hour after Dan's departure she answered a knock at the door of her suite and admitted a short, bustling man of an exceedingly nervous nature.

"Madam, I am Maurice of the Manhattan," he began.

"Yes, come in. Mr. Huntington said to expect you."

"That business we shall cover momentarily, Madam O'Lee. At the moment I am most perplexed on another matter. In the hall I just found lurking a most officious woman and one of those smelly photographer fellows. They insist upon seeing you and refuse to leave. How they gained entrance, I do not know, but it is the policy of the Manhattan not to allow our guests to be so disturbed. Had I gone for the house detective they would have just pounded on your door and made a horrible disturbance. The Manhattan does not like publicity of this type."

"Well," Liberty mused, "it's a problem. If you leave now, they will still demand to see me, won't they?"

"Yes, madam, that is a distinct possibility."

Liberty thought a moment. The Manhattan didn't like publicity, but the Central Pacific could use all it could get. She would just have to bridge the gap between the two.

"Show them in, Maurice," she said, as firmly as she could. "I shall handle it."

Before he could protest she turned, went into the Louis XIV parlor and stood there, poised and waiting. Maurice, seeing her from the foyer, shrugged; the lady did seem capable of handling most any situation. He opened the door and a couple barged in. The woman, in her thirties, was dressed mannishly in tweeds, string tie, and a small tweed hat with a feather in its brim. She wore no make-up and had her hair tied in a bun. She might have been pretty, Liberty thought, but she was obviously working hard not to be.

"Carrie Parsons," she barked, *"Times!* This is Dickens, my photographer."

Liberty asked curiously, "Hasn't he a first name?"

Carrie Parsons blinked. As a woman reporter little respected in her profession, she usually had to bully her way into an interview and wear the subject down. She was good at bullying. She had already bribed her way into the Manhattan, flaunting Dickens as a kind of male appendage. Now however, she decided she might just have to alter her tactics. This woman was clearly not her typical prey.

"Mark," she allowed, "Mark Dickens."

"All right, Carrie Parsons and Mark Dickens," Liberty said graciously, "I am Liberty O'Lee. What is it that you wish?"

Carrie studied her.

"An interview and some pictures, Mrs. O'Lee."

"I see. Are you aware that is against the policy of this hotel?"

"That's the key word, Mrs. O'Lee. Policy. Policy be damned. You are paying rent on this suite. It's your home, as long as you're here. There's no way this hotel can stop me from seeing you."

"Very interesting point, Miss Parsons. But I respect the hotel's rule, because it keeps every other reporter in town from barging in on me as you have done."

"They wouldn't have the brains to get in," Carrie boasted.

Liberty smiled. "No, I don't think they would, though I suspect 'brains' isn't the word you'd prefer to use. Well, Maurice, we must now face our problem. I trust you will agree with my solution. Miss Parsons, I will grant you five minutes and one photograph—although the blasted things scare me to death. In exchange you are to make no mention of this hotel whatsoever."

Carrie nodded in quick agreement then motioned for Mark to set up his tripod and flash pans. Maurice beamed. Five minutes and out. Liberty's solution suited him fine.

"At the railroad station you mentioned a reception, Mrs. O'Lee. May I learn where, when and for whom?"

Liberty thought quickly. "I'll answer your question in reverse order. My husband and I will host the reception to honor Mr. Collis Huntington of the Central Pacific Railroad. Friends, business associates, and the gentlemen involved with the Union Pacific Railroad will be honored guests. It shall be tomorrow evening."

"Where? Here at the Manhattan?"

"When will this article appear, Miss Parsons?"

"If accepted, tomorrow afternoon's editions."

"Yes, well, I insist on the rule of this interview. I do not want the event marred by gawkers and gate-crashers. Next question."

Maurice sighed deeply in the background. His opinion of Liberty was further bolstered.

"I was told of your stylish clothing, and the dress you have on is stunning. Would you mind being photographed in the gown that you will wear for the reception and telling me what it cost?"

Liberty's brows arched. Neither request would help the Central Pacific.

"You may say that the gown was designed by Miss Lizzie Garland, official dressmaker to the First Lady. If you wish to describe it in your article you may do so when this young man takes my photograph, but the price of it is no one's business but my own. The gown is airing out in that bedroom. It's the one across the foot of the bed."

Carrie giggled, so unusual a sound from her that Mark blinked. "Mrs. O'Lee," she said, "are you keeping the price of the gown from your husband?"

"Not at all," she said honestly. "Mr. O'Lee knows exactly what I paid for my wardrobe. Now, your time is running quite short."

While Carrie was in the bedroom looking at the gown, Mark expertly posed Liberty and told her to remain absolutely still for thirty seconds after the flash had been ignited. The flash was brilliant. The room filled with white smoke and stench, and Liberty's vision was so blurred she had to rub her eyes for several minutes. "My goodness, Mark," was all she could say.

Meanwhile, Carrie Parsons came back starry-eyed and a little baffled. She had examined all of Liberty's

Lizzie Garland-designed wardrobe—gowns which Liberty had been preparing to hang up when Maurice had knocked. She knew that there was more money invested in those dresses than she would probably earn in five years. She was beginning to think that this interview might be more important than she had anticipated.

"Just a couple of more background questions, Mrs. O'Lee," she said brightly, "and then we will be out of your hair. What is your own family background?"

Liberty had taken a seat. Her eyes were irritating her. She had a fear she had been blinded, knew the fear to be irrational, but was anxious nevertheless. It was difficult to remain alert. She answered almost by rote. "I was Liberty Wells. I'm married to Daniel O'Lee, who is the chief engineer for the Central Pacific, and we have one son. Naturally, we live in Sacramento, California."

"And your own family?"

Yes, Liberty thought, my own family. What could she say about her father? Somehow, it hurt her too much to think deeply about him. "I have no immediate family," she said. "My father, A. G. Wells, owned a plantation in Corinth. He was a colonel in the Confederate army and was killed at Shiloh. Now, please, I must ask you to go. Those fumes are horrible."

She nodded at their thanks and goodbyes, not feeling she had gained from the interview at all. Then she realized that Maurice was still there, and she still had to face the ordeal of planning the reception. Suddenly, all the fun was going out of things. She just wanted to lie down and take a long nap.

"Maurice," she said softly, "could we possible go over the reception arrangements later? I know you don't have much time, but . . ."

"For any other I would have to say no, Madam O'Lee," he grinned. "But would you trust Maurice to make all the arrangements for you?"

Liberty couldn't help but grin. "So you can steal me blind? I think I'm blind as it is."

The dour little man actually laughed. "Mr. Huntington warned you about me, did he? Madam, as to your vision, you shall soon recover it. I assure you—I have seen the camera flashes before. And as to my stealing from you—well, I shall not. You are too much a woman of taste and dignity. Allow Maurice to prepare a reception dinner on his own and I promise that it shall be as dazzling as the gown Madam intends to wear—and at a lesser cost than let us say Mr. Huntington's wife would have gotten out of me."

Liberty smiled warmly. "Thank you, Maurice. I am so much relieved."

That evening, the dinner hosted by the William Ogdens was a rather tense affair. At Durant's suggestion the party was kept intentionally small—six couples and Huntington. The thirteen place settings disturbed the superstitious Mrs. Ogden and she barely spoke during the meeting. Ogden, as well, was quiet. He had misgivings about the electoral meeting schedule for the next day.

Liberty, seated between the two Union Pacific men, began to see in them similar habits and characteristics. Each was a lone wolf, brilliant in economic plotting but ruthless in social relationships. Both were hard-backed sons of Connecticut upbringing. Both had been at the Mohawk-Hudson junction in 1836. Now, each was trying to wrest control of a railroad.

Liberty had been briefed on the others who would be present, but recognized them as pawns who would not be moved from their squares that night. So she turned her full attention and charm on Thomas Durant.

Durant was in a bestial mood. Of the thirty directors to be elected, seventeen were New Yorkers, and he had been cornered into giving Collis Huntington their names for the reception's invitation list. But the brunt of his anger rested on the absent Randy Porter. He had received no word from young Porter. He knew nothing about Liberty that he could use to his advantage. He did not enjoy the relatively powerless position he was in.

Nevertheless, the dinner conversation went more or less as he directed it. Most of the guests were his people, firmly under his thumb. Henry Poor, secretary to the railroad commission, hammered railroad talk at the Huntington-O'Lee contingent all night long. Major General Dix first tried to impress them with his credentials—among other things, he had been secretary of the treasury for two months before Lincoln's inaugural—then cautioned that his war duties would not give him much time to devote as a director of the Union Pacific, even if elected. Like the Ogdens, John J. Cisco said little. The New York banker had been General Dix's assistant secretary during his treasury days—the desperate days of the Pony Express scandal—and only clarified points in the general's story about them.

Sly Collis Huntington had the feeling the entire dinner had been rehearsed, but that he had come out of it with more information than Durant ever intended for him to garner. Then, as the farewells for the evening were being said, it was time for Collis to put his own well-rehearsed scene on stage.

The play needed Liberty as its star.

While Dan went to the cloakroom for her wrap,

and Collis busied himself with Mr. and Mrs. Ogden, Liberty singled out Durant.

"Before we say goodnight, sir," she said with a show of nervousness, "I wonder if I might have a private word with you."

Durant was instantly on the alert. He had been expecting a response from the Central Pacific people all evening, but thought it would come from Huntington. He nodded and indicated that they could take seats in the dining room alcove.

"Thank you," Liberty smiled sweetly. "This is a matter unknown to Mr. Huntington, and I would appreciate that it remain that way. I have a great deal of interest in my husband's future, Mr. Durant. A great deal of interest. He may just be an engineer, sir, but his interest in this railroad is just as strong as that of Mr. Huntington or yourself. But what good will the Central Pacific be unless it can link up with the Union Pacific? This is the important matter my husband came to discuss—and yet we've hardly touched on it this evening."

In spite of himself Durant laughed. "Mrs. O'Lee, in all my long political years, I have never heard an issue put more plainly. True, we did not confront the linking matter tonight—we just, shall we say, became more acquainted with each other."

Liberty spoke earnestly. "Under my maiden name, and with my own capital, I purchased Central Pacific stock. So, you see, my interest extends beyond my husband's career. I have strong reasons for supporting the Union Pacific's recommendation to the president, through General Dodge, on the Omaha terminus."

Durant silently chortled, but kept his face like stone. "Mrs. O'Lee, I'm afraid that is only a rumor."

"I do not believe in investing my money in rumors, Mr. Durant," Liberty said. "Had Mrs. Lincoln not told me of General Dodge's recommendation and that the president will soon announce his decision on it, I would not be wasting my breath with you. But it does concern me that Omaha is one hundred seventy miles from St. Joseph and a hundred fifty miles west of the Mississippi & Missouri's railhead in Iowa. It does concern me that the first branch line to reach Omaha can win the right to build toward the Central Pacific."

Durant sat back. "I am curious, Mrs. O'Lee, as to why you would have so much concern for the Union Pacific."

Liberty eyed him without blinking. "Because I also hold two hundred shares of Union Pacific stock, sir."

Durant openly gasped. "You? But that's $200,000 worth!"

"Really," she laughed, "I am not that big a fool. I, like everyone else, have made only the ten percent down payment. Oh, here comes Dan with my wrap, so I must finish quickly." She took a carefully folded sheet of paper out of her clutch purse. "I had the notary public in the hotel draw this up for me, Mr. Durant. It is the proxy for voting my stock. Would you be so kind as to vote for me? As I know none of the gentlemen, I leave the choice entirely up to you."

"I—I—" Durant was at a loss for words. To refuse would be ungallant. But he still felt he was being suckered in some way or other.

"Thank you," Liberty smiled, pressing the paper into his hand. "Until tomorrow night at the reception, then."

It was only seven in the evening on the Pacific coast. Randy Porter had read the telegram several times since he'd received it the day before and was still unsure of how to answer it.

What damning things could he say about a woman

who was letting him use her house for his secret rendez-vous with Lydia May? If something damning was what they wanted—he wasn't even sure about that.

Sitting before the fire, holding Lydia May's hand, he stared into it, as though the burning logs would supply the answer.

"You're a long way off tonight," she murmured.

"Just thinking," Randy said, with a sad smile. "We may not have too many more evenings like this. Your mother will be home next week and then Liberty soon after that."

Finally, Lydia May thought, her heart starting to pound, he's going to kiss me.

"How is she, anyway?"

Lydia May's heart sank again. "Mother? Well, *she's* fine, according to her letter, but grandma Pamela just isn't the same, and—"

"That's good." Randy definitely seemed distracted. "Do you think Liberty will mind our having imposed on her this way? I mean, even though she said it would be all right?"

"No, not Liberty!"

"How can you be so sure? What do you really know about her?"

"I know everything about her."

He grinned, but it was a shallow grin. He felt dirty and cheap inside for what he was about to do. "Okay, Miss Smarty Pants, if you're so wise, just tell me one thing you know about her."

She squeezed his hand playfully. "I won't. I'll just say that I wish I were as fabulously rich as she is."

Randy went rigid. "What do you mean?"

She nestled against his arm. "If you were a woman, you would understand. She has a home, a child, and a husband she doesn't have to meet secretly . . . and so much, much more."

Just then Tau Ti came bursting in.

"Old Master Howard come up walk now. You shoo-shoo, Master Randy."

Randy went on what little information he had gained. His heart was not in it. He fully realized that Lydia May was speaking specifically of spiritual rather than monetary values, but a sense of family obligation worked in him to distort the truth. The telegram had been signed by his father. Perhaps Liberty was indeed money-wealthy, he rationalized. He wrote out a brief return wire, feeling surly as he did so.

When it arrived in New York the next afternoon, Robert Porter personally took it to Thomas Durant. Although the board meeting was due to start in ten minutes, Durant sat behind his desk staring at a copy of the afternoon paper. Without comment he took the telegram from Porter and read the two-word message:

"Subject rich."

He studied the newspaper article and picture again and whistled. "I'll bet she is—plenty rich, and beautiful too. Randy's just confirming what I see here. Huntington's a lucky bastard, Bob. If we had that woman fully on our team, I'd be tempted to make her the ruddy damn president of the line. You should meet her."

"I shall," Porter answered coolly, "tonight."

"What?"

"Uncle Oliver and I received invitations this morning."

"Damn, she doesn't miss a single bet, does she? What did Oliver say?"

Robert grinned mirthlessly. "That as an old railroad man he wouldn't miss it for anything in the world. Naturally, he thinks that it is a Huntington trick to smoke him out of the tender car."

Durant laughed. "When he sees Liberty Wells O'Lee it is his groin that will smoke. And I think he might begin to see, as I am slowly seeing, how this revision of the Railroad Act, which almost assures the Central Pacific a monopoly on the federal loans, has come about. We have been fearing the wrong person. Huntington is the real puppet. He's dangling from strings held by very clever female hands. While I'm in the meeting, Bob, get in touch with Silas Seymour. I want the colonel here in time to crash the reception."

8

Many invitations went neglected by their New York social-register recipients until Carrie Parson's newspaper article came out. It told them that Mr. and Mrs. Daniel O'Lee were not the "common Irish folk" they'd suspected them to be. Carrie, for one thing, had painted a glowing portrait of the "famous" gown Liberty had chosen to wear—famous because Mary Todd Lincoln's dressmaker had designed it. Hardly a prominent man's wife on the list wanted to pass up the opportunity of seeing it.

"Besides," the mayor's wife said to an alderman's wife in an afterthought, "the Manhattan has never to my knowledge put on a shoddy affair."

Prior engagements were abruptly cancelled.

Maurice, a painstaking and exacting artist, had outdone himself in developing a railroad motif for the ball. At the main door of the Hudson Room the surprised and delighted guests were greeted by a maitre d' costumed for the occasion as a railroad conductor. Waiters, dressed as red caps, pushed New York Central carts that had been skillfully converted into portable bars. Colorful railroadiana abounded everywhere. On just twenty-four hours' notice, Maurice had acquired authentic railroad silverware, glasses, ashtrays and the like—all there to capture the fancy of laymen still impressed with the newness of this form of luxury transportation.

The buffet table itself was one long train, with a three-foot-high locomotive sculpted out of liver paté and railroad cars carrying artful creations from Maurice's kitchens.

The display, drawing responses ranging from amusement to lively interest, was an instantaneous success. Then—when the "redcaps" began wheeling out vintage champagne and glasses were lifted in smiling toasts—Liberty knew the gaiety of the evening was all but assured.

She stood on the receiving line with Dan, in her bustled carnation pink faille gown the frank envy of a hundred matronly guests. But her graciousness was totally disarming. Dan, a bit stiff at first in his formal tails, was so proud of her that he too began to relax and make everyone warmly welcome.

Collis Huntington could not have been more pleased. Sixteen of the newly elected Union Pacific board members were present. William Ogden was conspicuous by his absence, which made Collis smile. He knew now that he had been quite accurate in his perceptions the night before: Ogden was being forced out as president and Dix was being prepared to replace him the next day. What would better serve Durant's purposes than a "non-working" president who would leave everything to the "working" vice-president, Durant himself?

The raising of Dix to the Union Pacific presidency had also kept General Grenville Dodge from attending, Collis noted. Dodge had obviously not attained a position on the board and feared that Durant had obtained such a stranglehold on the organization that even Oliver Ames wouldn't be able to control him.

At the beginning of the second hour of the reception, the "conductor," in a booming voice, announced a new arrival:

"Ladies and gentlemen, the First Lady of the United States, Mrs. Abraham Lincoln!"

Two hundred voices gasped, then fell silent. Even the palm-shrouded orchestra let their music filter away into nothingness.

Collis gazed at Liberty in utter astonishment.

"How did she know?" he exclaimed.

"My God, I don't know," Liberty replied. "I sent her an invitation by special messenger just as a friendly gesture. I never dreamed she would come to New York!"

"It's a coup, Liberty," Collis grinned. "A real coup. You have just knocked New York society right on its ass!"

The short, plump Mary Todd Lincoln appeared a bit apprehensive as she gazed at the New York faces staring at her. She was well aware that she was not a well-liked woman in this city. Then her eyes lit upon Liberty and her face broke into a warm smile, revealing the true beauty that photographs were seldom able to capture.

As Mrs. Lincoln started towards her, Liberty instinctively began to applaud. Following the lead of their hostess, more and more guests began to applaud, so that the First Lady had an ovation before she reached Liberty.

No one missed seeing that it was Mary Todd Lincoln who quickly took Liberty into her arms and warmly kissed her on each cheek.

"You take my breath away, Mrs. Lincoln. I am so pleased."

Mary Todd's eyes twinkled. "Father thought it might be fun for me to come and also get in a couple of days shopping in New York. I do love a good party. Besides,

Father has a little surprise for your party. And he sends his love to you."

"Oh, Mrs. Lincoln, you're all the surprise I need. But it's making me forget my manners. Allow me to present my husband Dan, and Mr. Collis Huntington."

Mrs. Lincoln took Dan's hand and looked him squarely in the eye. "I knew who you would be the moment I came in the door and saw you. You are the same cut of man that I married." Then she turned to Collis. "From what Liberty had told me, Mr. Huntington, I feel I know you already. Would you do me the honor to act as my escort for introductions?"

"It would be my honor, Mrs. Lincoln," he beamed, offering his arm.

For her husband's sake as well as Liberty's, Mary Todd Lincoln was on her best behavior. She'd come, in part, to meet those editors, publishers, financiers and manufacturers who had opposed the president, often vitriolically. Instead of biting back at them, as was often her wont, she was a beaming display of diplomacy, using her wit not so much to explain the president's actions as to persuade his opponents to offer him more patience and trust. She also did a bit of politicking beyond the call of her wifely duties.

John A. Dix was still one of the most powerful figures in the Republican Party in New York State. Even though Lincoln had appointed him a major general, it was widely believed that he favored swinging New York to Salmon P. Chase's nomination.

"At last," Mrs. Lincoln said to Dix at one point in the evening, "a face I already had a name for. General. Mrs. Dix, how pleasant to see you again. General, Father knew that you would be here and wanted me to express his deep appreciation for the manner in which you are quelling the draft riots here in New York." Then she laughed. "You must be doing a remarkable job, or I doubt that he would have allowed me to come to the city."

"Please tell the president that I, in turn, appreciate his kind words."

"General," she laughed, "I will simply report your reply. Too many people already accuse me of 'telling' Father too much as it is."

As Collis escorted her away, Dix turned to his wife.

"It is odd, my dear, how you can gain an impression of another from a single word. Hear how she calls Abe 'father.' I had always considered the woman an aloof snob, but no one could mistake the warmth and love in her voice when she speaks of him that way."

"I have always admired her," Mrs. Dix said sincerely. "I think I would still be devastated with grief if we were to lose a child. I also know I wouldn't be able to face some of the men here if they said about you what they have said about the president. How openly they are trying to replace him with the likes of Salmon Chase!"

"It is reported that I am one of those men, my dear."

"I am aware of that, John."

Dix laughed. "Do you know what I see on your brow whenever the name Salmon P. Chase is mentioned?"

Mrs. Dix smiled and shook her head.

"Rigid lines of defiance."

"Really, John," she chided, "is it that bad?"

"Bad enough to make me question the wisdom of going against Lincoln's renomination. Aha!" he chortled. "My, how that did soften down those pretty brows. Have I told you lately how much I love you?"

She took his hand tenderly. "Once a day for forty years, but you can increase the dosage any time that you like, doctor!"

It was true that his wife's reaction had General Dix concerned, but it had been the First Lady who had tipped the scale in his lengthy mulling over which Republican candidate would draw most support in the upcoming election. If she wasn't winning friends that night, she was at least starting to mend some badly damaged fences.

Collis Huntington was also tremendously impressed by Mrs. Lincoln. Indeed, he wondered now if he could not have saved the money he'd spent in buying Union Pacific stock in Liberty's name. For in listening to the First Lady's conversations with various groups, he was gaining almost as much information through her as Durant would have to reveal to Liberty.

A great deal of information came through the banter Mrs. Lincoln exchanged with Oliver Ames and Thomas Durant.

"No, Mrs. Lincoln," Oliver said, "I am not a part of this railroad."

"Now, Mr. Ames," she chided, "you can't pull the wool over my eyes. Shovels are a major part of any railroad. A major part of living, I might add. Particularly your shovels. I'm reminded of a time when my father passed a neighbor clearing his field—this is when we Todds were living in Illinois. Well, this man's shovel snapped in two as he attempted to force out a boulder, and my father, a man of few and very dry words, picked the two parts up. 'This ain't no real shovel,' he said. 'Got no diamond.' 'What d'ye mean by that?' the farmer asked him. So my father scowled and said, 'It ain't no real shovel if'n it ain't got no diamond with the letters A-M-E-S on it.' "

Oliver Ames tilted back his bald head and roared with delight. "Madam," he said, "I was under the impression that Mr. Lincoln was the master of such tales, but that is priceless. And a wonderful advertisement for me, I might add. May I repeat it?"

Mrs. Lincoln grinned slyly. "Only if the source is given credit with each telling sir."

"To be sure! To be sure!"

"And now, Mr. Durant," she said quite seriously, "I have a tale to tell to you and Liberty's guests. If you would be so kind to soften the orchestra and if you, Collis, would give me a simple introduction . . . ?"

Durant and Huntington blinked at each other, suddenly aware of the true purpose of her visit, but not wishing to get their hopes up too high.

When the music stopped, Collis clapped his hands for attention.

"Ladies and gentlemen, a moment please. Gather round! I would like to introduce a charming lady who has done Mr. and Mrs. O'Lee, myself, and the Central Pacific the honor of attending tonight. Our own First Lady, Mary Todd Lincoln!"

The applause was polite, it having crossed several minds that a political speech on behalf of her husband's renomination was coming.

"Thank you, Mr. Huntington," Mrs. Lincoln said, a little too loudly and stiffly. She cleared her throat. "My goodness," she said. "Abe never told me that public speaking was such a frightening chore."

Her honesty brought chuckles and a splatter of encouraging applause.

"Thank you," she sighed. "If you don't mind, I won't make this a speech. I'll just direct my husband's intentions to Mr. Thomas Durant. You're all free to eavesdrop, because we aren't in Washington." The laughter became warmer and friendlier. Her comments were not going to be political, after all.

"Mr. Durant, Father didn't think he would be in-
fringing on Liberty's lovely party by giving you some
good news a few days in advance. Just about now, if
he is still not upstairs rough-housing with the boys,
he will be sitting down to sign the executive order
naming Omaha as the eastern terminus of the Pacific
Railroad Act."

There was a momentary silence and then thunderous
applause and wild cheering from the crowd.

Mrs. Lincoln waved her pudgy arms in the air to
silence them.

"Now, Mr. Durant, this will make sense to you, if
not to many here. I know it doesn't make sense to
me, but, like a good housewife and mother, I am
only repeating what Father told me to say." She
paused. All night long she had been purposely por-
traying her husband as a man and father and loving
companion. Now, she wanted to use his title to under-
line for many present that he also wielded great
power. Knowing the ground she now stood upon, her
voice rang out clear, crisp and with commanding
authority.

"The president, using the power of the executive
order in his determination to see a rapid commencement
of the Union Pacific, is declaring that the railhead
may begin before an eastern connection is joined."

Durant nearly fainted, but recovered himself by the
time the thunderous applause began to fade.

"Grab your glass!" he shouted. "Grab your glass!
I would first like to propose a toast to our First Lady
for bringing us this exciting news!"

"Here! Here!" a chorus of voices rang out.

"And then, I would like to propose a toast to the
chief executive of this land, whose recognition of the
need for a national railroad link has never been ques-

tioned—The president of the United States of America!"

"Here! Here!"

"And now an announcement of great importance." Durant was now going to put himself out on a limb, but he would never have a more opportune moment to capture the ears of New York's most influential editors and publishers. He picked a date out of his head that he knew would strike panic among competitors striving to get to Omaha first.

"With great pride," he bellowed, "I announce that the groundbreaking for the Union Pacific at Omaha, Nebraska, will be held on December the third."

During the mixed reaction that followed—wild joy for some, deep worry for others—Robert Porter made his excuses, took his wife and left the party. Porter was bewildered. He could not see why his Uncle Oliver had permitted Durant to make so rash a statement. There was no way the Union Pacific could start building in December. Durant would likely make them all a laughing stock and lose the whole railroad. But Porter said nothing. Thomas Durant had made his own noose. Let him hang.

Collis Huntington also enjoyed seeing Durant in a noose, but he didn't want him actually to hang. He wanted the Union Pacific to stay in business so that he could compete with it rather than with an unknown quantity; what he mostly wanted was a certain amount of control over the entire enterprise. Durant's rash promise had given him a lever he could use on the future, if he had Liberty jiggle it a bit more now. After a quick conference with Liberty, he left her to her work.

"Well, Mr. Durant," she beamed, "are we in the railroad business?"

"Deeply into it," he chuckled, "thanks to your brilliant little strategy of getting Mrs. Lincoln up here."

"Me?" Liberty said, feigning innocence. "Why, Mr. Durant, I had no way of knowing that Mary Todd would ever accept my poor little invitation."

"You're not fooling me with that act. And isn't it about time we became Tom and Liberty?"

Liberty sobered. "I would think it high time, because what I wish to say now is quite serious. You're not fooling me about that ground breaking ceremony, Tom. It was a a clever public relations gesture, but what will it gain?"

"You must be kidding. It will put the Union Pacific out front."

Liberty scoffed. "For what, Tom—a few miles, at best?"

"What are you implying?"

"Look around you, Tom. This party will cost me about half as much as I paid for a down payment on the stock. Do you think I bought that stock, or threw this party on a whim? You will soon learn that I do not do things that way. I dig deeply for facts. Tell me if I'm wrong, but at the present time the cash balance of the Union Pacific is less than $200,000, correct?"

"Jesus, how did you learn that?"

"That's immaterial," Liberty said stonily. "It is, however, one of the reasons I bought the stock and threw this party. You will have to look as if you are tying in with the rich and advancing Central Pacific, because three fourths of that money and the stock is really yours. Do you have the other ninety percent of the stock option money?"

Durant glowered. "I think you are getting into areas that don't concern you." He started to walk away.

"Come back here," she barked. "I could announce what I know right now and ruin you forever."

"I see," he said thoughtfully, "that is your game, is it?"

"Don't be simple! I don't want to lose my investment, but I loathe men who have the audacity to think that women do not have brains. I have now been around enough railroad talk to know that you do not have enough capital to build five miles of track. Don't get mad if I say your whole structure is wrong. What you need is a holding company like The Associates."

"And who in the damn hell are The Associates?"

Liberty grinned. The mouse had bit the cheese. "The holding companies that remove all the detail accounting for construction and material costs from the books of the Central Pacific. Why else do you think the Central Pacific is nearly a year ahead of you? Don't let Collis know where you got the information, but you would be a fool not to learn about their success."

She turned and left him alone in deep thought. He could not help but feel that she could grow to be more trouble than she was worth. Seeing that Oliver Ames was standing alone, he went and reported on the conversation.

"Brilliant," Ames mused. "It sounds similar to what those hotheads tried to form in 1859 in Pennsylvania. I don't recall its name, but it was approved by the Pennsylvania state legislature as a holding company specifically intended to finance the construction of railroads. Get George Train out there tomorrow to check on its status. I see the First Lady is about to leave and that will signal a grand exodus." He chuckled. "Delightful story! Delightful!" Then he sobered into a dollars-and-cents businessmen. "Get Maurice to reserve me a small, private room. I don't think I am fooling Collis Huntington, so invite him and his engineer to join us. I'll have the carriage take Mrs. Ames and your wife on home."

"And Mrs. O'Lee? Do you want her at the meeting?"

"Oh, no!" Ames chuckled. "Smart women make me nervous and brilliant women make me quake like New Hampshire aspen. But she makes me feel like I am deep center in an earthquake. Be a gentleman and see that she is escorted to her room."

That was no problem for Thomas Durant. He already had his man pegged and a scheme was developing in his mind.

"Silas," he said, encountering Colonel Seymour a few moments later, "how do you find the party and the hostess?"

The colonel grinned broadly, his pencil-thin mustache turning it into almost a leer. "Charming on both accounts. I take the lady to be about twenty-one to twenty-four—the age when a woman is really the most desirous. I've spent the entire evening enthralled by her. For the life of me I don't know what she could possibly see in her husband."

"Ames wants to meet with her husband and Huntington. Will you escort her up to her hotel room, if I arrange it?"

Seymour pursed his lips, devilishly. "Love to oblige, but can you trust me? You know my reputation as a womanizer."

"I'm counting on it," Durant said, quite seriously. "The woman is onto our stock scheme. If she were compromised, shall we say, then the scale might level out. But she's got to be cooperative, Silas. I don't want another situation on our hands like that fifteen-year-old chambermaid in Washington who yelled rape."

"Really, Tom," Seymour said, genuinely hurt. "That little slut was colored and came into my chamber while I was still abed. It was a frame-up to extract money from me and I refused to pay."

Durant shrugged and walked away. He knew Seymour's reputation too well to believe that fable. The man was incapable of getting a good night's sleep unless he had at least one woman before retiring.

Liberty was glowing with happiness. Mrs. Lincoln had asked her to accompany her shopping the next day, and the prospect was exciting. Her glow continued as she stood and said goodnight to her guests, giving all a feeling that their personal attendance had added to the affair.

She was not surprised to hear from Collis of the private meeting, for that had been Collis's intent on having her talk with Durant, but that they had bagged Ames as well made the night utterly triumphant.

"I shall be delighted," she enthused, "to have Colonel Seymour escort me to my room. It shall give me an opportunity to personally thank him for recommending Dan."

"Liberty," Collis said softly, taking her hand, "I don't know if man has ever created the proper words to express the admiration I feel for you at this moment. You have just been unbelievable. Get a good night's sleep; you deserve it."

As Liberty and Colonel Seymour went through the lobby to the grand staircase, the other hotel guests could not help but turn and stare. The immaculately groomed and uniformed colonel evoked a certain regal splendor that could only have been matched by a princely head of state. His egocentric nature told him that every female eye in the ornately stuffy cavern of plush and mahogany were envious of Liberty being on his arm.

Liberty too felt all eyes upon her.

As they were ascending the grand staircase, William Waldorf Astor and his party emerged from another of the hotel's ballrooms. Astor stopped short and watched the couple climb all the way to the gallery. Frantically, he waved over a page boy.

"Son, can you tell me who that dazzling creature might be?"

"To be sure, Mr. Astor. That is a Mrs. O'Lee who entertained the First Lady in the Hudson Room tonight."

Astor gasped. "Mrs. Lincoln was here?"

"Made quite a stir, sir, coming and going."

"Was my aunt in attendance?"

"I think not, sir."

"Good," he chuckled. "Then we can't crow at each other over who erred on this social coup." He pressed a coin on the boy and continued to stare upward. "Extraordinary," he breathed. "But the staircase does not suit her at all. Someday I shall build a staircase and hotel that will do justice to a creature like that. Creature? That, my friends, is what the Europeans say that we lack—you have just witnessed American royalty in its purest sense. I must send a note of apology for not having accepted the invitation this evening. Extraordinary!"

Turning to the next flight of stairs, Liberty explained, "My room is on the third floor, Colonel. 308."

"I know. Your husband gave me the key."

Liberty laughed. "I'm glad that he did. I'm still in fantasy-land and never even thought to ask for it. I hardly want the evening to end."

He didn't comment until they had cleared the next few stairs and were on the third floor landing. "It needn't have to, you know. Look ahead!"

A room-service bellboy had just stopped in front of Liberty's door with a heavy-laden cart.

"What is this?" she cried.

"Everyone was aware that you have had neither food nor drink all evening, and Maurice sent you up a small sampling of his art."

"It's monstrous," Liberty laughed. "It would take a full year to eat!"

"Well, as the meeting may go on for a couple of hours, you might take pity on an old, tired army colonel and invite him in for a bite."

"You are hardly old, and look anything but tired, but the invitation is gladly extended. I owe you so much for the opportunity you gave Dan. And, oh my, I am suddenly starved and hate to eat alone."

Liberty's excitement was such that a few bites and a sip of champagne fully sated her. She felt restless and desired the return of Dan and Collis so that they could relive the whole evening in words.

For a time, she stood looking down at the gas-lit street, only half-listening to Colonel Seymour ramble on about himself. It was beginning to snow, making fairy-like halos around each street lamp.

Seymour came to the window and drew her soft hand formally to his lips. "That is to thank you for the evening, so far." His voice was low with heavy emotion, yet his hand was icy cold. As his dark eyes went over her, Liberty suddenly understood why Mrs. Durant had said the man made her feel uncomfortable. His gaze seemed to pierce right through her clothing and examine every pore of her skin. No man had ever looked at her in quite that manner. It gave her an uneasy feeling.

Seymour's eyes lingered over her breasts. The soft faille dress clung to her nipples, and the colonel marvelled at the rise and fall of her bosom as she breathed. Like fresh picked fruit, he thought.

"More champagne?"

"No. I shall wait for my husband and Mr. Huntington."

"No need for that. Durant informed me that the meeting would go on past midnight."

Midnight! Liberty was shocked. Collis had anticipated no more than an hour. Durant had something up his sleeve and she sensed now that Seymour was in on it.

Silas Seymour watched her and waited. He was not malicious, merely implacable.

"Do you know what will keep them so long, colonel?" Liberty asked at last.

"It really matters little to me. They can talk all night, as far as I'm concerned." He winked. "The manner in which they got rid of their wives could also suggest business of a different nature. This is wicked old New York, you know."

His inference annoyed Liberty.

"You are being uncouth," she answered angrily, tossing her great cloud of brown hair. "Such a thought would not cross Dan's or Collis's mind."

"Indeed? Are they so pure that they haven't cheated on their wives before?"

"I beg your pardon," Liberty said icily. "We are hardly well enough acquainted for this discussion."

"Ah, really?" said Seymour. "Do I detect a tone in your voice which makes you fear the truth of my statement—where your husband is concerned?"

Liberty blushed hotly. "You're quite mistaken!"

"Ah, why are women such fools to hold onto their silly pride? They should do as their husbands do and let their emotions rule their desires. Haven't you ever longed for a man other than your husband?"

Liberty turned sharply from the window, her voice charged with indignation:

"You are base and vulgar, sir! There is no man in my life except my husband."

"Up to this moment, that is," he said evenly.

Liberty looked at him steadily, her soft green eyes hardening with contempt. Then she laughed.

"And you think you are the man who can change all that, don't you?"

"There is not a man alive who could teach you the true art of love better than I."

She was disgusted with him. She was used to Dan's simplicity and the charm and sophistication of men like Collis. This uncouth colonel was irritating, and she said something she knew would hurt his vanity: "I have no desire to learn what you have acquired in the gutters of life. No decent woman would. Perhaps you'd best leave before the snow forces all the street walkers indoors."

He flushed angrily. Only then did she see how dangerous a man he might become.

"I'm getting tired of this game of cat and mouse. I desire you and intend to take you to bed—tonight!"

It was a threat—no, it was more like a promise. She could not deceive herself. She was dealing with a man who could not be talked out of rape, because he would not believe he was committing rape. This was a forceful, domineering, egoistic man! A man such as she had never had to confront before.

They stared at each other like the bitterest of enemies. He saw in her eyes, hatred and confusion. But as he continued to look at her, he ignored her expression and admired the new flush of beauty her anger brought to her face. She was proud, and proud women don't talk. He felt that she wanted to be forced, so that she could later soothe her own conscience.

"Damn you, woman!" he roared. "You know you want it as much as I do!" He rushed to her and

grasped her by the shoulders. His voice was trembling
with emotion. Yet its tone was intended to convey irony,
and was partly successful. But there was nothing ironic
in the steely grip of his hands on her shoulders. Even
if it cost her her life, she refused to cry out in pain or
show her feelings on her face.

As his fingers closed savagely over her shoulder and
she feared that he would begin to shred the delicate
fabric of her dress, her body seemed suddenly invaded
by a warm, loving sense of protection. From the depths
of her soul surged up Kai Soong's words. They seemed
to act as armor preparing her for the worst. She relaxed,
almost to the point of being limp. As though Kai Soong
were in the room advising her, she put a hand on Seymour's chest, but did not shove him away.

"Please, the dress," she said softly, without a trace
of fear. "I can do it myself."

Seymour backed off, chuckling at what had brought
her to bay. To keep the dress from being ruined, she
would submit. He would have to remember that ploy
for another time.

As Liberty began to unbutton the bodice, she closed
her eyes. Whether it was because she had recalled his
words, or just because she was in need of help, against
the black of her closed eyelids the fierce Chinese eyes
seemed to stare back at her and take command of her
mind.

Because the dress had built-in breast supports, it
revealed her torso as soon as she had slipped it from
her shoulders and left it dangling at her waist. She
stood still, motionless, concentrating on the eyes danc-
ing in her imagination.

Seymour could only stare at her body with wonder.
Her breasts were high, perfectly round and up-tilted in
a way that moved him greatly. They had been perfectly
made for her beautiful womanly figure with its narrow

waist and flaring hips. Never had he seen lovelier breasts. He was mad with desire to touch them, savor their apparent softness, feel their touch against his cheeks and lips.

Something compelled him to look up. He started. Liberty held him in an unblinking, narrow-eyed stare. Her green eyes glinted like a cat in the dark, then altered from emerald to deep black. Seymour was unsure of what was happening, but for the moment he was unable to tear his eyes away. An eerie dread crawled into his brain, suggesting that she was not the same creature standing there a moment before.

"Touch them!"

The command that broke the silence made him blanch. The voice had been low, fierce and tinged with a bit of Oriental accent. Gingerly, he reached out and started to cup each mound in a palm.

"E-e-e-you!" he screamed, pulling his hands away and shaking them. "What in the hell—?" He looked down at his hands. They were as red as if he had placed his hands on a hot stove.

"Hell, exactly, Colonel Seymour," Liberty answered. "It has been foretold that no man shall ever possess me until my husband has left this life."

"What kind of witchcraft is this?" he demanded sharply.

Liberty smiled, her eyes mere slits. Seductively, she walked bare-breasted into the foyer, picked up his hat and stood by the door awaiting him.

He instantly reasoned that it had to be some kind of a womanly trick—a powder or salve she had put on her breasts to make them so fiercely hot. But when? And where did she get it? He had had many stunts pulled on him and still had overcome them. Painting an 'I am master' smile on his face he went into the foyer.

"Are you sure you want it to end this way?" he asked, taking his hat in one hand and reaching up to fondle her breast with the other.

When Liberty did not comment, or back away from his advancing hand, it gave him a feeling that all was not lost, as yet.

But her skin was as cold and uninviting as a touch of a reptile. Slowly he drew his hand away. He was puzzled, confused and frustrated. He jammed his hat onto his head and slammed out of the door.

Liberty stood for a long moment before she started to tremble. She was frightened. Frightened as she had never been before in her life, but not of Silas Seymour. She was unsure of how to explain what had happened. She had felt no extreme heat or extreme cold, but a voice had told her to plant such suggestions in Colonel Seymour's mind. It had worked! But how had it worked? She went immediately to bed, but was afraid to close her eyes. Afraid to see Kai Soong's eyes. She forced herself to stare into the darkness until her lids became too heavy to support themselves.

Colonel Seymour remained standing outside her door a full fifteen minutes, the key to it still in his possession.

Not since the age of thirteen, when his mother's scullery maid had refused to come to his room, had Silas ever been denied. Here, finally, after thousands of conquests since, was a beautiful woman provoking him to a new and exciting challenge. That tiny waist! That amazing alabaster skin! Those fiery green eyes! Standing there, his heart beating rapidly, he became obsessed with the idea of barging back in and taking her by force.

Suddenly it was too late. He heard voices on the stairs, and recognized one as Huntington's. He quickly darted to the end of the corridor, turned the corner and waited. The tones of the voices suggested anger. The colonel strained to hear them better but gained only a word here and there.

"Damn . . . key . . . late . . . probably asleep . . . backstairs . . . night porter . . . Goodnight."

The speaker was Dan O'Lee. Seymour raced along the corridor to the backstairs exit, with no real thought in his mind, only a heated vision of Liberty's loveliness. There, he pulled into the shadows of the third-floor landing—and waited.

Soon, Dan O'Lee's figure loomed in the exit doorway. Seymour heard him curse the darkness; he had obviously drunken a bit too much at the meeting. The colonel watched him as he began to fumble his way down the stairs.

Intoxicated as he was and in need of sleep, Dan had not wanted to awaken Liberty. He intended somehow or other to get down those stairs to the lobby for a pass-key. With both hands on the outer rail he cautiously planted each dark, downward step. At the second-floor landing he paused. The lighted area below seemed a million miles down into a deep hole and he had to close his eyes for a moment to keep from swooning. After taking several deep breaths he started down again. Something lodged between his legs. He tried to keep from tripping, but felt a shove on his shoulders that toppled him to the side and forward. With a crash, his head hit the wall. Then he was tumbling downward, unconscious, his body gathering speed as it fell, his limp body stopping at the base in an oddly twisted state.

Calmly, Colonel Seymour returned to the third floor and carefully stuck the key under the O'Lee's door. His heart was still pounding, even faster now than before, and he wondered if at this moment he was not quite mad. But he smirked as he thought to himself:

"As foretold, you cannot be possessed by another as long as your husband is of this life. I shall see you, Mrs. O'Lee. I shall see you very, very shortly!"

Within the hour a night porter found Dan and quickly summoned the house doctor. Liberty and Collis were aroused, informed of the accident and advised to remain upstairs, as "we will be bringing your husband up shortly."

Collis blamed himself. "He was pretty far gone," he groaned. "I should have gone for the key."

Liberty didn't know what to think. She was nearly hysterical. "Why didn't he knock?" she cried. "Why didn't he? The key was right there on the foyer floor!"

"How did it get there?"

"I don't know!" Liberty struggled to think. "I guess Colonel Seymour recalled that he had it and slipped it back under the door."

She sprang up to answer a knock at the door. The doctor came in swiftly, followed by four bellboys carrying Dan on a stretcher. She saw no signs of blood, but Dan was pale as a sheet.

"How is he, doctor?" she demanded fearfully.

She was rudely ignored. The bellboys carried Dan on into the bedroom, then left, and the doctor shut the bedroom door behind him.

Collis muttered, "He'll be all right, Liberty—he's just knocked up a bit, that's all." He kept on muttering. "Nice people, these New Yorkers. That doctor reminds me a great deal of our friend Durant." He cursed under his breath. "That man Durant is cold and bloodless. Picked my brain apart and didn't want to give anything in return."

"Collis, please," Liberty cried impatiently. "I couldn't care less about Durant at this moment."

"Liberty," he said sternly, "don't you think I'm concerned, as well? I'm trying to keep up some type of conversation so that we aren't just sitting here dreaming up things that may not come about. Dan's going to be all right—I told you that."

Liberty sank into a chair, aimlessly lifted her hands, then let them drop. "Some ending to our perfect evening," she said bitterly.

"He'll be all right," Collis repeated.

"I hope so." She kept shaking her head. "Tell me how he got so drunk. It isn't like Dan to drink that much."

"That amazed me, too. If I didn't know Maurice's bartenders better, I'd say that Dan's drinks were mixed to purposely loosen his tongue. Of course, as long as the discussion was mainly about finance, he couldn't do much more than just sit there and listen while he drank. But out of the blue, Durant launched into a discussion about where he thinks the two railroads should link up. He talked about the Humboldt River. His suggestions were wild, as if he were purposely goading Dan into an argument. Drunk or not, Dan countered them with the sound logic that Utah was still up for grabs and we'd be far east of the Great Salt Lake before the Union Pacific was across Nebraska. That let out the Humboldt River. Durant wouldn't buy it, and wouldn't let us go, even after Oliver Ames excused himself for the night. Finally, we just had to be rude and walk away from him."

Liberty opened her mouth and then shut it again tight. For a moment she was tempted to tell Collis about Colonel Seymour. But what seemed suspicious to her at one moment seemed innocent the next. After all, what reason would Durant have for arranging Seymour as her escort and then getting Dan drunk? It didn't make sense; she couldn't see what Durant had to gain by it. No, she decided to keep her experiences with Seymour that evening quite to herself.

The doctor came out and delivered a terse report.

"He's awake. Nothing broken, thanks to his inebriated state." He sniffed. "Badly sprained wrist and ankle, though. I'll check on him in the morning."

Liberty and Collis wordlessly looked at each other and then went to the bedroom.

Dan lay staring at the ceiling, a puzzled frown on his face.

"Are you all right?" Liberty whispered.

"Not by a damn sight," he growled, "and that sawbones can't tell me different."

"You mean you think you have more than sprains?" Collis queried.

"It's not that at all," Dan snapped. "He's trying to tell me that I fell because I was drunk. I say I was tripped and shoved and he says it was all an hallu . . . hallucin . . ."

"Hallucination?"

"What in the hell is that, anyway?"

"A nice way of saying you were in a stupor and you imagined it."

"No," Dan insisted, "I was there, remember. I've gotten pretty damn drunk in my day, but no matter how drunk I get I remember things. I bet I can recite every stupid argument Durant made tonight, and every argument you gave me, Collis, coming up the stairs and to the door."

"Then you're saying that you were attacked?"

"Yes. I don't know why, but I have a good idea by whom."

"Who?" Collis and Liberty chorused together.

"Brass buttons! When my head turned, before hitting the wall, I remember seeing a flash of a double row of brass buttons, like those bell hops wear who work in the lobby. I say it was one of them. He meant to rob me, but got fooled because I didn't have a cent of money on me."

Liberty's head swam; she felt ill. Dan's getting pushed, the key under the door, the brass buttons—all suggested that Colonel Seymour had done it. Should she tell Dan? She couldn't. The colonel was far more dangerous than she had imagined. Even to inform Collis of his acts that night would lead to an unpleasant, costly rift with Thomas Durant. To say anything to Dan could easily trigger his temper and lead to a violent fight, causing at the very least an unaffordable scandal.

She felt alone. She would say nothing about the incident. She took a deep breath and said, "Gentlemen, the party is over. Dan, I will sleep on the couch, so I won't disturb you. Collis, I will see you out."

Dan was groggy and falling asleep before they closed the bedroom door, and Collis turned to Liberty.

"I have a strong feeling that something is bothering you," he said. "Would you care to discuss it?"

"Yes," she alibied, "I would. I am a mother, who is suddenly starting to miss her child very much. When can we go home to California?"

Collis Huntington was a genius in measuring other people's lies. For once he decided not to press the point. In a way he welcomed Liberty's desire to get away. After what he had seen at the meeting, he wanted to separate Dan and Thomas Durant as soon as possible.

"You have been brilliant, Liberty," he said, "and so has Dan. You both deserve a rest. I have to stay on a few months, but we can start checking shipping schedules for the two of you tomorrow."

"Thank you," she sighed, "and goodnight."

At least she would feel a little safer with three thousand miles separating her from Silas Seymour.

* * *

Mary Todd Lincoln, given half a chance, could spend money like a whirlwind. Her budget for renovating certain rooms in the White House was in her opinion "stingy", and she took the close supervision on her in Washington as an insult to her bargain-hunting abilities.

"The man's name is Livermore," Mrs. Lincoln complained to Liberty in the hansom cab, "and he watches my every purchase with an eagle eye. I have just been dying to get to New York to prove what an old fool he really can be."

Liberty was only half listening. She had slept fitfully and had come near to sending a message to cancel her breakfast and shopping trip with the First Lady. It had taken Dan, who believed she was worried only about his health, to badger her into going.

Liberty had gone with reluctance. She had dressed simply, determined still to wiggle out of the trip after having had breakfast in the Columbine Room. But the First Lady was dressed even more simply, as if wishing to blend into the crowd and go unnoticed.

Mrs. Lincoln pounded on the roof of the cab with her umbrella for it to stop.

"Come, child, for an experience such as you have never had before."

Mary Todd's plan for that day did not include the fashionable shops. Second Avenue's second-hand stores had caught her eye, and she sought out scores of them. With Liberty, she pawed her way through dust and cobwebs to examine various pieces of furniture that were neither antiques nor "modern"—and thus had gone unwanted and some of them Mrs. Lincoln liked, however; she was hawk-like in her selections. Because she paid cash, no one had reason to ask for her name and she gave the address of a local mover who would pick up her purchases.

"You see, Liberty," she chuckled, "if they had known that chair was going to the White House, the man would have demanded at least fifty dollars. I don't think I've lost the horse-trader sense my father instilled in me."

A light snow that had fallen was melting fast and the sidewalk was turning slushy. Mary Todd stopped short when she saw one shopkeeper putting articles out on it for sale.

"The man is an idiot," she whispered. "He's putting those two lovely chairs right in the water."

She marched over and examined the chairs indifferently, as if they were the worthless castoffs the man obviously took them to be.

" 'Elp yah, lady?"

Mary Todd pursed her lips. "They looked finer from a distance. The fabric is shot and this one has a split leg."

"Got more inside just like 'em."

Mary Todd shrugged and motioned for Liberty to follow her in. The four the man showed them had equally deteriorated seat and back cushions, but the structures were sound.

Mrs. Lincoln sighed, as if greatly disappointed. "Only four?"

"How many yah want?"

"How many are in this set?"

"One time there were twenty of 'em. Folks around here don't need more'n four to six 'round a kitchen table. Nor do they like these fancy types. Who ever heard of a table big enough to seat twenty at once?"

"I'm a music teacher," she lied. "Matching chairs would be nice for students giving a recital. I can't afford much, though. How many have you left?"

"All of them—in one condition or another. If your hubby's handy, he can fix the broken ones."

"How much?"

He scratched his chin. "Oh, say a dollar each on the good ones, fifty cents on t'others."

"I would like to examine them, to determine which is which. I only charge twenty-five cents an hour and have to watch my pennies."

"Now I understand that, lady. I got plenty of violins and such, cheap. You just look around while I gather the chairs up."

Mrs. Lincoln winked at Liberty. "If they were in twenty pieces, I would snap them up at that price. I just wish getting them recushioned was going to be as inexpensive. Liberty, look! Could that massive thing actually be a headboard?"

Liberty puzzled over the piece, because only a portion of it was visible. Mrs. Lincoln tried to move away some furniture to get a better look, but it was impossible.

"Got 'em over here," the man called.

Mrs. Lincoln gave the chairs a quick and expert examination. "Fifteen dollars for all?" she said. "I'll have them picked up tomorrow."

The shopkeeper scratched his chin. "Well . . ."

"Done!" she grinned. "Now, I know this may be a lot of bother, but could you clear things away so I might be able to see this headboard over here?"

With Mrs. Lincoln's money in his hand he didn't mind at all—fifteen dollars was his average income for a week.

"It's a whole bed, you know," he explained as he moved things this way and that to clear a path to it. "Springs are in a shed in the alley, but Lord only knows what happened to the canopy. Huge monster's been here gathering dust for a good ten years." He laughed. "Eight foot long, it is. Only man I knows could fit a bed that size would be Abe Lincoln, and he ain't said 'Harry Dunlop, I've need of it.' Well, there she is!"

Mary Todd Lincoln stared. She could already picture the bed in her husband's bedroom—the mahogany polished to a mirror finish, a new canopy of starched muslin, and a downy, feather mattress that he could stretch out full-length on and never have to sleep cross-wise ever again.

"Magnificent," Liberty enthused. "Has it a history?"

Harry Dunlop chuckled. "Little lady, I've a competitor across the street who has the furniture with the history and a price to go with it. Harry Dunlop's furniture only has a future, at best."

"My husband is also a very tall man, Mr. Dunlop," Mrs. Lincoln said softly. "Dare I venture to ask the price?"

Dunlop considered a moment. He would be glad to be rid of the cumbersome thing that nobody seemed to want. "If I don't have to oil all those damn springs before you take it away, I say a hundred even."

Mary Todd gasped; she had expected a price four to six times that. Dunlop, misreading her, pursed his lips.

"Well," he drawled, "there are matching night-stands somewhere here about. I'll throw those in for good measure."

"That's very kind," Mrs. Lincoln said, opening her purse to finalize the sale before he could change his mind. "Please make out a receipt I can give the delivery man who comes to fetch it."

"In what name?"

"Mary Todd," she said, as she had been saying all along Second Avenue.

It was quickly done and Mrs. Lincoln left floating on a cloud.

Harry Dunlop put the money in his safe and went back to reading the *Tribune* front page to last. It was a habit he'd formed to wile away the morning hours, usually quiet in his shop.

At first ignoring the artist's sketch of the two women on the society page, he chuckled at Horace Greeley's dry reporting of the elaborate affair that had taken place at the Manhattan the night before. Harry wished he had known Mrs. Lincoln would be there. He would have loved to have gotten just one glimpse of the president's lady, for he greatly admired Mr. Lincoln. Then he studied the sketch of the ladies more carefully. He frowned, "Well, I'll be damned," he muttered aloud.

He turned and gazed at the headboard, and a slow grin spread across his face.

"Old bed of mine," he chuckled, "you got yourself a future. You are now Mr. Lincoln's bed."

By the time they returned to the Columbine Room for lunch, Liberty was nearly exhausted. Mrs. Lincoln, however, was already making plans to visit fabric shops during the afternoon, and she had every intention of keeping up with the First Lady's frantic pace. They were just finishing tea when Colonel Seymour entered. Liberty saw him stop abruptly and stare at her, as if he couldn't believe his eyes. She was lunching with Mrs. Lincoln—not grieving over her husband's "misfortune"? He spun on his heel and left the restaurant.

Liberty had paled. Mrs. Lincoln put down her cup and looked at her in alarm.

"What is it, child?" she said. "Are you all right?"

"Did you see that man who just left?" Liberty murmured.

"Yes, Colonel Seymour. I was hoping he would not intrude upon our luncheon. Men like that make my skin crawl."

"Mrs. Lincoln, I've just got to talk to someone about him. Someone who won't repeat the story."

Mrs. Lincoln eyed her apprehensively. "Oh dear, I hope it's not seamy," she said. "Father says I am a better talker than listener. But give me a try."

Hesitantly at first, and then with her renewed anger making the words flow smoothly, Liberty recounted every aspect of the incident, even the mystical nature of Kai Soong's "suggestions" to her. She ended by reporting what was Dan's belief as well as her own— that the accident was no accident.

Mrs. Lincoln heard her out, her small, soft mouth trembling, as one nearly incredible detail followed another.

"I hardly know what to say, Liberty," she said at the end. "I admire the way you handled the situation, although it could have been highly dangerous."

"But what am I to do now?" Liberty groaned. "He can deny everything, if accused by me or by Dan."

"Your plan to go home seems the wisest, as I see it." Mary Todd shook her head sympathetically. "But with your permission, I would like to discuss the matter with Abe on my return."

"Oh, no, that would be so embarrassing."

"Leave it in Abe's hands, child. He will know the best way to handle a man like Silas Seymour. Now, do you wish to continue on with me or go back to the hotel?"

That matter hadn't been in question. But now, with Seymour lurking about, Liberty also felt safer staying with the First Lady for the rest of the day.

* * *

The election of the officers went exactly as Collis had predicted. Dix was the unanimous choice as the president of the Union Pacific—all sixteen directors voting being Durant's men.

That night, while the new officers drank lavish toasts to him, Anna Judah knelt in prayer a few blocks away. Ted Judah had slipped from this world.

Liberty saw the obituary notice in the morning. She had been up since dawn, packing to sail for home that afternoon. It was Dan who brought it to her attention just as she was answering a knock at the door to let Collis in.

"Libby!" he cried. "Come quick!"

Liberty and Collis looked at each other in alarm, than raced to the bedroom. In bed, Dan held a newspaper toward them, his face ashen.

Liberty groaned as she scanned the article. Then she thrust it at Collis, and started to run from the room.

"Where are you going?" Dan called.

"Where else?" she sobbed. "To Anna!"

Collis Huntington read the article slowly and turned to the window. His main reason for staying in the east had just vanished. Ted Judah had been a major threat to him: Judah could have betrayed his dream by selling it to others. Now he was no longer a threat. Both Huntington's rule of the Central Pacific and the fantastic future of The Associates were assured. He couldn't help but smile.

Anna Judah, in private inconsolable but in public a woman of tearless strength, was just leaving the Metropolitan Hotel lobby when Liberty came flying in, almost missing her.

"Liberty," Anna cried, catching her in her arms, "how kind and sweet of you to come."

"Oh, Anna!" she sobbed, "I am so sorry!"

"Come," Anna soothed. "We can sit over here—out of traffic. I have a little time before my train leaves for Greenfield. They have taken Ted on ahead. My, what exciting things I've been reading about you in the papers."

"I wished I'd have known where you were staying, Anna. I would have loved to have invited you to the reception."

Anna smiled thinly. "It's just as well that you didn't. I might have been tempted to attend just to spit in Collis Huntington's face."

"Anna!"

"I'm sorry. That was more Anna Pierce talking than Anna Judah. Ted and I were good for each other in that respect. He tamed my youthful temper and I calmed his terrible . . ." Her voice caught and she turned away. Quickly she regained control and turned back. "And what, pray tell, are you up to now?"

"Dan and I are going home this afternoon."

"I see," Anna said slowly. "Will Dan get Ted's job?"

Liberty hung her head. "Collis says so."

Anna reached out and lifted Liberty's chin. "Don't be embarrassed, Liberty. At least Dan will make them stick to Ted's principles and build a good railroad. But, frankly, I feel sorry for him. There has not been a man born of woman who can make those four men see eye to eye on anything. Watch them, Liberty, for Dan's sake. I have first-hand experience on how they can change a man into something he never was before. They will use you until you are dry—and Collis Huntington is the worst on that score—and then cast you off as though they had never heard your name. But enough of this talk. What are your plans?"

Liberty smiled. "I think they have already been made for me. If I'm under the weather at sea it's likely to be morning sickness rather than sea sickness."

"Oh, Liberty, how marvelous for you: I just pray it will be a fine new baby. Now, I really must go. This is one train Ted would never forgive me for missing."

They stood and embraced. Then Anna Judah held her at arms length and looked her square in the eye.

"Liberty, learn all you can about that damn railroad. Dan is going to need you now, like he has never needed you in his whole life. He's a babe in the woods—like Ted was in many respects. He's a railroad man, not a power broker. God gave you a good brain. Use it on more than just raising children." Then she sighed. "Although I wish now I could have used mine on at least one."

She kissed Liberty quickly and fled.

9

As enthusiastic as Liberty had been to get home, Sacramento soon seemed drab to her. At first she ascribed her depressed moods to a wearying pregnancy, but, with Anna Judah gone and only an occasional visit from Lydia May Tedder, she began to see her problem as loneliness—induced boredom. Her days and nights in Washington and New York had been filled with things she had to do and learn to be of help to Dan and Collis. Now she had nothing. Even the Sacramento *Union* couldn't hold her interest.

When she tried to follow Anna's advice and learn more about the railroad, Dan became edgy and irritable.

"Damn it, Libby," he growled, "I get enough Union Pacific talk during the day, if I get any talk out of Charles Crocker at all. I'm glad Collis is getting back next week. I lay out a grade level plan, but Crocker won't put a crew to work on it unless Montague or Porter lays it before him. Behind my back he calls me 'Judah's ghost.' What in the hell does he mean by that?"

"I would take it as a compliment. I'm sure the other men do as well."

"Other men?" he roared. "Liberty, there is hardly a man around who knows who in the hell Ted Judah was! Because of the low-end wage Crocker pays, we have to train practically a new pick-and-shovel brigade every other day. They can make more money joining the army. Hell, today I was waiting for a dump cart to bring a load of fill. Not my job, but young Porter took sickly during the morning. And who should bring the cart along but a skinny twelve-year-old boy, who has been working for Crocker for seventy-five cents a day and board. I did some checking. There must be twenty to thirty kids of that age on the crews. The man has no scruples. Child labor to do this man-killing grade work! I'm hungry. When do we eat?"

"Right now," Liberty answered dully. This was Dan's type of railroad talk. Well and good. But it was not the sort she could make helpful contributions to.

Yet it was the only kind that Charles Crocker wished to place before the board meetings.

"Leland," he fumed, "you and Mark and Edwin don't face this desperate problem daily. I'm out there! You say hold down on expenses. I've gone to the bottom of the barrel to find men so hard-pressed by circumstances that they will work twelve hours a day, six days a week, for a dollar a day. We have no influx of Irish immigrants to haul off the ships as they do in Boston. I say we have to find our own source of cheap labor."

His brother Edwin scoffed. "Like your idea on the peon masses of northern Mexico, Charles? Word of your miserly nature must travel very fast. You haven't even be able to lure them north."

Charles ignored his brother, who was becoming too independent in his mind. "Well, I have a plan we can put before the War Department that will only cost us board and no wages. The *Union* says the army's capturing more Conferedate soldiers than they have compounds to hold them in. Leland, let me push for five thousand Confederate prisoners of war, with a few companies of Union infantry to serve as a guard detail."

"No wages," Stanford mused, "and a work force of five thousand. . . . Too bad you didn't think of this before Collis left for the east, Charles."

Crocker made a nasty gesture. "That's how far such a plan would have gotten with his suggesting it. What in the hell good is he to us, anyway?"

Mark Hopkins roared with mirth. "Charles, you can't be serious. What Collis and the O'Lees have done for the treasury of this enterprise in the past several months is unmeasurable."

"Bull!" Crocker exploded. "If the treasury is so fat why did I have to dip into my mercantile till last week to meet the payroll and buy supplies?"

"Patience," Hopkins advised. "Rome wasn't built in a day, nor are government subsidy checks that quickly issued. I tell you, we'll be reaping a harvest of gold soon that will make the Comstock lode look like pocket change."

Charles Crocker could only believe what he saw with his own two eyes.

Another saw something with her own eyes, but read into it what she wanted to believe.

When Anna Judah sent Lydia May Tedder the notice on Ted's death, she included as an afterthought the article on Liberty's reception. The handwriting and postmark on the envelope was recognized by Selena the moment Liu Ma put it in front of her breakfast plate and she quickly shuffled it under a stack of other mail.

Selena felt what she was doing was within her rights as a mother and protector. Lydia May had been deeply shocked by the announcement of Ted Judah's death in the *Union;* her grief had been renewed when Liberty returned home in late November. Selena was not about to have her daughter upset a third time, what with the holidays so near and her annual Christmas Eve dinner party pending.

"Mostly R.S.V.P.'s," she told Nazareth, when he asked after the mail, and scooped up the stack and went to her private den.

She crumpled Anna's note and the obituary article together and threw them into the roaring fire. But she looked at the sketch of Liberty with the First Lady, and read the rather lengthy article by Horace Greeley several times before touching them to the flames too. Watching the paper curl into gray ash, Selena seethed with jealous rage. How dare Collis Huntington pawn Liberty O'Lee off as a California aristocrat? What gall! No wonder Californians were looked on with scorn, if *she* was held out as a prime example of their culture and society! Selena had a good mind to write to the First Lady and tell her that she had been used badly by a social climber who couldn't even get in the front door of most respectable Sacramento homes.

She had not even considered inviting the O'Lees back for a second year. She was under no obligation to Lydia May or the Judahs this time around. But there was one person she had intended to invite and now intended to snub, hopefully into social extinction. With deliberate calm, she struck the Huntington name from her guest list. Then she purposely left the list unguarded on her desk for Liu Ma to see.

As usual, the houseboy grapevine spread the message—it hardly needed decoding—with utmost efficiency. Because peerage snobbery was rampant among them, Liu Ma couldn't help but lord it over Wang Wu that his "master and mistress" had fallen in disgrace.

Wang Wu hid his face in shame, until he learned that Tau Ti's household was not to be invited either. Wang Wu could hardly believe this news. To him Liberty O'Lee was the greatest lady in the entire city. He took the shame of both families personally on his slender shoulders and kept his ears open for any gossip against Selena Tedder.

Elizabeth Huntington took the rumor dismally, but considered herself too much of a lady to openly show her hurt. She took to her room with her decanter of brandy for the holiday season.

Liberty might not even have recalled Selena's annual event if Lydia May hadn't made such an issue over the snub to her. Lydia May even raised the issue with her father.

"Child," Nazareth sighed. "it is your mother's party, after all. You wanted young Porter invited and to get your mother to agree to that I had to back away from my insistence that your grandfather and uncle be invited. I don't think you should press your mother on the O'Lee invitation. You just might lose what you have already gained."

Lydia May childishly hid her embarrassment by avoiding Liberty all together before the holidays. This hurt Liberty more than Selena's churlishness. She tried to put the entire Tedder situation out of her mind by getting things ready for little Daniel's first Christmas, but she couldn't hide her feelings from Dan. And, though Dan was silently glad that he would not have to socialize with Selena, he did what he could to cheer her up.

They had planned on just a small tree for Daniel. Early Christmas eve Dan came carting home a five-foot silver spruce and a dozen cans of paint from Hopkins & Huntington Hardware. He planted the tree in an oaken bucket of sand and had it standing in the center of the foyer before Liberty saw it.

"Oh, Dan," she cried, "it is utterly gorgeous, but how in the world will we ever decorate it?"

"With genius," he chuckled. "I picked one that was still heavy with cones. While you prepare and string some popcorn, I'll dab a bit of paint onto each cone."

"And ribbons," she enthused. "I have a whole drawer full of hair ribbons I can tie into bows for the other branch ends."

She raced upstairs and brought back the whole drawer. While Dan spread papers on the floor and prepared to start painting, she brought the corn and long-handled popper to the drawing room fireplace, so that she had a clear view of his handiwork.

Inwardly Dan sighed with relief. For the moment he had been able to take her mind off of what was happening at that hour a few blocks away.

A knock at the door almost made it all come flooding right back.

"Merry Christmas!" Collis Huntington greeted them gaily. "Is this a private party, or can any old street bum come charging in?"

"Collis!" Liberty gasped. "Of course you can come in, but whatever are you doing here?"

Collis reached back around the door jamb and hauled into the foyer a basket laden with champagne and food.

"Frankly, dear friends, I am asking permission to turn this into a real party. Aha! Tree trimming time. I love it! After Wang Wu finishes our tree it always looks like a love offering to Buddha!"

"But Elizabeth . . ." Liberty began.

"To friends I don't mind admitting that she is so damn drunk that she won't feel the hangover until after the New Year is rung in. It is her subtle way of showing that she is not hurt in the least by not being at Selena's little bash this evening."

Liberty's mouth gaped open. Dan said quickly, "The party sounds fine, but you'll have to help with the tree."

"Wouldn't miss it," Collis chuckled. "I string a mean popcorn rope."

"I'll go get Tau Ti and have him set up some tables and chairs here in the foyer. We'll have the party right where we're working."

Dan raced to the kitchen, and Liberty looked sadly at Collis.

"I'm sorry," she said softly. "I didn't know that you hadn't been invited either."

Collis laughed. "Best thing that could have happened, as I see it. This will be like old times in Washington—the three of us together. I've missed that, Liberty. I've missed having you around."

Huntington hadn't realized exactly how much he had missed Liberty until seeing her that evening. She was as ravishing in a simple housedress as she would have been in a Lizzie Garland gown. He had tended to think of her as a tool useful for bringing about his wishes. Now he saw her as a very desirable woman. He wanted more than anything to kiss her at that moment, but Dan and Tau Ti came bubbling back, full of party excitement.

Party or not, this was the first time that Collis and Dan had been able to have a private conversation since Collis' return. Almost automatically, they began to speak of the railroad.

"Crocker considers himself a man with country

storekeeper skill," Collis said, "but somehow he has little conception of keeping a railroad stocked in advance."

"Or of needs," Dan amended. "It has taken him three months to grasp the fact that one mile of track, with side spurs and switches, requires one hundred tons of rail, approximately twenty-five hundred crossties and two to three tons of spikes and fishplates."

"Fishplates?" Liberty interjected. "What are they?"

"Honey, those are the slotted bars that connect rail ends and permit climatic expansion and contraction of the metal."

"Liberty," Collis said, "I wish Charles had asked the same question. The first four miles will have to be redone because he talked Porter out of using fishplates. You have made him see the light on that, haven't you Dan?"

Dan shrugged. "I've made Montague and Porter see the light, but I don't think they've swayed Crocker as yet. The man still refuses to talk to me face to face."

"Swine," Collis growled. "Got a solution?"

"Sure, if you can swing it. Get me back Nazareth Tedder. Crocker will listen to him and he can act as a go-between."

"Children," Collis scoffed. "I am surrounded by children both here and back east. Crocker and Durant should be put in a cell together for the duration of our building. I swear I expend three-fourths of my time trying to talk sense into their thick skulls. Durant doesn't have the first shovel full of grading accomplished and is back to the same old fight of stopping us at the Nevada line. Do you know I had to nearly twist his arm to get him to help me fight the Pennsylvania and Massachusetts ironmongers who were attempting to form a trust that would boost mill prices."

"Can you blame him?" Dan chortled. "After he learned that we even outflanked the army and navy buyers to get our hands on those sixty-six thousand tons of rail set aside for military use?"

"Hell, it'll be another six months to a year before he requires rails, and I want them coming in here at an average of ten thousand tons per month. I want a time schedule so down pat that it will keep your supplies eight months to a year ahead of your needs."

Dan shook his head. "A good thought, Collis, but there are not that many ships coming around Cape Horn. If you off-load at Panama, ship by that miserable little train across the Isthmus and then reload, you've got the surcharge rates for four handlings by the stevedores as against two on the Cape Horn run. That'll cost—and cost plenty. It's a time versus money issue, and I don't know how to resolve it."

Collis got up and circled the tree, methodically draping a popcorn rope over the branches as he went. A sly grin played about the corners of his mouth, and his hawkish nose twitched with devilment.

"I shall tell you both something that not even The Associates are aware of as yet. With my penny-wise philosophy I have always maintained that the low delivery costs on the Cape Horn run were the only way for us to go . . . and not only for the rails. We are practically a non-manufacturing state. We have to rely upon the east for our wheelbarrows, horse-drawn scrapers, two-wheel dump carts, shovels, axes, crowbars, mattocks, quarry tools, iron rods and blasting powder. The rails weigh fifty pounds to the yard. Those other supplies weigh near the same, but take up bulk space in a ship's hold. And, frankly speaking, we are not the only people in California or Oregon who desire things shipped from the east."

Unsatisfied with his last several popcorn loops, he redid them, without a break in the story.

"After you left New York, I began to spend the early part of each evening prowling along the Manhattan and Brooklyn waterfronts. When I just about had a scheme set in my mind I walked into the ship brokerage offices of E. B. Sutton. The man is a wily New Englander and took me for a western patsy. I told him, 'Well, I want to get a good ship, a good steady ship—safe. You go out and run around and give me a list of what you can find.'

"He immediately gave me a list with three or four ships on it. He said, 'You can have this one for so much and this one for so much.'

" 'Such a price', said I, gasping, 'is too high. I can't take one of those ships. I am in no hurry,' said I, sounding greatly disappointed. 'Ships are coming in all along.'

"Well, he called me back a few days later. He had gone out and compiled a listing of twenty-one available ships. I methodically took down the price of each as he spoke, amending it as I talked each price down and then took interest in another.

" 'Well,' said I suddenly, 'I'll take them.'

" 'Take them?' he said, 'take what?'

"In my best nasal New England tone, I said, I will take all those ships if they are A-number one.'

" 'Well,' said he, 'I can't let you have them. I thought you wanted only one. I will have to have two or three of them for myself and other customers.'

"I shrugged, 'Not those, you won't.'

"Well, those ships will take about forty-five thousand tons of rail, Dan. I've got them sewed up tight on a three-year lease. Mr. Sutton told me afterward, "Huntington, you would have had to pay at least ten dollars a ton more if I had known you wanted all those ships.'

"That would have been four hundred and fifty thousand dollars. And . . . that is exactly what I am paying for the three-year lease to keep our shipping charges minimal. There! Didn't I say I strung a pretty mean rope of popcorn!"

"Very successful," Dan agreed, "very successful, indeed." And he was not talking exclusively about Collis' business expertise. He marveled that the shrewd man could be so humorless around all others, and so warmly human when he was with him and his wife. He saw Huntington's gregariousness at least part of it, as stemming from the man's very unhappy home life, never once considering that he and Liberty gave Collis something that no one else was capable of giving him—a sounding board for his excellent ideas.

Just before Collis left for the evening, he turned to Dan.

"The railroad office car arrived today. We are getting far enough out to use it now. I'm afraid, Liberty, that it will make you a widow for days at a time."

Dan's face beamed. "That's just great. We'll start saving two hours a day, not having to deadhead the men back and forth. Now we're beginning to sound like we are really building a railroad."

"More than that," Collis grinned, "we're going to start getting a little more efficient in our work. I made arrangements in San Francisco to get you some adequate office staff to take the paper work off your shoulders. An early Christmas present, you might say. Goodnight to you both, and a very merry Christmas."

They happily chorused his cheer. With his arm about her waist, Dan stood and looked at the tree.

"Loveliest one I've ever seen," he whispered.

Liberty nestled close without answering. She was very content, very content, indeed. She suddenly felt that Selena Tedder was the loser that evening, and not Liberty O'Lee.

She was both right and wrong.

Collis Huntington trudged back toward his spiritless home, forced to do something to bring his words into action. He actually hadn't done anything yet to get Dan an office staff, but he soon would. Only when he was about to depart had he realized he wanted to stay —wanted to be with Liberty. Every boast, every story, had been for her benefit and not Dan's. She was the type of woman that he needed by his side—a woman as forceful, dynamic and success-oriented as himself. He knew he could never fully have her. But he could make arrangements to give her back a spark of the life she had had in the east.

Or was it a spark more for Collis Huntington? His spirits had been pretty low when he decided to barge in on Liberty and Dan. Outwardly, he would not admit that Selena's snub had bruised his ego far more than it had his wife's. He considered himself the prime mover of the Big Four. Where would they be without his expert money-management in the east? Would they have cheaper rails? Would they have a greater government subsidy? Would they have anything?

He was hurt mainly that they had all gone ahead and accepted Selena's invitation and not boycotted the affair out of respect to him.

Well, he had raised Liberty to great height before to bring down opponents—and he considered Selena Tedder far easier prey than, say, Thomas Durant. But to use Liberty again, he had to subtly subdue Dan O'Lee.

He stopped before reaching his door, turned and marched back to the telegraph office at the Sacramento Line depot.

His message to Kai Soong was captured in two words, "Mai needed"—but Calvin Culmer's key-box began to chatter with an incoming message before he could pass the paper slip through the wire cage.

The droll telegrapher's eyes widened as he laboriously wrote down the arriving message. He sat for a long moment after the chatter ceased, studying his own written words.

"Well," he gulped, "ain't that sump'tin else, Mistah Huntington. I just had the President of these United States on t'other end of my key."

"Is that a fact?" Collis said drily, believing rather it was an Army messenger relaying a war department order.

"You just listen, Mistah Huntington. 'Mrs. Lincoln, the boys and I wish for you a joyous Christmas and the Lord's blessing for a prosperous New Year. "Father" A. Lincoln.' Well, I never."

"Who is it addressed to?" Collis asked cautiously.

"That Mrs. O'Lee, Mistah Huntington."

"Oh," Collis said, pursing his lips. "She would be at the Tedder affair tonight, Culmer. But as you got two chink runners sitting here, I'd also send a copy to the O'Lee house in case they have left the party already."

"Good thought, Mistah Huntington. Now, what can I do for you?"

"San Francisco wire, Culmer," he said, passing the message to the man.

Culmer scowled. "Only two words, sir? Still gotta charge yah as though it were the full ten. That'll be twenty-five cents."

Huntington shrugged, as if he couldn't fight the system, and left. He would have given anything to be a mouse at the Tedder mansion when the telegram was delivered.

Collis would have been greatly disappointed. Selena took the telegram from Liu Ma and read it a single time. Without altering her expression, she tossed it into the fireplace.

"Some people just have no taste," she said to Jane Stanford. "Imagine sending a Christmas greeting in a telegram."

Jane Stanford nodded her agreement and steered the conversation back to the topic it had been on before the interruption—namely, herself.

This gave Lydia May a chance to slip away without having to ask to be excused. Once out of her mother's line of sight, she raced for the atrium. Deep in the shadows of the rubber-tree plants she found Randy.

"Did you have any trouble getting away?" she asked.

"None. They are nearly all sound asleep from Governor Stanford's long-winded stories."

"Come—let's walk out into the garden."

"No," Randy said, "it's too cold. Let's stay here."

"Very well. But I hung some mistletoe in the garden. Of course, if you had a mind to, you could pretend I'm standing under some right now."

Randy looked at her and a hard glint appeared in his brown eyes.

"I could," he said grimly. "And I shall!"

But it was Randy who broke free of the embrace.

"Oh my!" he whispered.

Lydia May laughed throatily.

"See what you've been missing?" she said. "Would you like to do it some more?"

"Much more!"

She leaned forward again, this time taking his hand and placing it gently on the cup of her breast.

"Lydia May!" he gasped.

"Don't tell me you haven't wanted to feel that for some time."

"I—I—no!"

"No?" Daringly, she rubbed his hand over the cloth until he could feel her nipple stiffen and harden.

The heat rose out of Randy's collar and beat about his face in waves.

"No," he said miserably, "we shouldn't be doing this."

She looked at him gravely. "You have been in California nearly a year, Randolph Porter. The most you have ever done is hold my hand and make 'goo-goo' noises. My mother is making it very hard for me to become your wife, but it takes only the two of us to make me your mistress—if you are man enough to try it."

Randy felt affronted, even angry. She was all but accusing him of lacking backbone. He took her fully into his arms, kissing as passionately as he knew how, exploring her breasts without her hand to guide him.

Neither saw the shadow dislodge itself from the foliage and return to the house.

The men were just emerging from the dining room as twelve-year-old Nathan Tedder idly crossed the foyer. Nathan looked forward to the next hour of carol singing and mock joviality with loathing. The whole affair for him that year had been a big bore. His 'Gramma Lady' had not come down from San Francisco, his 'Grandpa' Tedder had not been invited, and there was no one in attendance his age. Because several people had seen fit to decline Selina's invitation that year, Nathan had been forced to eat at the main table— and that had been the biggest bore of all. He wished there was some way he could bring the whole thing to a crashing end.

Selena came bubbling out of the drawing room, shepherding guests in the direction of the music room. In between polite comments to the joining men, she kept looking around. Nowhere did she see Randolph Porter or Lydia May. Their absence rankled her.

"Nathan," she said, on an overly sweet note, "have you seen your sister?"

"Sure," Nathan said candidly, "she in the atrium letting that guy kiss her and play with her tits!"

Selena's back stiffened. A sudden silence fell over the foyer. Selena's voice dropped to a spiteful crispness.

"To your room, young man!" she breathed, her wrath growing by the moment. "Nazareth, get that Lothario out of my house. Lydia May is restricted to her room!"

Then, as if nothing had happened, she waved her hand at her guests and marched into the music room. The guests had no recourse but to follow. To make their excuses and leave right then would have only increased the embarrassing strain.

Nazareth stood until the music room door closed and then went into the hall that led to the atrium. He was trying to formulate words in his mind, being a little unsure of how to handle the situation.

Halfway down the hall he saw Lydia May enter the house and throw herself angrily upon a chair. Nazareth approached her with a frown.

"Where have you been?" he demanded.

"Out in the atrium with Randy," Lydia May said. "Any objections?"

"Several, if your brother's report is correct. Where is Porter?"

"What did that nasty little snitch tell you?" she demanded hotly.

"It isn't fit to repeat, young lady. Now answer my question."

Lydia May looked startled. She was unused to hearing such an angry tone in her father's voice. She knew that Nathan must have seen all and reported all. But she felt she could get around her father, as she always had before.

"He's gone. I sent him back to the boarding house."

"Well," Nazareth sighed with relief, "at least you came to your senses before real damage was done."

"It wasn't my senses, it was Randy's. I would have gone all the way, but he's too much of a prude and gentleman."

Nazareth felt like slapping her, but held his temper. "I don't want to hear any more. Your mother has restricted you to your room."

"That won't help. Loving Randy is something I can't help."

"But letting you make a mistake with your life is something I can help, and I will!"

"How? In two years I will be twenty-one and can do as I please."

"That's two years. In the meantime I can go to Charles Crocker and tell him I don't like having the boy around. He'd be fired in an instant."

Lydia May yawned.

"You don't have that kind of clout, father dear," she drawled.

"Why, you little . . ."

"Exactly! If I have to become a slut and only his mistress I will become it. Mother shouldn't mind. It will be like history repeating itself."

It was out now. She had said it.

Nazareth didn't answer her. He stood very still and his mouth tightened slowly into a hard line. Lydia May realized that he was not going to scold, that there would be no scene. But the silence was infinitely worse.

Then, ever so slowly, Lydia May stood up. With deliberate grace she smoothed out her dress and turned back toward the atrium.

Nazareth ran his tongue over dry lips.

"Where are you going?" he demanded.

"To Randy," she said simply.

"You'll make a fool of yourself," he said. "He's already turned you down once tonight."

"I know. I'm not going to let it happen again and have a loveless life." She turned and looked her father full in the face. "A life like your life," she added softly.

Nazareth stood there foolishly watching her go. The crash of the atrium door, as Lydia May slammed it, awakened him from his reverie. He could not, nor could Selena, continue to live her life for her. For once she had to fall down and not have them there to instantly pick her up and soothe her wounds. He just prayed that Randolph Porter was as much of a gentleman as she portrayed him to be.

He avoided the music room and went upstairs to his study. Sitting at his drawing board he tried to lose himself in his plans for a new building.

Near midnight Selena came storming in.

"Where is she?" she snapped.

"Gone to Randy Porter."

Selena's jaw dropped a little.

"And you didn't go after her? What kind of a father are you, Nazareth?"

"Perhaps a very poor one," he said grimly. "But she was going to go—tonight, tomorrow, next week—and we wouldn't have been able to stop her."

"Maybe you couldn't, but I can!" Selena said sternly.

"No, Selena," he said calmly, "I forbid it. If you don't want to be hurt by her, just let it ride for to-night."

She started to protest, but the look on his face told her that it would be a losing battle. She sniffed and fled to her bedroom. She would handle the situation her way the next day.

By two o'clock Nazareth was beginning to fear that he himself had handled the situation very badly. Perhaps Randy wasn't that honorable after all. He rose stiffly and started downstairs to go in search of her. The house was dark, quiet and still, except for a shaft of light streaming from beneath the dining room door.

Quietly, he opened the door and entered. Lydia May sat at the far end of the massive table, a whiskey decanter and glass before her, her lovely face as cold and still as death.

"Lydia May?" he whispered.

"So—" she said heavily, "you come to gloat over your drunken daughter?"

"Hardly."

She sank back into the chair, her face ashen, her mouth so numbed by the drink that she could hardly speak.

"You lie! You did come to gloat!" she accused him. Then her voice broke into a thin, hysterical whimper. "Oh God, he wouldn't even let me into his room! Indecent, he said it was. His boarding-house reputation at stake. Fool! No! I was the one who made a fool of myself by ranting and raving. Men from the other rooms started laughing and egging him on. Mrs. Bellamy came to kick me out. Called me a society tramp." She sobbed.

Nazareth stood very still and waited.

"Randy wouldn't come from his room—the bastard!" She got up from the chair and had to use the table as a support to help herself around it. "I got drunk," she said. "Randy doesn't approve of a woman using strong spirits, but I . . . I . . . I think I'm going to be sick."

Nazareth started for her, then stopped himself.

"Daddy," she cried, "help me to my room."

He shook his head. He had vowed that if she stumbled, she would have to pick herself up. If he continued to baby her, he would be doing it for the rest of her life. He opened the door and went out. As he stepped into the hall, he looked into Selena's stricken face.

"You—you heard?" he said.

"Yes," she sneered. "Yes—I heard. Damn Randy Porter's wicked soul for playing with her emotions that way."

"I don't think you understand, Selena. I think he acted quite honorably."

"Naturally, you would. Out of my way. I am going to see to my daughter's immediate needs and then tomorrow I am taking the children to San Francisco, with or without your approval."

He leaned forward, looking into her face. "Oh, you are a vain fool, Selena," he said bitingly. "I think the young man has proven his worth, and I am about ready to give my consent to their marriage. But it is Lydia May who now owes him an apology. Let her wallow in her self-pity tonight. It might take some of the Buttle-Jones arrogance out of her."

Selena looked at him contemptuously, a tight smile on her lips.

"She will not marry as common as I was forced to marry," she said, "and that is final." She spun on her heel and marched into the dining room.

Nazareth didn't move. Strange, he thought, Selena's words seemed no longer to have the power to hurt him. He sensed that in continually trying to run their daughter's life she would stumble and fall repeatedly. But he had no inclination to pick her up, either.

Liberty saw Dan for only two weekends in January and February. But he seemed so content with the progress of the railroad, and the return of Nazareth as a part-time consultant, that she refrained from speaking of her own lonesome state.

To a certain extent, what Dan could not give her she was getting from Collis Huntington. With Elizabeth becoming more and more dependent on her afternoon brandy, Collis took to having tea with Liberty and using her as his sounding board. Perhaps it was Liberty's advancing pregnancy that kept the gossip from getting blown too far out of proportion.

"I don't know," Collis complained, "every time I seem to have this outfit on a firm footing, another enemy Leland made as governor pops up to knock us back. How do we fight this latest little bit of anonymously written garbage?"

Liberty sat silent for a moment, staring at the pamphlet Collis had brought for her to read.

"It's so unfair," she said at last, "and so untrue. The title makes me sick—*The Great Dutch Flat Swindle*. Swindle? Can right-thinking people believe this assertion that the Central Pacific has no intention of building beyond that foothill mining camp?"

"San Francisco investors are believing it and so are some of the state legislators who refuse to pass any type of bill supporting us. Our enemies, Liberty, seem commensurate in numbers with the lengthening of the railroad."

"That's because they don't know what it takes to build a railroad. If they could see your stockpile of supplies, and how they were used, reason would suggest that you intend to go far beyond Dutch Flats."

Collis looked at her lovingly. With each passing day the monster he had created was beginning to devour the creator. Dan's flesh had been very weak and Mai Ling had but to smile to rekindle their passionate affair. But Liberty's pregnancy prevented Collis from gaining any rewards for his efforts. He could share her companionship in the parlor, and there alone. His frustration was great. Still, he enjoyed being with her.

"Well," he grinned, "you might have something there."

"I know I do. The problem, as I see it, is that everyone of you continue to treat these legislators as neighbors and friends. Why don't you start treating them as we did the people back east?"

Huntington pursed his lips. "Throw a big party as we did in New York?"

"No," she insisted. "You want money out of them, so it can't appear to be extravagant. I was thinking of something along the lines of taking them on an excursion to the railhead. How far out are you?"

"They'll pass twenty miles this week."

"Good. That gives time to lobby on the ride out, let them see the construction and really nail them down on the way back."

"No party?"

Liberty frowned. "That has got to be carefully thought out."

Collis laughed. "Does that note I detect in your voice mean that you are applying for a job?"

"Really," Liberty giggled, "I thought you would never ask. I would love a job. Lord knows, I need something to do rather than just serve you tea."

"Excellent! The legislature sits the third and fourth

week of March. I think a Wednesday would be good, to break up their week."

"Oh, Collis!" she chided. "You are losing your knack. You might be pleasing the men, but would send them home to very unhappy wives and children. I say a Saturday—that way, we turn the voices of excited children into our greatest lobbying force."

"As usual, Liberty, I bow to your intelligence. Work up a suitable invitation and plans. I'll wring the money out of Mark, even if I have to float a bond."

"Which reminds me, Collis, I still have those Union Pacific bonds. You had better take them and have the name changed."

Huntington frowned. It had been his personal money he'd spent on these bonds, and he didn't want his associates learning of it quite yet.

"No, Liberty, if you don't mind, I would prefer to keep them in your name for a time yet."

Liberty shrugged. The bonds didn't really concern her and her mind was already racing with plans for the excursion. It seemed so good to have something worthwhile to work on. Her health had never been better. With this pregnancy there had been so little illness and discomfort that she hardly felt pregnant at all. She foresaw no problems in playing hostess for Collis' event.

She did not take into consideration what Jane Stanford and Mary Crocker might have to say on the matter.

"But Leland," Huntington said grimly a day or so later, "no one is trying to push Jane aside."

"I should hope not," Stanford said thinly. "As I am president of this line my wife should be the official hostess that day. It is her wish to have Mary Crocker as her co-hostess and all plans to date presented to them for approval or alterations as they deem appropriate."

"Now who is being pushed aside?" Collis exploded.

"This was Liberty's idea to begin with and I asked her to plan it in lieu of Elizabeth. Damn it, man, it's set for this Saturday and two-thirds of the legislature have accepted already. The plans are set, as far as I am concerned."

Stanford sat tapping his slender fingers on his desk. His wife had convinced him that the simple affair would be a humiliating disaster. She had been outraged that the invitations had been sent to the wives, coyly suggesting that they could bring along their husbands and children if they wished. The clever twist had struck Jane and Mary as tasteless, lacking the formal dignity of a business occasion. The governor all but believed that they were right.

Mark Hopkins saw the danger signal of the tapping fingers, and again felt compelled to step into the breech.

"Seems to me," he drawled, "we're going to be getting a lot of good publicity for damn few dollars expended."

"Hang the expense!" Stanford snapped. "I agree with Jane that it should be an auspicious occasion."

"Trouble with Jane," Hopkins said slowly, "is that she still thinks you're the governor of this state. Ain't so, Leland. Fred Low is, and he's a man of simple tastes. Everyone in that legislature is a man of simple tastes. Now, we're asking them to pass a bill guaranteeing to pay twenty years interest on $1,500,000 worth of bonds. That would give us the use of a good deal of money at a time when we gotta admit money is pretty pinching tight. Leland, I think you better make Jane see it square out that she ain't well-liked by the men we are asking to pass that bill or the governor who will have to sign it."

Stanford banged the desk. "I fail to see what my wife has to do with this at all!"

"Well," Hopkins went on, dry as ever, "as I say,

they are simple men who don't live in too lavish a style. It still kind of rankles them, Leland, that the governor's mansion you ordered built ran over its budget by about $80,000 because of all the alterations Jane kept insisting on. 'Jane's Folly' is what they dubbed it, Leland. Let her put on a big spread come Saturday and they're only going to say, 'There goes Jane Stanford spending money that could have been put into rails and ties.' Sorry if the truth hurts, Leland."

Throughout, the tattooing fingers had slowed. Now they came to a dirgeful stop. Stanford sat glowering into space. Deep in his heart he knew that his aggressive, extravagant wife had probably cost him the renomination more than his association with the railroad had. She saw her husband as presidential timber which was also the way he saw himself. But Stanford was fundamentally a realist. He would not gain national attention unless he made the Central Pacific a success. He would not be able to make it a success without being able to dip into the state treasury. It was time for him to compromise.

"If the plans are that far along, so be it. I shall still expect Jane to act as official hostess."

Liberty roared with mirth that this matter had tied up a board meeting for over an hour. She had no desire to act as the "official" hostess, only to see that the affair ran smoothly.

The weather was on Liberty's side, even if Jane Stanford and Mary Crocker weren't. March 19, 1864 dawned spring-like and balmy. An hour before the promotional train was scheduled to leave, a crowd had begun to gather, anxious to get seats.

Awaiting them was the locomotive "Governor Stanford," burnished and polished to a high luster, decked out with pom-poms and all manner of banners and flags. Behind it on the platform car a Union army brass band blared "Oh, Susanna" and like spirited melodies.

Some families had mysteriously doubled and tripled over night, as neighbors "loaned" their children to invited guests. It meant that an additional five cars had to be rolled up and locked into the train. Though these cars too were soon overcrowded, no one seemed to mind. A great and joyful adventure was anticipated, and when the skyrockets went off and the "Governor Stanford" started chugging away on its twenty-two mile journey to the end of the main track, it was fully delivered.

Charles Crocker was waiting by the new granite quarries when the train came to a stop. He took charge of a tour meant to show all the passengers—the interested adults and the small children who followed him as if he were the Pied Piper—just how a railroad, was put together. In the picnic atmosphere, he had to shout often to be heard.

"Now, way up the line, there, folks, you'll see a bunch of men with picks, shovels, scrapers and the like. Because it takes some little time to prepare the roadbed this area was prepared yesterday for today's demonstration. Now, I want you to pay attention to these next twenty men. Notice how they work in sets of two, a man on each side of the track. They're bedding a tie every fourteen feet and we call them the "joint-tie men." These next men are the "fillers" and they bed the intervening ties. It's all worked out scientifically.

Crocker waited, letting everyone get a good look at the exactness and teamwork necessary for the job. Then he nodded to ten men waiting at the sides of a rail-laden platform car.

"Here comes a job that really separates the men

from the boys," he chuckled. "There will be five stalwart "iron-men" to each rail. Now listen and watch closely."

With a loud "Away she goes" from the foreman, two rails were drawn forward from the car, walked up to clear the last-lain rail and, at the word "down," dropped into place with a precision only acquired by long practice.

"Each of those rails weighs seven hundred pounds," Crocker explained. "That's a hundred and forty pounds per man and everyone has to carry his own load. Ladies, watch your ears, because the head spikers and back spikers don't care what they say out here in the wilderness. The head spikers are going to gauge the width and drive six spikes into each rail. The back spikers will finish banging them into the ties. These next men, called "screwers," will screw up the fishplates. Before anyone asks, fishplates are what join the rails and let them move with temperature changes. Oh, I nearly forgot. See those men with the crowbars? Before all the spikes are firmly down these "track liners" make sure that the tracks are in perfect alignment.

"Off to the side you might notice that cart taking new ties up ahead and dumping them—always keeping the supply well ahead of the joint-tie men. Those fellows who look like they're sowing wheat from their canvas pouches are "spike peddlers"—they're dropping spikes along the way, exactly where they'll be needed. They don't have to look to see if a spike has an imperfection they've become so expert at it they can feel one with the hands. For you children, I've had the spike peddlers gather up a couple boxes of spikes we can't use and you can help yourself to them as a souvenir of this day. Feel free to watch the men as long as you like, and when you tire, the Central

Pacific has made arrangements for some refreshments."

The children, lured by the thought of getting a spike, raced back to the train. Many women ambled along, chatting about 'how interesting' it all had been. But for the moment, a majority of the legislators stood transfixed, awed by the process and lost in their thoughts. It was not mentioned aloud, but the message had been gotten across: you don't go to this kind of work to build just forty miles of rail to Dutch Flats.

While Crocker's demonstration had been underway, Liberty had been busy arranging a lawn party. On the grassy right-of-way, she'd had recruited houseboys spread out a few dozen army blankets Collis had procured. On them were placed baskets of wine and beer, cheese, ham, roast beef, fried chicken and the like, replete with pickles and other trimmings. For the kids, she had root beer.

"What a lovely picnic," Harriet Low, the current governor's wife, enthused to official hostess Jane Stafford as they watched the proceeding's from afar. "How utterly appropriate for the occasion. How much fun! You are to be congratulated, Jane."

"Not at all," Jane Stanford replied icily. "Anyone might have thought of it." She let it go at that.

Elsewhere, Leland Stanford beamed, and later Governor Low had a few words to say to his wife:

"You know, dear, I always thought Stanford a mediocre man. But what he's done today makes me think he has learned how to manage his affairs and will make a go of this damn railroad, after all."

Still later, Charles Crocker, who was growing more and more expansive as the successful hours tripped by, paid a totally unexpected compliment to a railroad representative who had hardly been seen. Perhaps he was annoyed at his wife, who went off to pout with Jane Stanford, he jumped on a platform car and bellowed for attention. Then he grinned sheepishly at the sound of his own voice.

"I guess now you know why the work crews call me 'Bull,'" he apologized. "They say they can hear me a mile down the track. . . . What I waited to say is—you know, we've got ourselves some damn fine engineers on this project, and one of those engineers has himself a right smart little wife. She's the one who put the bug in Collis Huntington's ear to give you all this demonstration, and she's the one who worked damn hard planning this little picnic. I'd like a round of applause for Mrs. Dan O'Lee."

Liberty, standing out on the grass, got an ovation that made her blush.

"Will wonders never cease?" she whispered to Collis next to her. "What got into him?"

"Show business," Collis chuckled. "He was proud as punch being able to show off his crews that way."

Liberty, smiling, waited for the applause to die down. "Speaking of crews," she said then, looking around, "I thought Dan would have joined us by now."

"This is just another work day out here, Liberty."

Her face mirrored her disappointment. "It's been three weeks since I've seen him."

"The office car is about a half-mile up that side spur," Collis said with more casualness than he felt. "Would you like to go along and say hello?"

Liberty scoffed. "In my condition I wouldn't be able to walk a hundred feet."

"Who said anything about walking? I can take you there on that handcar—if you don't mind doing part of the pumping."

Liberty instantly brightened. "Oh, Collis, yes! What would I do without you!"

He took her by the hand and started to walk toward

the spur. "The question is, Liberty O'Lee, whatever would I do without you? You've become very special to me—you know that, don't you?"

"The feeling is quite mutual, Collis. I shall always cherish your friendship."

In his heart, Collis hoped they would have more than just a friendship before the day was out.

A slight knoll completely hid the advance work party from the view of the train site they had left. The office car itself sat quiet as Collis braked the handcar from its run down the incline. At a far distance to the left grading crews were at work and on the horizon ahead Liberty could make out the tiny figures of surveyors. But the office car was apparently deserted.

"I don't think we're in luck," Collis said. "Dan is probably out with the surveyors."

Disappointed, Liberty shrugged and said, "Well, as long as we're here, I think I'll just go in and gather up his dirty clothes to launder. Maybe he'll come back while I'm still here."

Collis hesitated. Now that he'd come this far with a scheme he had in mind—now that it was working perfectly—he had second thoughts about it. "Liberty, I—I —well, suit yourself."

Liberty climbed up the metal steps and entered the car's cool, dark interior. Along each wall were drawing boards and wooden filing cabinets arranged so neatly that she paused, amused at man's perverse nature. Dan was never this orderly when he did his work at home. He usually left the tidying up to her or to . . .

Frowning at a thought that had occurred to her Liberty went on through a narrow kitchen area to a green curtain that blocked off what Dan had described as "cramped sleeping accommodations, like you could never imagine."

She lifted the curtain. Burlap bagging covered the windows and it took her a second or two to adjust her eyes to the dark. She looked at a cot. For a startled, embarrassed moment, she thought she had walked in on a crew member in a kind of writhing sleep in the buff. But this man was hardly asleep and he wasn't alone.

Liberty wanted to scream. Dan's head and shoulders were obscured from her view by the writhing body of Mai Ling pressed joyously down on him. She shuddered and tried to turn away, but the blood had drained from her and she stood transfixed. They hadn't noticed her, or if they had, perhaps it was too late for them to stop. She saw Dan's enormous erection. She watched Mai Ling pump herself down on it in faster and faster movements. She heard their gasps of pleasure, Mai Ling's a more prolonged sob. A stab of pain hit Liberty's stomach; for a wild moment she thought it was her baby kicking and, in her anger, wanted it dead.

Then, almost instantly, it was over. Dan gave a tremendous, thrusting lurch deep inside Mai Ling, who suddenly screamed in ecstasy, laughed outright then fell limply on his chest.

Liberty too went limp. The pain left her stomach, as did her anger, her fear, her grief—everything. She felt nothing.

She turned to go, and Dan saw her then.

"Liberty—oh, shit!"

Slowly, she turned to face him. Mai Ling had quickly got up from the cot and was standing there, gazing at her, making no attempt to cover her nakedness. How odd, Liberty thought, with a strange grim, inner smile—she shaves herself, all over. Only when she saw Dan fumble with a blanket to cover his groin did she speak. Her voice was as hard as nails.

"What do you think you're hiding Dan?" she sneered. "I've seen it before—and it's not worth all that much."

She turned in a new blind rage to leave again—and found herself staring into the leering face of Collis Huntington. Wordlessly, she brushed past him. Already, she sensed Collis's complicity in an artfully arranged scene that had left her devastated. With lady-like calm she returned to the handcar, trying to keep herself from bursting into hysterical tears.

Collis came racing after her, his only desire now to salvage what he could from Liberty's unhappiness. Behind him he left a benumbed and embittered Dan O'Lee. Collis had assured Dan that Liberty was not up to making the trip that day and because of the demonstration he and Mai Ling could enjoy a holiday. Dan had been duped before, but never with so much to lose.

Liberty remained quiet and aloof as Collis began pumping the handcar back toward the train.

"I'm sorry," he ventured.

"Are you, Collis?" she said icily. "Why do I have the feeling that you were fully aware of what I was going to walk in on?"

"Oh, really, Liberty," he blustered.

"Don't give me that!" she snapped. "I'm not some Durant or Ames you can codfish over. What's your game, Collis?"

Collis Huntington was not used to being snapped at; it shocked him into something near the truth. "My game?" he snapped back. "My game, if you care to call it that, was played for your benefit, Liberty O'Lee! I don't deal in rumors. I thought it best to let you see the facts with your own eyes."

"Oh, Collis," she said with scorn, "you are just too, too kind."

"Liberty, please," he begged, "I was only doing it for you. You're too kind and sweet and good to be hurt the way Dan's been hurting you. Forget him! He went running right back to that chink once you were pregnant again. He doesn't deserve you! He doesn't appreciate you, as I do. Liberty, Elizabeth is nothing but a lush and Dan a womanizer. They are doing nothing but pulling each of us down to their level. Together, we could fight them, Liberty. We could be a team that would set the world on its ear. Just say the word, Liberty. Just say the word!"

She couldn't find an apt word for him; nothing she could think of crawled low enough. Fighting down spasms of bitter gall, she saw to the gathering of the picnic baskets and the boarding of their guests. It was a jolly return trip for most. Earlier, Liberty had arranged with the engineer to keep to a time schedule to show that it could be done. The train reached Sacramento, with colors flying, at exactly 5:01 p.m., as promised.

Deboarding at the station, Leland Stanford was jubilant. He had been assured that the bill would pass and Governor Low would sign it into law.

Charles Crocker was jubilant. He was no longer looked upon as a mere seller of ladies' garments, but an actual railroad contractor.

Liberty, standing in her gloom, saw them as preposterously preening adolescents.

"Liberty," Collis insisted, "I'll see you home. We have matters to discuss."

"Thank you, no, Collis. I wish to think this out alone. Any further discussion between us at this time would be futile."

"Go to the devil!" he snarled and stormed away.

Liberty stood for a long moment, unsure of what she really should do next. The carriages bustling about the train created a traffic jam. In the distance she heard the first warning whistle for passengers to board the San Francisco steamboat.

She listened to the steamboat whistle for a long time. San Francisco. Kai Soong. Could she face up to the strange Oriental mystic who had so unnerved her? Could he help her now if she spoke to him? A kind of desperate hope soared through her.

She turned quickly on Tau Ti. "Go home! Tell *amah* look-see baby. Mistress go—home tomorrow—maybe!"

With her skirts flying, Liberty raced the two blocks to the river wharf and went up the steamboat gangplank just as the crew was preparing to lift it.

She stood at the rail, watching the Sacramento harbor recede in the distance. Collis had told her to go to the devil. Maybe, she thought, maybe that's just what I'm doing.

San Francisco was locked in fog. A chilling rain pelted through it.

Shivering on the Embarcadaro's cobbled sidewalk the next morning, Liberty began to feel foolish. She had Kai Soong's name, knew his tong house was on Grant Avenue, but lacked the street number. Because of the weather, cabs were in short supply. When she finally was able to catch the attention of a driver, her request was met with instant abuse.

"Grant Avenue?" he sneered. "Lady, you must be balmy. Ain't gonna catch me down among those chinks on a day like today. Can't see a dozen feet ahead of me."

"Please," she begged, "take me as close as possible."

He shrugged and clucked the horse forward through slippery wet streets. It had to fight to gain traction up Nob Hill. Halfway down the steep eastern descent, the driver pulled to a halt, demanded twice the fare Liberty thought just and pointed through the rain.

"Couple of blocks that way." Then his voice took on a note of concern. "If'n I were you, lady, I'd put that shawl up over my head and look as much like a chink woman as possible."

Liberty did as directed, but mainly for warmth and to keep the rain from her head.

It was smell, rather than sight, that told her she had left one world and entered another. Nor could she really put the admixture of odd aromas into a describable category. The hunger pangs that had overcome her in the hansom cab turned to near nausea. And the non-pedestrian fog world of a couple of blocks back was suddenly transformed into a swirling rush of blue-trousered humanity.

Five minutes earlier, or five minutes later, she might have avoided the mad scramble of workers pouring forth from the porridge restaurants and teahouses on their way to work throughout the city. Now their swift-moving silence was eerie and frightening. They jostled her, and each other, without raising their eyes from their shuffling feet. Liberty had an irrational fear that they meant to do her harm and tried to get out of their way. In doing so she collided with a short, stout man clad in a robe rather than work trousers. He grasped her by the arm to keep her from falling, which frightened her still further; her body went rigid. Seeing that she was occidental, his almond eyes rolled in disbelief. He barked at her in Chinese and she understood not a word.

Fighting down her fear, she managed to gasp:

"Kai Soong! House of Kai Soong!"

The man started and looked at her narrowly. What business could she possibly have with Old Master Soong? Did it bode good or evil? Liu Luang was unsure of himself. He was one of the lowest of 'tong' agents and could use the good favor of Old Master Soong, but he was with very little English to learn of her needs.

"You there!" he called in Cantonese to a hunched figure scurrying by. "Come to me, Ta Wang!"

The figure stopped and came back bowing low, his coolie hat keeping his face in deep shadow.

"I am most late, Master Luang."

"Silence, or you shall be permanently late. I have need of your English word, Ta Wang. Learn from this woman who she is and why she has need of Old Master Soong."

Liberty was looking from one to the other in alarm. Her arm was beginning to hurt in Luang's steely grasp, but, she reasoned, it would do her little good to try and break away.

Without raising his head or eyes, Ta Wang muttered in a high, sing-song voice:

"Master Luang wishes name and reason you seek Old Master Soong."

Liberty let out an audible sigh. At least, she could now make herself understood.

"I am Mrs. Dan O'Lee and my business with Kai Soong does not concern your master."

Ta Wang quickly translated. Liu Luang studied the words carefully in his mind. Her name meant nothing to him and her manner of not wishing to give information readily left him doubtful. He knew he must handle the situation most carefully.

"Ta Wang," he said slowly, "you will take the woman to the house of Old Master Soong. If she is known and admitted, you must say that you delivered her as a favor to your Master Luang. If she is not admitted, you must give neither of our names. I shall send word that you will be late for your work. Now tell her, and off with you."

Ta Wang mumbled at Liberty and motioned for her to follow. He was so bent, and had such a timid little shuffle, that Liberty felt she was following a little old man. Whether he meant to show her the sorrows of his people, or simply to make short cuts, he went through alleyways littered with garbage, snarling mongrel dogs and the noise of Chinatown coming fully awake for another endless day.

Finally he slowed and indicated that they were to cross the street. Halfway down that block one house stood apart, surrounded by a ten-foot-high brick fence. Three stories tall, it appeared even taller due to the upward sweep of its roof eaves. Its windows were heavily barred and the massive wrought-iron fence gate was locked.

A houseboy, Chou Nu, started scolding Ta Wang the moment he answered the banging of the brass knocker on the gate.

"What son of a pig-dog are you to come to this door? To the back, one of the gutter born to a nameless mother!"

Ta Wang stayed stooped over and muttered the reason why he dared to approach the venerable front entrance.

Chou Nu looked at Liberty. Without a word, he turned and hurried up to his master's bedroom on the second floor.

Kai Soong listened to Chou Nu's report with a deep scowl on his face.

"It is still early morning, Old Master. Do you wish me to send them away?"

"No! Let them in. I shall dress."

"Shall I tell the cook to—"

"Tell the cook nothing," Kai Soong said. Ask the one who brought her to await my pleasure. And take this ginseng porridge away. I do not want any this morning."

After Chou Nu had left, Kai Soong walked around his room, hating what he knew he must face. He had forbidden Mai Ling to return to her pleasures with Dan O'Lee, and that she had disobeyed him was the only reason he could fathom for the wife to pounce on him at such an unsocial hour. He must discipline Mai; but he didn't know how. He had attempted to turn her into a son and man, but could not change her heart and her body. Suddenly he missed his dead wife. He felt somewhat helpless without her. She had been a good woman and a fine disciplinarian, always keeping the house in good order. After she died, everything had seemed to go wrong. He had not been a good father. He had made numerous business mistakes. The House of Soong was the oldest and most powerful tong in Canton and his negligence was bringing shame and discredit to it.

Now he wished he had a full family counsel to discuss the problems of a daughter who was becoming too wild and westernized! He had never felt so empty and forlorn. His wisdom, his gifted inner sight that was so helpful to others, were failing him when it came to Mai Ling.

Slowly, he began to dress and let his mind concentrate on Liberty O'Lee.

Liberty sat fidgeting in the living room. The room seemed overdone in Chinese paintings and scrolls. It was furnished in very expensive teakwood tables and chairs, but they were horribly uncomfortable and gave the large room a deserted, almost ghostly look. Her feeling of unease was induced as much by the attitude of Ta Wang and Chou Nu. The coolie remained near the door, straw hat in hand, his shaven head and queue now sinisterly exposed. Chou Nu stood guard, his black eyes flashing back and forth, as if both Ta Wang and Liberty would steal everything in sight if he blinked.

Kai Soong descended the staircase regally, attired in a gown, slippers and queue cap all of flaming scarlet. He kept his deep-set eyes away from Liberty, nodded for Chou Nu to leave, then went directly to Ta Wang.

As soon as his slippers came into Ta Wang's downcast view, the latter began to mutter his name and the reason for his humble presence in that house.

"Have you English?"

"Yes, Old Master Soong," Ta Wang said. "That is how Master Luang had me gain the information from her."

"The incorrigible dog," Kai Soong mumbled angrily. "Afraid to face me until the water was tested by another." He tossed a coin down to the floor and asked, "Do you not fear me, one who bears the name 'bandit king'?"

Ta Wang left the coin lie there, although it would have put meat in his porridge for a month. "It was my duty to do as Master Luang ordered me and without thought of reward, Old Master Soong."

Kai Soong's stern look softened. At first glance he too had thought he was addressing an old coolie. And the name Ta Wang did indeed mean "bandit king." Ta Wang's dialect was cultured Cantonese, not rough Hunan peasant, and there was respect and decency in his voice.

"Stand," Kai Soong ordered, "I would truly look on you!"

An amazing transformation took place in Ta Wang. He began to unbend until he was ramrod straight and of an equal height to Kai Soong. His eyes turned glowing black and no longer wavered in trepidation. His golden face, lifted up, appeared smooth, as if he had not needed to shave more than a dozen times in his life.

Looking on, Liberty gasped at his new youthfulness. Both men totally ignored her in their continued appraisal of each other.

"I find you with some twenty years, correct?"

"Twenty and two, Old Master Soong."

"How long America?"

"Four of those, Old Master Soong."

"Your English comes in those four years?"

"No, Old Master Soong. From the days of my middle school from the Jesuits in Canton."

Kai Soong frowned. "No Chinese schools?"

"Both, Old Master Soong. By day to fulfill my filial obligation to my ancient grandfather, by night to appease the wishes of my father."

Kai Soong was momentarily perplexed.

"Bandit king?" he mused. "Am I to learn how you came by such a title?"

Ta Wang blushed deeply, but did not drop his eyes in shame. "Old Master Soong, it is naturally not my family name, but the one given me in disgrace to bear in my exile."

Kai Soong pursued the matter no longer. He was aware that no man alive could be forced into disgracing his family further by revealing his true identity. It was an honor code several thousand years old that he could admire and respect. He was suddenly glad that he had worn scarlet. The spirit of the young man had lifted his spirits and given him a sense of good omens.

"There is no disgrace," he said warmly, "in atttempting to right the wrongs in one's life and regain a place in the circle of the family. What have you done in America to accomplish such an aim?"

"Little," Ta Wang answered quite honestly. "I am an errand boy in the Buttle-Jones house because I have the English. Master Luang arranged for me to work there. I go to see Lady Pamela's tenants on the Barbary Coast and collect rent money from them."

Rent money? Kai Soong pulled at his stringy beard and drooping mustache. It was not the first time he had run into the stupid management of talent by Liu Luang. Here was a lad with apparent breeding, education and deep-rooted filial respect who was being wasted by collecting payments from the secretly owned brothels of the arrogant Englishwoman. Kai Soong was determined not to let such talent go to waste.

Liberty had become increasingly irritated during the Chinese conversation until she heard Lady Pamela Buttle-Jones mentioned. Until then, she had assumed Kai Soong and Ta Wang were talking solely about her, as if she were an object to be disposed of. Now she grew confused. She looked questioningly at Kai Soong. For the first time since her arrival, he looked back at her, briefly. Then he continued to address the coolie.

"You are released of your contract with the tong of Luang," he said softly to Ta Wang. "Pick up your coin and go to the kitchen for tea."

After the youth had gone, Kai Soong advanced on Liberty as if his mind were churning with great decisions. He offered no greeting. Thrown into a quandary, Liberty jumped to her feet and blurted out:

"I want my husband back!"

Kai Soong looked shocked. "Back from what, Madam O'Lee?"

Liberty stared at him for a moment and then shook her head despairingly. "From your daughter. I was unaware that she was back in Sacramento until I caught her with my husband yesterday."

"My wife's daughter," Kai Soong said after a sigh, "was born in the Year of the Sheep. She should be a woman of peaceful nature. But now I begin to suspect there is an evil spirit in her that is brought out by certain occidental men . . ."

"That is superstition!" Liberty said hotly. "She is a wanton hussy who will use her body to its fullest to lure a man!"

He crossed his arms and closed his eyes. "Ah, Madam O'Lee, it is such an easy thing to accuse another when one is inflamed with notions of one's own virtue. Are you suggesting that you have never in your life used your body to lure a man?"

"Never!" she snapped, and then hesitated. Her mind swirled with memories she had thought long-buried. Try as she might she could not keep the youthful face of Dan's dead brother, Burke, from swimming into her mental vision. She tried to swing her eyes away from Kai's, but they held her in a deep, penetrating gaze.

"Never?" he said, almost sadly. "I see the name Burke O'Lee burned into your soul as surely as if it had been put there with a branding iron."

"All right," she cried, "but that was long ago. I met Burke early in the war—it was over long before I met Dan, believe me!"

Kai Soong would not relent. "I see more men. I see three in blue. They are in the army."

"Oh, no," she moaned, "what kind of a devil are you? I didn't lure them! If you can see so much, can't you see that they were Union soldiers who raped me in Mississippi?"

He remained silent for a long time.

Liberty stared at him, rapt by the power he had to enter the most secret chambers of her life. She did not understand this power—she feared she never would— but she could not deny it, for Kai Soong was proving it again and again.

"And so you have good reasons," he said softly,

"that allow you to pass yourself off as a woman who has known only her husband?"

"Yes," she said. "In a way, that is quite honestly true. When I am myself—when you do not—do not . . . ." She trembled. "When you do not remind me of it . . . I have no feelings of having slept with Burke. It was the war—I was physically attracted to him. I know now only that it was a youthful and dangerous thing to do."

"Oh, I believe you, Madam O'Lee. Can you believe that my daughter may be going through a youthful and dangerous period in her own life?"

Liberty's back stiffened. "I might have believed that at first, but not now, not after what I witnessed!"

"I see," he mused. "And you are here to ask me to put an end to their renewed affair."

"Yes!"

"I wonder, though," he said slowly, "if you are willing to pay a price for my help."

Liberty caught a sudden, smoldering look in Kai Soong's eyes. Had she interpreted it correctly? She was sure she had. Her eyes narrowed. "If you are suggesting what I think you are suggesting, are you aware that I am pregnant?"

"Quite," he said gravely. "But I am an expert in such matters. You are a beautiful woman, Madam O'Lee. If you wish further to discuss the terms of my proposal, you may follow me. If, however, you wish to handle my headstrong daughter and your overly sexed husband on your own, please feel free to leave at once."

Again, Liberty found herself staring into Kai Soong's now impassive eyes. When he had called Dan overly sexed, a vivid picture of what she had seen in the railroad car had come flashing to her mind. She could not bear to look at it, and yet she had to—it was as if Kai

Soong were forcing her to. Her mind raced. Did he
have some magical potion to give her that would make
Dan forget Mai Ling? She *couldn't* handle the situation
by herself. Suppose she did have to submit to Kai
Soong's desires. Would she lose her self-respect any
more than she had when she'd been raped by the
Yankee soldiers? And this time—because she did believe Kai Soong would help her—she would be gaining
something important in return for giving him his mere
moment of pleasure.

Stoically, she rose and followed him. The rear wall
of the living room was panelled in mahogany. Perhaps
Liberty was beyond surprise, for she did not react
when, at a touch of Kai Soong's long finger, a panel
swung open, revealing his private den beyond it.

The den was obviously his pride and joy, his old
world recaptured in the new. He spread his gowned
arms wide to indicate his most cherished possession to
her—a black-lacquered teakwood kang, as wide as a
double bed, with a low tea table placed in its center.
Liberty blinked at the table setting. As if in anticipation
of this moment, Chou Nu had already placed on it Kai
Soong's water pipe, along with watermelon seeds, tea
and sweetmeats. On each side of the table was an em-
broidered pillow bearing the dragon-like symbol of
the House of Soong, so that Kai Soong, while napping
on the kang or dining, would always be reminded of his
heritage. In a commanding corner sat a golden replica
of the Chinese god of longevity, with plates of fresh
fruit set before its crossed legs. The god, with its searching almond-shaped eyes, was placed facing a small,
round window overlooking a bamboo garden—so that
it could forever look out on stillness, peace and tran-
quility.

Incense was smoking up from a burner.

Liberty sniffed. "That aroma," she commented, "it's oddly familiar."

"Perhaps," Kai Soong smiled. "I have reason to believe you may have smelled it in your tea during your first pregnancy, Madam O'Lee. Please sit. The aroma is actually coming from that bubbling water pipe. Will you partake with me?"

"Certainly not!" Liberty exclaimed. She pulled herself to the edge of the kang. "If it's the herb Mai Ling gave me, it will put me to sleep instantly."

"Hardly." He chuckled, then put one of the pipe's thin bamboo shoots in his mouth and sucked the smoke deeply. Liberty watched for the effect. There was none apparent. After exhaling, Kai Soong continued: "The opiate my daughter put in your tea did nothing more than relax the muscular spasms you were experiencing at the time. Once you were relaxed it was the *quientau* mixed with it that made you sleep deeply. This is a sleeping agent made from the venom of the cobra snake. At the time, I assure you, I allowed her to have it for the benefit of your health."

"And not for the further seduction of my husband?"

Kai Soong chuckled deep within his throat. "To face such a problem as we face, Madam O'Lee, a certain amount of levity is useful. Please join me now. The drug will help relax you for our discussion."

Liberty hesitated.

"It is written that to be unsure is but a step on the road to understanding. Naturally, this is a new and uncertain experience for you. But you have come to me for assistance, is it not so? Then part of my terms are that we smoke together."

Part of his terms, Liberty thought cynically. And yet, wouldn't the opium help her get through the ordeal? She took one of the pipe's reeds in her mouth and drew on it. Instantly she recognized the sweet taste, and, a moment or two later, the warm, relaxed feeling that came over her. She waited. The feeling was good. Indeed, it was wonderful. Slowly—slowly enough so that she could perceive the interesting event—the gates of her body and the doors of her mind swung . . . open. She took a second puff. Wider went the gates and doors. A third. She was in a world of infinite bliss. And yet, she could hear and see clearly every small thing Kai Soong said or did.

Kai Soong drew from his own reed at the same time. He waited for the room to fill with a certain amount of smoke. Then he put down his pipe and took hers from her.

"It's my intention, this day, to calm us and not drop us into a state of mindlessness. Now, please partake of the tea and sweetmeats. I think you will find that I have the finest Cantonese cook in all of California." He laughed. "Of course, the man is also an excellent spy for my eldest brother in China. As you are the first non-Oriental woman to grace my home, his poor brain must be buzzing with a million questions."

"As is mine."

"Yes," he mused, nibbling at a watermelon seed. "As a telegram will travel faster than your return boat, I shall send one. I assure you that Mai Ling will no longer be with your husband upon your return. I cannot, however, take responsibility for the mood of your husband over the matter. There is a boat that leaves at ten o'clock this morning. I would recommend that you be on it."

"And that is all?"

He rose and slowly walked to his moon-window to gaze out at the bamboo garden. "All," he said softly, "except for one minor request."

Yes. Here it comes, Liberty thought. The request. What must I do?

"I desire that you bare yourself for me, as you did for the man in New York."

Liberty gasped. "You knew about that!"

He chuckled, without turning. "It was in your mind as you entered this room, Chu-chee. But my desire is to see all of your body and not just your lovely breasts."

Wishing it over quickly, Liberty jumped up and nearly tore the clothes from her body. Then she stood proud and rigid, determined not to make a single sound to let him know that she was ready.

Kai Soong turned slowly and stared at her nudity with deep admiration and longing. For the first time in fourteen years he felt desire stir in his groin.

"You have reason to stand proud, Chu-chee," he whispered. "You are one of the loveliest women I have ever beheld."

He stood and let his eyes absorb every portion of her body; then he slowly turned back to the moon-window.

"But it is as I predicted," he said, almost gruffly. "No man shall possess you as long as your husband is alive on this earth. Please, you may dress."

Liberty stood benumbed and confused. With trembling hands she began to slip back into her petticoats and dress. What would this strange man do or say now? What?

With his back still turned, Kai Soong began to speak even as she dressed. His voice had a mystical quality to it.

"I would speak of the man-child that you carry within your womb. It is important that this child bear a proud name, for he will be born in June, which falls in the Year of the Horse. His destiny will be in moving men to his desires."

Only then did he turn and come back to stand before Liberty.

"Have you been thinking of a name for the child?"

"Not really. I was rather hoping for a girl."

He smiled. "Am I correct in stating that your paternal grandmother had a strong desire to keep her family name alive through your father?"

The opium was now making Liberty giddy. She giggled. "I don't know how you come up with these things, but she was a Grace who gave my poor father a name he loathed until the day he died. Alexander Grace Wells. He hated it so much he just went by the initials A.G."

"It is your filial duty to honor your grandmother's wish, your father's memory and the continuation of your own name. Alexander Grace Wells O'Lee seems proper."

Liberty shook her head. "The child will hate me forever."

Kai Soong said slowly. "I think not, for the events in his colorful life will reduce the name to a simple Wells Lee."

"O'Lee," she corrected.

Kai Soong shrugged. "You shall see, you shall see. Now, I shall have Chou Nu order my rickshaw to take you to the boat. As I cannot promise that you will fully regain your husband's love, I shall send you a new houseboy in a few days time to protect you from his well-known temper and wrath."

Liberty started to protest, but he stopped her with a wave of his hand.

"Our destinies seemed locked together, Chu-chee. You must learn to respect my wisdom, for to fight it would be futile. Please wait in the living room while I go for Chou Nu."

She was alone for only a moment. The houseboy came bustling out and motioned for her to follow. She hesitated a moment, expecting Kai Soong to come and bid her goodbye, but the front door was already open and Chou Nu began making hissing noises for haste.

The rickshaw was waiting. Liberty climbed in. Chou Nu locked the front gate. She sat staring at Kai Soong's strangely silent house until the rickshaw coolie got between the pulling tongues and ran her away from it.

10

Back in Sacramento, Liberty thought for a time that Kai Soong was going to be proven wrong about Dan. She needed no protection from his "wrath." He was sound asleep in the spare bedroom when she got home that Sunday evening and was gone again at dawn. At worst—and it was bad enough—she was hurt by his silence.

On Tuesday, a beaming Wang Wu brought in the new houseboy. To Liberty's surprise and delight, it was Ta Wang whom Kai Soong had sent. The onetime humble and ancient-looking coolie had undergone a further renovation. He now stood youthfully tall in a sparkling white jacket, blue trousers, and mirror-polished black shoes. Not a single strand of hair strayed from his glistening queue.

That Ta Wang was to replace Tau Ti darkened the latter's face with shame until Wang Wu told him he was being transferred to the House of Soong in San Francisco. Tau Ti nearly swooned with rapture at that honor. He was so anxious to get to San Francisco and begin his exciting life with the master that he fairly raced through the house explaining Ta Wang's duties to him.

Ta Wang was enraged at what he saw.

"This house is a disgrace, you slovenly pig. We are but eight days from the New Year and you have done nothing to prepare for its coming."

"It is a western house," Tau Ti shrugged, "and so there is no need."

Ta Wang glared at him. "It is our home away from China. Even though we are servants, the old customs must be maintained. You had best remember that, or you will not last the hour in the home of Old Master Soong." To underscore his distaste, he finished in English. "As I shall run the house in my fashion, I have no further need of your instructions. Wang Wu will take you to Mai Ling for your boat ticket."

Liberty, coming into the room, couldn't help overhearing the last and looked at Wang Wu with a questioning scowl.

He hung his head in embarrassment and muttered. "The daughter of Old Master Soong acts as a tong agent, Madam O'Lee."

"Yes, but she is apparently still in Sacramento," Liberty said impatiently. "I would think she'd have left by now. Kai Soong promised me that—"

Ta Wang interrupted her. "She is the new private secretary and mistress in the house of Master Collis Huntington. Madam Huntington left yesterday for the east where she is to visit her family."

Liberty delighted, kept a straight face, though Ta Wang's usage of the word mistress amused her. Mistress, indeed. She hoped Collis burned his fingers royally on his new Chinese firecracker.

She bid Tau Ti goodbye, giving him a personal going away bonus wrapped in lucky red paper. Then, when they were alone, she turned with a smile to Ta Wang.

"Ta Wang, I am so used to communicating with

Tau Ti in sign language that you will have to help me break the habit."

"I am here to do what ever you wish of me, mistress."

"Please, don't call me that. Nor Madam O'Lee either. Make it Mrs. O'Lee or better yet just plain Liberty."

Ta Wang frowned.

"It is not proper," he said sternly. "It shall be Mrs. O'Lee or Miss Liberty."

"As you wish. Did Tau Ti inform you of all your duties?"

"He did, but there are a few things I would like to change."

"For the better, I hope."

It was the cook and the kitchen that Ta Wang wanted to attack that very day. He didn't ask, he ordered, but the cook, who'd held Tau Ti in contempt, was pleased to comply with a voice of authority respectful of the old ways. He took down the paper-and-cloth image of Tsao Wang, the kitchen god, which had been dirtying all year above his stove; he smeared the god's mouth with honey and burned him so that he would ascend to heaven with sweet words. Then he pasted a new image of Tsao Wang above the stove.

"Ping," Ta Wing said, addressing him in his Hunan dialect, "I am most pleased."

Ping Soo sighed. "Yes, it is clean and Tsao Wang smiles again. But these foreign kitchens have no cockroaches, the servants of Tsao Wang. In this Year of the Horse, I do feel something must be done about it."

Ta Wang agreed and took the matter up with Liberty. Liberty hated cockroaches but, as she was never allowed into the kitchen anyway, gave the cook permission to have them, in the hope that the peace and harmony Ta Wang had brought with him would continue.

The food improved immeasurably. Still, it was not up to the standard Ta Wang thought proper.

"It is not your fault, old one," he advised Ping Soo. "You can work only with the ingredients available. This day I take our pay to the tong agent and shall place a suggestion at her feet."

Ta Wang was happy to go to Mai Ling, who, on her father's order, was forbidden to come to the O'Lee house for their pay. He had seen the girl just once, when he'd arrived in Sacramento, and had been immediately chagrined that circumstances had so lowered him in life that he could not sue for her hand. Still, he had hopes that the Year of the Horse would alter his destiny, perhaps he would be restored to grace and be able to woo her. In the meantime he saw no harm in looking upon her and dreaming.

Encountering Mai Ling at the Huntington home, Ta Wang said:

"Forgive this lowly one, daughter of the Old Master, for making a bold suggestion. The New Year approaches and there appears to be no adequate shop in this city selling festive foodstuffs. Ta Wang has learned there are a hundred Chinese cooks in Sacramento. It would seem that the company agent might win many *kowtows* by suggesting a good shop be opened and supplied weekly from San Francisco."

Mai Ling that night wrote her father a very lengthy report, giving Ta Wang full credit for an "excellent suggestion."

On the twenty-ninth of the month the O'Lee house had been thoroughly cleaned. It also had a pronounced Chinese flavor in the kitchen. Two large cockroaches were roaming loose; smoked pork and guts hung from a wall; two live fish were swimming in a tub, and a fat hen was cackling under the cutting table. All these were Chinese customs, indicating the prosperity and other attributes of the house. Then, from the new Chinese market, Ping Soo had happily obtained all the food he needed for a fine New Year's dinner—sea slugs, bird's-nest, shark-fin and other dried delicacies shipped directly from China by way of San Francisco. Ping Soo had never enjoyed cooking in America as much he did now. He was putting his fifty-three years of skill and ability to their truest test.

By the thirtieth everything was prepared. Hopefully, Liberty sent a note out to Dan, asking him to please try and come home for the dinner and the weekend, telling him he'd likely find the changes in the house "delightful." His curt reply was: "Will try."

But Dan didn't come for dinner.

At first, Liberty was sure it was his knock at the door she heard. Maybe that was because the knock came only a few minutes after she heard the arriving whistle of the "Governor Stanford" locomotive. Or maybe it was just wishful thinking on her part, bound for disillusonment. In any event, she prepared herself to receive him. She checked the dining table, which was candle-lit and set for two; one of the spring flowers was drooping in the vase and she fixed it. The Chinese staff had set up their own feast in the kitchen; she motioned for them to be quiet—everything must be a surprise for Dan.

When she opened the door, a rail-layer from Dan's crew stood there.

"Evenin', ma'am," he said doffing his sweat-stained cap, "Mr. O'Lee asked me to drop this note off."

"Thank you," Liberty said, trying to smile and hide her disappointment. "Are you off for the weekend?"

"No, ma'am, only the evenin'. Old Bull Crocker's

got us goin' heavy on a seven-day week now. Have a good evenin', ma'am."

Liberty slowly closed the door and opened the single sheet of paper:

"Detained on business with Collis. Don't hold dinner."

Damn him, she silently stormed. To hurt her was one thing, but to hurt the servants was quite another. They'd worked hard to get things ready for him. She crumpled the note into a tight fist and went into the parlor where Ta Wang was laying a fire.

"Ta Wang the dining room and kitchen tables are not to my liking. Put them together and tell Ping Soo not to send a tray to the *amah* in the nursery tonight. She is to join us."

Ta Wang gaped openly. For want of something better to say, he stammered. "Her name is Madam Soo, Miss Liberty."

Liberty blinked. "You mean she's the cook's wife?"

Ta Wang grinned. "For many years. She had herself smuggled to America when their last boy was safely married off in China."

"But," Liberty stammered, "they hardly ever speak. Good Lord, they're even in separate bedrooms!"

"As it should be, Miss Liberty. Americans do not like to hire married Chinese couples, because the women are here illegally. So Ping and Ma-yang appear not to know each other."

"That is ridiculous and will be stopped at once. You said that the New Year's dinner was for relatives and guests. We shall be their guests, Ta Wang!"

"But the master," Ta Wang started to protest.

"Will be detained," Liberty said, neatly tossing the crumpled note into the fireplace. "Now see to the resetting of the table."

As the four later stood behind their chairs, Liberty listened to Ta Wang's traditional words and found them striking home.

"At the table of the New Year's feast everybody must leave his sorrows and worries behind his chair before he sits or his woes will be doubled in the coming year."

All suddenly heard the squeal of the picket fence gate as it opened and slammed shut. Ta Wang beamed. "It must truly be New Year's for a guest to arrive as we are to begin. I will go."

"Another plate! Another plate!" Madam Soo scolded her husband. "It is bad luck not to have whoever it is join us!"

Liberty had no idea who the visitor might be. She'd all but given up on seeing Dan that night. Moments later, Ta Wang ushered in a shamefaced Wang Wu.

"I beg your pardon," he stammered, "I was unaware you were about to dine."

"Wang Wu," Madam Soo clucked good naturedly, "a lie on one New Year will keep your tongue sore with boils until the next. Repent! Repent!"

Wang Wu hung his head and grinned. "It is true, Madam Soo, that all of Sacramento has smelled your husband's excellent cooking these past two days."

"Then you will taste of it," Ping Soo beamed. "Unless Ching-yoo has prepared a grander feast at the Huntington house."

"I will humbly taste of it," Wang Wu quickly accepted, "for Ching-yoo does not cook this night. Master Huntington is in San Francisco on business and Mistress Mai Ling is taking dinner elsewhere."

They had been conversing in Chinese.

"Would someone please tell me what is going on?" Liberty demanded. "Perhaps then we can all find a way to sit down and eat."

Obediently, if thoughtlessly, Ta Wang translated Wang Wu's last words. Liberty's legs almost gave out on her, the news so stunned her. She sat down heavily. There was little doubt in her mind that Mai Ling was taking her dinner with Dan in the railroad office car. She felt as if she could not bear the pain of it; she felt as if she wanted to die.

They were all looking down at her. They were silent now and seemed embarrassed. Slowly Liberty lifted her head. "Well," she said mustering a smile. "I'm seated, at any rate. Will you all please join me now?"

She was hardly aware that the fifteen-course dinner contained two soups and Ping Soo's specialty— the eight-treasure rice, a sweet dish piled high in a huge Kiangsi bowl, containing red dates, lotus seeds and sweetmeats of assorted colors buried in the rice in an intricate design. But she ate it. She ate everything of the dinner she could, as they all did, stuffing themselves to the endless delight of Ping Soo, who had created it all and would have rushed to the kitchen to prepare more had anyone showed the slightest inclination to ask him. But the feast was plentiful, indeed too plentiful. At its end, the table looked hardly touched.

"It's a shame to let what's left go to waste," Liberty said. "What of the other servant's at the Huntingtons, Wang Wu? Wouldn't they like to partake of some of this?"

Wang Wu rose and kowtowed deeply toward her. "It would please them very deeply, Madam O'Lee."

"And please their stomachs even more," Madam Soo chuckled.

"Then why don't you all help Wang Wu cart it over to them?" Liberty insisted. "I wish nothing more than to go in and sit by the fire and let all of this food digest. I think I ate for four, instead of two, tonight."

Aware that she had hardly eaten enough for a sparrow, the Chinese nevertheless all understood. They stood and kowtowed her respectfully out of the room.

What Ta Wang learned from Wang Wu during their trip to the Huntington-house so greatly shook him that he roamed the streets of Sacramento until well after midnight.

Mai Ling, one goddess of his dreams, was a wanton she-devil casting her curse upon Miss Liberty, his second goddess. In his present condition he felt helpless to save the one or give comfort to the other.

Returning to the O'Lee house, he saw a large drunken man letting himself in the front door. A lamp still shone from the parlor window and he realized the dangerous situation Liberty was now in.

Like a jungle cat stalking its night prey, Ta Wang skittered around to the back of the house. He stopped just once, to remove his shoes in the kitchen.

The house was deathly still. A lone night owl screeched far off. The kitchen door made no noise upon opening. Ta Wang slid along the hallway wall toward the shaft of light streaming out from the parlor. Then he was close enough to hear their voices.

He heard Liberty and her husband, Dan.

Liberty had tried to ignore Dan and continue on with her knitting, but her hands began to shake so that she dropped the needles in her lap.

"It so happens that I know Collis is away in San Francisco," Liberty said.

Dan ran a hand through his mustache, giving it a shaggy and unkempt look. It made his face much fiercer.

"I said," Liberty began again, "that—"

"I heard you!" Dan snarled. "Don't be a bore."

"I'll not have you lying to me, Dan O'Lee!" Liberty said flatly.

"And I'll not have you going behind my back to that damn Chinaman! My life is of no concern to him."

"Or to me, it would seem."

"Damn right!" he spat.

The tears were there in the green eyes now. Miserably, Liberty shook her head.

"I want you to give her up, Dan."

"It's too damn bad what you want, Lib. While you're pregnant, I'll do what I want."

Liberty blinked away her tears as her brows arched. "And after the child is born?"

"Hell, you'll probably just get pregnant on me again!"

"No, Dan," she said coolly, "you will never touch me again as long as you continue to see that—that—"

"Concubine," Dan supplied. "Oh, that wasn't what you wanted to call her, but simpering little ole Liberty Wells O'Lee wouldn't dare use language like that since ole Collis made her think she's a 'lady' of some kind or other." He strode over and towered above her. "She's not what you're thinking, at all. I'm the only man in her life."

"Oh, you blind, simple fool! She was with you tonight only because Collis Huntington is out of town!"

Dan brought the back of his hand swiftly around and caught her squarely on the side of the head. The blow was so sudden, catching Liberty so unaware, that it toppled her from the chair and sent her sprawling with an audible gasp.

In an instant, Ta Wang came flying into the room, leaped in the air and came down jamming his feet through Dan's legs, flipping him off balance. Ta Wang expertly jumped away, clawed his arms about in a graceful motion and awaited Dan's counter-attack.

Dan leaped frantically to his feet, and stood for a moment in total puzzlement, his body trembling with rage.

"Who in the hell is this?" he growled.

"New houseboy," Liberty gasped, staggering to her feet. "He must have thought you were a robber."

"Damn chink," Dan snarled. "If the damn bastards learned English they would know better."

Ta Wang remained poised in his *hwarang-do-kung-fu* stance. "My English is good enough to know when a lady has been attacked," he said through clenched teeth.

Dan's lower jaw dropped.

"Get him out of here, Liberty, before I'm tempted to kill him!"

"Don't be foolish," Ta Wang said softly. "My hands and feet would never allow you to get in a single blow."

Dan felt uncomfortable. As a young prospector he had seen Chinamen fight each other in the strange fashion they had and it had been savage and brutal. But he could not let the chink rule him in his own home.

"Liberty," he barked, "are you going to do as I say?"

Liberty walked to the parlor door and turned.

"I think not, Dan," she said evenly. "Not until you do as I say. Ta Wang, there are bundles of fresh clothing in Master Dan's bedroom. Please bring them down and place them on the front porch for me." He didn't move, so she added: "Go! I shall be perfectly all right."

"Are you kicking me out of my own house?" Dan demanded.

"Yes," she said, quietly but firmly.

He sensed a new power in her, impassive, immovable.

"You can't do this to our marriage," he said, his heart plunging.

Liberty laughed aloud, shortly, with a sound under the laughter that desolated Dan. He felt its infinitely derisive and bitter harshness.

"How quickly you place the blame on my shoulders," she said. "I find that to be horribly amusing." Then, striving to remain detached but succeeding only in making her voice uneven and breathless, she said: "When the child is born I shall go home to Trail Back. I hated it once. Detested it. It was repugnant to me to be an owner of human flesh and see white men use the black wenches as if this were their due. And now? I find you and your Chinese love of the same ilk." She paused, and now her voice was stern: "I do not intend to become her leavings."

Dan stomped past her and out of the house. The anger he felt toward Liberty turned inward. That night had been the first he had been with Mai Ling in three weeks—and they hadn't had sex. But his pride was too great to admit that to Liberty. Let her find it out on her own, he brooded. She would have to come crawling back and seek his forgiveness, because he was not about to crawl to her.

How rapidly did the months roll by! With each passing day Ta Wang became an ever-important voice among the houseboys of Sacramento.

Time was long on his hands, for he had Liberty's house so well organized that his duties were minimal. Even the birth of Alexander Grace Wells O'Lee in mid-June did not add to his tasks—only to those of Madam Soo.

To take up the slack, he convinced Mai Ling to let him assist her with her tong agent duties. She was grateful, because there were many who resented taking orders from a woman, and she loathed having to straighten out domestic problems. Under Ta Wang's firm control the houseboys soon learned not to talk back. But there was little bitterness or resentment towards him. He grew to love and admire his people, treating them as his father had treated his family in old China—with a firm tough hand that could also pat with affectionate praise.

The only bitterness Ta Wang held in his heart was toward Dan O'Lee. He could not fathom how a man could continually refuse to come and view his new-born son. Had it been a girl-child, he might have understood. But a boy-child was the proudest possession a man could have on earth.

He could see that Liberty was torn between sending for Dan and holding to her determination to leave him once Wells was old enough to travel. Because of his deep respect for Liberty, Ta Wang finally gathered enough nerve to place the problem before Mai Ling.

"Hush!" she whispered. "He is in the next room. I will talk with him when the meeting is finished."

Ta Wang did not like the sound of the angry booming voices coming from the closed chamber and quickly departed.

"Damn it all," Charles Crocker roared, "the word is crisis! And the silver strikes in Nevada are causing it. For every thousand workmen we've signed up this spring, only a hundred are left at the end of each week. The others just take off—we give them free transportation to the end of the line, and whammo! they take that hundred-mile walk across to the boom towns."

"No word from the war department?"

Crocker looked disgusted. "They're afraid putting Reb prisoners to work would look like slavery."

"Our recruiting of immigrants in the east isn't working either," Collis Huntington advised.

"Well," Crocker mused, "that about boils us down to our last manpower resource. I say hire some Chinese."

"You must be crazy!" Dan exploded. "I will not boss Chinese!"

"Really, Charles," Hopkins said drily, "they are too frail for such hard labor."

"Nonsense," Crocker shot back. "My houseboy Ah Ling works harder and longer hours than any white man I know. Besides, how in the hell do you think they built that Great Wall in their country, unless they got some real muscle in those scrawny arms?"

"That could be," Stanford interjected, "but we are all missing an essential point. The California legislature passed a law back in 1848 forbidding further importation of Chinese. Our source of supply would be only what is at hand, and I doubt that any houseboy will want to give up his easy life for the one you're suggesting."

"Leland," Crocker insisted, "don't be an ostrich. You know as well as I do that the law is rarely enforced and Kai Soong has new labor coming in illegally all the time."

Edwin Crocker spoke up. "I don't think we should involve ourselves if it is illegal. The fines and all, you know."

His brother laughed derisively. "Fines? Edwin, only the ship captain gets fined, and it's a five hundred dollar pittance—if he gets caught. That's nothing to the profit he'll make from a cargo of chinks crammed into his hold. I say we start negotiating with Kai Soong for some cheap labor."

"No," Dan insisted, "I will not be responsible for work done on the road by chink labor. From what I've seen of them, they're not fit, anyway. I don't think the Chinese could build a railroad."

"Well," Crocker growled, "it's just one more thing we don't see eye to eye on, Mr. O'Lee. But I am a reasonable man, and am willing to make a little wager. If this board will let me hire fifty Chinese for a tryout, I'll pit them against any of our crew you want to put in competition. If I lose, we'll drop the idea and you and I will keep thrashing out labor problems at the site. If you lose, you won't say one word, no matter how many chinks I see fit to hire."

"Deal," Dan grumbled. "When?"

Crocker smiled. "Say first thing in the morning. Kai Soong sent me fifty laborers three days ago that I've been training out on the old Sacramento Line sidings. Or is that rushing you too much, Mr. O'Lee?"

"We'll be ready," Dan said, and stomped from the room.

"Psst!" Mai Ling hissed, motioning him to follow her into the parlor.

"Not now, Mai. I've got to get back to work," he said shortly. He had not seen her since the end of March and had come to believe, as Liberty had implied, that she was now Collis Huntington's mistress.

"It will only take a minute, Dan. I have word from your wife."

Dan stared straight ahead. Only a slight quiver of his nostrils betrayed his rage that Liberty would contact him through her.

"You have a boy-child, who is nearly three weeks old. Is that not important to you?"

"Not as important as building my railroad," he said grimly, and marched away.

At the work site, the crew that Dan picked thought that he and Bull Crocker had gone over the edge.

"Now, boys," Dan reasoned with them, "a little spurt by you in the morning will show up these coolies and put an end to Crocker's crazy idea. Just go easy on the booze tonight, that's all I ask."

At dawn the Chinese marched through the camp like a weird procession of midgets, their blue cotton pants flopping, dishpan-shaped hats shadowing their grave faces, delicate hands hidden in billowing sleeves.

"Hey, Bull, you formin' a circus?"

"Lookee, they ain't got no hands to pick and shovel with."

"Don't need 'em. They do it all with their buck teeth!"

"All right, you blarney-kissing bastards, let's show 'em what men with big round balls can do!"

Dan had felt he could win his bet in a single day. The first night's report was disturbing. The Chinese shovelmen took smaller bites in a bank, and their barrowmen trundled lighter loads to the fill, but they worked methodically, without breaks for gossip or smokes. Two or three times a day a younger Chinese plodded among them with two kegs at each end of a bamboo pole slung over his shoulder. The barrels held hot tea. Each workman sipped a cupful, then bounced back to the job. By dusk, the coolies' right-of-way was longer and smoother than the one Dan's crew had made.

"Well?" Crocker grinned, triumphantly.

"Well, nothing," Dan growled. "It's only grade work. What about track laying?"

Crocker's grin widened and he walked away.

Next day the white crews stepped up the pace, cutting down breaks and voluntarily halving their lunch hour. On the Chinese crew Crocker increased the 'iron-rail men' from five to seven, so that each Chinaman was lifting a weight no more than his own. They took to using the sledge-hammers, which were long-handled and heavy, in pairs. At first they were not as productive as the whites in laying track, but on the grade work, which the whites despised, they pecked methodically on. By the week's end Crocker's crew had built the longest stretch of grade of any gang to date on the Central Pacific.

"I'll give them that much," Dan said grudgingly to his men and Crocker.

Jim Stowbridge, the hot-tempered Vermont Irishman who was the iron-rail foreman, was not about to give the Chinese anything.

"The boys and I don't see it that way," he complained. "Don't know what you're payin' them, Bull, but if it's equal to our pay, it ain't fair. Seven to the rail and two to a hammer is five more than we got. We've all agreed that we want a $2-a-day minimum from now on, with board thrown in and no Sunday work, or you're not about to see our faces come Monday morning next."

Crocker shrugged. "All I can do, boys, is take your demand to the money men in Sacramento. What do you say, Mr. O'Lee?"

Thinking about it, Dan had to admit that the Chinese experiment had proven successful. Besides, he didn't think there was a white man on any of the crews that was worth any two dollars a day.

"I say, Mr. Crocker, that I am a tired engineer who hasn't seen his new son and hasn't had a weekend at home in months. I'll work with whatever damn crew you have for me come Monday morning."

Crocker stuck out his hand. He was a rough, abrasive, slave-driving man, but was hard-rock honest enough to see that they both would win on the bet.

Dan shook Crocker's hand, glad to have that battle finally over.

It was the one he faced at home that still bothered him.

Preparing to take the work train back to town Dan came up with what he thought of as a crafty idea to get Ta Wang out of the way. In his dark moods, he'd come to despise Liberty's "protector." Knowing that the Irish gandy dancers would do anything for an extra drink dollar, he hired six of the burliest and told them he'd like them to be at the Golden Nugget Cafe right after sunset. Then he hired a Chinese to take a message on ahead to Ta Wang, telling him Mai Ling wished to meet him at the Golden Nugget at about the same time. He wanted the gandy dancers to "detain" Ta Wang. With their feelings running high against the Chinese, they didn't need much persuasion to take on the job.

In town, Dan got a shave and a haircut, then took his time strolling home. It was nearly dark when he walked through the picket-fence gate, went up the porch and rang the bell, twisting the knob with great force. He hadn't tried his key, first because he was all but sure Liberty had changed the lock, and then—in his subsequent anger— because he was determined to make her come to him. His feelings thus in a turmoil, he stood back and waited. He heard, after a moment, Liberty coming. Good, he thought—Ta Wang had taken the bait and left.

Liberty slid back the bolt and opened the door a crack. Dan thrust a foot forward, but she did not attempt to close it again.

"Dan!" she whispered. "Come in!"

Then he was inside, grinning at her, nervous perspiration making little streaks run through the talcum powder on his closely shaven face.

"Libby, honey—" he began, then blurted, "I've come to see the kid!"

"It's your right," she said evenly. "Come. He's up in the nursery."

"He got a name?" he asked, lumbering after her up the stairs.

"Alexander Grace Wells O'Lee!"

"Your old man's name, huh? Godawful mouthful, if you ask me."

"You were not around to ask," she said coolly. "In here. Madam Soo, you may go down to supper now. Mr. O'Lee has come to see his son."

"Want to see both of them," Dan demanded, going to the crib first. "Good lord, Libby, this can't be little Danny. He's really grown a spell, I'd say. Damn, he's going to be a big handsome devil." Then he went to the crib and peered in, as if not knowing what to expect. He could not keep the disappointment from his voice.

"Wee, ugly little mite. Head appears twice the size of his whole body. He's not deformed or anything, is he, Lib? Libby?"

He turned to find that he was quite alone in the nursery. His temper instantly flared and he stormed across the hall to Liberty's bedroom door. He didn't even attempt to see if it was locked, but reared back his booted foot and crashed it in. The hinges squealed and popped.

"Oh, Dan, Dan," Liberty moaned, "must you always be the barbarian? The door was not even locked!"

"But it was shut against me," he stormed at her. "Who do you think you are to walk away from me and close a door in my face?"

"And who are you to come blithely in to see your child after he's nearly a month old?"

"I came because you sent for me!"

"Never! I wouldn't bring myself that low!"

"Damn liar!"

His swift, panther-like movement caught her off guard. Before she could gasp he had her in his arms, his mouth clinging to hers fiercely, fighting for possession. His big hands, about her waist, were like hoops of steel.

She did not want him, not this way. Her mind raced with terror. She tried to twist aside, digging her nails into his face until they left bloody furrows. He only tightened his grip more securely. Vainly, she hammered at his chest with her fists. But she would not give in. She kept using her nails, her hands, even her teeth, until Dan spat at her:

"Yeah, that's what I've come to like! Treat me rough!"

He might just as well have mentioned Mai Ling's name for the devastating effect his words had on Liberty. Suddenly, her strength was gone, her will power sapped away. What he had come to like from Mai Ling she would not ape if her life depended on it. She went numb. Dan slammed the door shut and threw her on the bed. In her dulled state, she was hardly aware that he removed her clothing with something that came close to tenderness. He was no longer her husband. He was a faceless man like the Union soldiers who had raped her, a man bent on sating his own maddened penis lust and no more. He might just as well have masturbated for all the ardor she returned.

"What the hell, Lib," Dan mumbled. "You once said that you should have the right to enjoy this as much as I. So enjoy!"

Liberty didn't bother to answer. She lay and let herself be used.

For many long moments Dan just rested silently atop her. He could see the tears squeezing through her eyelids, held tightly closed as if to blot his face from memory. A sickness began to eat through him. Somewhere inside him, he knew that he had been trying to play God, and that the game was over—it was a fool's game that he'd had to lose.

He rolled away and swung to a sitting position on the side of the bed. His shame increased and he finally came face to face with his fear. He was incapable of being a family man. His own family background had ill-prepared him for it. He now had two sons. Was he treating them any differently from the way his father had treated him and his brother Burke? His father had been charming, but irresponsible. How he'd treated his mother Dan didn't recall, for she'd died when he was small. But he guessed now that it was probably the way he himself had treated Liberty in the last several months.

He wanted to apologize, but knew no apology could atone for what he'd done.

"I'll sleep in my room," he said gruffly, pulling his trousers up to his waist as he rose. He cursed the broken door, vowing to fix it in the morning as the first outward sign of his intent to change his ways. He was not aware of how tired he was from all his battles—with Crocker, with Liberty, maybe most of all with himself. Within seconds after he was in bed, he was snoring deeply.

For Liberty sleep was impossible. She wanted to rise and plunge her body into a tub of purifing water, but she ached too much to move. Her lips were bruised and swollen; her face still burned from Dan's slaps; her legs and ankles hurt.

Lying in bed, she knew she should leave Dan. She hated him. And yet, she knew she wouldn't leave him— for the sake of the children who needed his support, and, yes, for her own sake. Because if she hated him, she also loved him, was touched by compassion for the spirit in him. Brutal as he could be, she still sensed something basically honorable and decent about him. In any event, loving him was something she couldn't help.

She'd been fighting this battle in the wrong way, she decided. She'd tried using her pregnancy as a weapon, and that hadn't been fair. Tomorrow, she vowed, I'll start fighting with a whole new set of rules.

* * *

Dan slept past dawn and awoke famished. Wrapping a robe around him, he crept barefooted into the hall, where he noted that Liberty's door was still closed. The aroma of coffee then hit his nostrils and he took the steps three at a time to get down to the dining room.

A single place was set on the oak table, with the Sunday *Union* neatly folded near it. Next to the newspaper was an envelope with Dan's name on it. After ringing the little silver bell for service, he tore open the envelope and read:

"Hate to disturb your Sunday, but Kai Soong is arriving on the noon boat to discuss labor. For some reason he wants your houseboy, Ta Wang, in attendance. My house at about one. C. Crocker."

Dan smiled and re-read the note as someone deftly poured steaming coffee into his cup. He rather doubted that Ta Wang would be in any condition to attend the meeting.

"May I ask your pleasure for breakfast?"

Dan looked up and froze. It was Ta Wang, standing tall and stoically calm. There wasn't a mark on him.

"Anything," Dan said, after a moment. "Anything the cook has prepared."

Ta Wang kowtowed deeply. "Perhaps you wish to read the newspaper while you wait."

Catching the meaningful tone in Ta Wang's voice, Dan picked the paper up immediately after he'd left. If he wondered why his men had not taken care of Ta Wang, he soon found out why.

"Heathen Attack!" the bold, front-page headline read. Scanning the article hurriedly, Dan learned that six Irish railroad men at the Golden Nugget Cafe the night before had been set upon by between twenty and thirty Chinese. There was no apparent reason for the attack, the article said. An accompanying front-page editorial screamed for the formation of a vigilante committee to rid the city of this "yellow menace."

Dan frowned steadily while he read.

A plate of pork chops, eggs, toast and fried potatoes was silently placed before him.

"Ta Wang," he said, without looking up, "have you seen this?"

"I have," Ta Wang replied calmly. "I also saw the disturbance. I was at the cafe on the request of Mai Ling, though, I regret to say, she did not appear. The article fails to mention that a coin has two sides. Last night the houseboy to the McKinleys was tortured by white thugs and left to die. You will find no mention of it in that newspaper. If I may be so bold to say it, the disturbing incidents will increase if more of my people are brought to work on the railroad. But that must still be done."

Dan looked up at Ta Wang with new interest. "Do you know that you are to attend today's meeting?"

"Yes. Two messages were delivered last night. One for each of us."

"Last night," Dan started. "Why wasn't I informed . . ." His words trailed off. It suddenly occurred to him that Ta Wang had to be back in the house in time to be aware of his behavior with Liberty. Then why hadn't he come to her aid? He decided the issue was too sticky to raise.

"Well," he finished lamely, "there was really no rush on the messages."

Ta Wang nodded and started back to the kitchen. Then he paused and turned. "Master Dan, do you wish Ta Wang to repair Miss Liberty's bedroom door after she awakens?"

That was too much. Dan exploded. It was the first

time Ta Wang had addressed him with a title of respect, but his anger put him past noticing it.

"All right," he bellowed, "enough of this cat and mouse game! You do have eyes and ears. You know I set you up last night. You heard me with Mrs. O'Lee. Why didn't you try to protect her, as you did the first time?"

Ta Wang eyed him as if it were a topic that should never have been mentioned.

"Because you were where you should have been, Master Dan. When two blind people refuse to listen to the sounds around them, or carry a tapping stick, a crashing of a door can make them realize their need for each other. I will see to the door."

Ta Wang left.

Dan sat silent for a long time. Then, "That chink is just too damn smart!" he muttered, stuffing a large bite of pork chop into his mouth.

By two o'clock Dan was again grudgingly complimenting Ta Wang on his wisdom.

Only he, Crocker and Kai Soong sat directly at the round table in the Crocker study. In chairs behind and to each side of Old Master Soong, Mai Ling and Ta Wang sat like palace guard-dogs.

Mai Ling's presence did not peeve Dan nearly as much as did Kai Soong's. The tong boss ignored both him and his daughter. But on nearly every point raised since the meeting began, he had held a whispered little conference with Ta Wang.

"Naturally," Kai Soong was now saying, "in the little time allowed me, I was unable to gather too accurate a picture. But from this tong and that tong, I feel we can supply up to three hundred workers by the end of next week. Is that sufficient, Mr. Crocker?"

"A drop in the bucket. Within six months I want at least two thousand and eventually, if it all works out, somewhere around fifteen thousand. And why don't you call me Charley?"

Kai Soong smiled.

"As many as that, Cholly?" he mocked. "When your own crews have never numbered over a thousand?"

Crocker's enthusiasm kept him from recognizing the insult. "Kai Soong, by this fall and winter we are going to be fifty-five miles out and starting into the mountains. For twelve solid miles we will have to make roadbeds out of ledges that rise a quarter of a mile above sea level, to say nothing of the tunnels that have to be dug. But that's not the half of it. Our supplies are coming in quite regularly to San Francisco, but the steamboat owners only ship to us when and if they feel like it. Ted Judah may have been a little crazy, but he was damn right about our need for the railhead to go west as well as east. I'll need every man I can scrape up to get the line to Oakland and then around the bay to Frisco!"

Kai Soong leaned back and whispered to Ta Wang. The young man whispered back.

"A new tong company shall have to be formed for such an undertaking," Kai Soong mused. "It will be expensive to administrate. I will need to know the pay offered."

Crocker tried to use the same argument on Kai Soong that the white workers had used. "So," he concluded, "because it requires more of your people, I think a $1-a-day is fair."

Ta Wang politely tapped Kai Soong on the shoulder and was given nodding approval to speak.

"That is the same as most receive as houseboys and cooks—plus, at least here in Sacramento, a bed and food. Your other crews receive $1.25 to $1.50

each day and two hot and one cold meal, for which they pay you seventy cents a week. Am I correct?"

"For the moment," Crocker scowled. "They're threatening to hold out for $2 and free meals. That would break us, just as surely as anything over a $1-a-day for your people would break us, because of the number needed."

Again Ta Wang whispered to Kai Soong.

"My young friend would speak again," Kai Soong sighed, "with my approval of his wise words."

"Sirs, when you speak of each day, you must keep in mind that each of your calendar months has a different number of days. Can we not simplify matters by using the standard thirty-day Chinese calendar and setting a monthly rather than daily wage?"

"Dan?" Crocker queried.

"Sure as hell would cut down on the bookkeeping."

"Bookkeeping?" Kai Soong smiled, keeping his gaze on Crocker. "There shall be hardly any required of you. The workers will have a tong agent right with them. He will be the bookkeeper and you will have only one payment to make to him in a lump sum."

"Now that," Crocker enthused, "I can readily go along with. Save us a bundle in weekly pay envelopes to begin with. So, hit me with a figure, but not too hard."

Kai Soong held up his hand for patience. He could see that this labor contract could make the California House of Soong of far greater worth than the Canton House of Soong, and he wished not to be rushed into a foolish mistake.

"Ta Wang has yet another question before we decide."

Crocker nodded.

"May I ask if the Central Pacific now has the re-

sponsibility for the hiring of cooks and mess facilities
for its crews?"

"Yes, we do. Also for the purchasing of the food.
Hell, the dime a day the men pay us barely covers the
cost of basic supplies. Those men can put away more
meat, potatoes and whisky than any I've ever seen before."

"The Chinese," Kai Soong pounted out, "eat little
meat, no potatoes to speak of, and are forbidden to
touch whisky. Therefore, I think the proposal Ta
Wang has made to me will be beneficial to us all. As
it is my intention to name him as the tong agent, I
shall make it his first responsibility to negotiate the
terms with you."

Ta Wang flushed deeply. The authority given him
was beyond his wildest dreams. He rose on shaking
legs, and fought to keep his voice low and business-
like.

"Gentlemen we cannot accept less than $35 a month
for each workman. However, since your cooks have no
experience in preparing Chinese dishes, we shall pro-
vide the cooks and mess facilities for our own people,
provided only that the Central Pacific will pay for the
supplies required."

Crocker sat back and pulled at his chin whiskers.
The monthly wage came to $1.06 a day per man and
he wouldn't have to pay the cooks—another saving.
He felt there had to be a catch.

"What kind of supplies?"

"Dried oysters, cuttlefish and bamboo sprouts, sweet
rice crackers, salted cabbage, vermicelli, Chinese bacon,
dried abalone, tea, rice, pork and poultry."

Crocker frowned. "Now, wait just a moment. Most
of that will have to be imported from China. Are you
asking us to pay shipping costs?"

"Ah," Kai Soong put in, smiling, "but, you see,

these foodstuffs are being imported already. Perhaps you are not aware of the San Francisco firm of Sisson, Wallace & Company? They have begun a thriving business in importing Chinese foodstuffs."

Crocker snapped his fingers. "Hell, you're right—and my brother Clark is a partner in that firm!"

"I am most aware of that, Cholly! Most aware! In China we say it is good to do business within the family. You then always know the face of the bandit who robs from you."

Almost imperceptibly, Kai Soong winked. Crocker smiled. In this wordless manner, the agreement was set.

"Now, then," Kai Soong began cheerfully, and he looked at Dan for the first time. "So that your household be not inconvenienced by the departure of Ta Wang, Mr. O'Lee, I shall replace him in the near future with Wang Wu. I trust that pleases you?"

Dan shrugged. "I suspect Ta Wang will be of great value as tong representative to the railroad. I'm sure Mrs. O'Lee will adjust to Wang Wu rapidly."

"Furthermore—and this should interest Mr. Crocker as well—I am sending my daughter Mai Ling back to Canton to work out a recruiting policy with my brothers."

"Very wise," Crocker said, nodding. "Mai Ling knows our needs well."

Dan cast a quick look at Mai Ling. Her face remained impassive. Then he stared at Kai Soong. The man was looking at him, he saw now, with a smile of cold hatred.

Liberty was proud of Ta Wang when she heard of his promotion—but then, she'd always believed of his capacity to grow. And in Wang Wu, whose life she had earlier saved, she had a devoted admirer, in seventh heaven now that he was able to serve her full time. Of one thing she could be sure with Wang Wu as her houseboy: no malicious gossip about her and Dan would ever pass his lips.

Not that there was any scandalous behavior in the O'Lee house to pass on during the ensuing months. Neither Liberty nor Dan ever mentioned his attack on her that one woeful night. Throughout the summer and early fall Dan came into town every weekend and found a home where he'd had none before. Because of the interest he began to take in the children, he won over Madam Soo's motherly heart. Because of the hearty pleasure he took on Ping Soo's cooking, the latter beamingly slaved to make weekend meals gourmet masterpieces. And because he found in Wang Wu a delightful sense of humor, and would joke with the boy until he nearly cried from laughter, he made himself a worshipful friend for life.

Wang Wu expressed an opinion as to why Dan and Liberty were getting along so well together. Their harmony, he confided to Madam Soo, was in keeping with the spirit of the Year of the Horse.

"It is well that they hold hands and kiss now," the boy explained importantly, "for next year brings the Year of the Snake."

Madam Soo boxed his ears for him. "For shame! Let us enjoy this good year fully and not speak of bad omens, Wang Wu—you are the only bad omen in this house!"

Dan, in truth, saw only good years ahead. Work on the railroad had never gone better, and he was not remiss in giving Ta Wang much of the credit for it.

"Lib, you're not going to believe what Ta Wang put into effect this week," he said one Saturday night. "It knocked the bejesus out of the white crews. Monday, the Chinese cooks and food supplies finally arrived from San Francisco. So that eve'ng, when the coolies trooped back to camp, he had them all strip down naked and take a bath in the Irishmen's old whisky kegs. Damn it, that's right, that's what he did! Would you believe he found enough of those kegs up and down the line so that every damn coolie had one to himself? He had the Chinese cooks fill them with warm water, and stack piles of towels and clean clothes near by. You should have heard it, Libby, those chinks sloshing and soaping and giggling and rinsing and toweling until you would have thought their skin was going to come off. Then Ta Wang passed around clay jugs of flower water that they dabbed on all the most important parts and then they slithered into their clean clothes. I thought it might be just a weekly ritual thing, like with the Irish, but damn, no. Every night it's been the same. Ta Wang has this rule: no bathee, no eatee!"

Later that night, Liberty rolled over and poked Dan in the ribs. "You know something, Mr. O'Lee?"

"What?" he grunted, half-asleep.

"I was right the first time. I think a woman should enjoy it just as much as a man, but I think it only fair to warn you to take advantage of my mood while you can."

"For Gawd's sake, Liberty—are you pregnant again?"

"Again, Mr. O'Lee. But this time it's going to be a girl."

"Humph!" he mumbled. "How can you be so sure?"

"Because during the week she gives me trouble like neither of the others. It's not a constant sickness, like with little Dan, and it isn't like it's no trouble at all, as with Wells. My morning sickness never lasts more than ten to fifteen minutes, but it's almost as if she's already demanding to be noticed. You know I loathe milk, but that little varmint has me craving it as if I were a calf."

"You're weird," he yawned.

She reached over and rumpled his hair. "And so will your daughter be, because she was conceived in a fit of passion and not a moment of tender love. She will be our wild one, Dan. I'll lay money on it."

His only answer was a snore. She bent and kissed him tenderly on the forehead. No matter the consequences, she was not going to let this pregnancy come between them. She would give of herself until it hurt—and then some.

11

By the fall of 1864 the Union Pacific's supply and financial problems had become awesome. Durant had three delivery routes available to him from the east coast to Nebraska. Like Huntington he could use ships to sail supplies to New Orleans, but this would add stevedore costs for a reloading onto Mississippi steamers and a second reloading at St. Louis for the trip up the shallow Missouri. The two available rail routes required almost an equal number of reloadings, and a final delivery would have to be made by either wagon train or riverboat.

Aside from the question of supply routes, the fact was that Durant did not have the capital or credit needed to build the first forty miles of track.

A rapid-fire effort was made to get the money. The charter of the Pennsylvania Fiscal Agency was purchased and the name officially changed to the Crédit Mobilier of America. Some $1,400,000 was invested in Crédit Mobilier, all by the Union Pacific directors. Of this amount, $218,000 was used to repurchase the outstanding shares of the Union Pacific Railroad & Telegraph Company. This not only reimbursed Durant for the $160,000-plus he had personally invested in the takeover of the railroad from the federal commissioners, but made him a majority stockholder in Crédit Mobilier. It also made Union Pacific a property of Crédit Mobilier, which acted as a holding company—in flagrant violation of the Pacific Railroad Act.

Now it was possible for Oliver Ames to come out of the woodwork. That fall he bustled around Boston selling $400,000 worth of Crédit Mobilier stock to friends and political contacts, and invested another $400,000 of the Ames family fortune in it. Quietly, he gained one-third of the company's voting stock, or voting options.

But before Durant and Ames could start tapping the 'golden' federal treasury they needed to pull off two further wily coups, so as to overcome the new conditions that Huntington had cleverly gotten added to the revised railroad act.

"I'll listen, Thomas," Ames said narrowly, "but the plan better be good."

Durant smiled blithely. "Our greatest problem is that the act states that all of the branch lines to the hundreth meridian must have one hundred miles of trackage approved by federal inspectors not later than June 27, 1866. They must be at the hundredth meridian by mid December, and thereafter construction is to proceed at a rate of not less than one hundred miles a year."

"I'm not worried about the *thereafter*, Thomas, just those damn first miles!"

"Exactly, and that brings me to our second greatest problem—Peter Dey. He may be a fine engineer, but will not budge an inch on his surveys. It won't mean trouble now, but it will later on."

"How?"

"Look at the survey map and I'll give you just one

example. Here, he wants to revise Grenville Dodge's route. Granted, it would be a hundred fifty miles shorter, but that's mileage and land and subsidy money we will lose when it all starts becoming pure gravy. Dey is too politically powerful to fire, so we will let him fire himself."

Durant took a sheaf of papers from his letter case and passed them to Ames.

"As you can see I wrote Herbert Hoxie on Union Pacific stationery offering him the construction contract for the first hundred miles of line. Next you will see his reply and request to extend his contract for the additional one hundred forty seven miles to the hundredth meridian. As my private letter to him instructed, his formal reply also includes the statement you and I worked out."

Ames read aloud: " 'I will subscribe, or cause to be subscribed, for $500,000 of the stock of your company.' Good! Good! How much is his fee going to be for setting up this dummy company?"

"He wants $10,000 in Union Pacific first-mortgage bonds. But if you note the third letter, he has already assigned his contract, at $50,000 per mile, back to Crédit Mobilier of America. On my orders Hoxie gave Dey the green light to get as much road-grade work done as possible before the ground freezes up for the winter."

Ames pursed his lips. "I don't see where all of this is leading."

"Right to Dey's downfall. There is no possible way I can get rails and ties to Nebraska before spring, although Hoxie has promised Dey he would have them during the winter. But in the meantime the grading will have to be inspected. Now, isn't it interesting that the revised act states that as long as a state of war exists, a military inspector must also be in attendance?"

Ames began to smile. "Silas Seymour! Yes! For Christ's sake, yes! But what would you have him do?"

"Scuttle whatever work Dey has done to date!"

"But the cost and delay!"

"Minimal in comparison to the overall picture. Dey has only been able to get riverboat roustabouts and farm youngsters for work gangs. Through a most ingenious barrister in Dublin I've been able to pay to the British government the fines on five hundred Irish prisoners who would have been sent to a penal colony in Australia. He will have them shipped to New Orleans by mid-February. It will take them at least a year to pay off their passage and fines. I'm negotiating for others and if a bunch of burly sod busters like that can't give us two hundred forty seven miles in twenty three months, then we deserve to fail."

"Oh," Ames chuckled, "we'll not fail, Thomas. Not with Silas Seymour on our side."

Liberty's request of Mrs. Lincoln had not sat well with Colonel Seymour. He considered the assignment degrading for a man of his worth and ability. Nor did he mind expressing that opinion to Federal Inspector Jesse Williams as they rode on horseback along the fifteen miles of embankment that Dey's crews had graded out of Omaha. Williams saw very little at fault, but Seymour found everything to his disliking. Williams held his silence, because the military had the final say and he was no engineer like Seymour.

"Bellevue!" Peter Dey exploded, "You must be crazy thinking the line has to run further south toward Bellevue."

"Peter, it grieves me to have to report that, you know. Such a pity that so much of the firm's funds had to be wasted for this unrealistic dirt pile. I'm sorry but it will have to be abandoned and a fresh start made in the spring."

Two letters of resignation were written that night, Dey to Durant, and Seymour to the war department. Then, with unmitigated gall and arrogance, Seymour wrote Durant:

"This day I have resigned from the army. I am settling into an Omaha boardinghouse and will assume at once the position of acting engineer. I will expect Robert Porter to be sent to me at once and shall begin work on the 'yellow peril' tonight."

Then he carefully constructed a telegram to Randolph Porter, praying the fool could read between the lines:

"Father in serious trouble. Delay your return east."

As the message was being tapped out, a Sioux brave was wrapped around the top of a telegraph pole bashing at the "singing wire" with two granite stones. When the wire snapped, the message was lost forever.

Randy might not have done anything about it anyway. After a summer of bliss, Selena's return was icier than the Chinook winds sweeping over the Sierras from Oregon. Received graciously in England and Europe, her meeting with the Porters in New York was like a stunning slap in the face. They had dined with Selena and Lady Pamela at the Metropolitan one night only and silently ignored them for the rest of their stay. Not even a thank-you note was sent to them by Mrs. Porter. It was never openly stated, but throughout the stilted meal it was quite obvious that the Porters, on direct orders from Oliver Ames, had no desire for their son to marry Lydia May. Robert Porter put it in blunt terms in a letter to his son:

"Should you decide to do anything foolish, we are prepared to forget we have a son and heir."

Nazareth, who had come to like Randy as a person and fellow-worker, advised just the opposite:

"To hell with my wife and to hell with your parents. If you want to marry my daughter, you have my blessing."

Randy hesitated. He lacked the will to go against his family and his great-uncle Oliver.

Selena saw that flaw in his character, but was unable to make Lydia May see it. Selena blamed it on her having too much Tedder blood. After her return, she began to place stumbling blocks in the way of their further courting. She felt she had been personally insulted by the Porters and had only Randy to strike back at. With their meetings constantly ending in a fight, Randy began to spend more and more time at the railhead camp and less and less time in town.

The work on the giant cliff was not going as Dan had anticipated, and he, too, had to reduce his weekends in town. Liberty didn't mind. The baby was giving her one devil of a time and she was quite content to spend days on end without seeing anyone. And that year it didn't hurt her feelings at all that Selena didn't invite her to the annual Christmas Eve dinner party.

Nor was Collis Huntington invited to Selena's or to the O'Lee's house. To everyone's surprise he arrived back from the east without his wife; to no one's surprise he began to spend more and more time in San Francisco after Mai Ling's return from China. The Jane Stanford-to-Mary Crocker-to-Selena Tedder gossip line chewed the situation raw.

Then, from a chance remark made by Nazareth, Selena was given a new bone to place before her pack.

"I can tell you," she simpered at them over tea, "it is thoroughly disgusting Nazareth. It's not bad enough that they have close to six thousand of those heathenish little men at the camp, but your husband, Mary Crocker, is closing his eyes to the fact that they have smuggled into the camp over a hundred 'singsong' girls and the smoking of opium is quite commonplace."

"Selena Tedder," Mary Crocker shot right back, "your facts may be correct, but not where my husband is concerned. I will take the matter up with him this evening, but you will find out that it is probably all the work of that Dan O'Lee. He, more than likely, has had the Chinese prostitutes brought in for himself. Everyone is aware of his taste for those yellow women—and with Liberty being in the family way again . . ."

Jane Stanford cut in with a short laugh. "And don't leave out, Mary dear, that Collis doesn't seem too concerned about the illegal importation of the singsong girls, since his yellow hussy mistress is the one doing the importing."

"Oh?" Selena exclaimed, gaining a bit of information she did not as yet have.

Jane Stanford smiled sweetly. She had overheard the argument between her husband and Collis Huntington on the matter, but she had never liked Selena Tedder, would never like Selena Tedder, and saw no reason to give her the actual facts.

"I must be running," Jane chirped. "Mary?"

Mary Crocker rose as if preparing to go and do battle. "Yes! Charles is at the store this afternoon, and I'm interested to know exactly what he does know!"

Selena smiled to herself. She knew the game Jane Stanford was playing, but also knew that Mary Crocker couldn't keep a secret if her life depended upon it.

Charles Crocker listened to his wife's carping. He was blunt in his response. "Of course I know, but I'm building a railroad and not running the Methodist Ladies Social Circle. It may hurt your sensitive ears,

Mary, but those Chinese men have sex urges that are mighty strong, and they are far less inhibited than the Irish workers. I would much rather have them working on the railroad and working on each other in their tents at night. I'm asking no questions about their women or opium, and I ask you to do likewise." He rose and took a battered pith helmet from the coatrack. "Now, my dear, the work train is waiting to take me out to the railhead. Dan has a most interesting and secret experiment for me to watch. I'll be gone for about three to four days."

Mary Crocker sat stunned. She could hardly go back and report to Selena Tedder that her husband not only knew, but was almost a party to such scandalous carryings on. Nor did she want to share the information with Jane Stanford. Had she queried her husband on the experiment, she might have had some real news to share with them.

The week before Ta Wang had come to Dan and asked him to go back with him to the Chinese tent camp. There, he proudly showed Dan a reed basket the Chinamen had woven out of the material that came packed around their foodstuffs.

The basket was waist-high and round. The eyelets woven into the top were located in the proper position of the Four Winds, and painted with symbols intended to repel the evil eye. Ropes ran from the eyelets to a central cable.

"We have noted, Master Dan," Ta Wang said, "that the white men are most afraid of hanging over the cliff in what you call bos'n's-chairs. It gives them no sense of security, dangling three hundred feet over that blue-black gorge. They hand-chip their holes badly, tamp in too little blasting powder, and scream to be hauled away before they have properly fixed and lighted the fuse. This basket will change all."

Dan examined the basket carefully, even to climbing inside and sensing the feeling of security it would afford.

"Damn good idea, Ta Wang," he said. "How many of these can you make for my men?"

"I was thinking," Ta Wang said slowly, "more of my own men. Master Dan, men of China were skilled at such work as you need on this cliff before the first Irishman was born. This is a small job compared to the fortresses that were built in the Yangtze gorges, or the stones that were carved and laid for the Great Wall. Baskets such as this have been used for high work since the Han Dynasty."

"Baskets, yes, but what about the explosives?"

Ta Wang laughed delightedly. "Master Dan, gunpowder is a Chinese invention. No man here has not as a boy set off firecrackers on New Year's and feast days. No instruction is necessary, because they are well aware of the latent dangers that can transform a handful of gritty gray dust into a lightning bolt. But they do not fear it until the fuse is set and lit. And no Chinese boy is foolish enough to cut a fuse too short. Give us a try, Master Dan."

"How many baskets have you made and how many more can you have by the end of the week?"

"Four ready now, twelve by the end of the week."

"Okay, Ta Wang, I'll get your Cholly Crocker out to take a lookee. The blasting crews want three days off for New Year's, so that will get them out of our hair."

For three days the wicker baskets bobbed like tiny gray kites against the skyline. The hand-drills chattered a tom-tom beat, and the powder blasts puffed flame. As the baskets were lowered over the next solid surface, a hoard of blue-trousered Chinese shoveled the blasted debris down into the gorge.

For those three days Charley Crocker stood far below and watched twelve well-coordinated baskets lower together, raise together and eat out equal portions of the mountain. It had taken the white crews over a month to blast out little more than a goat trail. In three days the Chinese were able to walk four abreast on the ledge and smooth it for track-laying.

"Jesus Jennie!" Crocker cried triumphantly, "order a hundred of those damn baskets, Dan! At this rate we'll conquer the cliff by spring!"

"Yeah!" Dan mused, "but the going gets rougher toward the summit."

"Why? This is solid rock here and it's tundra facing up toward the gap."

"Yeah," Dan repeated, "and that's far more treacherous. We'll have to shore up the mountain-facing with redwood and spruce. That surface can be like quicksand after the winter freeze is gone. I didn't think we'd be that far along, so you'd better have Randy Porter revise his schedule and get the wood ordered."

"I'll do it, but it will have to go through Leland."

"Why?"

"Our titled president is beginning to act like he was back minding his mercantile store and counting every stick of penny candy that goes in and goes out. Last week he jumped on me because our import charge for Chinese food ran $6,000 for the month."

"Crap on him," Dan scowled. "That's a dollar a Chinaman for the whole month. We spend that per week on the other crews."

Crocker winked. "I'll tell the kid to slip the lumber voucher to him gently. I'm going to go back to town now. Damn fine experiment, Dan! Damn fine!"

Ta Wang was equally pleased. That evening, at tong company expense, he distributed a supply of opium, a rack of pipes and "yen she gow" scraper tools to the mountain workers. Each bucket man was given a chit allowing him one free hour with one of the 'singsong' girls.

Then, out of gratitude, he took a pipe and supply of opium to the railroad office car. Dan, at first, laughed at the suggestion that he smoke with Ta Wang.

"Master Dan," Ta Wang reasoned, "you have seen my men smoke and the Irish drink their whisky. Who arrives at work the next day with the swollen head and the sick stomach? No Chinese! After the last thirty hours of dangling over the cliff-face my basket men need this recreation. Besides, the free opium and girls the basket men receive this night does not go unnoticed with the others. When more baskets are woven, Ta Wang will have no difficulty filling them for you."

"You wily yellow bastard," Dan grinned, "let me take a try at that stuff. Ever since Huntington got blue-nosed about whisky for the Irish it's made me crave the damn stuff more. I've watched your smiling 'drunks" on Saturday nights and envied them. What am I supposed to do?"

Ta Wang was a patient and well-informed teacher. When he had Dan reeling from the opium effects, he produced his second gift of gratitude.

Dan blinked and tried to focus his eyes on the scantily clad singsong girl Ta Wang had brought into the railroad car. His drugged senses saw her as one of the most exotic, sensual creatures he had ever encountered. But a warning light in his brain flashed a caution signal.

"Hey, you crafty devil," he slurred, "you don't fool old Dan. Last time you thought I was cheating on my wife you tried to beat the hell out of me. You out for my job?"

"No job," Ta Wang answered calmly. "She is called only Lotus. It is a flower that lasts but a single night, Master Dan. A flower that lasts a single night is far different, because it is gone and forgotten in the morning, except for the fragrance it leaves behind."

"Yeah!" Dan gasped, and his voice sounded to him as if it were returning to him from a deep tunnel. "Am I ever in need of the night before and not the morning after!"

Dan saw Lotus only once, and was offered opium by Ta Wang only once, but as the Chinese work force grew to nearly ten thousand it became necessary for Ta Wang to bring in additional company agents to help him supervise, and these agents were, like most creatures on earth, desirous of their own place in the sun. A casual word from "Master Dan" guaranteed him an opium pipe that never went unfilled; a sly wink assured him of a flower that lasted but a single night. Because it was for "Master Dan" Ta Wang was kept innocently in the dark. Had he known the monster he had created out of a single bowl of opium, he might have been tempted to kill Dan on the spot.

But, although the Chinese workers kept this knowledge from Ta Wang, they slyly leaked it to the white workers. The Chinese mastery of "rock work" had been a cruel blow to Irish egos, but to have the chief engineer constantly in bed with yellow women was one thing they couldn't stomach. They consulted among themselves to find the best man to confront Dan as their spokesman. They chose Nazareth Tedder.

Nazareth was aghast to learn that so much had been going on around him without his knowledge.

"Well," he demanded of Dan, "are these accusations true?"

Dan had already inhaled two pipes of opium that evening and had no desire to have Nazareth questioning him on the subject.

"It's none of your damn business!" he said, flatly.

Nazareth bristled. "I feel that it is, if we are to continue having a working relationship. I do not condone the heathenish practices of the Chinese any more than I condone the whisky-drinking of the Irish. I want the women, whisky and opium out of these camps or I shall be forced to tender my resignation at once."

"Naz," Dan said, his head bobbing and his tongue slurring, "You don't understand your own problem, do you? Ole Selena gave so much of her lovely ole self to the boys in the gold fields that she didn't have anything left for you. You prob'ly don't even know how to get it hard any more, do you? Well, with Libby pregnant again, Dan O'Lee doesn't have that problem. Do what you think you have to do, Naz, but I'm expecting someone shortly."

It was the first time anyone had ever flaunted Selena's past in Nazareth's face, and for three years he had feared that this was the man who would dare do it. But it was no longer in Nazareth, as it might have been in his over-zealous youth, to challenge Dan to a duel. He now realized that he had a far superior weapon to use against the likes of Dan O'Lee—his wife.

The quick, desperate charge of Selena's carriage across Sacramento to the Crocker mansion was born of frustration and despair at what was happening to her world.

Selena simply brushed Ah Ling aside. Giving Charles Crocker no opportunity to get in a word she demanded the firing of Dan O'Lee, Crocker's rejection of Nazareth's resignation, and an immediate end to the opium-smoking and womanizing by the Chinese.

"Selena," Crocker said slowly, "I have never been partial to your husband, as a man or engineer. I never wanted him in the first place and am most happy to accept his resignation. Now, I'm going to tell you, just as I told my wife, keep your damn nose out of my railroad business and forget the Chinese!"

Selena was not about to do either. By refusing her demand, Crocker had given her a cause to champion. Within the hour she had bags packed for herself and Lydia May and had boarded a steamboat for San Francisco. It was February 17th, two days before the Chinese New Year.

It took Selena only about ten minutes to convince Lady Pamela to join her cause and back it with money and her social power. Lady Pamela was more than happy to help. The increasing number of Chinese whorehouses was greatly reducing the revenue from her own establishments. That very day she saw to the renting of the American Theatre for the night of the nineteenth and had handbills printed for distribution. Oddly enough, Chinese were hired to pass out the announcements of the formation of the Anti-Coolie Labor Association.

The meeting was a rousing success, stirring passions to such a degree that the men and women in attendance marched out of the theater on Chinatown, pelting the New Year's Eve paraders with rocks and filth. San Francisco society matrons reverted to their gold-rush beginnings and howled out indecencies that made even Barbary Coast toughs blush. The police looked the other way. It became sport to set fire to Chinese business establishments, dump chamber pots on the doorsteps along Grant Avenue, and cut off as many queues as could be captured.

The Year of the Snake thus began with very bad omens for the Chinese.

Selena next brought her crusade back to Sacramento, where it was less violent, but still effective. Hypocritically, since none of Selena's women supporters wanted to lose the services of their cooks, houseboys and gardeners, the crusaders met every arriving steamboat and so intimidated the incoming Chinese workers that it took days for Ta Wang to quiet them after they reached camp.

Leland Stanford was finally forced to confront Selena and persuade her to back down. But Stanford picked an ill-advised moment to express his views. Selena cut him short with a single phrase and showed him to the door just as her afternoon tea guests were arriving. That day she was entertaining a San Francisco newspaper editor who had always opposed Stanford and the building of the railroad, two Methodist ministers who had taken a stand against the building of Buddhist shrines at the work camps, and an Irish labor organizer who felt his people were being denied jobs.

"Gentlemen," Selena said sweetly, "how nice that you are arriving just as our ex-governor is departing. Mr. Stanford, who for many years was himself ill-disposed towards the Chinese, has been trying to get me to back away from our crusade. I'm not going to suggest that he has a profit motive now, but I do want each of you to hear the answer that I gave him. I told the good president of the Central Pacific that there is not a Chinaman's chance in hell that I will stop until every last one of those heathens are sent back to where they came from!"

Selena had sounded a battle cry that was echoed in newspaper editorials, sermons, street talk and banner headlines: "Not a Chinaman's Chance!"

With Nazareth gone, Dan suspended any further work on the trestle that would connect the cliff with the point at which the Summit Tunnel bore was to begin. Instead, he sent five hundred Chinese, with supplies strapped to their backs, around the mountain and up to the summit to use their basket-magic in starting the bore. The tunnel—the first of ten to be bored—was to be 1,659 feet in length. The rock proved to be extremely hard. The blasting powder shot back out of the holes, merely chipping the surrounding rock. The rock, glazed with razor-sharp ice, had to be carefully watched so that it didn't chew through the pulley ropes. Progress was tedious and slow—seven to eight inches a day— and now not a single day seemed to pass without one seeing, floating far below in the foam-flecked eddies of the American River, the remnants of a wicker basket, the waterlogged top of a conical hat, and a frayed rope end. Dan and Crocker did not keep count of the coolie casualties; that was Ta Wang's responsibility.

Then, as if the Year of the Snake wanted to announce its arrival with a vengeance, heavy, wet spring snows began to fall. In one night thirty inches of snow fell on the summit camp tents, and no work could be done on the bore the next day. By mid-day the snow had reduced the cliff work to a snail's pace and it, too, had to be suspended. Then the wind rose and began to pile drifts fifteen feet high. The base camp took on the guise of an ant-hill on a bleached sand dune. It would be days before work could commence again, so Dan turned his thoughts to other pressing matters.

"Randy, what about my redwood and spruce for the shoring face? Once we get to that level I'll need them that very minute."

"Dan," Randy complained, "these aren't Yankee forests. Those trees are four, six, eight feet in diameter. You're calling for fifteen-foot lengths for the retaining beams and it's hard for the Chinese lumbermen to handle them. Stanford is already complaining about the cost of dragging timber down to the mills and then back up here."

"That's just too damn bad! Once we're rid of this

snow it will only be a week to ten days before we reach the tundra base. You get your ass back down to Sacramento and tell that clown Stanford to operate that mill double time if he has to. What in the hell is that?"

The whole office car shook on its tracks and the air was filled with a rumbling, like the report of a hundred blasts being set off at once.

They stumbled outside to be greeted by the sound of thousands of voices rising to a piercing wail. Dan turned to where the original sound was coming from, stared in horror, then screamed for Ta Wang.

"Quiet them," he yelled, "or they'll bring the cliff down on us!"

It was like talking to the wind. The Chinese couldn't control their fear as they helplessly watched the entire summit camp become a moving part of the avalanching mountain. The rush of snow increased, cascading down to the canyon three hundred feet below. As the great cloud of snow dust billowed ever larger, it created a sullen roar that thankfully kept them from hearing the five hundred death cries from within its wake. The silence that followed was far worse than the noise of the avalanche itself.

An hour later, Dan was still standing there, devastated by what he'd seen.

"Don't mention this in Sacramento," he told Randy Porter dully. "Just don't mention it."

Randy went to the mills in Sacramento in a daze. He had trouble asking Leland Stanford for the lumber. And Stanford, in turn, had difficulty in listening to him. A different sort of lumber issue was exciting the ex-governor.

The mills, built along the banks of the Sacramento River so that the logs could be floated to them, was adjacent to the steamboat docks. An enterprising ship's captain, who had been transporting the Chinamen, had gone up to the railhead, curious to see what they were working on. There he'd found a large chip of redwood, which he'd taken back to China to show to a furniture merchant. Redwood was unknown in China. The chip greatly excited the merchant, who promised to buy all the redwood the captain could bring him. The captain had just finished signing a very lucrative contract with Stanford when Randy arrived.

Stanford was not about to cancel the contract, even if the same wood was needed by the railroad. Randy's request, when he finally heard it, put him in a rage. Then he tried to figure out how he might be able to meet both demands. But there seemed no way of doing it until the spring thaw came and gave the lumbermen a chance to fell the trees faster.

Stanford scratched his whiskers and looked around. There just had to be an answer.

"What are all those logs stacked over there?" he asked the mill foreman.

"Spacing logs for between the rails so they don't get bent during shipment from the east."

"What do we do with them then?" he asked.

"Nothing much." The man shrugged. "Sell them off now and then as fireplace logs, if we find time to saw them up."

"They appear to be a good fifteen feet long, wouldn't you say?"

"Yep! Eighteen to be exact, Mr. Stanford."

"Well, that will solve a couple of problems and use up waste material. Fill O'Lee's retaining specifications with those beams and let Captain Farraday have the number of whole redwood logs he requires for shipment. Now, Randy, does that take care of your problem?"

"Yes, sir," Randy muttered, and walked away.

Stanford turned back to the foreman. "Can you fill O'Lee's order within the week?"

"No problem on that, Mr. Stanford. Those logs are cottonwood and will not eat up my blades like the redwood or spruce. It'll be like going through melted butter."

"Fine! Fine! That's what I'm here for, to keep everyone happy."

From Omaha, Silas Seymour took the Hollander Overland Stage to Dutch Flats. There he rented a horse and rode over the Donner Pass and down into the work camps. He was a sight that made the Chinese stop, stare and giggle.

Seymour bumbled up to the railhead, his umbrella at full balloon and a bedroll puffing up from his saddle like an immense denim bustle. His sparse goatee and a black top hat gave him the appearance of a high-plains Don Quixote. His arrival could not have come at a better time to veer the Central Pacific toward tragedy.

Charles Crocker was at home in Sacramento with the flu; Dan was disabled in the office car bunk with freezing chills and burning fever. Seymour was given ample opportunity to pick Randy's brain without anyone knowing exactly who he was or why he was there.

He was greatly impressed with the progress made on the cliff but chuckled to himself at the problems the Central Pacific faced with the boring of the Summit Tunnel. He was amazed that the loss of five hundred workers had barely dented the progress up the cliff. Already the locomotives could chug up nine miles of the twelve-mile climb, their main cargo being the back-beam braces and cross-hatch boards for the three miles of retaining wall that would be required.

In the three years that Randy had been on the job he had never felt like a traitor until Seymour's arrival and after three days of Seymour's questioning he knew he couldn't play the role any longer.

"I'm sorry, Colonel Seymour," he said miserably, "I just can't go along with what you and my family want me to do. These are hard-working people who are striving to build a railroad, when you haven't even started on the Union Pacific yet. I don't think it's fair for you to try and stall them until you can get a start."

"Stall?" Seymour lifted an eyebrow. "Whatever are you talking about?" He put a pained expression on his face, and lied expertly. "I have no connection with your family or the Union Pacific. I am an authorized military railroad inspector, with papers to prove it, and am here for that purpose and that purpose only. Now, you have made an honest mistake and I shall accept your apology without it being uttered."

He let a long silence descend between them as he sat on the platform car picking knots out of the cottonwood boards with a pen-knife.

"As my time here is limited," he said at last, "when do you anticipate the construction of the retaining wall will begin?"

"Why?"

Seymour sighed, as if dealing with an imbecile. "I have gone over the construction plans you obtained for me and they do not conform with government standards. I've taken the liberty to alter them. Here!"

"I'll have to go over these with Dan O'Lee when he is better."

Seymour scoffed. "Are you not an engineer, my boy? If at least a half-mile or so of the wall is completed before I leave, then I will sign a release for track to be laid below it. I can't alter my schedule because of one man's illness. You'll just have to leave that three miles of track unlaid until I can get back again in midsummer."

Randy shrugged, took the plans and went to report to Dan. Fate decreed that he didn't mention Colonel Seymour by name, but only referred to him as "the federal inspector." Dan, who had never had more than a half-dozen sick days in his life, was in no mood to be bothered.

"Then get started," he coughed, "and just leave me alone!"

The Chinese did not know wood and Randy was vastly unfamiliar with the construction of retaining walls, especially one that had to be forty-five feet high and built in three stair-step sections.

Colonel Seymour was very familiar with wood, especially soft, knotty cottonwood. Under normal circumstances this wood might have held back the tundra for a couple of years—the redwood and spruce would have for a couple of decades—but the alterations he had made in the plans would speed up deterioration considerably. Faulty constructed, the porous cottonwood would absorb the spring runoff at a greater rate, swell, expand, buckle and collapse as the upper tiers became too great a weight for the lower tiers to support. His technical changes would paralyze work of the railroad for several months.

With deliberate calm Seymour watched Randy instruct the Chinese on the job. Then as the latticework wall went up along the still-frozen mountain facing, he surreptitiously picked knots from the boards further to enhance the erosion process as soon as it began.

Finally, when the wall was nearly a half-mile along, Seymour stole the no longer needed blueprints from Randy's tent, restored them to their original condition, returned them. When the error was revealed, the colonel would be long gone and Randy would be scapegoated for it.

Unfortunately for the colonel's scheme, the weather took an unseasonal turn and deterioration set in even more quickly than he'd expected it to. For several days the temperature climbed to near ninety, dropping back at night to the low thirties. The melting runoff soaked the tundra and cottonwoods by day, freezing and splitting them by night.

On the day that Colonel Seymour planned to depart, Dan forced himself up and back to work. He informed no one, hitching a ride up the cliff on the locomotive and then walking the last half-mile to the retaining wall construction site. Weak and exhausted, he leaned on the wall for a moment, grasping at one of the horizontal beams. Water all but oozed through his fingers. He shook his head in confusion, fought to focus his eyes, then peered closely at every beam, joint and lattice.

"Jesus Christ!" he rasped. "How in the hell did this happen?"

He stumbled along until he came to Randy and a carpenter crew.

"This isn't the right plan or right wood," he insisted.

"The federal inspector," Randy started, but Dan cut him short.

"Get your ass down this mountain and bring him and the blueprints back up here. Damn idiot has given us a disaster zone. Move it! Hey, you chinks! Drop what you're doing and come with me. Maybe we can shore some of this mess up long enough for me to figure out what to do with it."

Randy scooted off, fearful that Seymour had conned him, yet not quite sure how. The work locomotive was only a third unloaded of that day's supplies and so he had to walk to the caboose, unhitch a handcar and cautiously brake his way down to the main camp. He grabbed the blueprints without looking at them and began a futile search for Colonel Seymour. No one seemed to have seen the man in the tall hat that morning.

Randy's frustration was no greater than Dan's. Only one of the eighty-odd man crew on the cliff knew English and his understanding was limited. He couldn't see why Dan wanted them to pound all the fifteen-foot-long beams up against the latticework, since this would block off the roadbed where track was to be lain. This slowed progress. Further, had Dan's mind not been feverish, he might have been aware of the compounded danger of the beams themselves. Dropped at an angle, they were pushing the lower part of the wall into the softening tundra and tilting the top forward, far out of alignment.

There was no warning—no initial rumbling or tremor or sound of timber tearing away from timber. It was as if an eighth-mile of retaining wall decided at the same instant that it could no longer remain attached to the tundra and began slowly to fold down on itself. Once released, the ice-age-ground granite pebbles of the tundra roared forth like lava, consuming everything in their path. In the batting of an eye, the work locomotive vanished under the gray-brown muddy surge. It bobbed to the surface halfway down the cliff with its shattered boiler hissing up a geyser of steam, then disappeared again. Eight platform cars went with it.

At the base camp, Randy stared up the cliff in horror. Then he peered for Dan. He was looking for Dan to tell him what to do. But Dan was no longer there. He had been swallowed up by the earth.

Randy panicked. "Shovels! Picks!" he screamed

frantically, then raced about, trying to get the awe-struck Chinamen to move. "Dig them out! Send back to town for Mr. Crocker! Do something! Do *something!*"

Then he collapsed on the ground, shredding the blueprints and crying as if the soul were being torn from his body.

It was the "Governor Stanford" that rushed back to town, full-throttle and signaling a disaster with short, eerie whistles while it was still a mile out. Scores of Sacramentans ran to greet it.

Charley Crocker, pulling trousers up over his night-gown, arrived at the station almost at the same moment the train screeched in. Leland Stanford ran the dis-tance in shirt sleeves. Liberty, who was returning home by cab from the doctor's office, had her driver veer about and rushed to the station too.

Crocker listened to the engineer's quick report and barked: "Part of that damn cliff's collapsed. If anyone here's a medical man or knows first-aid, get aboard. Everybody else back."

"Mr. Crocker! Mr. Crocker!" Liberty called, wad-dling up as fast as she could. "What is it?"

Before Crocker could soften the blow, the engineer blurted out:

"Avalanche, with your husband right in the middle of it!"

Liberty paled. Automatically, she put up her hands for a lift up to the platform car.

"What do you think you are doing, woman?" Crocker demand.

"I'm going with you," she cried.

"In your condition? Don't be foolish!"

"Help me up!" Liberty demanded. "And get this train rolling!"

Crocker didn't argue.

The train, with Crocker, Stanford and Liberty on board, made the return trip to the railhead in less than an hour. But the rush had been in vain. Standing horror-stricken on a platform car, the three saw the cliff side and gorge swarming with blue-trousered men using shovels and picks and bringing blanket-clad bodies back to the base camp. There was no need for the medical men; those who had fallen, injured, had been promptly suffocated in the churning mud.

In a trance, Liberty let herself down off the car, keeping her eyes on the jagged hole that had been left near the cliff's summit. She could not believe what she saw. This had been Dan's pride and joy. On his weekends at home, he'd discussed with her at length the engineering problem and his proposed solution for it. The cliff couldn't have failed him; it just couldn't have!

Ta Wang sorrowfully approached her.

"How did it happen?" she asked him numbly. She couldn't bear yet to ask about Dan himself.

"I'm not sure, Miss Liberty."

Liberty refused to look at the bodies being lined up, one after another.

"Have they found him?" she asked then, her voice thin and shrill.

"Before you arrived." Ta Wang hung his head. "Master Dan is dead, Miss Liberty."

Liberty screamed. "Take me to him! I just want to see him! I want to see him!"

"But, Miss Liberty," Ta Wang pleaded, "other sections could still come down. . . . And you can't see Master Dan. He's—his body is—" He did not go on. Dan's body had been buried too deeply in the avalanche to be dug out, but he could not bring himself to tell her this.

"I want to go," Liberty cried hysterically. "Something is wrong here! Something is terribly wrong! I want to know everything that has been happening around here lately!"

The engineer of the second work locomotive refused to take Liberty up the cliff until he saw the fire in her eyes. Then, when he was ready to pull out with her and Ta Wang, Charles Crocker swung up into the cabin and demanded to know what was going on. The engineer only nodded back towards his two passengers.

"Mr. Crocker," Liberty stormed, "don't you try to stop me too! I went over these plans with my husband a hundred times and I refuse to believe the wall he wanted built could have just collapsed. Call me a meddlesome wife if you like, but I . . . I . . ." She burst into tears. She knew Dan was dead now; the fact had just hit her with brute force. But she would go on—she had to go on!

"Mrs. O'Lee," he said soothingly, "I'm as troubled as you, because I gave my final approval to the plans. Get rolling, Davis. Ta Wang?"

"All I know, Mr. Cholly, is that Master Dan was down bad sick. Master Randy's been handling the construction crews and following the orders of that federal inspector."

"Federal inspector? I wasn't aware one was here. Must not be too good if he didn't smell out this tragedy before it struck."

He regretted his words the moment Liberty gave him a look of cold hatred. He remained silent until, refusing to go any further, the engineer let them off at a point still a couple of hundred yards from the scene of the disaster.

They were able to walk the rest of the way—at least to that part of the precarious retaining wall which still stood.

Though every moment they remained there was a

moment of danger, it didn't take Liberty long to spot a glaring cause of the wall's collapse. She felt, knocked upon and sniffed at a section of horizontal beam. Stunned, she turned to her companions.

"This is cottonwood. Dan wanted redwood and spruce."

"How can you be sure?" Crocker demanded.

"Mr. Crocker, I was raised in Mississippi. We use cottonwood for fencing there. It's the least durable wood God ever created. Where did this come from, Ta Wang?"

"The mill."

"Was my husband aware of it?"

"As I said, he was down with the chills and fever."

Liberty began to walk along a ledge, ignoring Crocker's warning. "This wall isn't as Dan designed it!" she gasped. "Come here, Mr. Crocker."

"Well, I . . ." he stammered.

"Come here!" she barked, and both he and Ta Wang sprang to join her. "You can't tell me that this is the plan you approved. Look! Those beams are laid against the mountain siding without base supports or anchor pinnings in the back rock." She looked up to the summit. "I can't tell from here, but I'll bet the upper two sections were built similarly. There was nothing to hold them into the mountain! No wonder they came down. This is sabotage and murder!"

Crocker, perturbed by Liberty's accusation, coaxed her out of the danger zone and back down the mountain. While workers were being evacuated from the area, he motioned for Stanford to meet him in the office car.

"Mrs. O'Lee claims that's cottonwood up there, Leland. What did you order sent up?"

Stanford faltered. "What young Porter requested."

"Cottonwood?"

The sequence of events got confused in Stanford's mind. "Yes. As I recall, we had waste material from the rail shipments and he said it would suit this purpose."

It was the first time that day facts would be either altered or omitted so as to make Randy Porter a scapegoat.

Liberty, hearing from Crocker of Randy's culpability, wanted further information and sent Ta Wang in search of him. As she sat waiting, she looked up to see a top hat come bobbing through the massed throng of silently staring Chinese. The top hat was so incongruous among the conical ones the Chinese wore that she stared at it until it came closer and she had a full view of the face beneath it.

"You," she gasped. "Mr. Crocker, this man is—"

Seymour cut her short with a doffing of the top hat, a flourish of documents from its interior, and his own self-styled introduction:

"Colonel Silas Seymour, United States Army, detached to the Federal Railroad Commission as an inspector and at your disposal to report on this unfortunate tragedy that I was in attendance to witness."

"Please step up into the office car," Crocker said. "We'll be most grateful for your eyewitness report."

"I wish to hear it as well," Liberty demanded.

Seymour turned on her archly. "Madam, are you an official of this railroad?"

"No, but I have just lost my husband who was its chief engineer."

"My sympathies," Seymour said briefly, "but my report is confidential."

Liberty tried to protest further, but Crocker whisked the colonel into the office car and slammed the door.

Alone with Crocker, Seymour was determined to

keep his skirts clean, no matter how the investigation progressed.

"Were you here in time to inspect the shoring material before it was used?" Crocker asked him.

"Most assuredly. Cottonwood, I told young Porter. Most undesirable."

"But the construction was allowed to go on with you on the scene."

"Yes, but only after I was assured that the plans had been altered and that this was only a temporary measure."

"Temporary?"

"But, of course! The cottonwood was to be used to hold the mountain in place only until the spring thaw was over and adequate shoring could be installed."

"Who made these changes in the plans?"

"Sir, I can only assume that it was the chief engineer. He was ill and I had only young Porter to act as a messenger boy."

"Did you have any reason to doubt that this temporary shoring would not hold?"

"We have had a few days of very unseasonable warm weather. Who could have counted upon that?"

"But still you let the construction go ahead."

"Oh, no, I strongly advised against it, but young Porter said that Mr. O'Lee insisted. I told him he could build all he wanted, but I would not approve track being laid on that area until a permanent and safe retaining structure was erected. Mr. Porter ignored me and bowed to Mr. O'Lee's wishes."

The scapegoat cloak was growing heavier about Randy's shoulders. Oddly, when Ta Wang brought him, Colonel Seymour was allowed to remain for his questioning and to a degree help Randy make a scapegoat of himself.

"Now, Randy," Crocker said in his best fatherly voice, "we know this has been a devastating day for you. But, first, I would like you to recall when you ordered this material from Mr. Stanford at the mill. After some discussion, Mr. Stanford recalls making a statement to you of this nature—'Now, Randy, does that take care of your problem?'—do you recall that?"

"That was it, sir."

"And you agreed?"

"Yes, sir."

"Fine! Now to the next point."

Cottonwood had never once been mentioned. The assumption was left that Randy was fully aware of what he was ordering and that Leland Stanford was the innocent supplier.

"I understand from Inspector Seymour that changes were made in the original plans. Is that correct?"

"Yes, sir!"

"Do you recall Chief Engineer O'Lee's instructions as to the changes?"

"Yes, sir. He said, 'Just get started and leave me alone.' That's all."

"One final question. May we have the plans?"

"I . . . I . . ." Randy stammered, not really aware of the implications of the question. "They . . . got torn up as I sat and watched that damn mountain come down."

Again he broke down into uncontrollable sobbing. Crocker nodded to Seymour that he had had quite enough questioning. Besides, it was now obvious that the poor lad had been badly used by Dan O'Lee, who had tried a very unfortunate short cut that had resulted in a most unfortunate accident.

Later, Crocker and Stanford agreed that they could not hold Randy fully accountable for following the directives of his superior engineer and were most grateful that Colonel Seymour had been there to witness it all and give them such valuable assistance with his reports. It was hard to face, the two had to admit, but Dan O'Lee, if he'd lived, would have had to shoulder the full responsibility for this terrible accident. They returned to Sacramento believing that Dan had full knowledge of the cottonwood order, had changed the plans and ordered the work over the strong objections of Colonel Seymour.

Seymour went back over the Donner Pass with a glowing sense of triumph. He had taken away not only the man of the woman who had snubbed him, but the Central Pacific's most irreplaceable asset since Ted Judah. And from his interviews at the base camp, he'd obtained still more information that could be used to hamper the construction of the budding railroad.

Liberty left the base camp in a state of utter frustration. Though somewhere in the recesses of her mind she was already mourning Dan, her grief would not surface. She had seen, at the camp, the blandly smiling face of Silas Seymour. Evil had radiated from that face —rank, gross, abysmal evil. Seymour was not a man born of woman; Hell had spawned him. She sensed lies, lies and more lies exuding from him. The investigation may have been completed, as far as Crocker and Stanford were concerned, but it wasn't for her—she would get to the truth if it took the rest of her life.

Remaining at the camp were hundreds of Chinese who believed, like her, in Dan's innocence and waited— silently—for what next the Year of the Snake had in store for them.

Dan's body was never recovered. On the day of a small, commemorative church ceremony, Kai Soong asked for permission to call on Liberty at her home.

"All things are foretold in the stars," he told her. "You may not think so at this moment, but your life is just beginning to bloom and mature."

Liberty was no less distraught than she had been the day of the disaster.

"But they are making it out as though Dan were responsible for the accident," she exclaimed. "I just know that they are wrong."

"Time will give you the answers you seek." Kai Soong said little more, and Liberty did not press him, though a dozen questions came to her mind to ask him. As he kissed her hand on leave-taking, his manner became urgent. "Promise that you'll not press this issue at this time. Your lunar aspects are unfavorable for impulsive behavior. You will only bring upon yourself further grief."

"I'll try," she assured him, and watched him as he left.

Kai Soong's mysterious prediction and warning soon came to fruition. Liberty might have done herself untold harm had she pursued the investigation at that time as energetically as she had intended. Two days after the Chinese sage's visit, her unborn baby began to kick violently in her stomach. The pains were premature, and she winced from them.

"Madam Soo," she gasped. "Please, it's time—send Wang Wu for Dr. Stanley."

Madam Soo and her cook husband quickly helped her to her bed.

It was April first. As the afternoon wore into evening, Liberty began to see irony in the date.

"Quite an April Fool's joke," she grinned, during a moment free from pain.

Dr. Stanley was not laughing. As if the child had a will of its own, it was refusing to be born. By April third Liberty's feet and ankles had swollen double their size and his fears increased. On the fourth, and again on the fifth, he tried without success to induce labor by every means known to him. Liberty's strength ebbed rapidly. Finally, Dr. Stanley quietly informed Madam Soo he would have to perform a caesarean section the next day, but feared its outcome in Liberty's weakened condition.

Madam Soo listened and silently scoffed. She had brought six sons and two daughters into the world and felt the doctor was incompetent.

She sent Wang Wu to the railroad camp to get some opium from Ta Wang to mix with her own blend of herb tea. Liberty recognized the flavor and odor immediately and turned her head away. Madam Soo persisted, almost forcing Liberty to drink several cups of the liquid. Liberty experienced a floating sensation and the drug coursed through her bloodstream and equally quieted the unborn child. For twenty-four hours, mother and child slept soundly. Dr. Stanley, when he found out what had been done, was furious with Madam Soo. He could not move Liberty to the hospital in her state. He left strict instructions that he be sent for the moment she woke up.

Madam Soo ignored the order. At three o'clock on the afternoon of April 6, 1865, she began gently to massage Liberty's belly to awaken the child and make it active. For an hour she continued the massage. At five minutes after four, Liberty came groggily awake just as her water broke.

"Give me a gentle little push, child," Madam Soo whispered.

Two minutes later, within the room and in the street outside, sound erupted simultaneously. In the room, Miranda O'Lee was vociferously announcing to the world that she was there to leave her special mark on it. Liberty was not even aware that she had been born until she heard that cry. Lifting her head to watch Madam Soo sponge the baby, she suddenly became aware of the outside tumult. She could make no sense out of it.

Ping Soo came bustling in with a kettle of steaming water, his dour face masked in a radiant smile.

"War over!" he cried happily. "They say war over!"

Liberty sank back on her pillow and whispered: "And so is mine. I don't want to go through child-bearing ever again."

Then, for the first time, the full truth dawned on her. She had no husband to give her another child. And all the tears that she had been storing up came flooding out. She had no time to feel joy over the ending of the hostilities; she was cleansing her soul and binding up her own wounds.

Selena Tedder stood triumphant. Her sense of victory was unrelated to the celebration taking place in the street. Though it had been going on for nearly three days and was still in progress while Lee surrendered to Grant at Appomattox, Selena was conducting her own surrender terms.

As much as Charles Crocker hated to crawl, he had no choice but to ask Nazareth Tedder to reconsider his letter of resignation.

"What of the Chinese?" Selena demanded.

"Well," Crocker lowered his eyes, "we need their labor to build the trestles, dig the tunnels and get us over the Sierras."

Selena stormed at him, "The war is over! Thousands of soldiers, from both sides, will be in need of that work!"

"But will they come out here to California to do it? That's the big question."

"No, Mr. Crocker, the question is will my husband return to work under the conditions as they now stand."

Crocker's face went taut with bitterness and fury. He could not for the life of him see how a big man like Nazareth Tedder could sit silently and let his wife do all the talking for him. Stanford had demanded Tedder's return at any cost. After what had happened they couldn't put Randy Porter in full charge and Crocker himself didn't have the necessary engineering skills.

"All right," he growled, "here are my terms. If Nazareth comes back at once, I'll start replacing the Chinese as quickly as we can recruit new men from the east. It may take as much as a year, though, you've got to understand."

"And the opium and singsong girls in the meantime?"

Crocker winced in anticipation of the grumbling that would cause. "I'll issue orders against it."

"Then that about settles everything," Selena crowed. She was rid of having to fear Dan O'Lee ever again, fully anticipated that Liberty would soon be departing, and could now begin to work on Nazareth to fire Randy and get him out of Lydia May's life. Moreover, she could take full credit for forcing Crocker to bring about a solution to the Chinese problem. She felt justified in thinking that she was back in full control. She could force her wishes on the Central Pacific in the same manner that she forced them upon her family.

Charles Crocker felt justified in making her promises that he had no intention of keeping. To appease Selena, he did run one recruiting ad in the Sacramento *Union,* but in no other paper. To Ta Wang he issued the following directive:

"Because the smoking of opium pipes and the use of singsong girls have become things of common knowledge, the smoking of opium will henceforth be per-

mitted only on weekends and outside the smell or eyesight of any white men. No singsong girls will be allowed in the Chinese camp unless they are clothed as
any other coolie laborer."

To the foremen of the white crews he issued a directive that contained a self-contradiction:

"Opium and singsong girls are hereafter forbidden in
camp. Any white worker who is caught smoking opium
or buying the favors of a singsong girl will be fired immediately."

Reading the directive, Nazareth thought it best not
to let it fall into Selena's hands. It was obvious that
Crocker was somehow going to let the practices continue, or why else would he have made such an issue of
them to the white crew members? For the moment he
decided to overlook the Chinese and their pleasures.
He'd become much more interested, since his return, in
the issue of Dan O'Lee. Had Dan really been responsible for the cliff disaster? . . . Nazareth received his
answer when the mill foreman couldn't immediately replace the cottonwood order with redwood and spruce.
He demanded to know why and uncovered the truth.
The truth would not bring Dan O'Lee back to life, so
Nazareth, for the moment, kept it to himself and
watched things very closely.

Miranda was eight days old and had the lungs of an
eight-year-old. Liberty could not produce breast milk
fast enough to meet the child's constant demands. A
wet-nurse had to be found, but Miranda already had a
mind of her own and stubbornly refused the strange
nipples.

So the house was in total bedlam when an unexpected
visitor arrived at seven o'clock the morning of April

fifteenth. It was Cloris Flounder, the widow from whom the O'Lees had rented the place.

She gave Wang Wu careful scrutiny, listened to the din cascading down from the second story, thrust the morning newspaper at him and scowled:

"This was cluttering *my* front lawn. Tell Mrs. O'Lee that Mrs. Flounder just arrived on the early morning boat and wishes to see her at once."

"Miss Liberty just have baby. She see no one."

"She will see me at once or pay the consequences!" she declared darkly, and pushed her way toward the parlor.

Wang Wu reluctantly ascended the stairs, reported to Liberty, and descended as if he felt he should have been more of a man in refusing to let this stranger impose upon Liberty's time and strength.

"Miss Liberty," he said coolly, "instructed me to show you to the dining room and offer you breakfast. She will be down shortly."

"I hope she can stop that cacaphony before she descends," Cloris Flounder said acidly, marching on the dining room without Wang Wu showing her the way. "Sounds to me like very spoiled children."

Wang Wu held his silence as he set her a place and poured her coffee. As if the servants were her's, Mrs. Flounder gave careful instructions as to the preparation of her breakfast, then went about inspecting the parlor and dining room furniture. Satisfied that the house was in as good a condition as she had left it, she sat down to sip at her coffee and open the newspaper that Wang Wu had left folded by Liberty's plate.

One look at the black-bordered headline made her sniff and shove the paper away.

"I say good riddance," she said to herself, as Liberty came into the dining room.

"Mrs. Flounder, this is a surprise," Liberty exclaimed.

"Really?" Mrs. Flounder snapped. "Hardly an original statement from someone who is three months in arrears on her rent."

"I beg your pardon?" Liberty gasped.

"Beg it all you wish, but facts are facts. The third year's lease payment was due on January eighth. When it became a month overdue I contacted Mr. Huntington and was informed by his private secretary that they knew nothing about it. Because life was becoming intolerable in the east, I decided to come and check on matters myself. The boat trip was ghastly, so I rested for several days with friends in San Francisco before coming down."

Liberty sank weakly into her chair. She didn't understand it. The yearly lease money had always been paid in advance by Collis Huntington and then, at Dan's insistence, taken out of his monthly pay checks. That a private secretary had been involved, and long before Dan's death, gave Liberty a clue as to Mai Ling's interference.

"I am sure," Liberty said softly, "that an error has been made. Perhaps, Mrs. Flounder, you are not aware of my recent loss."

"Quite aware," she stated. "Why else do you think I came down as soon as I was able to travel? Being a widow myself, I am well aware of how quickly the income vanishes. I can ill afford to grant charity. I need the income on this property."

"You shall have it," Liberty exclaimed. "I shall personally contact Mr. Huntington and see to it that . . ." She stopped in mid-sentence, the glaring headline from the newspaper on the table catching her eye.

"Oh, no!" she wailed. "It can't be true!"

"Mrs. O'Lee," Cloris Flounder insisted, "it is im-material to our discussion at hand."

Liberty ignored her and began to read aloud: "At 7:22 A.M. today (4:22 A.M. Sacramento time) the president of the United States died from a gunshot wound he received in his head last night while attend-ing a performance at the Ford Theatre. Many in this city are suddenly silent with grief for a man they did not like, diligently fought and now greatly miss."

"Mrs. O'Lee," Cloris Flounder said tartly, "I have read the article and hardly need a re-reading. My rent is of more concern to me than that man's fortunate death."

"There is nothing fortunate about any man's death," Liberty said sadly, "especially when his life personally touched your own."

Cloris Flounder knew nothing of Abraham Lincoln ever having touched Liberty's life. She had no qualms about speaking her own mind. "Good riddance, I say, and shall scream from the housetops. He was going to be too easy on the southern states and I say they should be whipped to their knees."

"Haven't they suffered enough?" Liberty asked miser-ably.

Mrs. Flounder sniffed haughtily. "Not when they brought the suffering upon all of us, or don't you agree."

"I was born in the south and married a Yankee, Mrs. Flounder. I have seen both sides of the suffering. I lost a father fighting for one side, and had a husband wounded for the other. Now, I have neither father nor husband, nor do I have a friend I learned to cherish as a great and compassionate person. Please leave me. I shall see that you receive your rent money at once. Just inform me where to have it sent."

Cloris Flounder, unmoved, rose to her feet.

"It needs be sent nowhere," she said coldly. "Now that you announce yourself a friend to Lincoln, I no longer desire you in my home. You shall be gone in three days time or I shall have the authorities throw you into the street. Three days and no more, do you hear!"

Liberty heard and watched her stalk from the house. She sat torn between bewilderment, grief and despair. She didn't have the money for the full year's lease to bargain with, even if Mrs. Flounder had been prone to snatch at such bait. Her immediate inclination was to wire her condolences to Mary Todd Lincoln, who had been one of the first to wire her after the Union Pacific had made sure the accident that killed Dan became national news. She needed advice from Mary Todd. But she couldn't ask for it, not now. Her despair deepened. Dan had always handled their finances; she didn't know where she stood. Not wishing to be beholden to Mrs. Flounder, she went to the room that Dan had used as his office. An hour later, shaken, she called Wang Wu in.

"I must find cheaper accomodations," she said dully, "and I must inform the tong agent that I can no longer afford servants after the end of this month. I am sorry, Wang Wu, but my husband has left me nearly penniless. I must cut back until I figure a way to get myself and children back to my father's plantation."

Again she thought of Mary Todd Lincoln. She, too, after so soon losing her husband, would have to pack and vacate a temporary home.

12

Years earlier Liberty had told a childhood friend that all she wanted in life was "a little cottage in Mississippi and a parcel of children." Now it seemed that's what she would have.

While she was still in Sacramento, Kai Soong refused to let her give up her servants, and she accepted his kind offer to pay them himself. She used most of her cash reserve to pay Mrs. Flounder her three months back rent, thus clearing her conscience on that score. Throughout the spring and summer she repeatedly tried to get a final accounting from Mark Hopkins on what wages were still due Dan. Her notes went unanswered. She grew desperate to learn if there would be enough money to get her back to Mississippi.

Daily, to save cab fees, she would walk to the Associates' office and try to see Hopkins in person. He was always conveniently out. She was also told that Stanford was busy building his new summer home at Palo Alto and Crocker was practically living at the railhead camp. She didn't ask for Collis Huntington; she had no desire to see him whatsoever.

One late August day, emerging from the office, she recognized the Huntington carriage pulling up to the

curb with Collis and Nazareth Tedder in it. Though she
altered her course to avoid a meeting, she was seen by
Collis, whose curiosity was piqued. In the office, he
queried the chief accounting clerk about her:

"Was Mrs. O'Lee just here to see Mr. Hopkins?"

"She was here, sir—is almost daily—but Mr. Hopkins refuses to see her."

"For what reason?"

"I'm afraid you would have to take that up with
Mr. Hopkins, sir."

Collis checked his bitter words. He and Tedder had
come to attend an emergency meeting of the Associates,
which Collis himself had called. Now he motioned for
Nazareth to follow him and barged into Hopkins's
office. Hopkins sat with his lips pulled into a thin
straight line. Leland Stanford stood at the window staring into space as if he'd just been assured by God
Almighty that the end of the world was at hand. Edwin
Crocker sat patting a forefinger nervously against his
lips.

Without a greeting, Collis launched into Hopkins.

"Why are you refusing to see Liberty O'Lee?"

Hopkins blinked, not expecting this particular issue
to be raised and unaccustomed to being shouted at.

"On my orders," Stanford said, turning stiffly. "The
woman keeps demanding an accounting of her late husband's last wages."

"Well?"

"There are none," Hopkins quickly supplied. "The
man's accident cost us a small fortune as it is."

"Am I hearing you correct?" Collis asked in disbelief. "You are refusing to pay out what was due O'Lee
because of our loss?"

"Quite," Stanford snapped. "The accident cost us
a very lucrative lumber contract with the Far East, a

locomotive, and who knows how much delay. Had he lived he would have been fired and sued."

Nazareth Tedder's anger blazed forth. He had held his silence too long.

"What manner of money-grubber are you, Stanford?" he challenged. "You were the one who changed the order from redwood to cottonwood. I have that straight from the mill foreman. When we started to tear down the remaining retainer wall it appeared to me then as if it had been purposely designed to collapse during the spring runoff. I questioned Randy Porter about it closely and found that the changes had been made by that federal inspector while O'Lee was ill. I put it all into a report for you to forward to Washington to have the incompetent ass fired. Didn't you even read my report? How can you stand there and continue to put the blame on O'Lee?"

Stanford took the tongue-lashing coolly.

"I thought it best to destroy your report, Tedder. Enough rumors are circulating about us in Washington without our adding to them by claiming that the military tried to sabotage us. The man is dead; the blame won't hurt him."

"Bastard!" Nazareth spat. "Either you instruct Hopkins to make restitution to Mrs. O'Lee at once, or I'm packing my bags for Washington to expose you and Colonel Silas Seymour."

"Seymour?" Collis exploded. "Jesus Christ, why wasn't I told this before? Stanford, you ass, don't you ever read anything any of us sends you? Seymour has been the acting chief engineer for the Union Pacific since last January. He wasn't even a military inspector when our accident occurred. You're so goddamn dumb you probably didn't even ask to see his papers."

"I will not be talked to in this manner," Stanford stormed.

"It's only the beginning," Collis roared back. "It's your damn big mouth and stupid decisions that have made today's emergency meeting necessary. How in the hell could you have told that *New York Times* reporter that you anticipated that the Central Pacific would be able to reach Salt Lake City during 1870? Why so late?"

"I see nothing wrong with the statement," Stanford said defensively.

"Oh, you don't. But then, you're not building the railroad or having to fight to finance it, are you. Did it ever occur to you to ask the opinion of Charley Crocker, Tedder or even Montague? No, you're too damn bull-headed to look at their plans. You don't see that construction down the Sierras' eastern slope will go right ahead, that we're not going to delay it until the Summit Tunnel is finished. Hell, that will put us into Nevada in '68."

"Tell that to the boys on Wall Street, Leland! Now that I know it was Seymour here it explains the rumor that our difficulties at the tunnel will hold the job up for years. Eighteen-seventy, bah! That so-called cautious estimate of yours is drying up our stock sales, in case you're interested. Durant is making sure that every banker and broker is being leaked the news that your date will all but assure the Union Pacific every bit of trackage across Utah and Nevada to the California line. But that's minor in comparison to what I got in the mail yesterday. Before I read it, Leland, tell me something. Don't you think the decision on the Couch-Fowle steam-powered drill should have been a board action, rather than you turning it down on your own?"

"Now it is you who have your facts incorrect,

Huntington! I was very enthusiastic about that drill and its ability to deliver a blow a second. That's five times faster than a first-rate hammerman can do it. I know that. But Strowbridge argued that we have only one steam-power machine, which will be required to pull the blasted rock out of the central shaft. Using a steam hammer up there would mean switching power off the hoist every time the hammer cut it. I finally had to agree with Strowbridge that it wouldn't work."

Huntington sighed indignantly. "First of all, Strowbridge is an old-fashioned blasting foreman who hasn't had an original idea in years. Second, I think the board should have decided if the purchase of a second steam-power machine might have been the financial answer. But the damage is done. I don't know what you said in your letter to J.J. Couch, but he leaked it to Durant. One of our biggest banking backers sent me the brochure that Durant is circulating on how they will use the labor-saving device to expedite construction through the Rockies. He's broadsiding it that the equipment will help the Union Pacific reach Salt Lake City in 1869, while Leland Stanford, Esq. and his 'Chinese chippers' will still be fighting their way through the Sierras."

"I can hardly be held accountable for the inaccuracies in their brochure."

Huntington ignored him. "Now for the most shocking news. Senator McDougall is greatly concerned over how our falling stock has eroded the faith of our 'friends' in Washington. The Union Pacific has tied President Johnson's hands, even he wanted to help us. Senator Wilson of Massachusetts, who has Crédit Mobilier stock in his wife's name, is successfully bottling up our bill to remove from the Pacific Railroad Act the clauses forbidding us to extend trackage beyond the California-Nevada line. Congress is *not* accepting Lincoln's executive order nullifying those clauses. Johnson *won't* sign a new order. Thanks to all of this rumor and gossip, we're right back where we started and losing ground rapidly."

There was a deathly silence in the room. Only Nazareth Tedder felt a note of elation. These men, Nazareth saw, were getting back exactly what they had been dishing out.

"When do you leave for Washington?" Stanford asked dully.

Huntington started to answer. Then a brilliant thought kept him silent for a few moments while he weighed its advantages and disadvantages.

"I can't possibly get away for two to three months. It will take that long to finalize all the details of the San Francisco city commission's $600,000 bond issue."

"We can handle that," Stanford insisted. "We need you more in Washington."

"No," Collis mused, "that won't work, and you know it. They only agreed to talk to me if I kept you and the Crocker boys out of the picture. But we do need to send someone with experience to Washington as soon as possible."

"Who?" Hopkins demanded. "With all due respect, neither Leland, Edwin nor myself can handle Washington. We don't know the place. You're the only one who does."

"Not really," Collis chuckled. "I'm thinking of someone who helped Johnson gain the vice-presidency and knows her way around Capitol's corridors quite well. Plus the sympathy she'll get as the widow of our late chief engineer should prove to be a mighty potent diplomatic tool."

Stanford gasped. "You can't be serious?"

"But . . . but . . . but . . ." Hopkins's mouth worked like a fish out of water.

Edwin Crocker frowned as he pondered the idea. Given the success Liberty had enjoyed for them in Washington before he thought it an excellent idea.

Nazareth smiled quietly to himself. For five months these vultures had ignored Liberty's pleas. Now they needed her. He prayed they would be sensible enough to vote her the challenge and that she would accept it, for she was exactly the right person to see that his report on Silas Seymour reached Washington.

"I suggest," Collis said softly, "that in addition to what back pay is due her husband, we offer her a year of his wages, in advance, to become our lobbyist. Congress convenes the second week in October. She should be able to make that easily. Mr. President, would you like it put in the form of a formal motion?"

"I do not," Stanford answered acidly. "I think it is absurd and utterly ridiculous."

"But, Leland," Edwin Crocker spoke up at last, and continued to speak, for ten minutes without interruption, on Liberty's proven abilities.

"Mark?" Collis demanded, when Edwin gave up the floor.

Hopkins shrugged. "You boys know how I hate to play poker with you—it takes me too much damn time to decide whether to draw to an inside straight or not. But I think Collis has just dealt us four cards of a royal flush and for once I'm willing to gamble on the fifth card being there."

"That makes it three, Leland."

"Then let it stand at that," Stanford said sourly. "The chair does not wish to vote on this matter."

* * *

Collis was amazed not to find Liberty at the Flounder house. It took him an hour, using the houseboy grape-vine, to find her new location—a far smaller cottage Wang Wu had found for her. His first words were an apology for the clerical error that had been made in her rent not having been paid.

Though he did not say so in so many words, Liberty soon figured out who had actually been responsible for the so-called error and why. She did not comment on the matter. Nor did she comment, or offer any form of hospitality, as Collis outlined the new proposal from The Associates. As badly as she needed the income, she refused to make a snap decision or even say when she might be ready to give him an answer.

To sweeten the deal, Collis tried a ploy that sickened her.

"I've been thinking about that Union Pacific stock that we bought in your name, Liberty. I'm astonished that Durant hasn't called for the other ninety percent due on it. By the time you meet him in New York for us, it should be about double what I paid for it. Sell it, return my investment, and keep the profit for yourself as a bonus."

The words "blood money" popped into Liberty's mind. She sensed they knew now that Dan had been killed and were trying to buy her off.

With cool reserve, she thanked Collis for the offer and showed him to the door of the cottage. She felt like spitting in his face.

Minutes after she returned to her tiny living room another knock came at the door. Thinking it was Collis with still another inducement, she waved Wang Wu away and went to answer it herself.

"Nazareth!" she exclaimed, completely taken aback.

"Liberty," he said sheepishly, "I hope I'm not intruding on your thoughts. I've been walking this street for twenty minutes, waiting for Collis' carriage to leave."

"Oh," she said, raising her brow, "you were aware it was his carriage?"

"More than that. I was at the meeting when your proposal was discussed."

Liberty thought. "Oh. Well, come in, Nazareth, but watch your head. This house was built more for people more the size of the Chinese than for us."

Nazareth looked around and smiled. He felt instantly at home. "This is a pioneer house built in the forties. It has the same floor plan as our log cabin in Tennessee. I admire your taste."

"Thank you," Liberty laughed. "Unfortunately, it's housing three servants and three children, and my taste is turning a bit sour."

She suddenly realized that this was the first time she had laughed in months. She also became aware that she was remiss in some duties she should have performed a long time ago.

"Have a seat, Nazareth," she said softly. "I—I'm afraid I've been a little tardy in thanking you for the flowers you sent when Dan died."

It was a subject Narazeth had hoped would not come up. He hesitated. "We differed on many points, Dan and I," he answered truthfully, "but I still admired him for many of his qualities . . ."

His words trailed off. Liberty was relieved; his simple silence was sufficient and she appreciated it. But Nazareth was thinking of how near he came not to attending the funeral. He had been resentful of Dan until he had seen the look of triumph on Selena's face when she learned of his death. The look alone had troubled, then moved him profoundly. He came to realize that Dan could have spoken out about Selena's past at any time during his three years in Sacramento, but had kept a gentlemanly silence. He liked to think that Dan's silence was out of respect to him. He had attended the funeral as a form of asking forgiveness from the man.

Without comment he handed Liberty his handwritten report on the accident. She scanned the pages. As he watched her bewilderment, alarm, then blind fury, he could almost feel the powerful will of Dan O'Lee enter the cottage and urge his wife to use the weapon that had been placed in her hands to free his name from guilt.

"What do you wish for me to do with this?" Liberty asked hesitantly.

"Get it into the hands of the proper authorities. The man is a murderer."

"Five months," Liberty said vacantly. "Why did it take so long for the truth to be uncovered?"

Nazareth said tensely, "Leland Stanford destroyed my original report. He'd probably find some way to keep a second one from reaching Washington. You're my only hope."

Liberty was perplexed. "Why, Nazareth? Why are you doing this now?"

Again, Nazareth hesitated. Once more he was being asked to speak on a subject he would have preferred not to discuss. Yet, searching himself, he found he had few qualms about sharing his innermost secrets with Liberty; somehow he trusted her. Slowly, then with growing determination, he told her of his early affair with Selena, of Lydia May's birth, of Selena's amorous adventures in the gold rush during her long separation from him. He mentioned Dan only as being a gentleman in not fully revealing the role he himself had played in Selena's past.

They were silent for some little time after Nazareth had finished speaking.

"I hope you don't mind my revealing so much of what has for so long been my so painful burden," Nazareth said then. "Dan might have revealed it to my enemies. He didn't. He was a remarkable man, Liberty. I—" He did not go on.

"I see," Liberty said. "Yes. Dan was remarkable . . . in many respects." She looked at him brightly as tears welled in her eyes. "I thank you for telling me this, Nazareth. I'm glad you felt you could trust me. You can, you know." She patted his hand, then fell silent again, lowering her head to think. When she raised it a few moments later, Nazareth saw that her tears were gone and that there was now a harder light in her eyes.

"I will take your report to Washington," Liberty said quietly. "I will also do whatever else I can for the railroad. I feel Dan would have wanted it that way. As for the rest of our conversation, I intend to forget it the minute you walk out the door. Thank you, Nazareth . . . again."

As Nazareth walked home, he felt himself walking taller and more freely than he had in years. He felt as if he had rid his mind of a ghost and that it would never come back to haunt him again.

Liberty found Washington a changed city now that the war had ended. No longer a tense fortress, it had become a rich and noisy haven for carpetbaggers, fortune seekers, con-artists and corrupt politicians now turning to a new and more promising form of the shell game. Freed slaves roamed the streets, having been told to come to Washington and ask for whatever they desired. Long lines of lobbyists snaked out of every governmental office seeking to dip into the golden pot left after the south's defeat.

After Lincoln's assassination Washingtonians had calmly accepted Andrew Johnson as the man to stabilize the government, but after seven months the air reeked with hatred for him. The new president did not live up to corrupt expectations. He gave a straightforward, honest "no" to every politician seeking greedy gain from the Union's victory. Liberty found not the railroad but the "reconstruction of the south" the central topic at all receptions and dinner parties. Because Johnson was not thought hard enough on the south on certain issues, he was being denounced as a usurper, tyrant and dictator. Because he was thought too harsh on other issues, he was being denounced in the same terms.

Liberty tried to be the person she had been here before, but her life too had changed. Her husband was gone, and so was that unusual man in the White House who had been such a warm friend and adviser to her. She felt a bit lost in the new bustle. Now she was more timid in asking for appointments, let alone favors. She was alone. She had no one to share her triumphs or failures with when she returned to the Willard Hotel each evening.

Her widowhood, which Collis Huntington had thought would work in her behalf, turned out to be detrimental to her. Before she had been a sexually attractive woman who was understandably out of bounds. Now she was fair game for every lecherous old power-broker who desired to pinch, feel or blatantly make his crude desires known to her.

October melted into November and December and still she was mostly appointmentless and frustrated. Time and time again she would sit alone in her hotel room and scoff at the words Kai Soong had uttered when he saw her off at the boat landing in San Francisco:

"It shall be a long journey with few immediate answers, young friend, but vastly rewarding when the end comes in sight."

Liberty had received few immediate answers indeed. The Department of the Army, because of Colonel Seymour's resignation, would not heed the allegations she wished to lodge against him. The railroad commission would not even inform her if he had been assigned to them as an inspector. Senators would not discuss the railroad bill revision with her unless she cared to talk it over in their private apartments, and her repeated efforts to see the president were being short-circuited somewhere between the White House and she didn't know where. Confused, frustrated, nearly bored to death, she wired Collis Huntington that the picture was growing blacker by the minute. Could he help? What should she do?

Huntington wired back five pages of such carefully detailed instructions that they made California's Senator McDougall laugh when Liberty shared them with him.

"It would seem," he chuckled, "Mr. Huntington has given you a license to do anything but kill. When do you want to tackle the state delegation?"

"At once," she said with new-found determination. "Time is running short and I, too, would like to go home when Congress adjourns for Christmas."

"As the senior senator I'll gather them together for lunch. But bear in mind that we have opposition within our own ranks."

The opposition melted away by the conclusion of the lunch. Liberty had narrowed her attack on two men—California's junior senator, whose home was in

San Francisco, and the congressman from that district. And attack them she did—in a most vulnerable spot.

"It would seem," she declared bitingly, "that the city commission was a little fearful to make a decision on their own and placed the bond issue before the so-called skeptical citizens of San Francisco. To the amazement of all, except the people of the Central Pacific, it passed overwhelmingly in last week's election. Now, as you both face rather stiff re-election challenges in 1868, Mr. Huntington would like to know what the Central Pacific can do to help you."

It was quite obvious that the two delegation leaders would first have to do something for the Central Pacific, but the implication was there that in the future they would not find Collis Huntington unwilling to listen to their own needs, financial or otherwise.

For the first time, the entire California delegation became a well-coordinated lobbying force for the Central Pacific. They had crucial votes to trade and Liberty had sheaves of U.S. currency to help them where vote trade-offs didn't work.

As moderate Republicans, far from the south and its problems, the Californians had not really feared the seating of the new southern congressmen—as, for example, the radical Republicans of the northeast did. But in both the Senate and House, the Californians now electrified the radicals by casting their votes with them. Now the radicals were in debt to California—even if they were reluctant to pay that debt by revising the Railroad Act.

On another battlefront, Congress had throughout early December pushed through a series of bills that President Johnson had immediately vetoed. On many of these bills the California delegation had been split. Since in most cases their votes were needed to override the veto, they were clearly in the driver's seat.

Liberty and Senator McDougall studied each of these bills carefully. They did not want a California vote changed unless it would eventually force open the hand of Senator Henry Wilson. Taking his orders directly from Durant, it was Senator Wilson who was still refusing to let the revised railroad act out of his committee.

Reluctantly, Wilson agreed to meet Liberty and Senator McDougall for lunch in a secluded Washington cafe. Hurting from the lobbying efforts directed by Collis Huntington, he still felt confident that he could charm any woman and he saw McDougall as a bumbling westerner. He found Liberty to be a hard nut to crack and McDougall foxier than he had thought. Finally, he was forced to reveal why he had been keeping the act in committee.

First he read them a letter from President Dix protesting that the Central Pacific's determination to press eastward from Nevada would jeopardize the Union Pacific.

"As Dix explains," Wilson said, "negotiations are well underway for a $20,000,000 loan from English, German, and French bankers. They have been led to believe that the Union Pacific would be laying the trackage through Utah and Nevada. Until that loan is secure, I don't want the revision coming to the floor. After that, it might be possible."

"And only the members of your committee know of this letter, Senator Wilson?"

"Naturally, madam. Any leakage on it could jeopardize the loan."

"I am curious as to how knowledge of it will not affect another provision of the act once it does come to the floor for debate."

"I'm afraid I don't follow you, Mrs. O'Lee."

"Because the eastern manufacturers did not want

foreign competition, they made sure that the act stipulated that all materials used in the construction of the Pacific railroads had to be made in the United States. I cannot help but wonder if the American bankers are not going to raise a howl over the Union Pacific purchasing those materials with pounds, francs and marks."

Wilson blinked at her in astonishment. In the months of hearing on the revisions that point had never been raised. He quickly recognized it as a torpedo that, if successfully launched, would sink the Union Pacific with the American financial institutions.

"Well . . . I . . ." he stammered, "it is getting late and I do have a personally sponsored bill coming before the Senate this afternoon."

"Ah, yes," McDougall said, leaning forward with interest, "and I haven't let you have a moment to lobby me on it, Henry."

Wilson laughed. "I anticipate little trouble with it, senator. After all, it is in the best interest of the nation to keep the Boston naval shipyard in operation. The war may be over, but the navy is in sorrowful condition and in need of almost a whole new fleet."

"Oh, I couldn't agree with you more," McDougall said expansively. "And the $40,000,000 price tag will keep a lot of your ship-fitter constituents happy all the way to the polls. Of course, it's not making the people of Baltimore or New York or Portsmouth very happy that their naval yards are being closed down. We've got a small ship builder in Oakland, you know. Now, he didn't get any war contracts, of course, but it sure seems to me it would be a whole lot cheaper to build ships for a Pacific fleet on the west coast. Oh," he added with devilish glee, "I think I forgot to mention Philadelphia, Henry. Lot of grumbling in the cloakroom, Henry. A lot of grumbling."

"Is this your way of telling me that you are going to stand in opposition to my bill?"

McDougall sat back, took a tally sheet from his inside coat pocket and slid it across the table.

"These are votes due me, Henry, whenever I decide to call them in. You might note that about half of them are ones that you are counting on today."

Wilson turned scarlet with rage. "You do that, and I shall personally see to it that the revision act never gets out of committee."

"Henry," McDougall said soothingly, "isn't it about time you stopped worrying about a $20,000,000 loan that Durant will never be able to swing and just make sure that Boston keeps its naval yard and $40,000,000 in work and prosperity?"

Wilson refused to comment. He even refused to share a carriage with them back to the Capitol. When the Wilson Naval Rearmament Bill came up for a vote, the two senators from California remained off the floor with five of their colleagues—but within hearing distance to keep a running tally sheet. Only when the Speaker, on the second roll call, had the clerk call out the names of the absent senators did the seven men enter and take their seats. It was clear to Wilson that victory or defeat rested in those seven votes. He caved in and nodded his agreement to McDougall. He had won for Boston, but lost for Durant.

Three days later the Central Pacific measure passed. The restrictions on its construction were lifted.

"Now comes the real battle," McDougall advised. "Johnson has already said that he will veto the bill. I don't think we can muster enough votes to override."

"If I could just get to him," Liberty cried in frustration. "I'm denied appointments, my notes go unanswered. Malcolm, who in the White House is purposely trying to keep me away from him?"

"Lord, child, I thought you knew. Besides Wilson, who was doing the most screaming against us on the floor today?"

"Senator Patterson."

"My dear, D.T. Patterson is not only the senator from Tennessee, he is Martha Johnson's husband. The good senator lives in the White House and acts as if he himself were the president rather than his son-in-law. In the war he was an aide to Grenville Dodge, which might enlighten you as to where he got his information to parrot the Union Pacific's every request." Then he smiled. "But I think I know a way we can slip you into the White House without his even knowing it. The bill won't reach the president's desk until day after tomorrow, so give me till then to work things out. You get one of your prettiest gowns ready."

Helen McDougall was quite pleased with her husband's plan. It meant that she could go home to California for a Christmas visit with her mother, something she infinitely preferred to another dreary Washington ball. She made plans immediately to take the train to St. Joseph's and the Hollander Overland Stage from there. It would be a hard journey, but well worth it.

It was quite a different White House that Liberty entered for the president's annual Christmas reception for the leaders of Congress. For one thing, much of the Lincoln furniture had been replaced. For another, two families rather than one now resided there.

On the reception line in the main entrance hall were the Johnsons' two surviving sons, Robert and Andrew, and a daughter, Mrs. Mary Stover. A third son, Charles, and Mary's husband had both been killed during the war. Next came Senator Patterson and his wife Martha, who was acting as the official hostess for the evening.

Senator Patterson took one look at the woman Senator McDougall had on his arm and quickly whispered to his wife. Martha, normally a charming and dignified person, reacted as if she'd been struck. Snapping at her sister Mary to take over her duties, she walked briskly over to Liberty and the senator and practically demanded that they follow her into the Green Room.

"What is the meaning of this?" she said angrily, once she had the doors closed.

"Meaning?" Malcolm McDougall said innocently. "My wife has departed for home and Mrs. O'Lee is a constituent who is in town."

"I'm well aware of who she is, senator, and of the reason you have brought her along. I wish for you both to leave at once!"

"Leave?" McDougall echoed. "Mrs. Patterson, I was invited here by the president of the United States. Only he can make such a request of me."

Martha turned on Liberty, her eyes flaring. "Madam, if you have any decency at all, which I strongly doubt, seeing the way you have been flaunting your body and money around Washington of late, you will kindly leave before your presence becomes a scandal and a slap in the face to my mother."

Liberty's temper rose instantly to the surface. "I am going nowhere, Mrs. Patterson," she said hotly, "until you explain the reasons behind those unwarranted remarks."

Martha Johnson Patterson eyed her. "My mother is an invalid," she said crisply. "She has been for some twenty years. At first, when my father told her of how you'd helped him get the nomination for the vice-president, she was grateful to you and admired you. We soon heard, however, exactly how it was that my father came into Mr. Lincoln's favor. The gossip hurt my mother. She is too much of a lady to discuss such a matter with my father, but it hurt her badly. Madam, you may have warmed the bed of one president and the bed of a prospective vice-president, but you shall not have a return engagement now that he is president!"

Liberty was aghast.

"I have never been confronted by such an insidious lie in my life!" she stormed. "I want facts and I want them quickly, or I shall turn this into a night that will find its way into the history books."

"Facts?" Martha sneered. "You will just keep lying to cover up your whorish ways."

Liberty's arm and hand automatically shot out and caught Martha with a stinging blow to the cheek. The young woman was so shocked that her mouth opened, but no words came forth.

"That wasn't for what you called *me*," Liberty said darkly. "It was for defaming the name of President Lincoln and your own father."

"You can't deny the facts," Martha cried. "I have the evidence from an eyewitness. Two years ago my father had dinner in your suite at the Willard and he did not emerge until after breakfast the next day."

Liberty frowned, trying to recall. Then she began to laugh.

"Oh, you silly goose, you should have checked your facts more carefully. Your father did have dinner with my husband and myself and Collis Huntington in our suite, and he did stay the night. But he stayed because of the blizzard that came down during the evening."

Martha scoffed. "That's easy for you to claim, what with your husband dead and Mr. Huntington not here to back you up."

"Then why not ask the other member of the dinner party?" Liberty insisted, through clenched teeth. "You may not, but I trust your father not to lie."

"Lie about what?" a stern voice said behind them.

Andrew Johnson entered from the Blue Room, thinking to pass quickly through the Green Room and get into the back of the East Room reception area without fanfare. He saw Liberty as she turned to face him, and his darkly handsome face broke into a quizzical smile.

"Well, well," he chuckled, "if it is not the mystery lady who ignores repeated invitations from the man she helped place in the unfortunate position of president."

"Father, D.T. and I thought it best and had your invitations destroyed," Martha quickly explained.

Johnson frowned. "Martha, I am beginning to resent the authority that you and your husband have assumed for yourself. But that is a family matter I shall discuss with the two of you privately. Now, what is this matter all about?"

"It doesn't concern you, father," Martha said piously.

President's daughter or not, Liberty was not about to let her brush the matter aside so casually.

"Well, it concerns me and my reputation," she emphasized. "Your daughter has accused me of having had an affair with you the night you stayed in our suite during the blizzard."

"Oh, Martha," he said sadly, "must you forever grab onto every rumor born in this town and try to protect me from it? Sometimes I think you really want them to be true, so that you will have a real sword to hold to my throat. Senator McDougall, by your presence, I would gather I have you to thank for bringing Mrs. O'Lee here. Now, I would ask a further favor of you, sir. Please escort my daughter into the East Room, so that I might have a private word with Mrs. O'Lee."

"No!" Martha spat. "I shall not leave you alone with this woman!"

"Martha! I am speaking as the president and not as your father! Either you do as I say, or you and your husband will be out of this house by midnight!"

Martha did not move. She stood glaring back at him, her large nostrils flaring in defiance.

McDougall shrugged. "I would rather go in by myself, if it's all the same."

He opened the door to the noise of the reception, confident that he had done his part in getting Liberty next to the president.

Andrew Johnson took Liberty by the arm and steered her to the door to the main hallway. Martha tried to follow, but he closed the door firmly in her face, then escorted Liberty quickly along the hall, up the back stairs and forward again to the pink and blue Queen's Room, which had become a favorite of the wheelchair-bound Eliza McCardle Johnson. Almost roughly he propelled Liberty into the room and up to the small woman seated before the marble fireplace.

"Mother," he said proudly, "I've brought someone up from the party to meet you. This is Mrs. Dan O'Lee, whom you've heard me refer to as Liberty in the past."

Eliza Johnson's dark eyes misted with tears. She refused to look up. "Andy, how could you?" she whispered miserably.

"To scotch rumors, dear, and to bring together the two women who have played vital roles in my life at various times. I want each of you to be able to hold your heads high above the gutter politics of this town and realize that you both had been the victims of a campaign to throw mud at me. It seems to have missed me, but slapped you both in the face and made you enemies without meeting. I'll not stand for that.

Now, let's all sit and get Martha's rumors settled once and for all."

Eliza McCardle Johnson, an ex-schoolteacher, had a knack for sizing people up quite rapidly, and she instinctively found an honest person in Liberty, which gave her comfort and pleasure.

Bound by her world of the wheelchair, she was thoroughly enjoying this break in her mundane life when Martha came flouncing into the room indignantly.

"I will not allow you to insult me one moment further," she declared icily to her father. "It is already a half-hour past the time you were to meet your guests."

"Martha," her mother scolded, "where are your manners? Can you not see that your father and I are also entertaining a guest?"

"Mother, are you fully aware of who you are entertaining?"

"Quite," Eliza said simply. "A lady like I always hoped you would someday become."

Martha's face stung from the words as much as it had from Liberty's slap. Wordlessly, she turned and fled.

"I suppose I should descend into the lion's den," Johnson informed his wife.

"Yes," she sighed, "but, Liberty, will you call again?"

"I would love to, but I also would love to be on my way home as soon as possible."

"What's to detain you, child?"

Liberty decided quickly that honesty was the best policy with this sharp-minded woman. "Waiting to see whether your husband is going to veto the revision of the Pacific Railroad Act."

"Andy?"

The President scowled. "D.T. informs me that they

don't have enough votes to override my veto, if I make it. It would be my first victory."

"Nonsense," Eliza snorted. "It would be your first real defeat. Why, Andy Johnson, after we were married you used to leave me and walk four miles to debate, you so loved the competition of it. Competition, husband! That's what this country needs to stir its blood again. Let these two railroads fight it out to the last mile to prove who can get there first. But if this dear child has anything to do with it, I would advise you to put all your money on her." Then she winked at Liberty. "He'll sign the bill, child, or I'll cut off his bedroom privileges."

Liberty couldn't help but laugh at the wry joke. It was quite obvious that these had been cut off throughout the twenty years she'd been an invalid. But she also cherished the woman for letting her know slyly that she was held blameless for any rumor connecting her with the president.

In the hallway, President Johnson suddenly veered to the left.

"Come," he said, "I want you to see something that may have caused some of the thoughts to enter my daughter's head."

Liberty gasped the moment she entered the bedroom and viewed the bed.

"We now call it the Lincoln bedroom," he said solemnly. "As you may have heard we had a bit of trouble getting Mrs. Lincoln to vacate the White House. I finally turned matters over to Martha, who, you have learned, can be a trifle brutish in her approach. Mrs. Lincoln insisted that no one else use this bed because it had become special to her, her husband, and a very special woman in his life who had helped pick it out of a pawnshop in New York. I'm sure Martha must have gotten your name of Mrs. Lincoln and has been adding things wrongly ever since."

Liberty touched the footboard as if the bed were a shrine. "It is inconceivable that anyone could picture him with anyone but his wife."

"Does that apply to me too?" He took a step forward and stopped. "I am just fifty-eight, Liberty, but I have been surrounded by rumors since I was thirty-eight. Only once in my life did I wish that the rumors were true. What would have happened if we could have been alone in the Willard suite that night?"

"Nothing," she said hesitantly.

"You're a widow now," he said pointedly.

"Yes, I am," Liberty answered. Disbelief surged to her mind. In a subtle way she was actually being propositioned by one president of the United States in a former president's bedroom. Then she added, firmly: "but you are not a widower!"

Johnson chuckled and then roared with delight. "If I didn't have so much faith in William Seward as secretary of state, I'd set this damn town on its ear by naming you to the position. Come, let's join the party."

"Please," Liberty begged off, "I would just as soon not have to confront your daughter for a third time tonight. I'll just have Senator McDougall's carriage take me back to the hotel."

"I'll agree on one condition."

"What is that?"

"That you come back here tomorrow."

"For what purpose?"

"Two, actually. First, to have lunch with Eliza and me and then to come into the oval office and watch me sign your beloved little bill into law."

Without hesitation Liberty stepped forward and

kissed him on the lips. The kiss did not call forth an embrace from Andrew Johnson. He took it for what it was—a much-cherished expression of genuine gratitude.

The next afternoon, feeling she had a mandate from Congress and the president, Liberty took a train to New York to see Durant. She hoped to make him agree to a junction point for the railroads in short order, so that she could be on her way back to California within a few days.

That hope was dashed by the news that Durant, Robert Porter and Silas Seymour had left for Omaha on the same day that the vote on the revision act had been announced. Liberty was irritated at having missed Durant, but now felt she had contributed enough to the cause. Something should be left for Collis Huntington to get done. She was growing very tired and homesick, and she wired that sentiment to Collis.

Huntington, untouched by the Christmas spirit, wired back coldly: "Bill revision great. Very busy on this end. Track Durant down."

Liberty felt put upon. In no way was she going to track Durant anywhere. She was even too exhausted at the moment to pursue the Seymour matter. She needed a rest before she could go on. She took a cab from her hotel to the train depot to wire Huntington from there that she was coming home on the next ship out.

She found the telegraph office at the depot packed with people trying futilely to get messages off in time for the holidays. A sign over the wire cage explained what the problem was:

"Due to Holiday traffic no wires received today can be delivered in less than 3/days—Eastern Seaboard;

5/days—Mid-America; 7-10/days—West of Missis-sippi." The sign-painter had added a wry touch at the bottom: "Wish them a Merry Christmas anyway, but don't mention the year."

Liberty, sighing, started to walk to the end of a long line. Suddenly, her eye was caught by the call board of a train scheduled to depart in two hours.

"Penn-Cen. RR: To: Scranton, Pittsburgh, Colum-bus, Cincinnati. Conn. with Ohio Valley RR: To: Covington, Louisville, Paducah, Memphis. Track 3. 4:10 PM."

The magic word had been Memphis. On an im-pulse, Liberty fought her way through crowds to a ticket window.

"Please," she begged, "if one were to take the trains listed there to Memphis, is there a line open to Corinth, Mississippi?"

The clerk studied his schedules.

"I believe," he said, "that the Georgia-Alabama-Mississippi line is operating again between Atlanta, Birmingham and Memphis."

"Good. That goes through Cornith. How much would it be for a one-way ticket from New York to Cornith?"

Now the clerk had to go into an entirely different set of books and do some arithmetic to figure it out. People behind Liberty, wishing only local commuter tickets, began to grumble and moan.

"That will be $25.80," he finally announced, tri-umphantly. "One-way, of course."

Liberty gasped in disbelief. "That is a horrible amount of money."

Someone at her side laughed derisively. "Really, Mrs. O'Lee, coming from your mouth that's almost a joke."

Liberty turned and saw a clean-cut young man who had sidled up to her.

"I beg your pardon. Have we met?"

"Hey, lady, buy your ticket or please get out of the way."

"Excuse me," Liberty stammered, opening her purse and purchasing the ticket hastily.

"No, we haven't met," the young man said, steering her out of the line, "I'm Carl Howard of the *Gazette*. You're a hard woman to trace down."

"Harder still, Mr. Howard, for now I must go and pack to catch a train."

"Oh, no you don't," he said firmly. He kept her arm in a steely grip. "I've worked too damn long and hard to corner you and get the truth. I'd like to know how much money you used to get that bill passed against the Union Pacific."

Liberty calmly freed her arm from the reporter's grasp, her eyes narrowing to pinpoints. She was angry at his intrusion, but had been carefully instructed by Huntington on how to handle the press at this stage. She aped the sarcastic answer Huntington might have given:

"I'm surprised to hear you speak in that way of the elected officials in Washington, young man. But I will be frank with you, and tell you that I brought from California a half-million dollars with the intention of using every dollar of it."

"And you're complaining about a twenty-five dollar train ticket?"

"Now we are speaking of my own personal money, Mr. Howard. That I watch most carefully, which I am sure is true in your case when you are not on your expense account. Good day, sir."

Actually, Liberty hadn't had a half-million available for lobbying purposes, but that was what Collis had wished her to imply and she had never had a chance to bring it out before.

She had bought the train ticket in a rush, and now she rushed back to her hotel to pick up her luggage. She felt that if she could not be in California with her children for Christmas, she could at least be back home on the plantation for the holidays.

As the night coach rattled across the Pennsylvania farm lands, she was not aware she had given an interview to a muck-raking reporter prone, at times to exaggeration. The morning *Gazette* headlined:

POLITICAL RR SCANDAL
CP Spends Millions to
Revise Pacific RR Act

The news was immediately wired to Thomas Durant in Omaha, who cryptically wired back the *Gazette* publisher, a personal friend and backer of the UP:

"Kill RR Scandal story. Our neck in noose if any investigation started now."

Publisher Harrison Davidson was not the kind of man who blithely took orders from the cut of a Thomas Durant. Immediately, he wired his old friend Senator Henry Wilson to ascertain the truth in his reporter's story. Wilson backed Durant. He shot back a two-word reply:

"All poppycock!"

An amazed Carl Howard found himself fired from his job. For seven years he would scrape together a minimal living on weekly newspapers, while continuing his private more sober investigations of the railroads. In 1873 he would be instrumental in breaking open the Crédit Mobilier scandal—but that was later, much later.

*   *   *

"Gone, Miss Libby!"

Liberty felt that if she heard that dreadful word one more time she would cry anguished tears. Home wasn't what it had been. The south she knew no longer existed.

"Your aunt, Miss Libby? She's gone. Died two years back."

"Her children?"

"Gone! Don't rightly know where, though."

"I just want to go home. Does Lem Parker still have the livery?"

"No, ma'am, gone, too. Carpetbaggers done forced him out for taxes and gibben his place to niggers."

Liberty recognized the big black man behind the forge at once. "Samuel, it's me, Liberty Wells. How are things at the Carleton plantation?"

"Ain't rightly knowin'," he said indifferently. "Gone from dere since freedom day."

"I need to hire a buggy and horse, Samuel."

He looked around hesitantly. "Ain't got none fur yah." Insolently he turned his back and went back to his anvil.

Liberty had come face to face with the 'freed' south and didn't like what she was seeing. The streets of Cornith were chocked full of loudly dressed black men who, under the urging of equally loudly dressed northern carpetbaggers and in the name of freedom, were behaving uncivilly to people they had known and worked for all their lives.

Worse, Liberty herself was vilified as a traitor. Whites who remembered her as having "run way with a Yankee soldier" slammed doors in her face, or crossed the street to avoid her approach. The hotel and boarding houses were mysteriously full for the night. Friends from her past were gone as surely as were her father and aunt.

Unable to rent transportation at any of the three liveries, she set off unhappily to walk the miles to Back Trail, where, even if she arrived at midnight, she knew she could find a bed.

Some distance along a dusty country road, a farm wagon passed her, then came to a hesitant stop.

"Miss Liberty, am dat ya'all a walkin' thar?"

Liberty shielded her eyes against the setting sun.

"Lord-a-mercy," she gasped. "Nathaniel, is that really you? Am I ever glad for a horse and wagon! My feet are beginning to kill me. Please take me home."

"Yas'um," he said. He was frowning deeply as she clamored up into his old cart.

The sight of Nathaniel, who had been one of her father's foremen, brought Liberty some reassurance that not all of home was lost. As if a dam had burst she began to chat freely, asking him of his family, of the families still around, and of Back Trail. The old black's answers tended to be uninformative, however, as if he were trying to keep something from her.

Liberty's chatter ceased abruptly on a puzzled note.

"Nathaniel, did we take a wrong turn? We should be on the Carleton land."

"Am, missy."

"Nonsense. Darrin Carleton always prided himself on his acres of oaks. These are plowed fields."

"Oaks gone, Miss Libby. Union soldiers done chop 'em all down back about eighteen-and-sixty-three."

"But the house! Where is their lovely old house?"

"Gone, missy. Ole Mistah Carleton done burn it down last spring when dey went to take it away for de taxes he done owed."

Taxes! During her youth in Cornith, Liberty had never been faced with the need to pay taxes. She knew little about them. She had no idea of how tax matters now stood at the plantation.

"The taxes," she asked hesitantly, "how were they handled for Back Trail?"

It was a heavy question. The old man had prayed he would not have to face it.

"By the new law," he said evasively.

Liberty didn't understand. She was about to question him further when she recognized the towering magnolia tree ahead. That was the boundary line for Back Trail. Her heart leaped in anticipation of the crest of a rise just ahead, from which she would be able to look down on the land of her youth once again.

Nathaniel pulled the horse to a slow stop at the crest and sat silent and forlorn. Liberty looked down on the valley with utter disbelief. It might just as well have been a foreign land that she beheld.

Gone was the two-storied brick house with its four white columns and shadowed veranda. Gone were the barns and stables. Gone were the slave huts. Gone as well were the chickens and cows and horses and pigs and quacking geese in the mill pond.

Replacing Back Trail's beauty and sweep was a checkerboard of fences dividing it precisely into two-and-one-half acre farm plots. On each plot sat a shanty, made mostly of Back Trail's brick and timber.

"Most folk are gone, missy," Nathaniel said softly. "Army took over afta they won and we got word of Colonel Wells's death. They say we all gonna get forty acress and a mule. Yah see what we got. No mules in sight, as yet."

So much sacrifice, so much waste. . . . Liberty had a sense of inadequacy. Who could be blamed for what had happened to Back Trail? No me, everyone. She had loathed the slave system, but this was not a responsible replacement for it. A plantation had thrived here, with a dynamic, inter-related life of its own. These individual little units would dry to dust and blow away. In to rush to rid the south of slavery, the north had unwittingly brought about as grim a master —poverty.

Liberty turned her back on the sight. She could never come home, because there was no home to return to. Home from now on would be only a memory— good or bad, depending on the moment she thought of it.

Silently, she slid down from Nathaniel's farm wagon and started back toward town on foot. The old man knew better than to offer her a ride.

He had seen many Mississippi women suffer disillusionment in the last few years. No old nigger could help them lick their wounds. They were mostly good folks, he thought, and Miss Liberty was one of the best—but they, just like him, were going to have to learn to face the new day.

13

A shooting war had ended in the south, but not in the west. As Liberty sadly made her way to Omaha, the army's massacre at Sand Creek of over six hundred Cheyennes was provoking new, fierce Indian raids across the plains. In one cold winter week alone, Sioux and Arapaho raiders burned Julesburg, attacked four army posts, and ambushed a large wagon train near Fort Bent. Scalping knives dripped blood again—and railroad workers were not immune.

Silas Seymour seemed hardly phased by the Indian menace. Working for the Union Pacific now, he seemed in no great rush in getting the shovel crews busy. By midsummer, 1865, the embankment finally reached Elkhorn Creek. The federal inspector shrugged and approved it. Tracklaying had begun in July and ambled west. By Christmas week the tracks too had reached Elkhorn Creek, at the leisurely pace of four miles a month.

It was this dawdling which had caused Durant to come west.

"Seymour seems to be determined to delay the work as much as possible," Robert Porter complained. "Twenty-four miles, Durant. That's all since July. At this rate we won't even reach the hundredth meridian by 1870, let alone Salt Lake City."

Porter was becoming an irritant to Durant. Seymour was moving in nice accord with his plans, but Porter's sly and secretive reports to Oliver Ames were undermining his, Durant's control.

"Robert," Durant said coolly, "Silas has no control over the weather and Indians."

"I am not talking of just this week," Porter said crisply. "Are you blind to what has been going on since we left Omaha? We have two thousand workers out in those tents to the right of the tracks who are beginning to believe the rumors that we are wintered in here. And do you know why they believe it? Because of the debauchery in the tents to the left of the track. Those whores and gamblers are the main reason we only average four miles a month!"

"Oh, Robert," Durant said airily, "you've got to take into consideration that our mob of bogtrotters from Ireland need to booze, brawl and fornicate—those are the pleasures they know."

Porter scowled. "That preacher from Omaha was quite correct when he said we weren't building a railroad, only a Hell on wheels."

Durant laughed. "I think, Robert, he was talking about the camp-sutler wagons that follow in our wake and the tent cities they're putting up."

"Tent cities, hell! Those people have begun to throw up whorehouses and saloons out of lumber they brought in from Omaha. That's our railroad land they're building on and Seymour won't let me do anything about it. My God, in a month they've already erected over two dozen buildings."

"By hiring away our workers at a better rate?"

"And wisely I would say. It stands to reason that the very saloons and whorehouses our people are building for them are going to strip them of their pay and force them to stay right here working for the railroad."

Durant sat and brooded.

"I've decided," he firmly announced, "that we will indeed winter here until spring."

"And do what?" Porter demanded.

Durant chuckled. "Tweak the noses of the good citizens of Omaha, for one thing. Let the hellions build all the brothels they want. We're going to build right alongside them and turn this place and not Omaha into our eastern terminal supply depot."

Porter shook his head. "Durant," he declared in deliberate tones, "that is totally unnecessary and a vast waste of money and effort. I have already let out many warehouse and supply contracts in Omaha."

"Which Silas has been cancelling right and left."

Porter glared. "He has no right. That is my area of responsibility."

Durant turned away without replying.

Just then Seymour came bounding into the office car, visibly upset.

"Tom," he barked, "that Mrs. O'Lee just rode into the camp in the caboose of our supply train. I don't think she saw me."

"What difference would it have made if she saw you?" Porter asked.

Both men ignored him, puzzling over why Liberty would be in Nebraska.

"Robert," Durant ordered. "Go fetch her. And for once keep your goddamn mouth shut!"

He then glared at Seymour. "Get back into the bunk area, Silas. As far as I'm concerned, I don't know where in the hell you are."

* * *

Liberty's legs felt frozen as she trod the hard ground. It was Wednesday, the third of January, an ice-cold day. A dirt clearing near the ignored track was crowded with burly Union Pacific workers who looked like they hadn't seen soap and water since summer. Some huddled around huge bonfires. Others were pushing into the already packed clapboard saloons, rather than freeze their feet in the temporary tents that were providing drinks. From inside all the saloons came the jangle of pianos, and much baritone and soprano laughter.

Pulling her hooded cape closer about her, Liberty managed to ignore crude remarks thrown her way, but couldn't help gaping at the flamboyant revelry.

A dance-and-drink girl slithered out of a saloon tent and sang out to a group of men, "Right oveh heah, honey. I'm Hot Hannah from Savannah and ah shake a mean leg." It was too cold to dance in a tent; Hot Hannah got no takers.

A pitchman strutted on a platform in front of Crazy May's Palace of Passion and Pleasure, hawking its wares.

"She's done it again, gents," he bellowed. "No one tops Crazy May for coming up with the unusual, the sublime, the best time in town. Better belly up to the bar now, boys, because in one hour—and continuing straight through until one this morning—Crazy May is proud to announce a Two-for-One night. That's right! Two-for-one. All black-jack games will pay double. All drinks and dances will be two for the price of one. *And then*—" he softened his spiel to a sensuous throatiness—"Crazy May's not going to stop there. All the fine fillies in her stable are also going to be available for the same price—Two-for-One!"

Trainmen by the score set up a hoarse shout and

pushed and shoved towards Crazy May's swinging doors. "Utterly disgusting," someone said, and took Liberty by the elbow.

She started, pulled away and looked into a face that was vaguely familiar.

"I'm sorry. Didn't mean to startle you. I'm Robert Porter and Mr. Durant sent me to fetch you."

"Oh," Liberty said. "How did he know I was here?"

"Train engineer told him," Porter lied. "Come along. This place makes me ill."

"It is unusual," Liberty exclaimed. She felt freer to gaze about now that she was being escorted. It was the variety of the signs that amused her the most:

LOTTIE'S LOVELY LASSES—All Irish or yr. money back.

SHAMROCK BALLROOM—Where the biggest hang out.

LITTLE EGYPT—100 belly-dancers.

ST. PAT'S—Only Irish whisky in town.

Porter whisked her between two buildings and she didn't get to see the other end of the dirt street.

"Well, we certainly don't have this problem in California."

"Wouldn't have it here either," Porter said darkly, "if our chief engineer didn't receive favors in return for allowing them to stay open."

Liberty's ears perked up. She didn't have to ask the name of the man Porter was referring to. It gave her a lift to know that Seymour was here. Perhaps now she could get something done about him as well as deal with Durant.

Durant was civil with her, almost too civil. After summarily dismissing Porter, he bantered about unimportant topics while Liberty sipped a steaming cup of chicken broth he had prepared for her. Still he couldn't keep the curiosity from his voice at finding her there in darkest Nebraska.

"I'm so sorry if I have made you come so far out of your way."

"Not really out of my way. I had some family property to see to in Mississippi. Besides, with the revision now law, Collis is most anxious to come to terms on a junction point."

"My dear woman, I must now advise you your trip was in vain. I do not have dictatorial powers. I can't just stick a pin in a map. I will have to wait until I have a chief engineer to guide me on the matter."

"You have none now?"

"No. That is the reason I am here. I am taking charge of the construction, but only temporarily."

"I was under the impression that Colonel Silas Seymour was your engineer."

Durant tried to laugh Seymour off. "Liberty, that comic opera bungler has tried to make many believe that. As far as I know he is still inspecting rail lines for the army."

"Hardly," she said shortly. "I talked to the army in Washington; he's no longer with them. I also learned that he was not a legal inspector when he came to California. We now have evidence that his alteration of certain blueprints caused the landslide that killed my husband."

"Liberty, you can't be serious!"

"Very serious," she said, eyeing Durant steadily. "Because of his inexperience, he was able to hoodwink Robert Porter's son, Randy, and for a while make Dan the scapegoat. To kill may not have been his primary intent, but I consider the man a murderer nevertheless."

Durant's worst fears were being realized. Ever since Seymour had told him all he'd done in the interests of the Union Pacific, he had feared the job had been stupidly bungled and would come back to haunt them. He could not, at this time, afford the scandal exposure would bring.

"Are you absolutely positive, Liberty? This hardly sounds like Silas."

Coldly, she gave him Nazareth's findings step by step, then, without mincing words, told him of the events in New York that had resulted in Dan's "accident" on the stairs.

Durant sat strangely silent. He was thinking. Liberty was a threat to him and to Seymour. Liberty was as expendable as her husband, but Seymour wasn't. Silas had to be protected at all costs. With the defeat of McClellan by Lincoln in 1864, Governor Horatio Seymour, Silas's brother, was the logical candidate for the Democratic party to put up against Andrew Johnson in '68. Durant was already anticipating the governor's victory. He reasoned there would be no easier way to win favors from him for the Union Pacific than by keeping brother Silas out of harm's way.

"Well," Durant said, at last, "this is shocking. Just shocking! I wish I could help, but . . ." He shrugged.

Liberty suddenly realized the futility of having raised the accusation in the first place. Durant was covering up for Seymour. He was lying. He would not expose Seymour, even to the point of admitting that he was in camp. She felt she had placed herself in a dangerous position and needed to back out.

"Perhaps," she said sweetly, "just being able to discuss it with you has helped more than you realize. I doubt that anything can be done against the man, but at least you are warned should he come around again."

"Well . . . ah . . . yes. I am terribly sorry for all of this and now must figure out what to do with you."

"I beg your pardon."

"The supply train does not return to Omaha until morning and accommodations here are . . . ah . . ." He paused and pondered. "Aha! I have it. The caboose. No luxury, of course, but the pot-bellied stove will keep you warm throughout the night. I will see that your dinner is brought to you. I would advise you not to be out after dark. There are some men in this camp who would kill a fellow creature for a few dollars."

Liberty had the sinking feeling that she was looking at one of them. She nodded and smiled, however, then asked for directions to the caboose. When she was given them but not offered an escort, her suspicions deepened into dread: she really was in the camp of the enemy, with no alternative but to step down to the spur siding and into their midst.

She thanked Durant and left. Then, just outside the office car, a shadowy figure approached her. It was Robert Porter, and he was shivering from the cold. He pressed a shaking blue finger against his lips for silence. Then he scurried Liberty away, unsure in his own mind what he was going to do next.

"You heard?" Durant glowered at the gunny-sack draped in back of the office car.

Silas Seymour emerged as if he didn't have a problem in the world. "Fully," he said.

"She can't leave here alive."

"Obviously. But it shall not be by my hand, nor can it be an ordinary, everyday accident."

"Don't get cute, Silas. She could hang you!"

"Yes," he mused, "thanks to Porter's idiot son. I think this is a job for Terence O'Bannon."

"O'Bannon?"

Seymour chuckled. "O'Bannon's our massive young track boss. He's an animal, Durant, an animal. He boasts about his penis being fourteen inches long and seven around. He's a cruel son of a bitch with the whores and he's broken several workmen's jaws already. They don't allow him in the houses any more."

"Wonderful," Durant commented dryly. "But I fail to see how this O'Bannon can help us."

"Oh, he'll help us, all right," Seymour promised. He grinned. "Of course, such an animal may have to be shot after he fulfills our wishes."

Durant's stomach churned. "Do it. Just don't tell me the details."

Robert Porter hesitated at the back door of Crazy May's. He knew he was taking a wild gamble. But, while lurking near the office car window, he had heard something of his son's involvement in the Seymour case, and this was the only place he could think of to take Liberty so as to learn more about it. He also had an inclination to save Liberty from the danger she was in.

He ushered her into a long, narrow corridor, slammed the door, then hesitated again. He had been in Crazy May's just once and wasn't sure of the way to her private quarters. Taking a chance, he elbowed Liberty up a flight of stairs and knocked on the third door on the right. From within came a gruff acknowledgement. Porter scurried them both inside and then stood panting.

Crazy May, wrapped in an Indian blanket and warming herself before the Franklin stove, turned and faced them in surprise.

"Well, Mr. Porter," she chirped, "what official railroad business do you come on this time?"

Porter stammered, "Not really . . . I . . . ah . . ."

Liberty stared at the small red-headed, freckle-faced

woman. Crazy May reminded her of someone. She had
a family resemblance to someone. Who? She couldn't
quite place her finger on who.

Crazy May was lengthily appraising Liberty too,
but for a different reason.

"Mother love us," she chuckled, "if you all be a
whore, honey, you're wastin' your pretty face on the
likes of the jackals we got around here."

Porter blushed deeply. "She is not a . . . ah . . .
this is Mrs. Liberty O'Lee . . . and . . . ah . . ."

"Trouble?"

Porter sighed. "In two words. Silas Seymour."

Crazy May made an obscene gesture with her hand
and arm.

"Then you brought her to the right place," she said.
She marched right up to Liberty. "Pleased to meet you,
Cathy. The name's really Maybelle, but don't ask me
my last one. I was with the Sioux for years, but that's
not what rattled my brains. Damn soldiers who rescued
me did that. Used me every which way but loose for
Lord knows how long and then dropped me on a
minister's doorstep in St. Joe. By then I thought
every man knew what his cock was for and tried to
get him to use his. Well, he didn't, and then I . . . ah
. . ." A memory cog in her brain began to slip. She
struggled back to the present. "Why . . . why are you
here?"

"Colonel Seymour," Porter repeated softly. "We
want your help in hiding Mrs. O'Lee away from him."

"Logical," Maybelle said, "and I agree. The man
is foul. Goods like her shouldn't be wasted. Let me go
check on my rooms."

They stood silent for a moment after her departure
and then Porter stammered:

"I'm . . . most embarrassed bringing you here."

"Please don't be," Liberty tried to reassure him.

"From what I've seen of this . . . area . . . you made a wise choice. It looks safe . . . I hope."

"My . . . my son? Please tell me?"

"What did you hear?"

He repeated everything that he had overheard. Unfortunately, as much as she wanted to, Liberty couldn't tell him what he wanted to hear, that Randy was free of taint in Seymour's infamous transaction.

Porter was crushed by the news. It was really not so much Randy's involvement that upset him, but the boy's utter stupidity in not remaining silent about what he knew. He vowed to wire Randy to return home at once. Meanwhile, Maybelle returned with one of her scantily clad girls.

"You go with her," Maybelle ordered Liberty. "They already know you didn't get to the caboose and are looking for you. Porter, sit! If they see you leave here they'll smell it out and bring their bully-boys to tear this place apart. I'm going out to start my two-for-one deal right on schedule!"

Liberty was led no further away than the next bedroom and Porter was left to stare dejectedly into the embers of the Franklin stove.

A half hour later Maybelle returned to Liberty with a dance-hall-girl outfit. "Best you put this on, Mrs. O'Lee," she said crisply. "It will help you blend in better."

"That's not going to do much good if Colonel Seymour comes looking for me himself."

Maybelle laughed and threw back the first layer of her own filmy outfit. A fancy derringer was slung about her waist.

"First of all, I doubt he'd have the nerve to come here, but if he does, I'm an expert with this."

"This must seem terribly strange to you," Liberty said, starting to undress.

"Honey, around here nothing is strange. It's a world with a single law—dog eat dog. Ain't a day passes but a dead body is found somewhere in the vicinity with pockets rifled of contents. Nobody pays any attention."

"How . . . how . . ." Liberty grew embarassed that she had even dared to start the question she had in mind.

Maybelle snickered. "The questions been asked a thousand times, so don't be embarrassed. Necessity, you might say. I was on the street broke, and my front man, Carter Hoyt, had been put off the paddle-wheelers for some very questionable card playing. We sorta drifted into a team. I'd find the men for him to play cards with and then I was the reward to hush them up with if he won too much from them. When we heard of this railroad camp we scraped together what cash we could and started out with one wagon, one small tent, a case of pretty damn rotten booze and one extra girl. Now, it's ten wagons, a big old circus tent, portable dance floor, ten roustabouts who act as teamsters, bartenders and bouncers. My girls number fifty and the booze comes in by the caseload."

Liberty laughed as she put on the dance-hall costume. "And they call you crazy."

Maybelle frowned. "Am sometimes, honey. Don't know if it was really the Indians, or the soldiers, or what. On the spur of the moment I'll do some pretty damn foolish things. Carter says that when I'm dolled up like this I act and talk like Crazy May, but when I'm alone I just go back to being a Tennessee hick."

"I was noticing that," Liberty said. "When I first saw you and heard you speak, you definitely reminded me of someone, but now I can't put my finger on it."

"Don't try, honey. I've been trying to put my finger on who I was for over twenty years and it only makes it go farther away. Here, I'll take your clothes and hide them in my room. No one dares go in there, unless they're with me. Later on, I'll have Luann bring you in a supper tray. Yep, I was right, you'd make a killing in this business."

Liberty turned to look into the square of mirror on the wall and was shocked at what she saw. Except for her pale face, the costume had changed her into something that she was not as artfully as the Lizzie Garland gown had changed her into a regal princess. But now she looked more like a whore.

When Luann brought the supper tray, Liberty didn't feel as if she had an appetite. She managed to put away a steak, parsley potatoes and toasted bread, however, and was just finishing her coffee when there was a discreet knock on the door.

Hesitantly, she said: "Come in."

Instantly, she recognized Crazy May's street barker. Now he was attired in a black silk suit that shimmered with sequins. He had oily black hair and there was a sleek handsomeness to him that at first glance Liberty didn't like.

"Good evening, Mrs. O'Lee," he said smoothly. "I am Carter Hoyt and Maybelle has told me all."

"Good evening, Mr. Hoyt."

His voice had a bitter edge to it, as if he considered her a nuisance.

"May's two-for-one night was a rousing success—in case you care," he said. "Other than that, we thought you should be told that we had a surprising visitor about an hour ago. Dr. Thomas Durant has found you. He made himself out to be quite a forceful man. He said that you are to be turned over to him by closing time tonight or no one will be allowed to open in the morning."

Liberty sighed with resignation. "Tell Maybelle to bring back my clothing. I'll go to him."

"No need," Hoyt said, a bit less coldly. "I think you'll find that it's Durant who's on the short end. Maybelle told him flat out that he would have to reckon with the Union Pacific workers not taking his closing order lightly. The crowd we had here tonight proved her point for her. She told Durant he is not to interfere with you tonight and that he's to make arrangements for you to return on the supply train in the morning. It's pretty clear that that's what he'll do."

"Thank god!" Liberty sighed. "Maybelle is really an extraordinary woman."

Hoyt eyed her. He seemed to warm to her for having said that. "That she is! I think her mother must have been a lot like that. Rock-hard pioneering stock that knew no fear."

"Her mother? But I thought her past was a blank to her."

"Mainly it is, now. We've been together for three years, and the first two were hell. Her nightmares were horrible, because of things in her past and the bleakness of the future. She would scream and rave at times, and at other times just sob and mutter. Here and there I was able to pick up unconnected little pieces of information."

"Did you discuss them with her?"

"At first, but it only seemed to make things worse, so I stopped. In the last six months, since things started turning golden for her, she hasn't had a single one of those nightmares. So I think now it's best to just let her past lie still."

"Perhaps you are right. But it's funny, that face, those freckles, that red hair—it's almost as though I've seen that face before."

"You ever been in this part of the country or Tennessee before, Mrs. O'Lee."

"No."

"Then it's unlikely you've ever seen her. I was able to piece together a little about a log cabin in Tennessee, a wagon train and a Sioux attack here on the Platte. This used to be big Sioux country until the army came in to push them back so they could build the Pony Express relay stations every ten miles. So it must have been somewhere around here that the Sioux captured her."

"How horrible for her."

"I'm not so sure. After I found her, I went to see that minister fellow that the army doctor turned her over to. Seems that when the army captured that Indian village she fought and screamed and didn't want to be taken away."

Liberty shivered. "What did the soldiers do—rape her to let her know she was a white woman again?"

Hoyt nodded sadly. "I think she must have been happy with the Sioux. She used to cry a lot about 'my men, my men.' Near as I can figure out she must have been with the Sioux for over fifteen years, so more than likely 'her men' must have been a husband and sons. The minister told me that every man, woman and child of that village were slaughtered. Only Maybelle and two other white women were brought back alive."

"That would be enough to make anyone lose her mind, even before the soldiers raped her. What I find sad is that somewhere she has a mother and father who don't really know what happened to their daughter."

"Not quite. I gather that her mother died on the wagon train and that she had older brothers—twins."

Liberty's heart began to flutter. She tried to sort out the many shipboard conversations she had had with Lydia May Tedder. She could almost recall her telling of her grandmother dying on the trek west, but there was something else about an aunt. For the life of her, it would not come back. More calmly than she would have thought possible Liberty said, "Were you ever able to learn her last name?"

"No. When I first found her she went by her Indian name—Man-tia—'Sunset Hair.' It was some time before she remembered May and only in the last few months that the full Maybelle came back."

"I think I know who she might be."

"Thinking is not enough, and I won't have you building false hopes in her that might not work out." Hoyt's tone was not defiant, just firm. "You're not a bad sort, Mrs. O'Lee. I take back some feelings I had about you. Now, it's time for me to open the black-jack table. You'll be safe, but I suggest you stay in this room."

After he left, Liberty thought hard. She recalled that Lydia May had told her she had been named for her paternal grandmother, Lydia Tedder, and her aunt. Liberty thought the aunt's name had been Maybelle, but she wasn't sure. If Crazy May was indeed Maybelle Tedder, then finding her here in Nebraska was a coincidence so extreme that Liberty's sense of reality was offended. And yet . . . and yet . . .

The evening dragged on. Putting the unanswerable question of Crazy May's true identity out of her mind, Liberty sought ways to amuse herself. It was impossible to sleep because of the din in the saloon below. She began to take ostrich feathers off the top of the bureau and stick them in her hair. If she already looked a bit like a whore, maybe she could improve the illusion. One look in the mirror told her her face needed rouging, so she dabbed some on from the open make-up pots she found. Then she added blue eye-shadow and some bright red lipstick. The change, when she cocked her head back and forth surveying it in the mirror, made her giggle with a small child's delight.

All this while, Crazy May's Palace of Pleasure had been bustling with overheard activity—from a burlesque show going on in the saloon below—to doors slamming on either side of her, as men entered and left the two-for-one girls' cubicles. Liberty, already costumed for a stripper's role, now got a wicked notion to partake still further of the sensuous atmosphere. Just for the fun of it, as the band in the saloon struck up a "take it off" rhythm and men exhorted the strippers to do just that, she stood in front of the mirror and jutted each hip in several artful bumps. She almost laughed out loud with the pleasure this gave her, swaying to the music, she felt young, lighthearted, more seductive than she had in years. A moment's pastime it was and that alone, she knew, but by gosh, she told herself with a gleam, make the most of it!

Suddenly, her room door came flying open. Liberty spun around and found herself staring at one of the largest drunks she had ever seen in her life. The man's girth alone frightened her. He was close to seven feet tall and wore a high fur cap that made him loom still taller. He had huge shoulders and arms and a massive, heaving chest almost bursting from his wool mackintosh. His bearded face and eyes were reddened from the cold and from all the whisky he'd drunk.

Terence O'Bannon stared back at Crazy May's gorgeous new whore with rising lust. He forgot the errand Colonel Seymour had sent him on. Whoever the prissy Liberty O'Lee was whom the colonel wanted him to rape didn't matter now. He wanted this girl before him.

Grinning and leering at her, Terence ran his hand down the front of his pants. He cupped his genitals and massaged them slowly. Wide-eyed, Liberty followed the motion. The man's pants could not contain his erection. Without taking his eyes from Liberty's face, he undid his buttons and pulled it out. Liberty stared at the huge thing in horror. It was as long and thick as a horse's. She lifted her eyes to the man's face and saw the brutality in it.

Terence held his hard, throbbing penis in his hand, pointed rigidly up at Liberty's face. He stroked it gently, "How much for this?" he croaked. Then he mumbled, "Won't hurt you with it, promise. Never mean to hurt nobody with it. It'll feel real good, you'll see."

Liberty's head spun. She could see that the man's raging lust would win out over his mock tenderness in the next instant or two. She cursed herself for having played her whore's part too well, but saw no chance of escape around him to the open door.

Nervously, she put her hand on her jutting hip and tried to continue her role. "Honey, I've been alone all night cause no sucker in this camp can afford my price. Can you? I get fifty dollars for one shot."

Would her gambit work? Liberty knew that fifty dollars was about six months salary to a railroad worker; she could only hope he'd realize this and back off.

Terence grew silent, staring at her and pondering. Then he shook his head like an angered bull and began to move up on her, his bear-like hands already reaching for her shoulders. A scream rose in Liberty's throat. She tried to scurry backwards out of his reach, then darted to one side. And then, suddenly, her impetus to scream was gone. Standing in the doorway, where Liberty could now see her, was Maybelle. She nearly fainted with relief.

"Terry, me boy," she heard Maybelle call softly.

The giant lumbered around to face her. Liberty saw Maybelle look down at the front of his pants, then run her tongue over her lips. "Mmm," she said. "May wants that, honey. May's never seen it that big. You got to give it to May now, honey, because I got to have it." Her voice had gone throaty. She licked her lips again, then fell on her knees in front of the man and took the whole head of the huge penis in her mouth. "Mmm, mmm, mmm," she moaned. The giant gasped, grunted, then moved to slide his erection in deeper. Maybelle took her mouth away. "My room, honey, oh quick—I want it in my cunt, I want it!"

She got to her feet and, as Liberty watched in wonderment and awe, pulled a now docile Terence O'Bannon out into her own room.

For a long time Liberty listened to the animal-like roars and gasps of pain and delight coming through the thin walls. When finally all was silent, she washed off her make-up, fell into bed, and slept a dreamless sleep.

Morning came. Liberty awoke to a cold, pearly gray dawn, hearing a gentle tap on her door. She sat bolt upright in bed and listened. All was quiet, except for the tap. Through the window, she saw the huge Terence O'Bannon blowing on his hands and walking up and down in front of the house. Beyond him, several other railroad men who'd apparently spent the night at Crazy May's were reporting morosely to a Union Pacific crew boss who shouted at them to move faster.

When she called come in, Maybelle entered, her face furrowed with lack of sleep but her eyes bright enough.

"We have just won a convert," Maybelle said drily, "With his help we will have you on that supply train when it leaves at seven."

Liberty's head sank and she couldn't stop the tears. "But . . . but you . . ." she sobbed.

Maybelle came and cradled her in her arms. "Hush, honey. I may have been doing it for myself as well. Had the big brute crying like a baby fore I was finished with him. I'm the first woman been able to sate him and he's not about to forget that for a long time to come. Don't hurt none, either, that he's the track foreman. He's gonna do what I say, not what either Durant or Seymour says. Now, here's what we must do."

Two hours later Liberty waited to join nine other Crazy May girls who would take the supply train back to Omaha and a return to whatever life they desired. Crazy May paid her girls so well that after a few months they had a nice enough nest egg to escape the life of prostitution.

"They won't be checking the girls aboard," Maybelle said. "This is routine. I send old girls out and new ones come in, all the time. Thanks for leaving me your dress."

Liberty grasped her hands. "It is I who should be thanking you—for a million things. Someday, and quite soon, the Union Pacific and Central Pacific are going to join. I'll be there that day, if for no other reason than to see you again."

Maybelle blushed. "Honey child, that would please me. You might think differently later, you being what you are, and all. But don't worry. If the day comes,

and you choose not to recognize me, I'll fully understand."

Liberty looked at her with loving tenderness. "That
will never happen, Maybelle, never."

"Oh, there's the train whistle. Bustle along and just
act like the rest of the girls. I'm off to my carriage."

Liberty held her and kissed her cheeks. Then, on
a sudden impulse, she said: "Lydia would have been
proud of her daughter!"

Maybelle broke away, blinking. "Why . . . why
. . . that was my mother's name, I do believe. However . . . ?"

Liberty looked up into the glowering eyes of Carter
Hoyt and was stunned by what she read in them. He
loved Maybelle, and desperately feared losing her to
her past. For the moment, Liberty decided it would
be best to fall back on a comment old Kai Soong
might have made.

"Oh, the name just came into my head as we embraced," she laughed. "I must have read it in your
thoughts."

With fiery determination, Carter Hoyt grasped Maybelle by the arm and steered her to the awaiting horse
and carriage, allowing no further goodbyes and giving
none of his own. Liberty, her face even more made-up
than she had done it on her own, joined the other
winter-wrapped girls for the walk to the waiting train.
She was kept in the center of the throng and boarded
it without question.

Ever since the dawn return of Terry O'Bannon,
Thomas Durant had been highly cautious and Silas
Seymour totally jealous. Terrible Terry had been able
to convince them that he had been with Liberty and
she had been able to sate him with no ill effects to

herself. To Durant it meant that she was healthy
enough to escape him, so he ordered a horse saddled
and left tethered to the office car platform and a lookout posted at 'Crazy May's'. To Silas it meant that
O'Bannon, not he, had had the experience of his life.
Seymour's mind seethed with images of what must
have gone on between the two. He was determined
that that night he would have Liberty O'Lee in his
bed, one way or another.

Five minutes after the departure of the train, the
guard alerted Durant that a small carriage had just
left heading west, being driven by a woman in wool
plaid. He might not have reported it, except for the
dress of the driver.

Durant quickly strapped a holster around his waist
and rushed to the waiting horse. Beating the horse
to a lather in the frigid air, he overtook and halted
the carriage in less than a mile.

"What is the meaning of this?" Maybelle demanded
harshly.

Durant blinked. "What . . . what are you doing
here?"

"The same as I do every morning, sir! A short ride
to clear my nostrils of the stench of your unbathed
legions."

"But . . . but that dress."

"Oh, isn't it just too, too divine. I purchased it
from Mrs. O'Lee."

"Whom I gather is still in your establishment, madam?"

She simpered. "Hardly. Perhaps, Mr. Durant, I
should have said that the dress was paid for in exchange for letting her have one of my girl's seats on
the supply train into Omaha."

Durant spun his horse about and rode off in a
cold fury. Back at the office car, he took over the

telegraphic key himself, while informing Seymour how they had been royally duped. Seymour mentally decoded the dots and dashes he tapped out and frowned.

"Thomas, I fail to see how stopping her from taking a train back east will really stop her. She will still have the stagecoaches west available to her."

"Oh, will she, now," Durant said with murderous intent. "You get that damn Indian scout you hired off the bottle and on his horse. I don't care how long it takes him, but he's to tell every tribe between here and Fort Bridger that the Great Iron Trail stops here for the winter until our chiefs can powwow with their chiefs in the spring. Tell them we want a fair peace and only a small strip of land. Tell them the Pony Express men and the stagecoach men are fighting us, because they want all the land. *All the Indian land!* Because of this the men of the Great Iron Trail will pay two rifles for the scalp of every passenger in a stagecoach, female scalps included. We will also pay for the scalps of Pony Express riders and for the cutting of the singing wires. That offer stands from now until spring."

"I can understand you going after her," Seymour said, confused, "but why disrupt the Pony Express and telegraphic service?"

Durant looked at him as he was beginning to look at all people, as beings so far inferior to his level of comprehending *his* railroad that it taxed his energy even to communicate with them.

"Seymour," he said icily, "I don't want her able to get any form of message to Huntington in California, today, tomorrow or ever. Do I make myself quite clear?"

Seymour got the picture then. "Quite," he said, and grinned.

14

Liberty was nearly exhausted when she reached Omaha; the fear of pursuit had always been with her. Quickly she changed clothes in her hotel room, grabbed up her luggage and headed for the ferry depot—bound for Council Bluffs and a return east. Her only desire now was to file an official report against Silas Seymour in Washington and catch a boat home to California.

The clerk in Council Bluffs looked at her railroad pass, then frowned at a telegram at his side.

"No good!" he said curtly.

"What do you mean? I've traveled extensively on that pass. Everyone has honored it."

"Can't here."

"Then I wish a ticket to New York, via Washington."

"Can't do that, neither," the clerk said, shaking his head. "Wire here says can't issue any eastbound ticket on this pass, no matter the circumstances."

"But I will pay cash," Liberty insisted.

"Next, please," he said dolefully, ignoring her completely.

A man in a dapper plaid suit and bowler hat stepped up close to Liberty and bowed.

"Harvey Tucker, madam, representing Ben Hollander. The company that was here first and is still here to serve the traveler's need. Railroads are trying to put us out of business, but Ben Hollander wants people to know that his stagecoaches are still here and he still cares. How can we be of service to you?"

"I'm not sure you can," Liberty said, although appreciative of his kindness. "I wish to get east so that I can catch a boat to California."

"Madam," Harvey Tucker said smoothly, "you are contemplating a week's return to the east coast and then an additional four to six weeks on the high seas. Are you aware that if you take a Hollander coach west you are but a week away from California?"

"I am well aware of it, Mr. Tucker. I have made that liver-shattering journey before. Now there's a threat of Indians, besides."

"Both problems easily solved by Harvey Tucker, madam. All trips west are now made by the new Concord stage, with its easy-ride springs. And we have telegraphic reports that the Union Pacific has made peace with the Indians until spring. Where are you headed?"

"Sacramento," she said wistfully.

"Lady," Tucker enthused, "I can have you on a stage for Fort Laramie, Fort Bridger, Dutch Flats and Sacramento within the hour."

"Those are my bags," Liberty said, pointing to them. She had made her decision. After what she had been through, she figured she could put up with a week of the worst Ben Hollander could dish out.

A few hours out of Omaha an eastbound stage passed along the report that twenty soldiers had just been ambushed on the Platte by Sioux and had gotten away only after a ten-mile running fight. The Concord driver took the news calmly. He said it sounded like an exaggeration to him and pointed out that he carried an extra rifleman atop the stage and four additional rifles in a rack over the six passengers' heads.

Nor did the news seem to frighten Liberty's five traveling companions. They had just seen four years of killing and felt they could handle a few Indians without difficulty. Four were tough Missouri farmland brothers who had returned from the war to find their fields burned out by the Yankees. Bitterly, they'd grasped at the only family they had left—each other —and headed west, lured by the promise of quick money. In Kansas City they'd been recruited by the fifth passenger, Harvey Landusky, a cattleman on the lookout for gunslingers. At one time Landusky's grazing land had stretched from the Canadian mountains to the headwaters of the Missouri. Now homesteaders were moving onto Montana land he considered his own. The Thomas brothers, Landusky figured, could help him force the homesteaders out, and he'd paid them well to take on the job.

As the Concord bumped along, Landusky's thoughts turned away from the adventure he was planning with the Thomases to the woman sitting opposite him. He studied Liberty and considered his prospects of bedding her. The moment she'd boarded the stage, he'd been aroused by the firm roundness of her buttocks. He longed to see the shape of her thighs and legs and wondered what they'd feel like wrapped around him. They'd be hot and white and smooth and as tight as a bear trap, he thought.

He did not put his thoughts into words until the stage stopped at Fort Kearney for the night.

"My boys have blanket rolls, m'am. But for protection, you might consider sharing a cabin with me."

Landusky was a tall, dignified-looking man greying at the temples; he tipped his wide-brimmed hat to her and smiled.

Liberty lifted her eyes and gave him a cool gaze. She remembered Fort Kearney quite well. Indeed, it was not unusual for travelers to share log cabins there in times of Indian danger. But she had sensed Landusky's examination of her throughout the day and had a clear view of what he wanted from her. Very slowly, she opened her cloak and showed him the derringer strapped to her waist. She had scoffed when Maybelle had advised her to take it; she was no longer scoffing.

"I see to my own protection, sir," she said meaningfully. She looked away without another word.

Landusky smiled and replaced his hat. He was a patient man. He did not expect instant gratification in his war with the homesteaders, and he did not expect it now. He would make no further advances to the lady at Fort Kearney; he knew that he would still have three more nights to win her over before they separated at Fort Bridger.

He did not get the chance to pursue his cause.

The attack came when the coach was still two days ride from Fort Bridger.

All that Liberty could remember of the moments preceding it was that she must have dozed off. She came to in the middle of a nightmare. Without warning, fifty rifles had opened fire from ambush. The driver and his outriders did not get off a shot. Four of the six horses went limp in their harness straps and fell, tripping up the two remaining ones as they stumbled on. The onrushing coach climbed the fallen horseflesh, careened wildly, then crashed over on its side. Liberty screamed. Inside, two of the Thomas boys, dead from the first salvo, fell on top of her, pinning her to the overturned side. Twisting her head desperately, she saw the other two Thomases clamber up to the topside window, drawing their six-shooters and cursing—only to get cut down the moment they showed their heads.

The rifle fire abruptly ceased. Liberty lay terrified under the two bodies. Moments passed.

"Where in the hell are those red-devils?" Landusky howled. He could not see from where he lay. He heard no sound of circling horses. That puzzled him. No Indians he knew fought like this. He waited several moments longer. Still no sounds. He'd lost interest in Liberty. Grimly, he used the butt of a rifle to smack a hole through at the floor boards large enough for him to crawl through. Again he waited, but heard nothing. "You're on your own, lady," he snarled at Liberty. He put a foot through the hole and worked his way to the ground. He made it only to the end of the coach. The quiet was suddenly blasted by more rifle fire. A scream of surprise was torn from Landusky's throat as a dozen bullets hit him and spun him crushingly to the ground.

In the ensuing silence, Liberty lay still and whimpered. She did not dare to struggle from beneath the bodies. At any instant, she expected hoards of red savages to descend on the coach, set it afire, scalp the only surviver, who was herself. But she would not move. She had seen what had happened to those that did. She lay under the suffocating weight of two bodies, and waited . . . and waited . . . and waited.

Nothing happened. An hour ticked by. Still all was quiet outside, and still Liberty did not move. Her mind began to whirl. The agonies of suspicion wormed their way into her. Who were these attackers? Why did they not show themselves? Ten thousand thoughts crossed her mind. She could not pin down one and make sense of it before another took its place. The face of a Thomas brother was inches from hers. Looking into its open, staring eyes, she thought she would go insane.

Night fell, and blissfully she slipped into unconsciousness.

"Lady . . . lady . . . wake up . . . it's all right now," a deep female voice said soothingly. "You can open your eyes now . . . it's all right."

Liberty came groggily awake. She opened her eyes and saw a sky full of stars. She was lying on her back on the ground and a woman who appeared middle-aged was peering down at her. Dazedly, Liberty turned her head and saw the overturned coach a few yards away. She looked back up at the woman questioningly.

"I am a doctor," the woman said. "Dr. Bertha Geddy. Can you hear me? You've had a shock, but you're all right now. We're going to take you into Fort Bridger. Just lie quietly."

Liberty started. "There was a dead man," she said hysterically. "I was looking into his eyes."

"Yes, we know," the woman soothed her. "I was on my way to the fort when we found you. We had a devil of a time getting you out. I work at the fort. I'm a doctor there. The fever will pass. You're in safe hands."

Liberty nodded and closed her eyes. She was burning with fever. She realized that now. She felt strong hands lifting her, and then she was unconscious again.

When she awoke, she was in a soft bed at the fort. She opened her eyes warily and saw Dr. Geddy standing over her.

"Good morning," Dr. Geddy said cheerily. "Do you realize you slept two whole days? "You must have been one tired young woman. Don't try to rise. Nothing is broken, but your shoulder is badly sprained. Still, I aim on keeping you in bed for a couple of weeks."

"I . . . home . . ." Liberty mumbled. "Must go . . . California."

"In good time. Now, Jim Bridger is here. Do you feel up to answering a couple of questions for him?"

Liberty nodded.

Jim Bridger, the famous scout who had built the fort named after him, had been warned by Dr. Geddy not to tax Liberty's strength. He really only needed confirmation for what he already suspected. After three brief questions he nodded for Dr. Geddy to follow him out of the room.

He scowled at her fiercely, his eyes two deep sockets in his heavily bearded face.

"Thunderation in hell, Berty, they were Mormons. Those people are the real savages. Well, this time we got ourselves an eyewitness. Jest let that despot Brigham Young try to blame this attack on the Indians."

"We don't have solid evidence they were Mormons, Jim," Bertha pointed out quietly.

"Didn't take no scalps, did they? Didn't fight like Injuns, did they? But they left us a clue like none of the other attacks before. She weren't denuded, now, were she?"

"No, but I fail to see why that makes them Mormon attackers and not just a band of outlaws."

Bridger chuckled. "After eight years of fighting an enemy, Berty, you learn his weaknesses, as well as his strengths. Now what did Brigham Young do during the Mountain Meadow massacre? Closed his eyes to the killing of a hundred forty folks he calls Gentiles. Dad-blamed murderer. But he buried the women fully clothed, that's the point. You see, Berty, it's highly sinful for them to look upon the nude body of a woman. Mormons it was. Outlaws'd probably strip and rape the lady, jest like Injuns, her being the good-looker she is."

"But this is Wyoming, not Utah," she protested.

"Tell that to Brigham," Bridger scoffed. "He's still mad as hell because I led the army against him in the Mormon War and got him kicked out as the territorial governor. As far as he is concerned, Fort Bridger is squatting on his Zion land. Well, I ain't about to pay any toll for wagon trains going through the South Pass. How many wagons in that Prevost train?"

"About forty."

"Been a right mild winter," he mused. "I think I'll tell them to be ready to move by about mid-February. Armed to the teeth, of course."

"What about Mrs. O'Lee?"

"I think we can talk one of those good Prevost people into taking her along to California." He winked, devilishly. "Seein' as how I aim to personally take this train through Zion, I don't think they will be refusing her. Now, I'm going to go see our schoolmarm and have her pen me a little letter to Salt Lake City."

Brigham Young ignored the letter Bridger sent, claiming no knowledge of the most recent attack. Still, his Mormon forces remained up in arms. Now that the Civil War was over, federal troops were back in Utah, harassing him. Under the command of Colonel Patrick E. Connor, a devout Catholic, they were trying to shepherd huge flocks of non-Mormons into the territory he felt God had given to himself and his polygamous followers. Young was not about to let that happen. If need be, he would use all the forces at his command to keep the wagon trains, stagecoaches and even the railroads out of Zion. He knew God would approve, for all the Gentiles he slew were no more than tools of the devil.

With the Mormon threat in mind, Bridger prepared the Prevost party well. Once the wagons had climbed up through the canyons and gorges to the South Pass, no man or woman was to go unarmed day or night. Scouts would be doubled, because Bridger, after the attack on the Hollander stage, now felt the Mormon danger keener than ever.

On the morning of departure he hobbled in to say goodbye to Bertha Geddy.

"Why are you walking that way?" she demanded.

"Old age," he grinned, trying to pass it off as nothing, although every step was pure agony.

"Humph!" she snorted. "Drop your trousers, James Bridger, and let me take a look."

Even through his mass of face hair, she could see his skin burn red. "Are ye daft, woman?"

Bertha grinned. "If you have something I haven't seen before, I promise to keep your secret. Now, down with them."

The old mountain man slowly let his buckskins drop to his knees and instantly knew the worst from her face.

"Land-a-mercy," Bertha Geddy gasped. "Your legs are spread wide by boils. How'd you come by them?"

Bridger scowled at his own stupidity. "Been trying out that leather saddle those railroad dandies sent me fur helpin' on their survey. Jest don't fit me right."

"Nincompoop! You had to keep trying though, like the stubborn jackass that you are, and cause the sores to turn into boils. Well, they have to be lanced and drained." Which she proceeded to do before he could protest further. "Lucky I noticed. These things pop on you and they would have been burying you on the trail with blood poisoning."

"Damn it, woman, finish and patch me up."

"And where do you think you're going?"

"I've got a wagon train waiting for me out there, unless you've forgotten."

"It will have to be put on Fergus Fowles's shoulders, Jim. You're staying off of a horse for a couple of days."

He opened his mouth to protest, but knew it would be futile. "How many days?" he asked through clenched teeth.

"Two—three at the most!"

"You win! It will take them two days to get up into the canyons, another day to climb to the summit. I can make it in half a day and meet them in the South Pass."

Bertha Geddy held her comment. Several of the boils already had the tell-tale red cobwebs of blood-poisoning and she didn't anticipate his going anywhere soon.

Fergus Fowles had been recruited at age eighteen as a Bridger scout and wagon master. In ten years he had guided over fifty trains up through the South Pass and knew it almost as well as Jim Bridger. But repetition had dimmed some of Fergus's youthful caution. He failed to put out any scouts the first two days, and, more negligently still as it turned out, failed to keep a watchful eye on the weather.

On its third night out, the Prevost party made camp at the base of a hill with a gorge halfway up it. The camp clearing had come to be called "Avalanche Camp" because of an accident that had befallen a wagon train there twenty-three years before. Now the gorge, in which bodies and wagons lay buried, was filled in by new growth. Jim Bridger knew who was buried there and so did Lady Pamela Buttle Jones and

Selena Tedder, for they—mother and daughter—had been on that fateful trip. But none of the three were present now—either to speak of the secret the gorge held or warn of its current danger to those parked beneath it.

Rain had started falling in mid-afternoon as a welcome relief from an unusually hot February day. By the time Fowles stopped the train it was hard to see where the rain stopped and the low-hanging clouds began. To the north, thunderclouds were rising rapidly to pass over the Rockies. But a reverse front, which had held the eastern plains in a blizzard condition, was swirling back to climb the same range. Somewhere over the craggy Tetons the climatic forces locked in titanic battle. Neither would budge. They moved southward together, smashing back and forth, unleashing massive lightning blasts that halved trees and reduced granite boulders to powder.

It was a storm like none of the train people had ever seen before. Hour after hour it came down, soaking through the canvas wagon tops as if they were paper. It was impossible to keep fires lit in the downpour.

The two weather fronts clashed finally at Granite Peak, some ten thousand feet above the train at Avalanche Camp. As if weary of their long, futile battle, they loosened their heavy moisture as one. In less than an hour ten inches of rain fell on the peak, turning ravines into streams, gullies into rivers, gorges into awesome torrents. And this water then came down to lower ground seeking the Sweetwater River runoff.

Liberty, traveling with the Dover family, couldn't believe her ears at first. The noise was deafening, like a locomotive's up close. She was looking out the front of the Dover wagon just as a tremendous lightning bolt

lit up the gorge and mountain. She'd never seen so
bright a light before and called for Mr. Dover just as
yet another bolt flashed.

Homer Dover stared in stunned awe. A wall of
water, twenty feet high and climbing, was moving down
the canyon, cleaning out the avalanche-filled gorge as
if the boulders were matchsticks.

"Flood," he croaked. He pushed Liberty out into
the rain and screamed back at his wife and children
to get out from beneath their blankets.

Liberty slithered to the ground and reached back to
take ten-year-old Melanie Dover from her father's arms.

"Start for higher ground," he screamed over the
ever-increasing roar, "I'll get the rest."

Liberty started to slosh away, but the child began
to scream in fear and beat her with her fists.

"Stop it," Liberty scolded. "You're maw will be
with us in a minute."

But the child was strong and broke from her grasp
when she saw her mother step down from the wagon.
Liberty screamed at her, but she was running towards
her already burdened mother now and would not turn
back. Liberty turned to face the flood alone. Gathering her skirts up about her waist, she started climbing
the hillside ahead of her. The ground was a quagmire
and for a while she kept slipping back further than
she advanced. Silt and debris from the hillside sluiced
down, as the wind roared hollowly between barrages
of thunder. Then she looked up ahead and saw the
first two wagons up the line begin mysteriously to rise.
She clutched at a bush and screamed over her shoulder, "Mr. Dover! Hurry! It's upon us!" The words
sucked out of her mouth and in that brief second the
flood came down and embraced her. She fought to
keep it from pulling her out into its fierce central
vortex. She saw wagons and horses floating by, pelted

by rain. She was crashed into a tree trunk and stunned, but remained clear enough in mind to wrap her arms and legs about it. The tree's closest branches were still a good six feet above her head and she let the water raise her in the vain hope that she would be able to grab one and pull herself still higher. The pine branches, as she'd suspected, were too flimsy to support her weight. The whole canyon was a raging white-water river now and still rising. The wagons were being floated away in small caravans, and Liberty could hear even through the storm the pitiful cries of those still trapped within them.

Then, without warning, the flooded ground yielded up the pine's roots and the tree toppled over into the torrent. Desperately Liberty kept a grasp on the branches, but it was as if a huge hand were pulling the entire tree down underwater to bedrock. She let go and, choking for air, fought towards the surface. For a moment she felt beaten, helpless; her head throbbed from the many blows it had taken and it was hard to keep her eyes open. Then, out of the corner of her eye, she saw an odd-looking wooden object hurtling towards her. It was the door of a royal carriage, an English-made carriage, perhaps. Not sure what it was, Liberty flung her body in its path and prepared to grab it as something to buoy her up. Her fingers caught at it, but even after twenty-three years the highly varnished wood was too slippery to hold. With a desperate thrust of her legs she managed to get her torso onto it, praying it would carry her along for a spell. It did not. The weight of her body instantly plunged the door beneath the surface into a strong, swirling undercurrent. Liberty's dress caught on a rusty hinge. Down she went with the door, choking and spluttering again. She opened her eyes to see how to claw free from the hinge, and for an instant thought she was at that point of death in which she'd been told one's past is revealed in strange images. The underwater current had washed the carriage door clean; she saw the same coat of arms she had seen in Selena Tedder's house. It was clear to her that that's what it was, and it was almost as clear to her, in her quirky mental state, that she was about to die.

Then, suddenly, the carriage door smashed into a bedrock boulder, tearing away the hinge and Liberty's dress with it. Again she found herself fighting to gain the surface. She came up just behind another fallen tree that had been partially uprooted but still clung to the bank. She grabbed a topmost branch. Inch by inch she worked her way down towards the trunk, reaching for branches which lay on the water like helping hands. She got to the mud-entangled roots and pulled herself ashore, or at least into shallower water she could stand in, for there was no shore. She didn't look back. She made her way up the mountain. When her feet felt a hard slippery surface free of mud and silt, she knew she was above the flood crest. She took a deep sobbing breath. You're alive, she told herself. Now stay that way until morning.

Two riders had been high in South Pass that night, distant from and unacquainted with each other but both with full vision of the flood.

One was a man Fergus Fowles had put no scouts out to see. At dawn—a bright, cheery one, with birds singing—he looked down at the ravaged Prevost party with smug satisfaction, then turned his horse toward Salt Lake City and his Mormon home.

The other rider felt awe and grief. He had seen the wagon train camp in the rain, but had decided not to go down and join them, for he'd been bound for

Fort Bridger on a mission of great urgency. Now, in a gorge where an avalanche he himself was thoroughly familiar with had once occurred, where a dark-green forest had later grown, was nothing but water surrounded by high canyon walls. Looking out across the entire basin, in some places piled fifty feet high with silt, he felt there could be no survivors.

Forlornly, he turned his horse back towards Fort Bridger. Sick at heart, he could hardly think of his mission. He snaked down off the pass, and plodded his way along what a day before had been a road and was now a foot-deep bog.

He moved slowly for about a mile, then stopped his horse in disbelief.

A woman stood in the bog ahead of him. She was bent nearly double and breathing like an animal. One mud-dripping sleeve had been ripped from her blouse and hung like a rag from her wrist. The other sleeve was gone entirely and the blouse was in tatters. Mud clung to her long, stringy hair, and scratches and abrasions covered her face. Her eyes were wide and staring.

It was Liberty O'Lee.

Theodis Tedder barely recognized her.

Theodis got down from his horse and plodded toward her. She was beginning to gibber as he approached, out of fear or joy he could not tell. Then, when he touched her shoulder, she began to scream.

The scream unnerved Theodis. He felt an impulse to slap her hard, and would have had her face not been so badly cut. Instead, he yelled at her savagely, "Stop it! Don't you know me? I'm Theo Tedder!"

The whiplash voice startled Liberty into silence. She blinked and dug her fingers into Theo's arm. She knew him now.

"How . . . how . . . why?"

"Enough time for that. Let's get you to warmth and medical attention."

Liberty nodded numbly. She let Theodis help her onto his horse. He climbed up behind her. Once in the saddle, she took hold of the pommel in a vice-like grip and did not speak as they rode.

Ten miles down the trail, when Theo halted for two fast-approaching horsemen, Liberty still had not said a single word.

Theo was quick to reintroduce himself to Jim Bridger and Bertha Geddy. Neither had recognized him, for he'd grown from a teenage stripling to a rather heavy-set man far from their eyes. But he knew them instantly. In his eyes, focused on the past, neither had changed in twenty-three years.

But the past had to wait on the present. Theodis gave Bridger and Bertha his version of the flood and the finding of Liberty. Throughout, Liberty still had not spoken.

"What's the matter with her?" Bridger demanded. "Bertha, can you tell?"

"I think so," Dr. Geddy said slowly. "Look at her eyes and the way she's holding that pommel. It's catalepsy. She must think she's still in the flood and must hold onto something for safety. She may have heard Theodis briefly, but I doubt that she can hear us now. Liberty!"

The word had no effect.

Bertha sighed. "This girl's been through hell twice, one time right after the other. Leave her. She's peaceful and I can't really do anything for her until we get back to the fort."

Bridger climbed up with Liberty and rode with her up ahead, while Theo, on Bridger's horse, dawdled alongside Bertha Geddy. A million questions about the past rushed through Theo's mind, now that the emergency was over. They had nothing to do with his urgent mission. Shyness held his questions in check.

"I—I—" he stammered.

Bertha smiled. "It's my little sister Pearl you'd like to ask about, isn't it Theodis?"

"Yes." He blushed.

"Twenty-three years," she mused. "It hardly seems possible. There we all were on the same wagon train—the Geddys, the Buttle-Joneses, the Tedders. My, my, how times have changed." Bertha shook her head. "Pearl is close to forty now. She certainly hasn't had the best of life."

"Is—is she still at the fort?"

"Oh, no, she left in 1858 when gold was discovered in Colorado."

"Then she remarried?"

Bertha said drily, "Long ago. She married one of Bridger's scouts before I could send her back to Ireland. She'd already had that horrible marriage of convenience on the wagon train, as you know. Imagine, she was just fourteen and starting on her third husband."

Tedder made a sour face. "Ours was not a real marriage."

"True," she sadly agreed, "but I venture to say she's had times when she wished she had held onto you."

Tedder frowned. "Had I not been so shy I might never have let her talk me into having Mr. Bridger annul our marriage. Even if we were as young as we were."

"Are you married now?" Bertha asked curiously.

"No."

Struck by his sober response, Bertha remained silent for a few moments. "It so happens," she said then, "that I received a Pony Express letter from Pearl last

week. First word out of her in three years. I can tell
you this much. She has three children—two girls and
a boy—but she isn't married now."

Theo picked up his ears.

Bertha went on. "No, you see, Frank Waller, the
scout she married, was enough to send any woman to
her grave. He chased after every squaw within a hundred miles. Pearl, after the children were somewhat
grown, gave up on him and took up with a farmer
named Seamus Colm. I take it Colm was a good
enough man, but—" Bertha shrugged, "he was killed
in a Cheyenne attack. Seems Pearl is doomed to her
troubles. She's living near the town of Denver now,
working Colm's farm for mere survival." Bertha
shrugged again. "She seems cheerful enough for all
she's been through. I will say that."

"But she has not remarried?" Theo repeated.

"Theodis Tedder," Bertha chuckled, "am I to believe that you came all the way from California just
to ask that question again and again? No, she is not
married now, and neither, you say, are you. Make of
that what you will."

Theodis flushed. "I had hopes of seeing Pearl, is all."
He was silent for a moment, then looked at Bertha.
"Actually, I had another reason for coming to Fort
Bridger, involving not Pearl but you."

Bertha looked at him, surprised.

"I'm on a mission for my brother Nazareth. I don't
know if you remember Nazareth, but—"

"He's your twin," Bertha said alertly. "Of course I
remember him. He was a regular little pepperpot whereas you were—well, sweeter."

"Yes, I suppose that's so," Theo said slowly. "At
any rate, Nazareth is now working for the Central
Pacific railroad and asked me to come and see you
specifically as a doctor. I'm to speak to Mr. Bridger

too. When I finish, you'll know why we couldn't trust this information to the telegraph. This past fall Chinese workers began to cut a right-of-way for the Central Pacific down the mountainside to Truckee Canyon. There have been blizzards in that area since December. It's hard to estimate how many Chinese froze to death or were killed in avalanches these past few months. But they had to be replaced—that's the main point. Two weeks ago about a thousand replacements arrived in San Francisco on two ships, both coming from the same area in China. Many of the Chinese on the first ship were sick when they were off-boarded. At first it was assumed it was merely sea-sickness. They all had diarrhea and were vomiting."

Bertha Geddy began to listen more intently.

"Well," Theo went on, "the weather was such that the second group, who seemed well, couldn't be shipped by steamboat to Sacramento. For three days they were kept in San Francisco's Chinatown and daily more and more of them fell ill. When the Chinese families they were staying with also began to take ill—the symptom was an inflammation of the intestines—the tong agents became concerned and called in doctors other than their own."

"I should certainly hope so," Bertha snapped. "It's cholera, isn't it?"

Theo nodded sadly. "And highly contagious. San Francisco has been in a state of panic. Large sections of Chinatown have been burned out by thugs and self-proclaimed vigilantes. They are allowing no new ships to dock and have the city sealed off.

"Sacramento has done the same, although they have not reported any cases as yet. But they are scared, because the main work camp there has over fifteen thousand Chinese, and the white work crews are in and out of town all the time."

"Any signs of cholera in the camp?"

"Not in the main camp. But at Truckee Canyon, where the new workers were sent, it started cropping up about seven days ago. No one can understand the delay."

"Whoever doesn't is a blind fool. Naturally, I am assuming the workers brought the disease with them from China. The one group was taken immediately to a high, frigid elevation. The bacteria just took longer to build up than in the crowded conditions of China-town. But what has all of this to do with me?"

Theo sighed. This was the hardest part. "The own-ers of the railroad, first of all, wanted to keep the news from the people of Sacramento. They tried to get doctors from San Francisco and Sacramento to come to Truckee Canyon and handle the situation quietly. The San Francisco doctors claimed to be too busy and the Sacramento doctors refused because they were afraid of bringing the germ back into town. Their only suggestion was to isolate the camp and let the disease run its course."

"Inhumane bastards!" Bertha muttered.

"It was my father who suggested you as the logical solution, Bertha. He remembers you from the wagon train as the gutsiest doctor he ever saw. I don't know if you'd be willing or not to—"

Bertha was thinking. "How soon can you get me there?" she cut in.

"Took me three days, but I had a change of horses and put in a sixteen-hour day. You'll have to have pack mules for your supplies. I'd say five days, at least."

Bridger had drifted back on his horse and had lis-tened intently to most of the discussion.

"Nonsense," he snapped. "You came the wagon route. I'll give you a trapper's map that will take you straight across to the Santa Rosa Range. The Winna-mucca tribe can float you down the Humbolt River and put you a half-day's ride from Truckee Canyon. You'll get where you're going in three days, without burden to man or beast."

"That's fine," Bertha said, "but it all depends on the patient I have at hand. I just can't desert her."

Liberty opened her eyes and stared vacantly at the ceiling. Her head ached. Every muscle in her body was stiff and sore. For the moment her mind remained blank about the flood and she thought she was coming to after the stagecoach attack. She tried to struggle up-right and a hand restrained her gently. Somebody said, "Quiet now." She turned her head. Dr. Geddy was standing by the bed.

Bertha smiled. "This is beginning to become a habit."

Liberty stared, frowned, and then remembrance flowed through her. She started up, thrusting the doc-tor's hands aside.

"Was Theo Tedder really here?"

"Yes."

The tension flowed out of Liberty. She sank back slowly until her head touched the pillow. "Thank God. I thought I was hallucinating it." She wet her lips. She said, "What . . . what is he doing here?"

Bertha told her.

"And you are going back with him to California," Liberty repeated dreamily when she'd finished. She closed her eyes. "Then I am going with you."

Bertha felt a surge of helpless sympathy. She said quietly, "You are hardly up to such a journey, my dear."

Liberty took her arm away from her forehead and

opened her eyes. There was anguish and desolation written on her face. She said emptily. "Am I cursed never to get home again? My babies need me and I need my babies. Bertha, please!"

"I'll talk to Jim about it."

Bridger was squinting over the map he had made when Bertha found him and told him of Liberty's request. He had Theo with him. Bridger's eyesight was beginning to fail him. Bothersome nuisance, he called it. He heard Bertha out, then did some thinking. Even though the inclusion of Liberty on the trek would be one more bothersome nuisance, he felt morally responsible to see that she got safely home. Yet all that day the reports from his scouts had troubled him. Something was brewing among the Mormons. The hundred miles his three charges would have to pass through was not really Mormon territory, but it was stoutly claimed by Brigham Young and the scouts had reported his raiders' presence. And Bridger was beginning to wonder if his suggestion about the Winnamucca tribe was wise. He could handle the Indians, but could Theo?

"You know," he said slowly, "with all due respects to you, Tedder, I been thinkin' I'd best take this party through myself. Course, Mrs. O'Lee will have to dress like a mountain man, same as you, Bertha. Those Injuns will let us through, if that's what they think we are. Same with the Mormons, it's just settlers they both hate."

"I'm sure that's fine with her," Dr. Geddy chuckled. "The poor dear would just swim about in one of my dresses."

"When do you think she'll be ready to travel?"

"If she had her way it would have been yesterday. Physically, she's just bruised up a mite. Mentally, I think the sooner the better is the right medicine for her. I'm all for tomorrow morning."

"And you, Tedder?"

Theo cleared his throat nervously. "I was just wondering . . . seeing as how you are now going along . . . if it were really necessary for . . ." His words trailed off.

Bridger grinned broadly.

"Would you be liking me to draw you a map on how to get to Denver, in the Colorado territory, son?"

Theo blushed deeply. "How in the world did you know that was on my mind?

"Ain't been a snoopy old scout on this earth a good sixty-two years for nothing, lad. Worst thing I ever did was annul your marriage to Pearl. In fact, I don't think I had the legal right to do it. Seems to me, you still got a good six hours till sundown, which would put you into the relay station at Rock Springs. Ride hard the next day and you might be gettin' yourself an invite to supper."

Liberty took the news of Theo's quick departure— he hadn't stopped to see her—with mixed feelings. She felt stronger now, up to telling him what she'd learned about Maybelle, and was disappointed that she wouldn't have the chance. Still, she was anxious to get home, and hearing that Bridger approved of her going along with him and Bertha filled her with joy.

Riding out of the fort the next morning, they soon reached the scene of the disastrous flood. For Liberty's sake Bridger would have preferred to cross the still rather spongy delta quickly and get up the side of Granite Mountain, but he had reasons for taking his time. He peered up the canyon wall and had his suspicions confirmed. "We'd best dismount and poke about a bit," he called out to his two companions. "We're being watched."

Liberty shuddered. She didn't want to get off her horse and look at this tragic place. She wanted to keep going and get the flood out of her memory.

"Sorry, Mrs. O'Lee, but we're traveling as mountain men and mountain men are curious creatures by nature. That's a Mormon scout watching us and we got to do what he expects us to do—which is to mosey around like we're looking for cooking utensils, rope, any little thing of value. Don't worry about the horses and mules; they've been trained to stand where you stop them. And try not to get het up about any corpses you might see—mountain men have a habit of taking such things in stride."

Liberty nodded. "I understand, Mr. Bridger. I'll do my best."

Actually, the sight of the buggy plain depressed Bertha even more than it did Liberty, the flood's sole survivor. She had come to know all three hundred members of the Prevost party while they'd awaited their last leg of the journey west. She'd done everything from doctoring their colds and mosquito bites to delivering their babies. It was hard to believe that all had drowned. It was hard to look at scattered wagon wheels and plow handles without recalling their owners and feeling sick.

Liberty, on her part, poked aimlessly for the better part of an hour, up to her booted shins in muddy water. Then, not looking where she was going, she tripped over something, fell and cursed. On her knees, she tumbled with her hands to find what had brought her down. Her fingers slipped over a varnished surface. Suddenly she was frowning. Could it be? She beat at the water with her fists so as to clear some of the mud

out of it and get a better look at the object. She stared
at it in surprised recognition. It was the mate to the
carriage door she had tried to ride through the flood's
torrent.

"Well, I'll be . . ." Liberty began, but did not finish.
Instantly, it re-occurred to her that the other door had
had imprinted on it Selma Tedder's crest—that is,
Selena Buttle-Jones's crest, she corrected herself. Possibly the carriage had belonged to Lady Pamela Buttle-
Jones, Selena's mother. Liberty didn't know. Curiosity
gnawed at her. She tried to lift the door out of the
water. To her amazement, it didn't budge. Though it
felt like wood to the touch, it was stone heavy.

"What in God's name . . ." Liberty said, exasper-
ated. She looked around to get some help from Bridger
and Bertha, but they were too far off to call to.

Nearby was a length of wood that she tried to use
to lever up the entire door, the pointed end of the wood
slipped under a veneered panel, however, and when
she pushed down, hoping for a crowbar effect, only a
piece of this veneer came to the surface. Now when
she peered down she she saw a gleam of metal. Her
breath caught. The metal was gold. Quickly she dug
away the rest of the veneer. It was all gold—the whole
door was gold!

Liberty rose to her feet. "Mr. Bridger!" she shouted.
"Jim! Come quick!" She was unmindful of the distance
now; she shouted at the top of her lungs.

Bridger came sloshing over as fast as he could.

"Jehosaphat!" he cried when he saw the golden door.
"Do you know what you've found there, gal? Do you
know? Here, let me help you with that. Easy now.
We'll just get it over here to dryer ground . . ."

The door weighed over two hundred pounds. Even
after, by struggling and straining, they'd tugged it free

of the water, Liberty stood looking at it in continued puzzlement. Gold it was, undeniably, but whose? And how did it get to where she'd found it?

Bridger stood there alternately scratching his head and chortling.

"Never forget the first time I saw it—or the last," he said. "This door was part of the prettiest landau carriage I'd ever seen. Right foolish, I thought, comin' cross prairie and plain in such fancy riggin', but the lady who rode its padded seats was a Lady—perhaps not in actions, but in name."

"Lady Pamela Buttle-Jones," Liberty supplied hesitantly.

Bridger scratched his chin. "Yep, that's it. Lady Pamela, it was. And that damn carriage of hers caused one hell of a problem with my first wagon train through. I had the gol-dangest group ever assembled, lass. Fightin' and feudin' like you'd never believe. Worst of all was this Lady Pamela and a man who turned out to be her husband that she thought was dead. Had ourselves a real Russian count, too, who gave my guide, Barry Fitzgerald, one rough time in his rush to get to the west coast. Fact is, though the train was snowed in, that count was in such a hurry to get on that he bribed one of Lady Pamela's coachmen to steal the landau and take him and four of his Russian wagons over the pass. They was halfway up the mountain when her husband—Lester was his name, as I recall—went right off his rocker. At that time only this Lester and Lady Pamela knew the carriage was packed with gold and he went tearing after them. Damn fool shot off his rifle and avalanched half the mountain down—on the carriage, the Russians and himself. Filled up the gorge that the flood has now cleaned out. Lady Pamela wanted the gorge dug out and had to confess why. Couldn't dig it out, though, not then. What the flood did in a few minutes would've taken a crew of men fifty years to do."

Liberty had been listening raptly.

"I'm confused," she said. "What did she have to confess to?"

Bridger looked at her startled. "Lass, aren't you aware of what's between these door ribs? It's not just gold—it's smuggled gold. This Lester had it illegal, I think, and Lady Pamela got it from him. He chased her all the way to America to get it back. But by then, she'd had her coachman melt it down and pour it into every cavity of the carriage. You've found just the one door. Lord only knows where the rest of the carriage is under this silt."

Liberty stood as if mesmerized.

"Just my luck," she said then, "to find Lady Pamela and Selena's gold for them."

Bridger had been raising a corner of the door to examine how the gold was laid into it. He looked at her as if she had suddenly lost her mind.

"What you talkin', lass? Ain't been their gold for twenty-three years. It's yours."

"Don't you mean ours?"

"Nope! Trapper's law. When we scavenge, what any of us finds is his to keep."

Liberty stammered, still not quite believing in her good fortune. "But . . . but I'll need your help to get it out of here."

"Yep. But that ain't gonna be too hard. Look here." He pointed to the door ribs. "The gold looks solid but it's in chunks under these crossbars. They're what's holding it in. I count twelve chunks. Now, that's easy. You, me, Bertha, we're going to take these chunks one by one and load them into the mule sacks I now got loaded with beaver pelts. We're gonna leave the pelts right here to make the room for your gold.

"That sound all right to you?"

"Y-yes."

"That's what we'll do then. . . . What's the matter now?"

Liberty shook her head. "Nothing. It's just that it's so much money. I never dreamed I would have so much money. Not of my own. I don't know if I'll be able to handle it. I don't even know how to go about converting it into cash."

Bridger scowled. "Lass, what with you being husbandless and all, this old man strongly advises you to say nothing to no one until you can snoop around and find the right person to give you some honest advice and counsel. The forest is full of two-legged wolves who would love nothing more than to steal this all away from you."

"Yes," Liberty said softly, "that is very good advice. I will think about it on the trip."

"Let's get a move on, then. . . . I wonder what them Mormons up there on the canyon will be thinking, seeing us pick an old door to pieces? Probably think it's three old trappers run out of their brains, which suits me just fine."

The deaths had started two days before their arrival, in Truckee Canyon, which was some ninety miles to the northeast of Sacramento. The Chinese felt that Tin How had gone against them in that horrible Year of the Snake and that they would all perish before the Year of the Sheep came in four days time.

Bertha, taking charge, immediately ordered a quarantine, isolating the sick and having their clothing quickly burned. The patients were then wrapped in wet sheets to help reduce the dehydration taking place in their thin bodies.

Even though Ta Wang protested that his cooks were very clean, Dr. Geddy insisted that all of their utensils be boiled sterile, along with the workers' rice bowls and chopsticks. Such measures alone put new hope into a camp whose inhabitants for weeks had been lying about dispirited, wanting to die.

Ta Wang brought Bertha an excellent interpreter and a battery of Chinese to act as nursing aides. Within a day of her arrival, she had organized and instructed the group in administering vital medications. Most of the hygienic work had been done in her first hours there.

"Miss Liberty," Ta Wang said in awe, "had that woman been born a man in China she would have been a feudal war lord. She barks and my people jump. And she has most strict orders for you to obey."

"Oh she has, has she?"

"I am to see you away from this place at once."

"I think Bertha is right," Jim Bridger advised her. "No use you staying round and catching this crud."

"And what about you?"

"Hell," Bridger scowled, "I'm old enough to die, but too damn mean to get this sick. Besides, I gotta wait and take Bertha back."

"Thank you. Thank you for everything."

Liberty grabbed him and kissed his bearded cheek.

He grinned and winked. "Don't be forgetting your pack mules, lass, or my words about what they carry."

"Ta Wang will see me safely home, Mr. Bridger, and then I know exactly who to discuss my problem with. Thank you, again."

Liberty had many questions for Ta Wang on the way home, and he expertly filled her in on most every railroad event that had taken place since her departure.

The tunnel work had been very slow, due mainly to the surplus blasting powder that Charles Crocker had bought from the army. Either it was old, or badly manufactured, but it was not doing the job.

"Because so many shiploads of this powder are already purchased and on their way," he explained, "Cholly Crocker will listen to no other solution."

"Is there a better one?"

"Ta Wang thinks so. In China many smokeless powders, such as cordite, are combined. These, with glycerol, are slowly added to concentrated nitric and sulfuric acids. After they are carefully mixed a new substance forms on top of the two acids. This layer is drawn off and washed, first with water, and then with a solution of sodium carbonate. We call it "Dragon Fire," for in small quantities that is its main use—to make the New Year dragon belch out a tongue of fire and smoke. It produces a burning gas three thousand times greater in volume than the liquid source."

"Liquid?"

"Yes, Miss Liberty, the substance is a heavy, oily liquid as colorless as water. It is my belief that it would be three times as powerful as an equal amount of blasting powder."

"Let me think on it, Ta Wang. I might be able to sneak it into my report on this trip. Well, I see the retaining walls on the cliff have been rebuilt."

"Some progress has been made, Miss Liberty. Oh, we have also completed the line to Oakland. Our supplies arrive much faster now."

They reached the railhead, which was now up to the Summit Tunnel mouth. Ta Wang was just taking the bundles off the mules and putting them on a hand-car for the trip back across a trestle and thence to the city when someone in the cab of the "T.D. Judah" locomotive began tooting angrily at them from the trestle's far side. Ta Wang looked across the trestle and smiled. Ignoring the toots, he turned the mules and horses over to a coolie for their return to Jim Bridger. Then he pumped Liberty across. They were met by a fire-breathing Charley Crocker.

"Ta Wang," Crocker roared from the cab, "you know we don't give no damn free passage on hand-cars to trappers coming across the pass."

Liberty stepped lightly from the hand-car, removed the fur cap and shook out her hair.

"Hello, Charley," she said sweetly, "nice welcoming committee."

"Jesus!" Crocker gasped. "You're supposed to be dead!"

"Pity, but I'm not. Who supplied you with your information, Thomas Durant?"

"Exactly," he stammered, still shocked to see her alive and equally shocked to see her outfitted like a mountain man. "When he got word of the massacre of the Hollander stage, he wired Collis that you had been on it."

She turned to Ta Wang. "Were you informed of this?"

"No, Miss Liberty."

"Well," she commented acidly, "it isn't often that a person gets to learn how quickly the news of her death hasn't spread."

Ta Wang felt obliged to come to the defense of Charles Crocker.

"Perhaps, Miss Liberty, my answer was too short. The blizzards and then the cholera have kept us rather isolated up here."

"Thank you, Ta Wang," Crocker said with uncommon graciousness. "And may I say, Liberty, that I thank God that Dr. Durant's report was in error."

"Someday, Charley, when I come to realize that this

nightmare is really over, I'll inform you of how errant his report really was and of the murderer he was protecting by it."

"Now, Liberty, you aren't still raking that old chestnut over the coals, are you?"

Liberty smiled, suddenly realizing how long it had been since she had given Colonel Silas Seymour a thought. "No, Charley, I'm not raking. I've pushed it out of the embers so that it can roast slowly and pop open when ready.

"And now," she added, "when can Ta Wang and a train help me get home?"

"We got a train," Crocker said, "that's just been off-loaded and is dead-heading back to Oakland. I'll tell the engineer to let you off in Sacramento. Oh, Ta Wang, while you are in town, ask Leland Stanford if he has any word from the governor on getting doctors to help up at the canyon."

"That won't be necessary, Charley," Liberty put in evenly. "Theo Tedder made arrangements for Jim Bridger to bring Dr. Bertha Geddy to the camp. She has already started to get things under control."

"Bridger," Crocker exclaimed, with boyish glee. "There is one man I have always wanted to meet. Think I'll go over the pass and check on things for myself. Welcome home."

Halfway across the trestle in his "Judah" locomotive, he stopped and looked back. Liberty O'Lee had never called him anything but Mr. Crocker, and that always a little nervously. Now it was Charley. It wasn't just the new name and her new buckskins that made her seem different. It was something he couldn't quite put his finger upon. It was as if she had been put through the fires of hell and now feared nothing except God Himself.

God and a Chinaman, Liberty might have corrected him.

"Ta Wang," Liberty said suddenly, as the train neared Sacramento, "please take my bundles to the house for me. Reassure Madam Soo that I am alive and safe and shall return tomorrow."

"Your wish is my command," Ta Wang smiled. "Old Master Soong shall be happy to see that you are alive, as well."

Liberty certainly hoped that was true, for she had much to lay before Kai Soong. She wanted his spiritual help in explaining the puzzling coincidences she had encountered—the finding of the long-lost Maybelle Tedder, if it was indeed she, and the discovery of Lady Pamela's ancient gold. And she wanted his counsel on what to do with that gold.

Temporarily, at least, all thought of Kai Soong vanished from Liberty's mind, for once on the flat floor of the Sacramento Valley the engineer suddenly opened the throttle wide. She was astonished to find the train roaring along at forty miles an hour.

"This is unbelievable," she breathed to the brakeman in the caboose.

"Ain't nothing," he boasted. "You should see the 'Governor Stanford' on this run. Tell me, they got that old smoke belcher up to near fifty-five. Steamboat captains yelling like hell, since we make it to Oakland in about two hours, which is ten hours less than them. But they're claiming we're just a freight line and won't let us put on passenger cars yet."

Liberty giggled. "Then, I'm quite illegal."

"Hell, Mrs. O'Lee, you ain't a passenger, but railroad family. Heard tell that you were dead, but glad you ain't. But this death sure saddens me." He handed her a copy of that afternoon's edition of the Sacramento *Union*.

The boxed headline blared: FAMED SCOUT KILLED IN FLOOD.

Liberty read the article in amazement.

"Salt Lake City—Brigham Young, president of the State of Deseret and leader of the Church of Jesus Christ of the Latter Day Saints (Mormons), today announced that word had reached him that a flash flood in the South Pass of the Rockies took the lives of famed Indian scout and wagon-train master Jim Bridger and upwards of three hundred other lives. President Young went on to announce that since his church had been in a boundary dispute with Bridger since 1853 over the place called Fort Bridger, he had taken steps to have the fort resettled by his people immediately and renamed Fort Smith, in honor of Joseph Smith, the man alleged to have been visited by God for the establishment of the Mormon religion. The military commander of the Utah Territory, Colonel Patrick O'Connor, was on a gold expedition in the Wasatch Mountains above Salt Lake City and was unavailable for comment."

Liberty couldn't help but laugh, which startled the brakeman.

"What's your name?" she asked.

"Mike Saroyan, Mrs. O'Lee."

"Well, Mike Saroyan, I am dressed the way I am dressed because I came by stage to this Fort Bridger. I was almost killed in the flood they speak of, but Jim Bridger was not. He brought me and a doctor to the Chinese camp, where she is working on their illness. This is all tommyrot, except perhaps the part about the Mormons taking over Bridger's land and fort."

"Damnnation," he spat, "they can't get away with it, can they?"

"I don't know. I just don't know."

Liberty sat back, thankful she would not be there when Jim Bridger got the news. Why was it, she wondered, that all the hard-working pioneer leaders who opened up the west world were being so quickly pushed aside by power blocks? It wasn't just the Mormons literally stealing Bridger's fort. It was cattle barons gobbling up homesteaders, and the large processing and smelting concerns gobbling up prospectors' gold claims. And it was men like Durant, Stanford, Huntington, Crocker and Hopkins—the avaricious takers, grasping at land, money, lives, anything they could get their power-greedy hands on.

They had taken her husband from her, and come back only to ask additional favors. They'd believed her dead, and had been so "grief stricken" they hadn't announced it. She saw them for what they were: bloodsuckers. Never before had her father's words on slavery had more meaning for her:

"Libby, girl, these slaves give us their work and their future generations. We give them food, lodging, medicine, and the assurance that we are here to keep those future generations together as family. You speak out against the slave system, child, and quite eloquently, but without understanding it. Someday, Libby, you're going to see real slavery in this world, and I don't speak of the blacks. We care for our people. Think back on that when you see men of power use their fellow men without care. Don't scoff. History is crowded with men who have misused other men to do their will. It will never change. But if you are ever given the opportunity to change it just a mite, don't hesitate."

Liberty left the train, tucked her hair back up under her fur cap, took the ferry from Oakland to San Francisco, and then hesitated. She had no money with her, only a few little chips of gold that had been loose in the carriage door. She looked at the long line of carriages and hansom cabs on the wharf; the unhappy faces of the drivers, who had lost most of their business in the cholera scare, made up her mind for her. She walked with determination up to the first driver.

"I want to go to the House of Soong in Chinatown," she said firmly, "but this is all I have for fare." She held out a chip weighing close to an ounce.

The driver looked at her suspiciously. He took the chip, weighed it in his palm, tested it with his teeth. Incredulous, he shook his head.

"Lad, I'll take it as fare, all right, but are you aware of what it's worth?"

"Quite," Liberty lied. "But I want to get to my destination fast, and it's worth it."

"Right," the man agreed, but was still curious. "Lad, I took some of the first ore out of Sutter's Mill. This piece has been processed and smelted. It ain't stolen now, is it?"

Liberty took a wild gamble. "You'll only learn that if you take me."

"Done," he barked, "but you sit up here to tell me."

The driver was not particularly concerned if the gold had been stolen or not. Business had been very bad and he would have taken it regardless. But he was curious to learn more about it. Liberty climbed up beside him and told him where she wanted to go.

"Chinatown? House of Soong?" he mused. He made an instant assumption. "Why would old Kai Soong want processed and smelted gold?"

"Don't ask me," Liberty shrugged, following his lead. "I only know that someone told me that was the way to get the best price for it from the Chinese. Easier to ship to China, I guess."

The driver nodded and remained silent for a few moments as the cab rolled on.

"Travel far?" he said then.

"Yes."

"Thought as much, by your dress. Knew you couldn't be from around Californy."

"No. Been over into Utah."

Liberty could almost hear the man's heart begin to palpitate.

"Utah," he said. "Ain't ever heard of no gold strike thereabouts."

"And you won't," Liberty said. Suddenly, her heart was pounding; the man was giving her an opportunity to trust him with a "secret." "Mormons control that whole area," she said. "I had to smuggle this out to an outfit in Nevada to process it for me. They don't want outsiders in their country, but I'm going back."

"That much gold, huh?"

Liberty hesitated for a moment, trying to recall the words in the newspaper report. The hesitation whetted the man's enthusiasm even further.

"It's in the Wasatch Mountains," Liberty said slowly, "above Salt Lake City. Even the Union army commander is out looking for gold. You mentioned Sutter's Mill. Mister, there's a thousand times as much gold in Utah, but the world will never know about it because the Mormons don't want it known. I hope that colonel makes a big find to open the area up. The Mormons are strong. Did you hear they took over Jim Bridger's land just cause he got killed in a flood? It will take a rush on their land, like 1849 here, to really get that gold away from them."

"Who said the gold and the land was theirs to begin with?" the man flared.

"They say God!"

"Well," he declared hotly, "they are God damn wrong. It belongs to Christian people like us. Would you be minding if I told a couple of me friends about your gold find?"

"Not at all. From what I understand there's enough gold in Utah to make a million men like us rich for life."

"Here we are," the driver announced in a state of nervous elation. "Shall I wait for you?"

"No. I can find my way back."

It was exactly what the driver had hoped the reply would be. He had a million plans to make, several dozen people to see, a hundred ears to whisper into. He would make sure that within the week the out-of-work and starving would be given new hope. In San Francisco alone, he knew close to two thousand men who would march on Utah for the opportunity of striking gold again. Mormons? They didn't worry him. The prospectors he knew had killed claim-jumpers before and would kill them again if need be. He turned his cab around and raced it back to the wharf.

Surprisingly, Kai Soong himself opened the door, his usually grave face aglow with pleasure.

"Never has a house been more pleased to welcome a wayward traveler," he said warmly, bowing Liberty in.

"Can I never surprise you?"

He grinned. "Not when Ta Wang had the good sense to wire me of your arrival."

Liberty laughed. "You could have made yourself sound exceedingly mystical by not telling me that."

"I could, I could," Kai Soong said with an understanding nod. "But is it not mystery enough that I was able to keep you alive in the hearts of some, while all others wished to believe in your demise?"

"I don't understand."

"Selena Tedder," Kai Soong said with a scowl. "I had to convince Collis Huntington that you were still alive, because Mrs. Tedder wanted to put your children in an orphanage at once. They are still with Madam Soo, but by court order under the custody of Mr. Huntington."

Liberty felt a sudden alarm. "I should have rushed to them first!"

"No. They are young and know nothing. One more day will not matter to them now, though it shall in the future. Come with me. It is the future you wish to discuss, is it not?"

Liberty nodded. "That, and the past, Kai Soong. I am still afraid of your powers, but . . . but . . ."

He smiled at her disarmingly and motioned for her to follow him into his inner room. Once the panel was closed behind them, he said to her gently, "Show me now what you have brought for me to see."

Mutely, Liberty showed him the gold chips.

"Ah," Kai Soong said knowingly. He did not take the chips from her, but said, "Perhaps the proper place to put them is in front of him." He pointed.

"Do you mean the idol?" Liberty said. "I liked him the first time I was here. He seems so happy, as if tickled about something." She went to the idol and put the chips down at its feet, smiling at its cheerful countenance.

Kai Soong followed her. "He has been blessing you on your journey."

"How has he been blessing me?"

"He is one of the high officials in the celestial world.

He controls people's ages and the time of their deaths."

"You mean he's a god of longevity?"

"A very occidental translation, but yes."

Liberty stood up.

"I have more gold than this, Much, much more."

Kai Soong only nodded.

Liberty knelt again and touched a chip with a finger. "Except for coins, I had never before touched gold in my life. It's so warm, as if it had a life of its own."

"You are treating it with proper respect, Chu-chee. You are giving it life and the god will give it longevity, making it multiply into a vast treasure."

"Shall I tell you how I came by it?"

"No," Kai Soong said, almost harshly. "You must not. Nor do I wish to read it in your thoughts. Its past is of no importance, Chu-chee. You must give it only a future. But before we discuss that, I have had my servants prepare a tub and clothing for you."

He clapped his hands and a panel was instantly opened in the east wall. A young girl entered, bowing low. She was dressed in a Chinese gown of light blue and wore a pigtail. Her pretty face, without make-up, glowed with health.

"This is Meng, the youngest daughter of my youngest brother. She is with us just two months. She will see to your needs, if you but follow."

Liberty went without hesitation. To rid herself of the heavy buckskins would be a relief, to bathe in a tub a luxury. When they reached the "bath-house" she promptly changed her opinion. The spacious pavilion with red-lacquered lattice siding was clean but quite open to the view of several coolies working in the garden.

Wang Wu came bustling from the house, his arms heaped with towels and his moon face smiling.

"Missy, welcome!" he chirped. "You fill Wang Wu's

heart with much pleasure to look upon you again. Meng bathe you now, yes?"

Liberty hesitated, looking out the lattice at the workers.

Wang Wu laughed. "They no lookee, missy. Old Master Soong forbids it."

Liberty still was uncomfortable, and the feeling grew as she came to realize that Meng intended to bathe her head to foot. She tried to shoo the girl away, but Kai Soong had been able to intimidate the girl since her arrival, certainly not a white woman. With hand signals and giggles she let Liberty know exactly what she expected her to do. And it was all done in almost ritual fashion.

As Liberty sat nude on a little three-legged stool, the girl pushed her head down between her legs over an oaken bucket. Hot oil was vigorously rubbed into her scalp and then rinsed away. Next came a lemony-smelling lathering agent that stung Liberty's eyes when she tried to open them. She gasped at the temperature of the first hot water rinse, relaxed a little when the second bucket of water was several degrees cooler, and gasped again as the third bucket of very icy water cascaded down on her head.

Deftly, Meng toweled out most of the moisture and sat Liberty upright. Now a lavender-scented lathering agent and sponge were used to soap every portion of her body. It embarrassed her to be bathed in this fashion. A large sunken tub was built into the floor of the pavilion. After she was subjected to three more rinses she was led to the tub and motioned to take the three steps down into the steaming water.

Liberty gingerly put a foot in and pulled it back quickly.

"That water is scalding!" she cried.

Meng merely giggled and pushed her in by the

shoulders. Liberty yelped. She felt like her skin was being boiled from the bone. Meng motioned for her to sit down in the water to her neck and relax.

"How does one relax when they're being cooked alive?" Liberty exclaimed. But within seconds the water seemed less hot and she could feel the tension and soreness ease from her limbs.

She was reluctant to leave when Meng motioned her out. Without warning she was doused with another bucket of icy water and then roughly toweled dry. Her body was scented, powdered and her hair brushed to a glistening sheen. Again she was motioned to rise and Meng held open a Chinese gown for her to be wrapped in. Liberty objected. She looked around and pointed to her underthings. Meng giggled and pointed to her own body as if to say she didn't wear such, so why should Liberty? The gown's silk was so soft and cool, touching her skin from neck to ankle, that Liberty stopped protesting and let Meng fasten all twenty of the buttons down the front.

She felt as if she were floating as she followed Meng back into the house and up to the secret panel.

Kai Soong sat on his kang puffing at his water pipe, the room already a little hazy from the bluish opium smoke.

"I anticipated the length of your bath, Chu-chee. Are you to join me again at the pipe?"

Liberty laughed. "I feel as if I myself have been smoked."

She walked to the kang, the silk molding to every sensuous curve of her body.

"The gown becomes you," Kai Soong said admiringly. "I hope you don't mind that it is one of my daughter's."

Liberty was surprised to find that she didn't mind. Out of courtesy she asked: "And how is Mai Ling?"

"I hope well. She is on business in China for me again. My eldest brother thinks that what I make in the morning must all be sent to China by that night. She will set him straight."

Liberty took a small puff at the reed tube. "In many ways I envy her. I wish I had the business schooling she has."

"Some must learn from books, others from practical experience, and still others are born with the knack. You, Chu-chee, are of this last class."

"I hardly think you are correct this time, Kai Soong."

He shrugged. "Have you given any thought to what purpose you shall put your gold?"

"Hardly. I don't even know its worth."

Even without having seen the bulk of her gold, Kai Soong quietly quoted her a very conservative estimate.

Liberty looked horrified. "However can I exchange as much as that without it becoming known?"

"That shall be my worry, Chu-chee. Your worry shall be its proper investment."

"I can't decide that alone," Liberty objected. "I just don't know—wait, a couple of possibilities just crossed my mind."

"Let me hear them, by all means."

"Several years ago Collis Huntington bought two hundred shares of Union Pacific in my name to force information out of the UP board. I was supposed to sell the shares in New York, return his investment and keep the profit for myself. I never got a chance to do that in the east and the certificates must have been destroyed in the stagecoach."

"That is no problem. The brokerage house and the Union Pacific will have a record of them. What do you now wish to do with them?"

Liberty sat back smiling. The opium was relaxing her brain so that she could think quite clearly now.

"I want to keep the shares," she said simply. "I want to return Collis's ten percent down payment, which came to $20,000, and pay off the rest of the money due. That will cost me $220,000, in all. How soon can I do it?"

Kai Soong chuckled. "Today. I can have money advanced to you to pay Collis and have my tong agent in New York handle the rest."

Liberty blinked. "You have a tong in New York?"

"Chu-chee, we deal in spices, silks and tea just as much as we deal in coolie labor. Loung Li is a cousin from my mother's family and can be trusted. But may I be so bold as to suggest that the certificates will give you no return on your money for some time?"

"Yes," Liberty mused, "that's true. But someday I feel the shares will be worth more than all of the gold."

"Of that I am sure, but you also need an investment that will make money for you in the present."

Liberty picked up a sweetmeat and nibbled at it. "This may sound fantastic, and I wouldn't know what the idea might be worth, but Ta Wang was telling me about 'dragon fire' and how it could be used in the blasting of the tunnels."

"Hum," Kai Soong said with a nod of approval. "Nitroglycerin."

"Is that what you call it?"

"That is what an Italian chemist by the name of Ascanio Sobrero calls it. He claims to have discovered it in 1846, although it has been used in China since the days of the Chou dynasty. I am aware of this because Ta Wang also mentioned it to me and I wanted to look into the feasibility of shipping it from China."

Liberty sat up. "Why ship it? Why not set up a factory and make it right here? Would I have enough money for that?"

"I'm sure you would, but who would run the factory for you?"

"Ta Wang. of course."

"Chu-chee, Chu-chee," he laughed, "and you say you are not a businesswoman. Right to my face you announce that you would steal my best agent away from me."

"Hardly steal. He is too intelligent to be wasted herding shovel crews around."

Kai Soong took a long, meditative pull on the water pipe. He fully agreed with her about Ta Wang's intelligence. Moreover, the thought of a dragon-fire factory here had occurred to him too, but he had not acted on it, knowing his brothers would fight the investment. They were beginning to fight him on all investments. They wished only for the money to keep flowing into the Canton House of Soong, plowing none of it back for the future.

"Chu-chee," he said softly, "for once you have shown me the future. If it is agreeable to you, I shall look into a partnership for such a venture. In that way your name need not be linked with it."

"Agreed," she said, then hastily added: "but I want Ta Wang also to have a fair share, because it was his idea."

He looked at her with loving tenderness. "You shall be very successful, Chu-chee, because those around you cannot help but be loyal and trustworthy."

Kai Soong rose and walked to the moon-window to gaze out on his bamboo garden. He felt as if his family umbilical cord had just been severed and he was breathing on his own for the first time in years. He would begin to build a second House of Soong, one that his Canton brothers would not learn about and be able to drain dry. He felt young and excited at the

prospect. He felt he had at last fulfilled all of the obligations for his past sins and was redeemed and set
free from the conditions placed on him by his brothers.

"Chu-chee," he whispered, "can you read my innermost thoughts?"

Liberty started to answer and stopped. Except for
the Chinese gown she was wearing, everything was as
it had been the first time she had come into this room.
At that time she had feared that she would have to
give of her body to regain her husband. She had been
shocked that she bared herself and Kai Soong had
done nothing but look away and foretell her future.

Now, as if hypnotized, she slowly stood and began
to unbutton the gown. She felt no fear of Kai Soong.
He no longer seemed a threat to her, mentally or physically. Something within her told her that they had
reached a plane of mutual understanding and trust.

She let the gown float to the floor.

As Kai Soong slowly approached her, he appraised
every detail of her body: hair, eyes, nose, lips, breasts,
waist and femininity—likening each to a Chinese flower
or bird. His voice was mesmerizing, lifting and falling
like an invisible piper playing in a mist-laden forest.
At first only his long fingernails came in contact with
her skin. Like gossamer, they explored the parts of her
anatomy that his voice sang praises to. Liberty could
feel the effect of those minute touches charge through
her body like lightning bolts. She was unable to tell
him to stop; either that, or she did not wish to.

Kai Soong waited, then gently stepped from his
gown and slippers.

"Behold me!" It was not an order; it was an invitation to touch him as he had touched her.

The gown, the beard, the drooping mustache, the
stern look, seemed now all to have been parts of a
disguise to hide the real Kai Soong. He stood before

her in a youthful ardor belying his forty years. His chest was muscular and hairless. His torso tapered down to a flat belly, slim waist and strong hips. The muscle-roped legs were those of a strong young man in his twenties.

Liberty's hands danced capriciously over his upper body, while a few inches below another part of him leaped with desire.

Kai Soong leaned down until his tongue contacted the rosy nipple of her breast. Liberty stood with her legs wide and breathed with delight. Whatever qualms and trepidation she'd been feeling vanished. She could hardly wait for the next delicious move he would make. Nor was it opium that was inducing her now miraculous sensations of desire. She was allowing his advances, she realized suddenly, because she desired them, nothing more and nothing less.

15

Lee-Soong-Wang Explosives, Inc. was generally thought to be owned by three Chinamen. Liberty, was content with its organization. Leaving most of the technical details to her better-informed partners, she quietly negotiated with Collis Huntington to get a land site for the factory. Because the Associates realized the factory's potential danger to the citizens of Sacramento, they agreed to lease railroad land at Donner Lake for its operation.

The Central Pacific had actually been intrigued by the new explosive's possibilities from the start. Heretofore, they'd been using three hundred kegs of niter and soda powder per day, army surplus materials which had to be shipped around Cape Horn in iron kegs to prevent spoilage. From $1.50 a keg, post-war profiteering had pushed the price first to $3.75 and then steadily upwards. The cost to the railroad was $15 a keg out of Boston when Lee-Soong-Wang gave the first demonstration of its "dragon fire." It proved to be an enormous success.

Now calling the nitroglycerin "California powder" so as to confuse the eastern competition, Lee-Soong-Wang showed that it could do a third more work than

400

the imported powders at a price equivalent to $2.60 a keg. They were given an order to supply seven thousand kegs a month. Huge sums of money were about to roll into Liberty's coffers.

Meanwhile, on another front, both Dr. Bertha Geddy and Jim Bridger made important decisions affecting their lives. Neither wished to return to Fort Bridger to fight Mormons—Bridger because he felt he was too old and Bertha because she would not go without him. Bertha, after stemming the cholera crisis, felt it was time for her to go visit her sister Pearl and consider setting up practice in the Colorado Territory. As for Bridger, Liberty found a use for his still valuable services. Putting a bug in Collis Huntington's ear, she had him hired by the Central Pacific to negotiate peace treaties and land-usage pacts with the Indian tribes along the railroad's route. What Bridger offered the California and Nevada chiefs and their braves—a lifetime coach pass for the former and free rides on platforms for the latter—cost the railroad nothing. But it helped them avoid the greatest problem facing the rival Union Pacific—constant attacks by Indians who did not want the iron horse to cross their land. Not a single Central Pacific employee lost his life to an arrow or tomahawk, after Bridger was hired.

The Year of the Sheep was considered by the Chinese to promise much prosperity. A month after its arrival, Liberty had her first private meeting with her two partners.

Ta Wang gave his report. It was not altogether sanguine.

"We have fulfilled the order for the first month, but the work is slow because each coolie must be carefully trained. Also, many of the ships' captains are refusing to transport the supplies I require from China. They claim it is too dangerous, but mainly it is because they are greedy and the freight charges are less than a human body in the same space."

"Are more Chinese coming in?" Liberty asked.

Kai Soong nodded. "Crocker has placed quite a large order, but for very menial workers. They will not be qualified to work in the factory or to do the blasting. What we need are Chinese already trained in the manufacture of dragon fire and its uses."

"But," Liberty asked cautiously, "won't they cost more, being trained, and will the Central Pacific pay a higher wage?"

Kai Soong grinned. "Occidential business questions, Chu-chee, that must be answered in an oriental manner. China is in a deep drought and famine. If we feed the families of skilled men while they are gone, they will come at any price. But yes, Cholly Crocker should be charged more for them. However, it helps us little, because whatever added profit we make must go directly back to the Canton House of Soong."

"Why?" she demanded. "Is there no way that we can recruit them without going through Canton?"

Kai Soong shrugged. "We could do this physically, Chu-chee, through Mai Ling. But the shipping masters' contracts with the Canton House of Soong are quite binding."

Liberty puzzled over the problem for a minute. "While I was in Washington," she said slowly, "I recall Senator McDougall mentioning a shipbuilder in Oakland. Are we in a position to purchase a ship and bring in not only the men you need but the necessary supplies?"

Kai Soong lifted an eyebrow. "Perhaps," he said cautiously. "I must think about it. With a bit of sleight of hand, perhaps. I will investigate the matter on my return to San Francisco."

Shipbuilder Samuel Fletcher had three new ships lying at anchor, apparently unwanted. Furthermore, the government contract he had felt assured of had gone to the Boston naval shipyard. He had been forced to reduce his labor gangs by two-thirds and no new keels were being laid in his drydocks.

A hard-rock Methodist ill-disposed towards Chinese, Fletcher at first saw no reason to yield on his prejudice when Kai Soong came to him. He knew of the man's reputation, of course; everyone in financial circles did. But he failed to see how the sale of just one ship—which was apparently all the Chinaman was inquiring about—could get him out of his present difficulties.

But Kai Soong was using a gambit earlier employed by Collis Huntington. After inquiring about each ship separately, he made a firm if lower offer for all three combined.

Sam Fletcher swallowed. "The ships are seaworthy, Mr. Soong," he stuttered. "If you'll take all three at that price, I can have them fully crewed and ready to sail in two weeks or less."

Kai Soong nodded indifferently.

"For the moment," he said softly, "that will be adequate. But I humbly wonder—when might I have three additional vessels?"

Fletcher was staggered. "Three more? I could give you one in a year, with my present labor force. A third of that, for all three, if I can afford to go back to full strength."

Kai Soong closed his eyes slowly. "If a deposit is required to give you such, please do not hesitate to name a figure."

Fletcher did so with no hesitation. He knew the cost of his product down to the last penny.

"Agreed," Kai Soong sighed. "An agent will be back today with the money for the vessels, their crews and the deposit."

"In cash?" Fletcher gasped.

Kai Soong eyed him coldly. "Naturally! I assumed that you were aware that I am only a go-between for the true owner. You may make out the necessary papers in the name of Lee-Pacific Lines."

"And the names for these first three ships?"

Kai Soong thought a moment.

"We shall call then the *Dan,* the *Wells,* and the *Miranda.*"

Fletcher shrugged and wrote them down. He didn't care what names the owners gave their ships, as long as they paid for them and ordered more.

Next, Kai Soong made out two carefully worded messages for delivery in China by the *Pacific Queen,* which was sailing from San Francisco that day.

The first was simply a sleight-of-hand lie. It was to his eldest brother, the Master of the Canton House of Soong, sorrowfully reporting the loss of a quarter-million dollars in gold aboard the *Hong Kong,* which had sunk during a typhoon. Insofar as the *Hong Kong* had indeed sunk, Kai Soong had support for his story. In stern words, he went on to inform his brother that since the loss had occurred during the Year of the Snake, the San Francisco House of Soong could not take responsibility for it; he then softly suggested that with the arrival of the Year of the Sheep the gods should more than double the profit they had lost.

The second message was to his daughter. Without the knowledge of her uncles, Mai Ling was to begin recruiting the finest gunpowder experts who were desirous of employment, place orders for the list of supplies enclosed, and take out a docking and import-export license in the Lee-Pacific Line name.

Finally, Kai Soong took from his safe the money to send to Fletcher—a quarter-million dollars that would have been on an upcoming ship to Canton had he not chosen to spend it otherwise.

His future, Kai Soong knew as he sealed the envelope, was not with his brothers but with Liberty O'Lee.

By the time the lupine blossomed in the Sierras, twelve thousand Chinese were laboring on the mountain's eastern crest and nearly half that number were blasting tunnels on its western side.

At first Crocker objected to paying the new blasters $2 a day. Then Ta Wang proved to him that by doing the work of three men each, they were actually saving him a dollar a day, and Charley Crocker shut up.

Liberty quietly bought a little cottage in Sacramento, desiring nothing fancier. Let others, like Selena Tedder, put their money into showplace homes; she was intent at the moment only in acquiring more money and more power, for herself and her children. Not even Dan's unpaid wages escaped her attention; she wanted what was due her.

"It's not only unfair, but illegal, Collis," she insisted. "My life was nearly taken three times, but I still accomplished more in Washington than any of you dreamed I could. I don't buy Mark Hopkins's statement that Dan's money will be paid out of railroad profits. You pulled that on Anna and Ted Judah. She's wealthy enough not to have to sue. I am not."

"Just settle down, Liberty," Collis soothed. "You do, at least, have the profit out of the stock I let you sell."

"Which is what I have been living on," Liberty lied. "That has nothing to do with the verbal contract I had with your so-called Associates. I want Dan's wages and that's all there is to it. If I don't get it by tomorrow, I'm filing suit. When I get finished in court, Hopkins and Stanford will regret the pennies they refused to pay me for the millions that it will cost them. You all seem to forget that I know where a hell of a lot of skeletons are buried."

Two hours later Mark Hopkins himself delivered $15,000 in cash to the cottage. The next day, Liberty's new houseboy delivered it to Kai Soong. A day after that it was in the hands of a San Francisco broker for the purchase of Central Pacific stock in the name of L. Lee.

Then, in mid-May, a sequence of events gave Liberty still another challenge to meet. It too involved a railroad, though not the Central Pacific.

Mainly to keep her body as youthfully attractive as Kai Soong's, she had been carefully watching her diet. One day her houseboy placed a distressing salad before her—the tomatoes over-ripe and rubbery. She shoved her plate away.

Madam Soo, who had become her constant meal companion, sighed deeply. "Is not fault of my husband. He cannot get good tomatoes. Is same at Chinese market or at Stanford Mercantile."

"That was never so before," Liberty protested. "The farms in the upper valley have always had two crops a year, and we always got them fresh."

"No longer," Madame Soo mourned. "It is a long trip by wagon since the trains no longer run. See, they are even selling the train's parts—it says that here in this newspaper."

Liberty took that day's Sacramento *Union* from her

and, frowning, read an auction notice. Because the wide-gauge Sacramento Line was no longer needed, the notice explained, its rolling stock, locomotives, ties, rails and right-of-way would be dismantled and sold on the steps of the state capital building.

Next to the notice was an advertisement announcing the last two days of Sacramento Line excursion trains running to Sutter's Mill and the former gold fields.

The information gave Liberty not one but two bright ideas.

The first was to pay a surprise visit to Howard Tedder, who was living alone in Sacramento. She had gone to see the old Tennessee man twice since her return— once to report on his son Theo's accomplishments and then to see if he wanted to send a letter back to Theo via Bertha Geddy. Both visits had warmed old Howard. He missed his family. Selena had made sure that he seldom saw Lydia May and Nathan, and Nazareth was too busy with railroad work and his own construction company to have much time for his father. Carefully, believing that in his loneliness he might be interested, Liberty told him of what was happening to the Sacramento Line.

"Yes," Howard answered slowly. "It's a shame. I recall the building of that line quite well."

"Now that they are going to tear it up and sell it off, I was wondering, as a favor to me, would you take that excursion run with me this afternoon? I would love to see it through the eyes of one of the men who built it. Ted Judah always promised such a trip to Dan and me, but time just seemed to run out."

It pleased the old man to be needed by someone. It pleased him even more, while they were riding the train, to find that Liberty was quite intelligent in her questions about the line, as to what deterioration had taken place, what it would take to bring it back into full operating condition and how much of the wide-gauge equipment was still serviceable.

He answered all her questions quite honestly and then asked a puzzled, "Why?"

Adroitly, Liberty managed to avoid answering. She began relating the tales she had heard about him and the other members of the wagon train Jim Bridger had brought out west more than two decades before. Tedder was pleased. He didn't think young people liked to hear nostalgic yarns and relished spinning them.

When the conductor announced that the next stop would be the Feather River Station, Liberty laughed.

"Can you tell me, Mr. Tedder, when you last saw the Herberts?"

"Herbert?" he pondered. "Oh, yes, the young chap that married his step-mother, with that big parcel of black slaves. They were from Alabama, I recall. Well, not since we split up down the Sacramento a piece."

"And I bet you didn't know you've been eating their vegetables for years."

"Didn't," he answered drily, "but can't say I've cared for them lately. Dried out and pruny, them as I cared to buy."

"That, Mr. Tedder, is because the railroad hasn't been running freight for a month and everything has been brought down by wagons."

"Don't say."

"I do say, and I have one more favor to ask of you. From what I understand, the Herberts' main farm is only a mile from Feather River. There is another excursion train coming along in two hours. Would you have the time to stop off with me and introduce me to them? I've heard so much about them that I'm curious to meet them in person."

Howard Tedder had all the time in the world. Besides, he told himself, it might be rather fun seeing people he had not seen in nearly a quarter of a century.

When they crossed the spacious fields, entered the plantation-style house and met the Herberts, they each saw them quite differently. To Howard, carrying his memories with him, Harmon Herbert was still an arrogant, muscular youth, who'd had the gall to marry his own stepmother; Mary Sue Herbert, in his eyes, was still a simpering southern belle who had tried to hold onto her slaves after freeing them.

Liberty saw them in their present form. Jim Bridger had told her a little about them, but not enough to matter. To her, Harmon Herbert was one of the most beautifully sensuous males she had ever encountered, but he seemed totally unaware of his powers. In his eyes glowed a love for his land, for the black farmers he worked closely with, and, most deeply, for his wife.

Mary Sue was rapidly showing her age, but Harmon looked at her as if the past twenty years had never been; and her eyes reflected back his love with equal ardor. Liberty felt an instant fondness for them. Although they lived only forty miles from Sacramento, the news they heard from Howard Tedder was fresh to them—they were living a romantic idyll far from the city's strife.

Harmon Herbert frowned, however, when Howard brought up the subject of the quality of his vegetables.

"Problem is, Mr. Tedder," he said, in the Alabama drawl he'd never lost, "we're close to a hundred farms that work close together. We stretch twenty miles to the coast range and another twenty up the valley. We was mostly cotton, till Sacramento began to grow and demand more foodstuff. No problem shippin' cotton, anytime. No problem shipping foodstuff either, even though some wagon had to come twenty miles for it,

long as the railroad ran to Sacramento. But no railroad means back to cotton next year, even though this
land will yield two vegetable crops a year."

"Do you sell in San Francisco?" Liberty asked.

Harmon Herbert looked at her as if she couldn't be
expected to understand geography.

"Near an impossibility, ma'am," he said politely.

"What about the steamboats?"

"Ma'am," he said, "the twelve-hour run on the
steamboats near ruins anything we've tried to ship
down in their holds. It's hot down there. Heat ages
it a week in a half-day run. Agents refuse to buy and
we're stuck with the freight bill."

"Aren't you aware that there is now a rail line to
Oakland?"

"No ma'am."

"Well, there is."

Harmon scratched his head, then shook it. "Ma'am,
that still don't help. We'd need spur lines twenty miles
west and twenty miles north, before we could supply
fresh produce to San Francisco, same as we used to
supply to Sacramento."

"Then that's what you shall have," Liberty instantly
declared. "Mr. Tedder, tomorrow, we are putting in
our bid on the Sacramento Line. If we are successful,
then you have a job of building forty miles of spur
lines."

Before anyone could comment there was a knock at
the door and they were interrupted by an aged Italian
farmer, his voice filled with pleading. Harmon Herbert
stood on the doorstep and spoke to him briefly. The
man was adamant about something. Liberty could not
help but overhear the conversation, although she understood little of the man's garbled English.

"Excuse me," she said to Harmon when he returned.

"I don't mean to intrude, but what did he say about forest land?"

"Mrs. O'Lee," Harmon said slowly, "it's a sad case. Several years ago I leased some land I homesteaded north of San Francisco to this man's son. The place is called Napa Valley. It's mostly forest, but the son cleared a few acres and planted grapevines. I 'spect he wanted to boast to his father. In any event he wrote home to Italy and told him of the great wine-producing land he had discovered. Pretty soon, the father has arrived on my doorstep. It seems he brought cuttings from every one of his grapevines in Italy, thinking the land here would be ready for them. But I don't have the labor to clear the land he needs and now he cries that his cuttings are dying back daily."

Liberty's mind clicked. One after another, ideas were coming to her like offerings of the gods. "What manner of lease would you grant him if the timber was cleared at no expense to you?"

"Lease?" Harmon frowned. "I don't want to lease —I want to sell it now. I have all the land I need. But he won't buy unless I pay to clear it. I just can't afford that."

"How many acres?" Liberty asked, keeping her voice calm.

"Over ten thousand."

"How much?"

"Ten dollars each."

"Unheard of. Say again."

"I have said."

Liberty's eyes narrowed. "Then say again, Mr. Herbert. I am not about to buy the Sacramento Line and put in forty miles of spur lines for your benefit without gaining something in return. You seem totally out of touch. Tomorrow, if you receive the news that I have purchased the Sacramento Line, come into town to negotiate. In exchange for the spur lines I will consider buying your Napa Valley property for two dollars an acre. If you decide to accept it, bring the Italian farmer with you so I can negotiate with him as the new owner of the land he wants."

Back on the train Liberty giggled out an admission to Howard Tedder.

"I don't even know if I have enough funds to buy the railroad and here I am making a deal on land as well."

"To say nothing of the spur lines you were proposing. Are you aware of their costs?"

Liberty sobered. "Yes, I guess I really am, from what I've learned in my short time in this business. Tell me, Mr. Tedder, am I being stupid?"

"Ain't heard a stupid word out of your mouth this whole day. Sounds mighty wholesome, if you know what I mean."

"If I bring this off, will you place the bid for me and become my general contractor for the spur lines?"

"Nothing would give me more pleasure."

"Oh! My name can't really be connected with it. We would do it all in the name of L. Lee."

"Mrs. O'Lee, I couldn't care less what name you use. I just pray it happens so I can begin to feel useful again."

"Then I'll give you your first chance to be involved. I hardly know what to bid tomorrow. Will you name the figure?"

"What if I am way off? It's been a long time for me."

"Longer for me in the other direction, Mr. Tedder. Longer for me."

They need not have feared. The Central Pacific had no interest in equipment and stock of an unusable gauge. No one else in California was interested in a defunct railroad. Howard Tedder, astutely ascertaining these facts, found his only competitor in the bidding to be a salvage dealer out of Oakland who knew nothing about railroads and soon dropped out. The hitherto unknown Feather River Corporation, chartered an hour before the bidding with Howard Tedder as president and one L. Lee as secretary-treasurer, won full title to the Sacramento Line for $18,000. The original line had cost close to two million.

At first Kai Soong was a little dubious about Liberty's new schemes.

"Of course, we can arrange coolie labor to build the spur line, but whatever will you do with the timber taken off those Napa Valley hills?"

"Sit on it. It shouldn't cost much to have the coolies set up a saw mill right on the site. We'll just stack and cure the lumber until Howard can figure out a good use for it."

"On some days you amaze me more than on others."

Liberty laughed. "Then I am going to amaze you even more."

"Not another scheme, Liberty. We do not want to spread ourselves too thin."

"Liberty?" she said, with a devilish little grin. "What happened to Chu-chee?"

"That is for our private moments."

"Like this weekend?"

"I do not understand."

"I told you I was going to amaze you even more. I'm inviting myself to Chinatown for the weekend—if you'll have me."

Kai Soong grinned. "Only if you leave Liberty O'Lee, the businesswoman, at home."

* * *

On receiving disturbing news from Robert Porter about the Union Pacific's lack of progress, Oliver Ames began to take a more active interest in the railroad. One thing he did was order Durant back from Nebraska to New York. More money and a harder-driving construction company were needed, Ames felt, to make up for the bumbling incompetency of the spring and summer before. Hillocks of rails, ties and hardware had piled up through the winter at a spot fast becoming the town of Fremont. With them were tons of perishable supplies.

Durant stalled, both on finding a new construction company and replacing Colonel Silas Seymour, whom Ames wanted fired. Ames quietly took the issue up with President Dix and wound up firing Seymour anyway. Through Dix's influence, General Grenville Dodge was released from the army to become the new chief engineer for the Union Pacific. And Dodge, with Ames's consent, immediately gave the construction contract to a reputable outfit known as the Casement brothers.

A jubilant Robert Porter greeted the Casements in late April. At last, he felt, he would be dealing with men of high moral character, *real* railroad builders. To a certain extent, his expectations were met—the Casement brothers did begin to whip the crews into shape. But Porter's demands that the whorehouses and saloons be shut down fell on deaf ears. The Casements, as long as the railroad got built, simply weren't interested in what he had to say about them.

Porter chortled about their lack of interest. He'd done his high moral duty, hadn't he?

Keeping up his civic-minded front, Porter went to town and stormed up the back stairs of Crazy May's. The girls in the hallway paid him no mind, and he entered Maybelle's room without knocking.

Maybelle awoke from her afternoon nap and sat up

blinking. "They're not going to do a damn thing about stopping you people," Porter said gruffly.

Maybelle grinned, dropping the blanket away from her bare breasts.

"So, you can just start planning to pack up and move right along with the railroad," he continued. He grinned, quickly got out of his clothes and crawled into her bed.

She cuddled him in her arms as if he were a little boy in need of comfort.

"I still don't know how all of this started between us," he whispered, "but you are the first woman who has made me feel like a man."

"Probably," Maybelle chuckled, "because I'm only the second woman in your life."

He was silent a moment. "You know that I'll have to continue to scream and rant against you in public."

"And quietly tell me the best locations to set up in?"

Porter frowned. "I don't know if they can do it, but the Casement brothers claim they'll be laying a mile of track a day within the month. You're going to be doing quite a bit of moving."

"Could be," she murmured, "now let's start getting some movement out of you."

Thomas Durant was beginning to mistrust Oliver Ames as much as Oliver Ames was beginning to mistrust Thomas Durant. For the moment, he kept Ames in the dark on certain financial manipulations he was undertaking. He controlled seventeen of the thirty Union Pacific directors; now he was going to give them and others an opportunity to become thirty-five new stockholders in Crédit Mobilier. Because he still had Liberty's proxy on file and two hundred shares of her stock were shown to be paid in full, he sent an oddly addressed letter to California. It was to Liberty's "estate."

"The man must still think that I am dead," Liberty told Ta Wang.

"What do you intend to do?"

Liberty tapped the letter thoughtfully. "I think it's best to let him go on believing that he is dealing with the trustee of the estate of Liberty Wells. I'll have Kai Soong handle the matter through Loung Li in New York. But it still strikes me as odd that Randy Porter hasn't informed them that I am alive."

"He is too busy thinking of the Tedder girl."

"That could be the answer. It must be terrible to be so in love with a person you cannot have."

Ta Wang nodded and turned away. He could not help thinking that Randy at least got to see Lydia May occasionally. It had been a very long time since he had seen Mai Ling.

"Liberty," he said slowly, having dropped the "miss" since they had become partners, "may I ask why you have never confronted Porter with what you learned?"

"His father helped save my life in Nebraska, Ta Wang. For the moment I wish to believe that Randy was duped by Colonel Seymour and Thomas Durant. If he is their spy, he is not a very effective one."

"Perhaps," he mused, "or perhaps they have not had need of him lately."

"Well, that's a problem for Collis and his associates to worry about, not me. I'll write out the instructions for this stock and you can deliver it when you go to San Francisco tomorrow."

"You do not go yourself?"

"No. Mai Ling is to arrive back today."

She needed to say no more.

"I think I go today and not tomorrow," Ta Wang said hastily.

Liberty grinned. "Does she know how you feel about her, Ta Wang?"

He flushed. "Whatever do you mean?"

"Oh, Ta Wang, whom do you think you are kidding? From the first day you came to me I was aware you were smitten by her. Why don't you speak out?"

"Is not proper."

"Would you like me to drop a buzzing fly into Kai Soong's ear?"

Ta Wang was aghast. "Never! I am not good enough to touch the hem of his robe, let alone consider myself fit to become his son-in-law."

"Nonsense! You are one of the finest, most attractive young men I have ever known. Frankly, I think you are too good for her. Give me one good reason why Kai Soong shouldn't know of your interest."

Ta Wang was silent for a long time, debating over a problem that was known only to his family.

"You must not mention my desires ever again, I beg of you, for I have killed a man within my own family and was exiled in disgrace."

"Did you have just cause to kill him?"

"Youth can always find a just cause after they have sinned, Liberty. But the man was my mother's brother, a wealthy and well-respected merchant who kept his evil ways carefully hidden from the eyes of the gods and my mother. In China, marriage contracts are often drawn up at a child's birth with the child from another powerful family. Such was the case for Fengmo Wu, my real name, and Linyi Kang. Do not laugh when I say that I was already eight when she was born. As is our custom, because she was already considered to be my wife, she was brought to live in my

father's house when she was ten. It was understood
that I could not have her for another five years, and
I did not want to, for my learning was more important to me then.

"Within half a year it was learned that Linyi was
with child. I was accused and Linyi lied and said I
was guilty. My father and mother were ashamed to
look upon my face. I was headstrong and obtained the
truth from Linyi in a rather unpleasant manner. I flew
into a jealous rage in learning it had been my mother's
brother who was the father and grew even more furious
when he continued to deny the charge. He was very
fat and I threw him into the goldfish pond. He could
not swim and although the pond was no deeper than
four feet, I walked away and let him drown. Of course,
he had not confessed and Linyi continued to lie. Because of the abuse I had given her, she was believed
and I was not. My father no longer has a son bearing
the name Fengmo Wu."

"And you can never go home again?"

"Youthful wishing made me think I might rise high
enough in America to go back, with my head held
high, but it is only a dream. My five-year contract is
finished in two months time," he said sadly, "and I
must go back still in disgrace."

"Ta Wang," Liberty laughed, "do you really think
that Kai Soong would let you go back? You are too
valuable to him and to me."

"He may have no choice. The contracts are controlled from China. None are renewed, because the
House of Soong loses power over those who stay here
too long."

Liberty had a thought.

"What about the Soos? I've had them for over four
years."

"Then their time is near too."

"Well," Liberty flared, "I'm not about to lose them. Tell Kai Soong that I want to talk to him about them and you. To hell with his brothers in Canton."

Liberty might have known that Kai Soong would have been well ahead of her on the problem. His concern with it had led him to ask Mai Ling to bring back personally information he sought from China.

Sitting on his kang, slowly puffing at his water pipe, he carefully read the updated report she had been able to gather on Fengmo Wu, alias Ta Wang. In the five years since Ta Wang had been gone, he learned, his next oldest brother had taken Linyi as his wife and, upon the death of his father, had become the master of the House of Wu. Ta Wang's mother had also died. The brother had taken his dead uncle's wife as his concubine to keep that money still within the family. He had no desire for the return of his brother Fengmo Wu, ever. Ta Wang, of course, knew nothing of this.

"Why do you take so much interest in this young man, my father?"

"We are much alike, Mai Ling. He has nothing really to return for. Nor do I, though someday, upon the death of my brother, I will have to return to accept my obligations to the family."

Mai Ling made a wry face. "My uncle shall never die as long as you live. His hatred for you is like Ta Wang's brother for him. Neither will move aside and give up what he has gained."

"Nor do I wish to move aside without knowing I leave this house in capable hands. I must look at you still as a son, who will inherit what I leave, but also as my daughter, who will need much help."

"That will be years in the future," Mai Ling said indifferently.

"Wise men plan the future and do not let it sneak

up upon them. I have been compiling a list, my daughter, of many servants who I feel will be of great value in that future. Most are due to be returned within the next year. We are going to extend their contracts."

"That is out of our hands, my father."

Kai Soong chuckled. "Nothing is ever really out of my hands, Mai Ling. I have yet to send to my brothers the list of the cholera victims. These few names I give you—you will please add them to that list. Then you will see to the forming of a new tong for these people."

"With the money for their coolie services staying right here in your own personal coffers?"

He nodded.

"Is Ta Wang on the list?"

"He heads it. He, however, will no longer be considered a coolie."

"No!" she cried, jumping to her feet. "I begin to see what you are about and I'll have no part of it. I have no desire to marry him or any man!"

Kai Soong remained inscrutable. That thought had not entered his head. He had quite different plans for Ta Wang.

"He shall be here tomorrow," he said sternly, "and you will conduct yourself as befits your station. Now leave me! You fill my heart with sadness, instead of love."

"You don't even know what the word love means," she said hatefully, and fled from the inner room.

Kai Soong sat very silent, dressed in his gown of silver-gray brocaded satin. He had wished this to be a real welcome home. Mai Ling had been greeted at the gate by drum singers and well wishers, many of whom who would be back within the hour for a feast. He wished he could cancel the feast. He was still wishing that when Wang Wu bowed his way in to announce the arrival of Ta Wang. Kai Soong's spirits lifted, but he kept his emotions from crossing his face.

"How is he dressed?" he asked quietly.

"As always, Old Master Soong."

"Take him to my rooms and outfit him with one of my gowns, Wang Wu. He shall stay for the feast and sit upon my right."

Wang Wu was astonished. He would not have imagined that Old Master Soong would give a coolie such a place of honor.

Ta Wang, too, was stunned, but obediently did as the master commanded. He was of an equal height to Kai Soong and so Wang Wu had no difficulty in gowning him, although the matching queue cap did fit a little too snugly. It had been five years since Ta Wang had been so attired and he had nearly forgotten how graceful a man could feel when his legs were not confined to baggy blue trousers. He walked downstairs with a poise and grace and pride that revealed his true breeding, perhaps for the first time since he'd come to America.

The other guests were already beginning to assemble and they gaped and whispered at his entrance. He was not recognized. They speculated on who he was and wondered if he had arrived from China with Old Master Soong's daughter. Most of the guests were older tong agents. They had felt for some time that Mai Ling should have been married long ago and hoped the feast might bring such good news.

Kai Soong entered quickly and motioned them to enter the dining area without pausing for introductions. Mai Ling, as the returning person, was the last to enter; since she was a woman, the only one present, they remained on their feet.

Kai Soong whispered softly to her, placing her on his left and informing Ta Wang to take the seat on his right. The honored seat had thus been taken away from Mai Ling, and now everyone was well aware that a great announcement was to take place.

Seeing his daughter's surprise, Kai Soong addressed them all in an unusually soft manner. "I have learned as I have grown older," he said, "that man must sometimes help the gods prepare for the future. And I have learned that the gods do not wish a debt to be paid over and over, for a soul has the right to its own true happiness. This morning it was my intent to take into my family a nephew-in-law. Events have made me alter that intent."

Mai Ling closed her eyes on a shudder. Pride had made her snap at her father. Never once had she thought it might be her cousin, Meng Soong, he had in mind for marriage to Ta Wang. She had insulted him and made a fool of herself. She sat quite still, her hands folded on her lap and smiling her lovely smile, but she felt shame.

Kai Soong's next words mystified many present.

"Tonight, honoring a custom that is older than the land from which we come, I ceremoniously break the rice bowl of one who is dead. His name shall no longer be mentioned lest it bring us bad luck."

He took Ta Wang's rice bowl and hurled it at the floor, shattering it. Then, in the deadly silent room, he took up his own rice bowl and placed it in front of Ta Wang.

"By custom, as a man with no son, I claim the right to place my rice bowl in front of any male and proclaim him as son of my loins, heir to my house, and brother to his sister. Henceforth this man shall be known as Ta Soong. All his former names and lives shall be as if they had never been. So does custom order. I have a son born to me this night. Come, eat, drink and rejoice with me, for the gods have made my heart bountiful with love."

Ta Wang was in a state of total shock, Mai Ling in a blind fury; but neither of their emotions were noticed by the guests. The announcement was far beyond their expectations. It would cost them much in gifts of money. For by law, this newborn son would have to reacquire the number of years since his actual birth, and each year would add another coin to their red-wrapped gift parcels. But they did not mind this. They left the feast with full bellies, joyful hearts and many prayers for the happiness of Old Master Soong and Young Master Soong.

Mai Ling held back her tears until the last guest had departed and then fled to her room without a goodnight or backward glance.

"Father," Ta Wang said, knowing he had to use the title or show great disrespect. He lifted his head and forced himself to speak quickly, to push out the words and have them said. "I am not worthy of this honor. I am not worthy of taking Mai Ling's place as eldest. I have killed a member of my family and must live with that shame."

Kai Soong thought of his mixed motives in the affair. He had wanted to put Mai Ling firmly in her place, to teach her how to eat the bitter roots of being a woman second to a man. But he'd also wanted to raise Ta Wang in his own right, for he'd be valuable to him with his new name and new position. He said gently, "What is done cannot be undone, my son. I have read the report of your life as prepared by your former brother. I hold you blameless for the entire affair."

"Blameless!" Ta Soong exclaimed in amazement.

"The girl Linyi confessed her lies before she married your brother. It did not matter to your mother and father, for they were already dead."

A shadow fell across Ta Soong's heart. His shoulders drooped and he turned his face away. "Then I indeed did die tonight," he said simply. "Fengmo Wu has no more home."

"Nor is Ta Wang any longer a coolie," Kai Soong said in the same voice.

"Both are dead," Ta Soong agreed.

They stood in long silence, understanding each other.

"I wish for you to marry, my son," Kai Soong said at last.

"Your every wish I shall obey, my father."

Kai Soong sighed. "I meant it when I started the evening by saying I wished you to marry my niece. Now, it is even more important. It will draw you into the family by two ties. And it will please my younger brother that I have found such a good marriage for her. She is a simple girl, but in time, if you wish, I shall grant you a concubine of your choice."

Ta Soong nodded. He would be now considered blood of Kai Soong's blood and Mai Ling would be his sister. That would be sufficient for him. He had no plans for taking a concubine.

He said, "That is for the future, my father. I shall be well pleased with the wife you have chosen for me. Now, I must return your robe and find lodgings."

Kai Soong laughed. "A new child does not leave his own home on his first night. Wang Wu has prepared a room for you and tomorrow tailors will come to see to your own wardrobe. The night has been long and I still have the papers to go over that you brought me. Over breakfast we shall discuss them."

Ta Soong kowtowed deeply. From out of the shadows Wang Wu emerged to lead him up the stairs. He could hardly make his legs move, he was quaking so. It had all been a dream and the reality was only then becoming apparent. Earlier he had ascended the stairs as a coolie; now he ascended them as a prince of one of the most powerful houses in China.

He took the candle from Wang Wu and entered the indicated door. Inside, he put the candle on a table and went to gaze out the barred window at the moon-lit bamboo garden below. His mind was so alive he knew that he would not sleep a wink that night.

He started at a slight touch on his back and spun.

Mai Ling posed in the candlelight, its soft glow making her nude body breathtakingly sensuous.

Ta Soong gulped. On many a long, long night, he had dreamed of this moment. And yet, though instantly hot with desire, he did not move.

"Shall I help you disrobe?" Mai Ling whispered seductively.

Ta Soong closed his eyes so as not to see her lovely rose-tipped breasts, her lithe legs and beautifully rounded thighs. "Do not tempt me, Mai Ling," he muttered.

"Don't you want me?" she cooed.

"I have always wanted you," he snapped.

"Then take me," she said simply.

At this Ta Soong, who had been staring down at the floor, looked up in alarm. "That I cannot do! We are now brother and sister!"

Mai Ling looked surprised. "Do you really believe in all that old-fashioned ritual?"

"I believe in respecting the trust your father has placed in me," he replied.

"Do you mean to tell me that you really believe that you will become his heir?" Mai Ling inquired next with some indignation.

Ta Soong said deliberately, "Somebody had to become his son. Why not me?"

Mai Ling blinked, then shot at him, "Don't climb too high too fast, bandit king. When I return to China I can saw the limbs out from beneath both you and my father. You take me to be stupid, but I have learned to control puny little men such as you. You weren't born tonight—you died, so you might as well lie down and let me have my pleasure with you."

Ta Soong marched staunchly to the door, opened it and waited for her to exit. Standing just outside was Kai Soong, who had been ready to knock.

Mai Ling walked past them both as if she were fully clothed and hadn't a care in the world. Wordlessly, Kai Soong bowed goodnight to his new son, his respect for Ta Soong soaring by the moment. It was quite obvious to him what Mai Ling had attempted and Ta Soong's apparent refusal of her gave him much to consider for the rest of the night.

The incident was not mentioned at breakfast. Kai Soong had been up before dawn, and houseboys had been rousted out to run the many errands he had devised during the night. Telegrams had been sent to Loung Li to purchase the stock for the estate of Liberty Wells, with an equal number of shares to be purchased in the name of L. Lee. This matter Kai Soong did not discuss with Ta Soong. Their talk centered mainly on wedding plans—Ta Soong was to be married three days hence—and tong business. The latter discussion awed Ta Soong, who had never been included in so high level a talk before.

There were approximated one hundred thousand Chinese in northern California at that time and more than three million dollars a month was being sent to swell the House of Soong coffers in Canton.

"Tomorrow," Kai Soong said, "you will return to Sacramento and find a suitable replacement to run the factory for at least three months. Please return by the evening train, for we have much more to discuss before you depart."

"Depart?"

"Out of respect to the family in China it is only proper that you present yourself after your wedding here."

Ta Soong asked quietly, "Shall my sister also make the journey, my father?"

Kai Soong frowned. It was just as he had suspected. Mai Ling had made certain threats that Ta Soong wished to avoid discussing. He replied, "Poong, my youngest brother, will no doubt be happy to greet his daughter and her bridegroom. Before you depart from China, you shall know my other two brothers equally as well. You shall have quite enough family to cope with at one time. I see no reason for my daughter to return with you."

Unbeknownst to them, however, Mai Ling had determined that she did not need to return to China to ruin Ta Soong. At the moment the two men were eating breakfast, she was delivering a letter to the captain of the S.S. *Yellow Sea*. She was little aware of the consequences of this, her petty act of revenge; she did not know she was planting a seed that, nurtured in anger, would explode into the bloody, senseless 'tong wars' that raged through Chinatown for the next sixty-odd years.

It was a summer of accomplishment for all:
For the Union Pacific, the Casement brothers began

laying track westward at the record-breaking pace of one mile a day. They would reach the one hundredth meridian before the fall 1866 deadline.

Also that summer the Central Pacific tracks entered Dutch Flats, sixty seven miles from Sacramento, and the tunnel work was progressing well.

Elsewhere, the Napa Valley land was cleared and Ernesto and his sons began to plant their precious grape cuttings; Howard Tedder began to lay spur line track out of the Feather River Station; and the Sacramento Line stayed in operation, with most everyone too thankful to get fresh produce again to question the hows and whys.

Late in the season, the L. Lee Wholesale Produce Warehouses and Farmer's Market were erected on Sacramento Line property. These businesses and the line itself were subsidiaries of a holding company, which charged the Herberts and other farmers freight to Sacramento, bought their produce out at wholesale rates and reshipped it to dealers in San Francisco and Oakland. The venture proved to be most profitable for Liberty, and she poured every cent of her profits back into Central Pacific stock.

The summer had its biting moments too:

It was a summer in which Mai Ling quietly bowed to her father's wishes and sailed for Europe, confident that she would be back in full command by her return in the fall.

It was a summer in which Oliver Ames saw Union Pacific money flow out faster than it was coming in and felt that Thomas Durant's reckless spending might ruin them all if he were not soon checked.

It was a summer in which Randy Porter finally decided that he would have to be a man after his own destiny—and came near to undressing Lydia May

Tedder on a picnic outing before she broke down in sobbing hysterics. For after nearly five years of pushing him towards that point, she suddenly had had second thoughts. Randy, unwise to feminine wiles, had in effect pounded his chest and bellowed at a time when Lydia May wanted begging and knee crawling. The contretemps ended in a screaming match, each accusing the other having been the teaser and tormentor. Two days later Lydia May induced her mother to take her on a shopping trip in New York.

Finally, it was a summer in which Ta Soong returned to China with a new wife and a new station in life.

The houses of the three brothers Soong stood within the same block. Wang, the eldest, lived in the ancestral home of his father and grandfather. Like the man himself, the house was large. In the eyes of Ta Soong it seemed seedy and in need of repair.

Wang Soong was a traditionalist. Out of respect to him as the head of the family, Kai Soong had written him a full account of Ta Soong's background and his reasons for accepting him as a son. The letter pleased Wang Soong and he sent for Ta Soong to visit him. The sight of the young man pleased him even more, for he was tall and very much like his brother Kai.

A maidservant came in smiling. She carried in both hands a plate of steamed bread rolls, very hot. They were made in the shape of peaches, the symbol of immortality, and each was sprayed with red dye.

"Long life, long life, new nephew!" Wang Soong called in a coarse, hearty voice. "Now my brother's house will ring with the voices of children."

"Thank you," Ta Soong said, "thank you for your acceptance."

"And how do you find your new wife, my nephew?"

"I find her as every man should find his wife, uncle. Simple and obedient, willing to do my every command."

Out of courtesy Ta Soong took one of the steaming rolls and broke it open. A dark sweet filling was inside, made of crushed beans and red sugar. "It is delicious," he said, and began to eat.

The man was pleased by this show of respect for tradition and custom. He wished that his eldest son were as courteous, instead of trying to ape his Uncle Poong. Wang Soong had little in common with his son. Now he began to envy his brother Kai Soong for having gained such an articulate and intelligent offspring in this young man.

When Ta Soong had finished with his dutiful report on the health of his new father, Wang Soong leaned forward. "I ought not to tell you," he said in a loud whisper, "but I do it because you are now a member of this house. Times have been very hard on the House of Soong. The coolies demand more now to go to America. The ship captains charge three times the price of two years ago. Were it not for the profit Kai Soong garners out of America this ancient house would dry up and blow away."

Ta Soong saw a different Wang Soong from the picture Kai Soong had given him. His new uncle was indeed fat, but the dishes on the square table in the middle room were of very common fare. The man's gown had a frayed hem and the kang on which he sat had been oft times repaired. What had the man been doing with the vast wealth pouring out of America for eighteen years? It was something that Kai Soong had instructed him to look into and he decided to hold his tongue until he could learn more. Had Mai Ling been lying to her father, and why?

"But," Wang Soong continued, "this is a day of

filial duty and not business. You must now pay your calls on your other uncle and your father-in-law. Tomorrow you shall see the counting house and the operation of the House of Soong."

"I shall look forward to meeting you again tomorrow, old uncle."

Wang Soong's clear black eyes took on a look of distance. "Would that were so," he said. "I do not go to the counting house. For five years my stubby little legs have refused to carry my weight and so all business of import is brought here to me. But if you have questions, my nephew, the door of my house is always open to you."

The house of Chou Soong was clean and tidy, almost spartan in its bareness. Ta Soong found this uncle snappish, sometimes amusingly so. He was a frail little man with two wives and six daughters in his household. He was embarrassed at having no sons and he was also hen-pecked by the family he did have. Consequently, Chou poured his life into the counting house, where—provided his brothers weren't around to badger him—he turned tyrant and lashed out at his clerks with an acid tongue. Considering Ta Soong little more than a clerk himself, he spoke bitterly against Kai Soong and his mismanagement of affairs in America. Further, he didn't tell Ta Soong that it was a good thing Mai Ling had not returned, because he would not work with a woman.

Ta Soong paid Chou what filial respects he could under the circumstances and left. He had a double duty to perform at the house of Poong Soong—as a nephew and as a son-in-law.

Poong Soong was the brother most like Kai Soong. At thirty-eight he was handsome, virile, the proud possessor of three wives, five sons and two small daughters. Meng was his eldest, the only child by his first

wife, and a blessing to be rid of, in Poong's opinion.
Looking at Ta Soong he shuddered to think that this
fine, serious young man should be saddled with so
simple a wife. As for Kai Soong, Poong hardly remembered him, having been only ten when his brother was
sent to America. He listened in bored silence to Ta
Soong's account of his brother, becoming animated
only when Mai Ling was mentioned. He was greatly
disappointed that she had not returned, he said, for
he greatly admired her, even though she was a woman.

Having paid his respects to Poong, Ta Soong left
for his hotel and soon returned with Meng and their
luggage. Meng's mother, Ying, saw to it that her daughter was greeted as a new bride by firecrackers, old
friends, and children who gave her watermelon seeds
to propitiate her fertility. Except for the eighteen years
difference in their ages, mother and daughter could
have been twins: both were small of body, mooned of
face, soft of speech and beautiful in a very simple
way. The genuine affection they showed for each other
touched Ta Soong deeply; he could not help but note
that there was little, if any, such affection where Meng's
father was concerned. It was almost as if Poong Soong
was greatly angered by Meng and was just waiting a
private moment to scold her. And it appeared to Ta
Soong that Meng was deathly afraid of him.

The welcoming home feast took up an entire day
and night. Ta Soong was up and gone by dawn. He
was scheduled to meet his cousin Tang in front of
Wang Soon's house. Although he was Wang's eldest
son, the arrangements for Tang to accompany Ta
Soong had actually been made by Poong. At the feast
Ta Soong had noted that the twenty-two year old man
dressed very lavishly, despite his father's claims of
near poverty.

Tang wore this morning a long robe of summer silk,

the color of foamy sea water. His dark hair was brushed to a high sheen, and his dark olive skin was smooth with health and good food. But his eyes were dark with inner secrets and mistrust.

Tang had a single idol in life, his Uncle Poong. His feelings became clear to Ta Soong as soon as he spoke.

"My Uncle Poong should have been the first born, my cousin. He is the real businessman for the House of Soong. My father is always too ill and my Uncle Chou too acid to deal with people properly. It takes a gifted tongue, like that of my Uncle Poong, to gain the best bargain."

"He seems to be doing well at it, cousin."

"Well! He never makes a mistake. I learn from him daily."

"Aha," Ta Soong mused, "then you work directly for my father-in-law."

"Almost as an equal," Tang announced proudly. "But my main duty is to bring affairs of business before my father's eyes for his approval."

In silence Ta Soong absorbed all of Tang's remarks, however unimportant they seemed. More and more he was sensing that something was terribly amiss. He wished that Kai Soong was not so many thousands of miles away. He felt suddenly incapable of handling the many matters that he had been instructed to carry out.

His worry grew as he was shown the counting house by Chou Soong. It was a dusty tomb in one corner of a large warehouse, sweltering hot even though the sun had been up less than an hour. Two dozen clerks wordlessly went about their chores, fearful that the least mistake would bring Chou's wrath down upon their heads.

Stopping here and there, to peer with a show of dis-interest at their ledger books, Ta Soong saw many gross errors and figures quite different from those Kai Soong had made him study in San Francisco. Because he did not comment, Tang whispered:

"I hate all of this bookkeeping. Do you understand it, Cousin Ta?"

"Not these, I don't."

A group of studious-looking clerks isolated in a corner caught Ta Soong's eyes. He started to walk towards them, but Tang put out a hand to stop him.

"Those men we cannot disturb. Even Uncle Chou is a little afraid of them."

"What is their purpose?"

"My Uncle Poong has a couple of small businesses outside of the family. They are his private clerks."

Ta Soong now noted the studious clerks were glowering at him, as if they would kill if asked a single question. He frowned, not knowing what to make of this, then moved on.

Tank next showed him the warehouse for the family merchantile business, the import and export sheds, and a vast area, called the "holding pen," in which the coolies gathered before being shipped. Less than fifty men sat huddled there in a wordless group.

"So few," Ta Soong mused. "When do more replacements arrive for me to return with?"

Tang shrugged. "I know nothing about that part of the business."

"And what are in those two large warehouses over there?"

"Empty," Tang answered, almost too quickly.

But as they were turning back, Ta Soong saw a heavily laden ox-cart pull up to the warehouse; the door swung open and the cart entered. He was being allowed to see what they wished him to see and no more. He saw no evidence of Poong throughout the day.

After lunch in a teahouse, Tang took him down to

the wharfs to see further warehouses, rice storage bins and another huge indoor holding pen where the coolies were stamped with a number, had their histories recorded in a ledger and received a cursory medical examination. That afternoon close to five hundred men were being processed. Ta Soong noted that they were being loaded on a ship he was unfamiliar with.

"Are they bound for America?"

"Australia, probably. Those are not our tong agents processing them."

"Are other tongs shipping coolies?"

"Many do. But we are the largest."

Tang then invited Ta Soong to visit the singsong girls, a pleasure he politely declined because of his recent marriage. When he asked his cousin to go on without him, Tang was happy to oblige. The day had been a burden to Tang; his new cousin might be quite a handsome man, but he considered him dull and stupid.

They took separate rickshaws from the wharf. When he was sure that Tang was out of sight, Ta Soong ordered his driver to return to the ship being loaded with coolies. There, claiming that he needed to know the ship's sailing time so as to post a message, he learned that it would sail at dawn for San Francisco.

"Not Australia?" he asked, on a note of puzzlement.

The first mate laughed. "Not with this cargo of chinks. They're Californy bound."

Ta Soong nodded his thanks and returned to the house of his bride's parents. Meng had been crying, but she passed it off as of little importance. Later, when he noticed that her arm was badly bruised, she claimed to have bumped her arm.

At dinner that evening he casually asked Poong if other tongs were shipping coolies to California.

"Some try," Poong answered indifferently, "but we usually catch them and put a stop to it. Besides, they would still come under my brother's eyes in California."

"Perhaps not," Ta Soong said in a quiet, reasonable voice. "My father must deal with over two thousand company agents of varying importance. Some could easily be importing coolies and keeping a double set of books."

"Near impossible, my nephew. Tang is a very clever recruiter and shipper and would know when someone was undercutting him. I suggest you learn more about the business before you foolishly speak out again."

Ta Soong had just learned a great deal about the business. Tang had lied to him twice that day.

When the house was dark and quiet, he dressed and slipped away. He had little difficulty finding entrance to the counting house, but some difficulty reading the ledgers by moonlight. The private ledgers of Poong Soong were the ones that he really sought and he poured over them until his eyes were weary.

The next day he spent secretly following Poong Soong about the city to see for himself what the ledgers had only implied.

That night again he went prowling, this time to the so-called empty warehouse. It was closely guarded, which intrigued him, since the counting house had not been. Keeping to the shadows he made his way about the huge building until he found a sleeping guard. One sniff at the man's breath told him that he would remain that way for some time and so he carefully borrowed his keys and let himself inside.

The entire interior had the same sickly sweet smell as the guard's breath. Row upon row, stacked ten feet high, were burlap bales of opium. In the back of the building was a large office. One whole wall of it housed ten large metal safes, and another wall was solid with clerks' desks and shelves of ledgers. The center of the room was filled with counting tables and weighing scales.

Ta Soong concentrated on pouring over as many of the ledgers as he could absorb, constantly praying that his candlelight would not be seen.

Sick with disgust at what he was finding, he slammed the books closed and returned home.

To his dismay he found Meng awake and weeping.

"Before you think the wrong thing," he whispered, sitting beside her and taking her hands, "I have not been with another woman until this hour of the morning."

"I am aware of that, my husband," she sobbed. "But it frightens me what you are about."

"Oh?"

"Tonight, after you left our bed, I went to the room of my mother. The heaviness in my heart had to be shared or I would have died. She listened, even though it was my own father I had to speak against, and gave me wise words. I am to be honest with the man who is my husband."

"Honest about what?" Ta Soong said curiously.

"My father sent me to America for only one purpose, to spy on the house of my uncle and report on his business dealings."

"And your reports were in the form of friendly letters to your cousin, Mai Ling?"

"How did you—"

"I found a folder of them tonight," Ta Soong interrupted.

"That is why my father beat me and twisted my arm. I am to continue filing these reports. Please, my husband, when can we leave? I fear for your life."

Although Ta Soong was beginning to fear for it

also, he tried to soothe her. "There is nothing to fear, Meng."

"Husband, you must have all the truth. Mai Ling informed my father all about you. He is but playing a game with you before she arrives from Europe. She . . . she has been my father's mistress."

Ta Soong had strongly suspected that. How else, without Mai Ling's help, could the records have been altered and the money diverted from the House of Soong into Poong's opium and private coolie trade?

Chou Soong's ledgers had been full of errors. The clerks could only have recorded from the false reports given them. The false reports were surely made up by Poong's private clerks sitting in the same counting house as Chou's clerks. Nothing, therefore, could escape the eyes of Poong and his henchmen.

"The other day," Ta Soong whispered, "I was down at the docks. The S.S. *Dan* is in port. Tomorrow I shall check on its departure."

"My . . . my mother . . ." Meng stammered.

Ta Soong thought for a moment. Any sudden move on their part would unmask the fact that the woman and daughter had talked, and Ta Soong was now convinced that Poong could be ruthless if need be.

"All right," he said at last, "perhaps it is best for us to start tomorrow by paying a dutiful call upon Uncle Wang. No one will question the mother of the bride going along to call upon her brother-in-law."

"I wish Uncle Wang were Uncle Kai," she said wistfully. "He would know better how to handle the situation."

Ta Soong soundlessly agreed. He had little faith that Wang Soong would do more than grunt and reach for another sweetmeat.

* * *

Poong did not yet fear Ta Soong, feeling that Mai Ling had grossly overrated his intelligence. He was, however, greatly distressed with his daughter. He learned less from her than agents he already had in San Francisco. He needed Mai Ling back. She was the only one he could really count on. He tolerated Tang, but only as a faithful lackey he could use to make his eldest brother do his bidding.

Poong was pleased that his wife, daughter and son-in-law would be out of the house that morning. He had many important things to discuss with Tang and several of his closest agents that day—things that were better discussed in the privacy of his home and not in a teahouse, the counting house or the warehouse. Ever since Mai Ling's return to China for the first coolies for the railroad he had been planning for the day that was near at hand. Although he lived well, his house was not a true measure of the wealth he had accumulated in the metal safes. He had wealth that would fulfill his dream. Only with Mai Ling had he shared this dream, and she had enthused over it.

Now, he had only a few days to start bringing his plans all together. By the time Mai Ling arrived from Europe he would have disposed of his two eldest brothers and be the master of the House of Soong. He did not fear Kai Soong. Over the past two years Mai Ling had been able to smuggle five hundred of his agents into California. One word from him and they would be able to recruit five thousand more and quickly bring down the House of Soong in San Francisco. What was captured from Kai Soong there was to be Mai Ling's prize.

At the moment Poong was dreaming his dreams, his eldest brother Wang sat in silent meditation. Ta Soong sat beside him. Wang was not trying to remember the words that had just come from the mouth of his new nephew; he was not even thinking; he was simply being all that he was. He was neither waiting nor expecting. Times were chosen and appointed. If one forced them, they were wrong. All the quiet strength of his decision would gather around the opportune moment, and then it would become right.

Soon he heard the footsteps of his brother Chou coming solidly through the courtyard. It was the first time in three years Chou had been inside his house and Wang took it as another bad omen for that day.

Chou entered, his arms heavy with ledgers, his face ashen.

"Are you ill?" Wang asked abruptly.

"I did not have the noodle soup for breakfast," Chou said by way of an opening remark.

While Wang waited for an explanation, he put the ledgers down on a low table and, bowing with respect, sat and started opening them with shaking hands.

"Today, my brother, after the first two hours of work, the soup boy came around with his kettle and bowls. Things being what they are, I cannot afford soup for my clerks, but our brother insists upon it for his. Today, within minutes after drinking their bowls, they grew ill and held their stomachs. One after the other they left for home, leaving the cleaning up for the next. Being a neat man, I went to put away their ledgers when the last left. I was amazed by what I found."

"I am not," Wang said stonily. There he had a sign that Ta Soong's words had been accurate. Rapidly, he informed Chou of exactly what Ta Soong had reported.

But Chou had become one who believed more in figures in a ledger than in the words of men.

"Here," he cried, waving two parchment sheets at Ta Soong. "I have two reports. Can you tell me the figure that my brother allegedly sent from San Francisco last month?"

"Not to the penny," Ta Soong said truthfully, "but I think Old Master Soong said that it was over three million."

"Aiyee!" Chou cried, "$3,127,000, to be exact. But here, this sheet, which is a very good forgery, claims only $127,000! My brother, there is a robber in our house!"

"Several," Wang sighed. "My brother, my son, my brother's daughter all seem to be in league against us, Chou."

Chou could only stare at him open-mouthed.

Wang Soong was no longer astonished: he was furious. He rang the gong for a messenger and sent him to get the several strong young men who guarded the gates at both his house and Chou's house. When they returned, each was given instructions and a purse of money. Still more armed men were required, and Wang knew where these men could be bought for a price.

The takeover of the warehouse was accomplished with such ease that only one of Wang's men was lost. But before the small army could storm across town to capture Poong he had gotten wind of what was happening and fled to a secret house he had owned and shared with Mai Ling. From there he was able to put out his own battle call and garner an army of fifty. Within the hour he had the warehouse back in his control. His axe-wielding henchmen had killed ten in the doing.

The rumor spread quickly that the House of Soong was under attack. Even though it had fallen on bad times of late, this house still supplied a great many Chinese with their wages and hundreds took to the streets to rally to its cause. But there were also Chinese who knew their money came directly from Poong

Soong and rushed to his aid. A pitched battle ensued, with no real generals to direct it. Throughout the night it raged; scores were mortally wounded, buildings burned and supplies destroyed—with nothing really gained.

Wearily, near dawn, the warriors broke away from each other to have a cup of hot tea and await further instructions.

Cunningly, Poong sent Tang as his negotiator.

"Traitor!" Wang screamed. "Capture him and cut off his hands!"

"Let us hear what he has to say first," Ta Soong cautioned.

Tang entered his father's barricades and bellowed his demand. "I say for you to surrender and let my Uncle Poong take his rightful place as the master of this house. You, father, have made it a mockery."

Wang eyed his son coldly. "And I shall give you the opportunity to take back my answer to him."

His answer was to return Tang in a basket, with twelve swords driven through his body. As Poong was staring down at his slain nephew, Wang's forces recaptured the warehouse and the safes of money and gold.

Poong retaliated the same day. He opened the safe in his own home and spread the money lavishly. Everyone now knew that the fight raging in the streets was for control of the leading tong of Canton. Lesser tong leaders chose sides quickly, then re-chose them almost hourly, depending upon course of the battle. They were not really interested in who won. They wished to weaken the whole House of Soong so as to increase their own power.

Under cover of night, Wang advised Ta Soong to take his bride and mother-in-law and go aboard the S.S. *Dan.*

"My nephew," he said sadly, "tell my brother that I do not know what the outcome here shall be, but it is advisable that he make a journey home."

Ta Soong was unaware that the captain had already been bribed to carry a message to one of Poong Soong's agents in California:

"The time has come. Bring down the House of Soong so that it might rise again."

16

The summer of accomplishment withered into an autumn of anguish and a winter of despair.

The very night that the S.S. *Dan* docked in San Francisco twenty tong agents were having a late dinner in the Celestial Garden teahouse to celebrate the fortieth birthday of one in their group.

"Today," the man so honored chuckled, after acknowledging their kowtows, "I have reached the halfway point in life . . ."

He never finished his sentence. Three nitroglycerin blasts reduced the teahouse to rubble in seconds and created a fire that destroyed three blocks.

On the same night there were ten murders in Chinatown. The police thought little about it. Murder was almost commonplace in Chinatown and along the Barbary Coast.

Kai Soong thought a great deal about the murders. Killed were ten more of his most valuable company agents. His grief over the loss of thirty old friends was compounded when he heard Ta Soong's report on Mai Ling and on the conditions he had left in China.

"No, my son," he said sadly, "it is not the time for

me to return home. First, we must see to the brush fires here, and then we will see to the forest fire."

"But how are we to know who is our enemy?"

Kai Soong smiled sadly. "The Occidentals say they cannot tell us apart. For once they are correct. Who knows which one among us is an assassin and traitor? As a boy, when my grandfather faced a similar problem, he baited his traps with red-paper-wrapped money. Ta Soong, I wish of you several things while I also bait my traps. The captain of the *Dan* is preparing to sail back to China by tomorrow night. Tell him I personally will stand all cost of the cargo he is to carry; it will presently be delivered to him. Then you are to take Meng and her mother to Sacramento; they will be much safer there than in Chinatown. Then go to the factory and find out for me who was responsible for letting that nitroglycerin find its way into the teahouse. If this war reaches out to the railroad crews, it could be the ruination of us all."

All night the houseboys of the House of Soong ran their legs ragged. Tong agents came and went and were reduced to messenger boys.

While Ta Soong was at the *Dan* accomplishing the first of his missions, Kai Soong was busy acquiring his cargo. A steamboat captain was rousted out, his crew awakened and a midnight run chartered for Oakland and back. Two dozen coolies went to Oakland and brought back many heavy crates. Half were delivered to the *Dan*, the other half directly to the front yard of Kai Soong.

"Whatever is this?" Ta Soong gasped when he saw what was in the crates.

They were axes.

"Another good business investment by our friend Liberty O'Lee," Kai Soong chuckled. "The handles were made from some of the lumber cleared from the Napa Valley land she bought; she had them manufactured in Oakland. Our shipbuilder, Mr. Fletcher, was induced to use his scrap metal and start a subsidiary foundry for making blades for axes, picks and shovels."

"But these blades are of ancient Chinese design," Ta Soong said.

"I designed them," Kai Soong said simply, "knowing our people working on the railroad would feel more comfortable with them. Now let us see if others of our people feel comfortable with them in their backs. If they wish ancient war, let us give them ancient battle weapons!"

Three hundred carefully recruited coolies sailed for China, with three hundred sharpened axes. All were between eighteen and twenty five, healthy, virile and strong. For thirty-five days they would be wined, dined and pleasured by singsong girls aboard ship. All had between three and five years to fulfill on their tong contracts. All were offered the same terms: their contracts would be paid in full for one year's service in the private army of the House of Soong.

The axes retained by Kai Soong were to be used in his tong war at home. This, however, was a war against secret traitors, and the coolies who fought it received different terms. They continued to get their regular daily wage, plus a five dollar gold piece for the cut-off queue of every traitor they uncovered and killed.

Chinatown ran red with blood that fall and the authorities looked the other way. They were content to let the Chinese handle their own problems in their own way.

The Central Pacific was not as tolerant.

* * *

"Goons," Liberty declared, "just a squad of goons."

"I'm sorry to bring my troubles to your door," Ta Soong said.

"They are also my troubles," she admitted. "Madame Soo, take Meng and Madame Soong to the kitchen and see to lunch for them."

Ta Soong blinked. "Liberty, you said that last in Mandarin!"

"A summer project," she laughed. "I seem to be dealing with more Chinese than American, so I've had Madame Soo start teaching me." Then she sobered. "Is your house wrecked?"

"Completely. This time I think Old Master Soong was wrong, Liberty. My wife and mother-in-law would have been better off staying in Chinatown."

Liberty grunted. "The problem is all over the railroad area you rented in. That's exactly where Charley Crocker is hiring his goons. Now that they can't find anymore gold or silver to grub for they are right back here demanding work."

"And what work he gave them," Ta Soong replied. "He does not see that it is best for the tong agents to police our own people. As it is now, two coolies can raise their voices a little too loudly over a game of *gen-fen* and the Irish clubs crash down on both of them. They claim as their excuse that the tong war is responsible for the rise in accidents and sabotage."

"Is it?"

"Possibly some of the accidents to individuals, to frighten a man into changing tongs, but not something as big as the collapse of the Bear Creek trestle. Even Nazareth agrees that it would have taken an engineer to know where to set off those blasts to weaken it—and all of the Chinese blasting men were a good seventeen miles away."

"Who was in charge of the final construction on the trestle?"

"Randy Porter and two white crews."

Liberty didn't reply, but couldn't help but wonder if the inept Randy wasn't up to his old tricks again. "Well, let's take care of other matters first. By tomorrow I should be able to move into my new house and you three can take over the cottage here."

Ta Soong started to protest, but a strange noise coming from behind a folding screen made him jump in alarm.

"Something else I have learned this summer and fall," she laughed. "Come and see."

On a table behind the screen sat a telegraphic sending and receiving set. Liberty sat down and copied out the incoming message.

"As the owner of a railroad I had little trouble getting the line put in, but never realized how valuable it would become. Some day you shall have to meet your second cousin in New York. Loung Li is a most remarkable man. An hour after the White House appointed General Dix as ambassador to Napoleon III's court, I had the news. Two hours later I had the news that he had resigned as president of the Union Pacific."

"Who replaced him?"

"Aha!" she chuckled, "no one as yet. Oliver Ames got himself elected to the board and he and Durant are in a power struggle for the presidency. Ames is quietly buying up shares of Crédit Mobilier and soliciting voting options from the stockholders who will not sell."

"Are you selling?"

"No, Ta Soong, I am quietly buying up all the shares Loung Li can get his hands up. I intend to make sure that Dr. Thomas Durant rises no higher in life than he already is, and, perhaps, even takes a tumble."

Ta Soong eyed the machine with great interest.

"If Old Master Soong had one of these in Chinatown, think how much faster it would be to communicate with him."

"I doubt that he would use it," Liberty said peevish-
ly.

"Have you quarreled with my father?"

"Not at all," Liberty replied. "Indeed, we never
quarrel."

"Indeed, how can two people quarrel when they
never see one another?"

"Now you are beginning to talk like him, Ta Soong.
At first it was he who wanted me to stay away, because
of the trouble in Chinatown. Then . . . then . . ."

"And then you chose to stay away?"

Liberty paused for a long moment before she answered. "Yes," she replied at last. "He was here when
he got word that Mai Ling had been killed in Canton.
I couldn't feel any sorrow, Ta Soong. I still can't feel
any sorrow and I think he expects me to soothe him
and comfort him over his loss. That would be hypo-
critical of me, and it would only make matters worse."

"Did he tell you of her activities towards the last?"

"No."

"Then it was his error that has led to the distance
between you, Liberty, not yours. His sorrows are many
because of her, but not because of her passing. Through
her knowledge and efforts, Poong Soong was able to
rob from his own family. And like all robbers, when
the House of Soong began to grow strong again, he
sacrificed Mai Ling to save his own worthless neck.
He escaped and is setting up his own family tong."

The telegraph began to chatter again. Liberty's writing kept slowing down as she took the message.

"You won't be needing the cottage," she said dully,
"the message was for you."

"Who could have known I was here?"

"It is also being received at the Sacramento Line depot. Kai Soong wishes you back in San Francisco at once. Wang Soong is dead, and Kai Soong is leaving for China on the first boat."

"Will you come to bid him farewell?"

"There was no message for me." She could not keep the hurt from creeping into her voice.

"Do old friends need messages to bring them together?" Ta Soong said sternly. "They do not, unless they have ceased to care for each other."

"I have not ceased to care for him."

"Then you have ceased to think, perhaps. Wang Soong was the eldest. Kai Soong is now the eldest. This could mean that he will never return from China."

Liberty rose and went to the window. She leaned her head on the pane. "I think that is why there is no message for me. We were spirits from two different worlds who were able to wash away each other's loneliness for a while. Neither of us could really live in the other's world, however."

Ta Soong groaned. "O Heaven, that has made you of two different continents!"

Liberty smiled at this. "You may blame Heaven, but it changes nothing. Tell Kai Soong, for me, that I wish him well."

When Ta Soong had gone, she sat down again to her reckoning. Again she was alone, but not lonely. From Kai Soong she had learned much, but mainly peace and contentment.

Kai Soong sat back, weary from the many matters he had been forced to go over with his son in so short amount of time. Looking around his inner room he realized that his weariness was not so much physical as spiritual. It was hard to define even where in the spirit it lay. Certainly his mind was not weary. Ahead lay the challenge which had always been his destiny, and now he had a son to share that destiny with. But he could not help but think that he had come to America as an exile and he was now returning to exile in China.

There were so many things about America he would miss, but those thoughts would have to be left behind or become added burdens on his shoulders. He faced enough burdens without taking some with him. A rebellion within a family cast shame upon the whole family, especially when it had become as public as this one. He would have to act quickly and firmly or lose the family reins even before he could grasp them. All concerns but that now had to be washed from his thinking.

"Chu-chee," he whispered, "thank you for wishing me well."

Ta Soong looked up from the account book he had been studying. "Did you speak, my father?"

Kai Soong started to answer in the negative and changed his mind.

"Yes, my son, one last instruction. See to the affairs of Liberty O'Lee just as studiously as you see to the affairs of the House of Soong."

17

The snows came early and drifted deep in the Sierras. The blizzards came early and similarly stymied the Casement work train on the North Platte.

The Central Pacific turned its Chinese into shovel men to clear away the fifteen to thirty-foot drifts. The Union Pacific sat back and let another hell-on-wheels town spring up about its camp. The UP was forty miles beyond the hundredth meridian—forty miles that the Casement brothers had not as yet been paid for; they were in no great rush to fight the winter weather.

Robert Porter had a solution on how the UP could keep moving through the winter, but no one was prone to listen to him. Too bitter a battle was being fought between Ames and Durant.

Durant, having little success in gaining proxy votes, put Pinkerton agents out to ascertain who some of the mysterious stock purchasers were so he could confront them directly. The Pinkertons were prompt, accurate and thorough. They tracked L. Lee down, reported back her true identity, and supplied a two-page resume on her business interests, partnerships and stockholdings.

Durant was aghast. Not only was Liberty O'Lee alive—she was far wealthier than he had ever imagined. Her stockholdings in the Union Pacific and Crédit Mobilier were nearly as great as his own, and the Central Pacific stocks and bonds she held in the name of herself and her children were staggering.

Oddly enough, Thomas Durant knew Liberty's worth better than she did. Each of her companies had its own Chinese accountant who passed profits along to the House of Soong. Ta Soong would bank them for her. Though she could get a profit statement whenever she wanted it, she was mostly satisfied with Ta Soong's reports that she was doing "extremely well."

Durant pondered the Pinkerton report for a long time. If the woman sided with Ames, he knew, he would never gain the presidency. He had to find a weakness. He had to find something that would discredit her in the eyes of the Central Pacific people. But that wouldn't be good enough, he mused, for she would still be able to vote her Union Pacific and Crédit Mobilier stock. Then, finally, he saw a way to do considerable damage both to her and Oliver Ames.

On official Union Pacific letterhead paper, he forged a carefully worded instruction:

"My dear great-nephew Randy:

"As you must be aware, from the many rumors afloat, I am challenging Durant for the presidency of this line. The rumor is also out, which Durant believes, that we will veer south from Wyoming to Denver and sneak into Salt Lake City by the back door.

"Once Durant is out, we shall do no such thing. Straight across Wyoming, Idaho and Oregon we shall come, leaving the Central Pacific sitting on

the Utah salt flats with their finger up their four
fat asses. Leave them to Brigham Young, they deserve each other. Pious hypocrites all.

"My reason for writing you this, is that you are
family. When you left us, I said someday I would
have need of you. The time is now.

"Now, this is in confidence, my boy. A wealthy
Chinaman by the name of L. Lee, at my suggestion, bought the old Sacramento Line. Out of the
earshot of the Central Pacific, he has been quietly
building north up the valley and will link up with
me in the Klamath Falls area of Oregon. He
should be there by spring and we by late summer
or fall.

"You are to make yourself known to him and
send me secret reports on his progress.

Your great-uncle
Oliver Ames."

Durant smiled. Now he had to sit back and see if
Randolph Porter reacted as he anticipated he would.

The letter crushed Randy. It was a stunning reversal
from the letter and Christmas check he had received
the month before. Then Oliver Ames had been gush-
ingly proud of the manner in which Randy was stick-
ing with the arduous construction problems of the
Central Pacific.

Ever since the "accidental" killing of Dan O'Lee he
had slaved to redeem himself by tireless work and
study. He had gained a pride in himself and his accomplishments. He was fearful that he would be once
again blamed when the Bear Creek trestle collapsed,
but Charles Crocker had stubbornly stuck by him

until an engineer admitted planting the explosives to create more jobs for white workers.

Now, he was torn between two loyalties—family and the railroad which had become almost like family. He had only one man he could trust with such a problem.

Charles Crocker read the letter several times.

"Why do you bring this to me, Randy?"

"I feel like such a traitor," Randy gulped, fighting to control his tears. "Uncle or no, it just doesn't seem fair to me. I've put four years of my life into this work. What right does he have to make it all for nothing?"

Crocker was deeply puzzled. He didn't think Ames could pull off such a stunt without a change in the Pacific Railroad Act. He was aware that the Sacramento Line had been sold and was being used as a freight line, but he was in town so seldom now that he was unaware of what freight they were carrying.

"All right," he said softly, "for the moment let me keep this letter and you say nothing about it. I'll go into town and do some checking."

Just as he got off the Governor Stanford, a freight engineer with seven platform cars of rails was chugging out of the Sacramento Line depot. Good naturedly, he sauntered over to the station master.

"Hey, Lem," he chuckled, "someone make an error? Those rails are heading north and not east."

"Ain't for you, Mr. Crocker."

"Oh, the old line doing a bit of repair work?"

"Don't no one tell me nothing, Mr. Crocker. But this I do know, cause I been here since Ted Judah built this line. Can't be just repair work, cause twice as many rails have been shipped outta here than took to build it in the first place."

Then it is true, Crocker thought. He kept his face stony. "Need to use your telegraph," he said.

"What's wrong with yours?"

"Nothing!" he said with growing impatience. "I just happen to be closer to yours at the moment. Get in there and tap out a message to Ta Soong. It's simple. Just tell him that it's urgent I meet with the owner of this line. Have one of your runners bring the answer over to my office."

Lem Purdy shrugged. "As you like, but I'll most likely have an answer coming right back."

"How's that possible?"

"He's one smart Chinaman, Mr. Crocker. He had a telegraph line strung into his house. He and the owner send messages back and forth all the time."

"The owner? The owner is here in Sacramento?"

Lem Purdy prided himself on being very exact. "Nope! Owner just left on that freight train for up valley."

"Get the wire off," Crocker demanded hotly.

Five minutes later he was in a state of rage. Ta Soong had wired back that such a meeting was impossible.

"Well," Crocker stormed, "we'll just see how impossible it is."

He went to the marshalling yards of the Central Pacific and rounded up fifty of his fiercest "goon gang" members. Then he commandeered a half-dozen wide-track handcars and screamed out his orders:

"If there are chinks up this line, I don't want a one of them coming back alive."

He went in and ripped the sending key from its wiring and stalked away.

Howard Tedder's original plan for two twenty-mile spurs had been greatly expanded upon as the work had progressed and Liberty's money had multiplied. That day, feeling like gloating, he had induced Liberty to come and view his handiwork. From the Feather Creek junction they headed due west, dropping off rails at a spur line that was being run right into the main Herbert farm. Eighteen miles beyond the track began a thirty-mile circle that would eventually come back to meet itself.

"Ain't a one of their farms," he exclaimed, with due pride, "that is now more than ten miles from the rail line. If they pick in the morning, you can have it in Sacramento by noon."

"And to the San Francisco markets by the next morning. Oh, it's marvelous. When will it be finished?"

"Spring. Just like I told the inspectors."

"What inspectors?"

"Railroad," Howard answered laconically. "Didn't have to go through all that mess when we first built this line. Looked at me like a fool when I said we planned on forty miles and it was now seventy."

"They probably thought you were going all the way to Oregon."

"Nothing up there I'd want. Well, the rails are delivered. Let's get this crew on board. I want them to help finish off the spur into the Herbert farm before the end of the month. Only got a crew of twenty there, and you'll have to talk to Ta Soong about replacing the foreman. He's a lazy one and it makes the whole crew lazy."

The foreman had been worse than lazy. He had been asleep when the Chinese workers had looked up to see the approach of the handcars. They were not paid to think, so didn't alert him. Fifty heavy clubs came down upon them as one, giving none even a chance to gasp as his skull was crushed. Their tools were gathered up, and, without having raised a sweat, the goon squad went back to the junction of the two spurs and began to take up a section of track.

"Why we doin' all this work lifting track?" one demanded.

"Do you wanta pump after that damn train?" the leader demanded.

"Not rightly."

"Then work! We let the train come back to us and derail. Then we got a few more chink heads to crush!"

But they had only one rail removed and the other just loosened when the engine came puffing over the crest of the hill.

The engineer saw the handcars on the track and began to brake down and blow his whistle all at once.

"What's up?" Howard shouted.

"Crew on the track!"

"Can't be!" Howard yelled. He moved to peer around the engineer, and instantly jerked back. "Ain't ours and they got a section of track up."

"Can't stop in that distance," the engineer screamed.

"Then open it up and jump it!" Howard shouted back.

"We'll crash!"

"So what difference does it make at what speed you do it? Give me that damn throttle! Get back over the tender and release the cars. No use having them pile up on top of us."

Howard pulled the throttle open slowly and dunked his head out the window.

"Goon squad," he snarled, now that he could see the burly Irishmen racing from the tracks to the handcars. He felt a hand entwine through his arm, and it was shaking. "Liberty, girl, forgot about you. Climb on back to the cars before he releases them."

Liberty shook her head. "I'm staying with you!"

Just then the fireman jumped out of the cab and went rolling away down the right-of-way.

Howard grinned. "Glad you stayed. Poke me some wood into the boiler."

He wanted to keep her busy, so she wouldn't think about what was going to happen. The manner in which the goons were yanking their clubs off the handcars told him that if the train crash didn't kill them, the goons were going to have a go at it.

"Here we go!" he warned.

For a second the left side of the engine dipped, grinding up the ties into wood chips. The right wheels squealed. Metal tried desperately to keep traction on metal, but the weight of the cab pulled it dangerously to the left. The cattle guard and left guide wheel caught on the exposed rail, shearing them off and sending sparks high. The rail buckled down on the end, up in the middle. The six-foot-high drive wheel slammed into it and spun crazily, trying to climb the buckle and thus tilting the engine precariously back to the right.

Howard Tedder could do nothing but keep his hand on the throttle. If the buckle straightened, they would be on clear track. If it snapped, they would plow up everything in sight.

The Irishmen sensed that the locomotive would make it, if not the freight cars, and frantically tipped their handcars off the rails to keep them from getting smashed.

The locomotive and tender car settled onto firm track before the rail snapped with a loud report. The freight cars had no way of jumping the gap now and began piling up in a grinding crunch of metal and wood. The coolies jumped to safety, still bearing their work tools, only to be met by a greater danger.

The goon squad now came screaming at them with

clubs flying and pistols blazing. The Chinese, out of instinct, instantly fought back with axes, picks, shovels and crowbars.

Suddenly, the Irishmen realized they were being slaughtered rather than slaughtering. Fighting their way back to their handcars, they held the Chinese off with gunfire while they got them back on the tracks. Then, frantically, they started pumping away. Two cars of six men each made their escape.

It took Howard all the way to the Feather River junction to throttle and brake down the engine. There he let the gears cool for a moment, then slowly made the wheels spin in reverse. He had just raised the speed to full reverse when he screamed and blew the whistle:

"Handcars on the track!"

Liberty looked out the fireman's window. "Don't brake," she yelled.

"But, Liberty!"

"Damn it, don't brake!"

The Irishmen must have thought the engine would come to a stop for them. They didn't slow in their mad pumping. The tender car tossed men and machines about as if they were toys a spoiled child had just tired of playing with.

"Liberty," Howard gasped, "do you know what we have just done?"

"Quite!" she said through clenched teeth. "I have just shown the Central Pacific their hired killers can be killed. Let's go see to our people, Howard, and then I want to learn what this was all about."

It took them two hours to see to the wounded, get help from the Herbert farm people in burying the dead and get back to town.

Liberty came down out of the engineer cab, followed by an ashen, quiet Howard Tedder. For two hours Howard had been in the presence of a changed Liberty

O'Lee. She had always been a strong and positive woman in his eyes, but he saw now that her strength now was as hard as steel, her resolve unquenchable.

She listened very quietly to Lem Purdy's report as to how the handcars had been stolen and who had given the order. Then, as if they were concluding a pleasant day's outing, she turned sweetly to Howard.

"Thank you, Howard. I wish to have a couple of words with Charley Crocker, and then shall see myself home."

Heads turned and lips began to buzz as she sailed through the Crocker's fashionable store and up the stairs to the office area. Liberty wanted these women to see her sooty and bloody and speculate as to how it had come about. A store executive rose to bar her way and she brushed him aside.

"Liberty," Crocker gasped, "what happened to you?"

"I ran into some of your goon squad out near Feather Creek junction."

"My . . ." He started to protest, but she cut him short.

"They're dead, as are about forty-five Chinese laborers."

"But . . . but . . . what were you doing out there?"

"That is no concern of yours, except to say that I was there with the owner of that line."

Interesting, Crocker thought to himself, but said: "You seem to know quite a few Chinaman, Liberty."

She had a strong urge to spit in his pompous face, but that would come later, she told herself.

"I am told," she said acidly, "that you desire a meeting with Mr. Lee. He shall be at my house at eight this evening."

"Good. I shall be there."

"Not just you. All four of you!"

"I don't know if—"

"You can get them there, Crocker. If not, he'll produce witnessess to prove that you stole his property and sent out your goons to do murder. If you've forgotten, your last words to them were, 'If there are chisks up the line, I don't want a one of them coming back alive.' Eight o'clock, *sharp!*"

None of the four associates had been in the old Caldwell home in years. None wished to be there now, although they all looked about in wonderment. The stuffy, over-furnished, heavily draped old mansion had been transformed into a simple abode that suggested its present owner's good taste as well as wealth. They were kept waiting in the parlor until the mantel clock struck the hour; when they were shown into the dining room.

At one end of the table Liberty sat quietly, in a simple but elegant gown. There were stacks of papers to her left and right.

"What is this?" Crocker blared. "You promised Mr. Lee at the stroke of eight. Where is he?"

Liberty rose slowly, her face emotionless, her voice as cutting as a diamond.

"I am L. Lee, and the question is mine. Why this attack against the Sacramento today?"

"Really, Liberty, I don't know—" Collis Huntington started.

"Sit!" she ordered.

As if she were Queen Victoria, they scrambled to take seats. With a finger she indicated a small stack of papers.

"These papers will indicate to your satisfaction that one Liberty Wells O'Lee, under the name of L. Lee, purchased the Sacramento Line railroad for the purpose of bringing produce into Sacramento and San Francisco. Again I ask, why this attack against it today?"

As one, they turned to Charley Crocker.

Face to face with L. Lee, and with the Oliver Ames letter in his pocket, Crocker sat back smugly.

"Produce only?" he said slyly.

She eyed him coldly. "That wasn't my question."

"But it's my point," he roared, banging the table. "Produce from where, madam? New York via Oregon? How clever to pass yourself off as one of your Chinese friends and make a side deal with Oliver Ames to build a railroad right under our noses and link up with him in Oregon. But you're found out, by God, found out! And I have the proof of it!"

"What are you talking about?" Collis Huntington flared, at the same time Mark Hopkins coughed, "What? What?" Leland Stanford puffed, "Proof? Proof of what? Why wasn't I told of this, Charley?"

Liberty wasn't sure of Charley Crocker's game, but she was not about to play by his rules. She crossed her hands daintily.

"I too," she said clearly, "wish to hear his proof."

"Why do you need to hear what you already know?" Crocker spat.

"You must be careful of how far you take this, Charles," Liberty said. She spoke in a quiet, dispassionate manner which he found disconcerting.

"What do you mean?" Crocker stammered.

"I can have legal action brought against you now," Liberty said. "Lem Purdy is well known for his inability to lie."

Her voice conveyed no threat; she'd merely stated a consequence to be expected.

"Charley," Mark Hopkins said softly, "isn't it about time you told us what this is all about?"

"I have already told you," Crocker said, biting out the words. "This woman has put herself in league with Oliver Ames to leave us sitting high and dry."

"Have I?" Liberty asked. Her voice full of music and wonder.

"Yes, you have," Crocker repeated, taking Durant's forged letter from his breast pocket. "Randolph Porter received this letter from his uncle and brought it to me practically in tears. He said it wasn't fair to take away four years of his life's work. Here, Leland, read it aloud for all of us."

Liberty's face didn't change once during the reading, although the four turned ashen and Stanford's voice quivered toward the end.

"And you actually believe that propaganda?" Liberty smiled slightly when he'd finished. She directed her comment at Collis Huntington.

Collis did not smile. His too-serious face reflected his painful inner battle between disbelief and wonderment. "Liberty," he began, and had to wet his dry lips. "I think it would be wise for you to speak to the charge."

"I shall not," she said firmly. "Had a proper investigation been made, you would have seen the absurdity of the charge. Crocker went off half-cocked, as usual, and lives and property were needlessly laid to waste."

Crocker flinched. "A few Chinese and Irishmen," he argued.

"Is that the same thing you said when the retaining wall collapsed? A few Chinese and an Irishman?"

"Let's not get into that issue again, madam!"

"But that is exactly where I intend to start," Liberty said, her voice cold again. "That letter, if Oliver Ames wrote it, makes the issue for me. Unless your ears are full of wax, as usual, you, too, would have noted the open admission that Randolph Porter was sent here so that someday he could be of service to the Union Pacific. 'The time is now.' Blindly, you covered over his mistakes and your own mistakes, in the death of my husband, even though later evidence proved his involvement with Colonel Seymour. I nearly lost my life because I placed that evidence before Thomas Durant in Nebraska. Now, and I think Collis would have to agree, you can almost hear Durant's voice in the letter. Ames is too—"

"Garbage," Crocker interrupted in his stormy impetuous way. "Can you honestly say that you are not in league with Oliver Ames?"

"No, I honestly can't," Liberty said, still mildly. "I, as Liberty Wells and L. Lee, have had quite a bit of correspondence from the man this winter. I intend to give him every proxy vote I have to keep Thomas Durant from becoming the president of the Union Pacific."

Crocker stared at her in stubborn refusal to give up his main point. "And you intend to link your railroad up with his, correct?"

"That would be impossible."

"Impossible?" Crocker cried with contempt. "You've already extended that line by some forty miles, have you not?"

"Incorrect again, Charley. It is closer to seventy."

He sat back startled. He could not conceive of what had happened under his very nose.

"Then wherein lies the impossibility?" Stanford demanded, on a dark glower.

"Gentlemen," she said in her sweet and reasonable voice, "you really are a worthless pack of imbeciles. So arrogant, so corrupt, so money grubbing that you strike and then ask questions. *That line is as it always has been—wide gauge!*"

In the deathly silence she rose, feeling a moment of

pity for the stupid, gawking looks that came over each of their faces. While they were still benumbed, she intended to make a few more points quite clear.

"Cars, track and personnel were destroyed today. You will make full restitution."

"I . . . ah . . ." Hopkins stammered. "Funds are short, at the moment."

To this Liberty, picking a report folder up from the table, replied with her usual coolness, "I do not wish to make you out a liar, Mr. Hopkins, but my records show that through Crocker & Company the construction to date has run about $23,000,000, but the actual outlay from The Associates is only about $14,000,000. Odd, that funds are short and no dividends have been paid on any stock from the first day to this."

"My God, Liberty," Huntington laughed, a little hesitantly, "Where did you come up with such an outlandish figure?"

Liberty smiled slightly and put down the folder. "I don't see Mark Hopkins laughing, so I don't think I am too far off base. But I think we have played enough cat and mouse games. Besides the restitution, I want an official investigation made into my husband's death. I want Colonel Silas Seymour unmasked. I want Randolph Porter sent packing, so that Thomas Durant knows that this latest scheme to ruin Oliver Ames and myself just didn't work."

Leland Stanford rose suddenly from his chair. "Go to hell, madam!" he bellowed. "You have no right to demand anything!"

Liberty pretended horror and surprise. She pursed her lips and sat down sadly.

"Well," she sighed, "you leave me little choice. I shall wire Oliver Ames and have him do the investigation from that end."

"You do what you wish," Stanford declared, "but the Central Pacific will not raise a finger to help you."

"Then," she said carefully, "I don't think I should raise another finger to help the Central Pacific. My money is better invested with the Union Pacific. I hope, Mr. Hopkins, your treasury is not too short of funds to handle the stocks and bonds I shall place on the open market tomorrow."

Ever the accountant, he automatically asked, "How much?"

Liberty patted the stack of certificates in front of her as if it were pitifully small. "Not much," she sighed. "Just a little over $7,000,000."

Hopkins's face broke into wrinkles of horror. He struck the table with both palms. "That can't be done!" he cried. "You would ruin us if you flood the market with that much in one day."

Stanford began to shake as the implication of Liberty's dumping her stock dawned on him. It would cause a panic and drop all other stocks dramatically. But, for once, he was speechless.

Collis Huntington stared at Liberty with renewed respect. She's got us by the balls, he thought, and she's not going to stop twisting.

Charles Crocker could only sit and stare. His mind refused to function.

Liberty said nothing. She quietly gathered up the papers before her and started to leave the dining room.

"Mrs. O'Lee," Hopkins gulped. "I think we would still like to talk to you further on this matter."

Liberty turned, smiling. "In the words of your illustrious president, 'go to hell.'" She sailed across the foyer, into the parlor, and slammed the door.

Huntington began to chuckle.

"I hardly see any humor in the situation," Hopkins growled.

"You wouldn't, Mark. Gentlemen, you have just had a taste of how that woman made you rich and prosperous. I had forgotten how astute she was in gathering her facts and figures to lobby our cause."

"She'll lobby us right into the poor house," Stanford sneered. "Something has got to be done. Collis, you were always close to her—can you talk her out of it?"

"You heard her terms."

"But that was before you rudely turned her down, Leland," Hopkins sagely noted.

"All right!" Stanford snapped. "Make my apologies, but do anything to keep her from selling that stock. Damn, how did she get her hands on so much in the first place?"

The question had also been puzzling Collis, but this was not the time to admit that to his colleagues.

He waited until they had departed before he knocked on the parlor door. Liberty admitted him as if nothing had taken place.

With a shrug she accepted his offering of Stanford's apology.

"Big of him," she said.

"Speaking of big," Collis inquired, with open admiration, "how in the world have you accomplished all this?"

"Collis, Collis," she said coyly, "you are the last person I would have thought would wonder about that. Didn't you turn $10,000 worth of borrowed hardware stock into a million before you ever thought of playing around with this railroad?"

"Yes, but . . ."

"But, nothing. Let's just say that I put the profit from that stock and the year's wage due Dan and me to just as good a use."

"With a little bit of oriental wizardry?"

"Yes," she said candidly, "Kai Soong was a great help. He made a little bit too, you know."

"I'm sure, knowing him. I was afraid that things would go from bad to worse after he left, but Young Master Soong seems far more ruthless than Old Master Soong."

A silence fell between them. It was time for them to discuss what they both knew was uppermost in their minds.

"Will you back off if they meet your terms?" Collis now inquired.

"I have been thinking of a couple more," Liberty said thoughtfully.

Collis sighed. "I figured as much."

"Yes, but they would both benefit the Central Pacific, if only those blind fools could see it. All winter Howard Tedder has been after his son with an idea so simple that Crocker thinks it's stupid. Collis, snows are going to come every winter. When the trains start running on a regular schedule, are you going to keep thousands of Chinese on the payroll to dig the drifts out? No! But the trains won't run on schedule either. Snowsheds, Collis. The snows will drift over them like so many more new tunnels."

Huntington frowned. "Sounds reasonable, but what has that to do with your not selling the stock?"

Liberty grinned. "I had to get you to land on the honey, mister fly, before I could clip your wings. First, the contract for the design and construction of the snowsheds is to be given to Howard Tedder—with no interference from Charles Crocker. Second, all the lumber for same is to be purchased from the L. Lee mills of Napa Valley."

Huntington sat back. In theory it sounded good, but he was also a very practical businessman.

"Are you aware of the millions of board feet and lodge-pole supports you are talking about?"

"Down to the last inch."

"Fine, but when could you start making delivery of cured lumber?"

"Make it a part of the deal first," Liberty said coaxingly.

Sweat burst out on Huntington's brow. He had been in Washington and New York so much lately that he was unaware of all of the accomplishments, of L. Lee. But he had to put his neck out, and he nodded agreement.

"You needn't have looked so worried," she laughed. "Every bit of lumber required is already cut, stacked and cured. I'm just damn glad to finally find a sucker to take it off of my hands. But if you tell your cronies that, I'll call you a liar to your face."

"Oh, Liberty," he roared with delight, "I taught you too well."

Liberty frowned. "But not yourself, it would seem, Collis. My next bargaining point is based on something I found out about this afternoon and evening. I shocked Hopkins with the information I had, but it was really quite easy to gain from the newspaper clippings I keep and the rather candid stockholders' reports that he puts out. I only had to put the two together, sifting the wheat from the chaff, to come near the truth. Someone who really wanted to ruin you could come up with the same information. Funny, Collis, you gave Durant the idea for the Crédit Mobilier, but haven't copied its success."

"No, but I have a sneaking suspicion I know what you are getting at."

Liberty said lightly, "Collis, to forestall any further complaints, such as mine tonight, about the way profits are siphoned through Crocker & Company, I think a new construction company has to be formed. Now, let me finish before you tell me how Charley Crocker will hit the ceiling. As with Crédit Mobilier, Crocker &

Company would stay as the general contractors in the books of The Associates. But the new construction company would be overall—Chinese labor, trestle contracts to Nazareth Tedder, snowsheds to Howard Tedder, and so forth. Their books must be kept separate, but deliberately entangled in a way to keep the finances of the Central Pacific from being traced as easily as I have just done."

Collis grinned. "And you would want a piece of the new company?"

"Quietly," she murmered. "Very, very quietly."

Collis nodded. "They are waiting for me at Leland's house. Shall I bring you back their decision?"

"No," she said slowly, "for I have no desire to go into these last two provisions until the matter of Dan and Randy Porter is finalized. They can decide all they like, but once and for all, I want action."

But her proposals were far more interesting to the big four that night than was the question about Randy Porter. They would have Randy brought down off the mountain in the morning, but right then they were too busy forming a contract and finance holding company, with themselves, naturally, as partners. After seeing the millions they could thus hide away, none of them, including Collis Huntington, wanted to give Liberty a piece of *their* pie.

Crocker reasoned that she would be getting a piece of the construction profits from the snowsheds—a contract out of his pocket.

Hopkins reasoned that she would make a few million out of the lumber supplied—which they would not share in.

Huntington was just being greedy for his own sake.

Surprisingly, it was Leland Stanford who did an about-face.

"The hour is late and it has been a trying night, but

I wonder if we are being wise in leaving ourselves open to another such night in the future. She made certain conditions and we have rejected them."

"Why not?" Crocker insisted. "She's rich in our stock, as it is."

"Very brilliant, Charley," Stanford sneered. "Stock she can sell at any time. I think we need a counter-proposal to keep her satisfied and out of the contract and finance company's affairs."

"Agreed," Hopkins said, "and I think I have it. Before we knew who L. Lee actually was, I noticed that the produce company he—or shall I now say she—owned was our biggest freight-shipper to San Francisco. Could she balk at the Sacramento Line receiving free freight on the Central Pacific, from Sacramento to San Francisco, for, say, ten years?"

"No more than five," Crocker demanded.

"Say seven." Huntington added a note of compromise.

"Agreed," Stanford chuckled. "Now get her to agree to it."

Several days later, when Liberty did agree to it, the big four thought they had pulled a very shrewd deal. Liberty held her silence. The spur lines would now allow the Herbert farms to double and triple their acreage and produce in those seven years. She would make millions out of the big four's short-sighted greed. She could not know that she would also be saving her reputation. Seven years later the Crédit Mobilier scandal would break. The books of the contract and finance company would be destroyed by a mysterious but opportune fire, which would not keep the big four from being looked upon as swindlers. Because they had kept Liberty O'Lee out of the company, she would not be linked with the scandal that would haunt them.

* * *

Because Stanford and Charles Crocker had conducted the original interrogation of Randy Porter and Silas Seymour, they bowed to the wishes of Mark Hopkins and allowed lawyer Edwin Crocker to handle the affair in a more detached manner.

The interrogation again took the form of a courtroom trial. Leland Stanford, less than happy to have his involvement pulled from the closet again, finally agreed that it was wise for Edwin to question Nazareth Tedder first. Nazareth's testimony did not vary from the time he had accused Stanford and reported the facts he had uncovered to Liberty.

The big four, sitting as judges and jury, were content with his report—except for Charles Crocker.

"A question, Nazareth, before you step down. Are you aware of the work your father has been doing on the Sacramento Line?"

"Why, yes, spur line work."

"And nothing more?"

"Not to my knowledge."

"For whom?"

"Why, Mrs. O'Lee. I thought everyone knew that."

Crocker pursed his lips and asked no further questions. He was put out that everyone knew about it except the people it really mattered to.

Then the key witness was questioned. Much time had elapsed since the cliff disaster, and Randy Porter became confused in many of his answers. At one point he gave the impression that he had concurred with the changes that Silas Seymour had made in the plans; then, a few questions later, he denied his previous statement.

Edwin Crocker, who loathed corporate law, relished

playing criminal prosecctor. He badgered and sneered, promised and threatened, soothed and snapped, until he had Randy's mind spinning.

"Now," Edwin inquired, "prior to his arrival at the cliff, had you ever met this Colonel Silas Seymour?"

"Yes. He got me this job. I met him at . . ." Randy stopped. He had been told that this was to be an inquiry only into the death of Dan O'Lee. Now he saw it leading up to the letter he had received and shared with Charles Crocker. He felt betrayed and his sense of family allegiance came back strong.

"And . . ." Edwin coaxed.

Randy set his lips and glared at Charles Crocker with unquestioned hatred.

"Well," Edwin said, "shall we take it that your silence speaks for itself? That you were sent here by your Uncle Oliver for rather questionable reasons?"

Randy still refused to answer. His heart was breaking. He had come to look on Charles Crocker as the 'mannish' father he had never possessed who might enslave him in his tasks and browbeat him when he'd done wrong, but who at least had never ignored him. Now Charles Crocker was ignoring him.

Leland Stanford cleared his throat, judiciously. "This is not a court of law, and it is not our intent to bring what we have heard into one. I think I speak for my colleagues in saying that it would be best if we consider your contract terminated at once. Make your departure quickly and we will immediately close the book on this whole affair."

Randy rose as if in a trance, but when he passed Charles Crocker's chair, he quickly leaned down and whispered: "Judas! Thirty pieces of silver won't keep me quiet about where the skeletons are buried!"

Crocker shook his head in bewilderment. He was being called Judas and yet Randy was speaking of thirty pieces of silver keeping him quiet. The boy's obviously gone batty, he thought. Congratulating his cohorts, he prepared to depart for the railhead.

Then, as he started to board the Governor Stanford, he stopped and contemplated how much Randolph Porter really did know. He stepped down and slowly walked to the supply-yard office. Ignoring the greeting from the Irish security guards, he went directly to Randy's small office and began to gather up his papers and files. Now, he thought, he will have nothing to base his claims on. No one would know of the over-charges Crocker had made against his own partners.

About to leave the office, the cot in the corner gave him a new idea. He had, to a degree, felt sorry for Randy and his plight with Lydia May. He had, with a sly wink, suggested that Randy install the cot for when he had to stay in town overnight. He did not know that the cot had not been used for the purpose that he had anticipated.

But now all he could think about was getting rid of Randy with the least amount of fuss. Lydia May, he thought, was his answer.

He returned to the guards with a grin. "Timothy, I've got some extra dollars for you and your boys to earn quietly. Half now, and half on completion."

"Always willing to oblige, Mr. Crocker."

He was quick with his instructions and pay.

Timothy Callahan liked the plan. He had always thought Randy a bit of a dolt for not just claiming the girl, if he really loved her that much. He sent his three brothers to fetch Lydia May and he went in search of Randy.

Only one of the brothers approached the Tedder house, the other two remaining on the borrowed supply wagon.

Liu Ma, the Tedders' houseboy, was skeptical.

Madam Tedder was shopping; Master Tedder had come home in a dark rage and had had words with his daughter.

"Who send you for missy?"

"Porter!" Sean Callahan said curtly.

Liu Ma had heard all the words between Nazareth and Lydia May. He knew Randolph Porter was being sent away and Nazareth had forbid her ever to see him again. But Liu Ma was a romantic, of sorts. Since Selena had stopped paying him for his gossip, he had stopped telling her of Lydia May's trysts with Randy.

"You wait! I get!"

Sean Callahan told the girl only what he had been ordered to tell her. Lydia May accepted it without question. Putting a shawl over her head to look like an Irish girl she went with them to rendezvous with Randy.

If he could have seen just a few moments into the future, Liu Ma would never have let the missy go. As the supply cart rumbled away Selena and Randy arrived at the mansion from opposite directions.

Both alit from their carriages, and Randy stopped her as she neared the front door.

"I wish—" he began, and could not go on.

To this universal cry of a youth eager to see his love one last time Selena remained cold and firm. She told him she'd pass his farewell message along but she would not allow a meeting. She was not sorry to see him go. At last she could get Lydia May to start thinking about other young men.

It was another crushing blow for Randy. He wandered aimlessly away and it took Timothy Callahan nearly an hour to find him.

"Where ye been, lad? Mr. Crocker's had me runnin' me legs weary to fetch you." Randy looked at him bewildered. "He's made arrangements for you to meet the Tedder lass."

Randy's sorrow turned into new hope. "Take me to her," he commanded.

"That I'll do, but we must act fast. Your train leaves in less than an hour."

Randy followed silently. What was there to say? Crocker was giving him a chance to see Lydia May, probably, he figured, to ensure his silence. It was up to him to persuade her to leave on the train with him.

In the first fifteen minutes of her wait Lydia May had been happy; then each passing minute added to her fears that Randy was not coming. She sat crouched on the floor of the abandoned freight car, paying little attention to the Callahan brothers.

"What in the hell is keeping Tim?"

"Who gives a damn? Gimme another swig from that jug."

"Another?" he laughed. "You got better than a quarter of it in you already."

"Keeps me from thinking."

"Probably the same as me," said the third brother. "Damn, she's a good looker. Before Tim gets here I'd like to get me a hand under that skirt for a feel."

"Hell of a time to get such an idea," Sean growled.

The thought stayed on Angus Callahan's mind and prompted him to action. He sidled up to Lydia May with a suggestive swagger and blew hot, sour whisky breath down into her face, whispering, "What you and your boyfriend going t-to be doing?"

The question and foul breath angered Lydia May and she turned her head away.

Angus had a violent temper. He grabbed Lydia May by the wrist and in a single motion jerked her to her feet.

"I asked you a question, you little bitch." He leered at her drunkenly.

"Let me go, you miserable fool!"

She swung at him with her free hand but Patrick Callahan was quickly there to grab it before it could collide with his brother's face. Patrick took both of her arms and pinned them behind her back while warning: "She's going to scream, Angus!"

"Naw!" Angus barked, planting a big paw over her mouth and nose. It had happened so suddenly, Lydia May hadn't had time to scream. Angus put his crotch up to hers and ground his hips around. She could feel his immediate arousal. "What do you think?" he cooed devilishly. "Bet old panty-waist Porter ain't got nothing like that."

On a twinge of alarm, Lydia May tried desperately to twist her way free.

"Sean, come help!" Angus commanded.

"You ain't gonna try it?" Sean asked incredulously.

"Shit, yes!" Still holding her mouth, Angus started ripping her dress off with his other giant paw. "If you want a piece of her, Tim, get ahold of her mouth. Patty-boy, hold her still and we'll give you thirds."

Now, as the dress was shredded away, Lydia May felt the terror of abandonment. It had been a fatal mistake to believe the men; she gave up all hope that Randy had sent for her in the first place. And it was nearly hopeless to fight them.

Angus began to breath heavily as he revealed more and more of her nudity. All his encounters had been with fat, dumpy Irish women who would plop down and accept his assault with yawning candor. He didn't take too kindly to the idea of doing it standing up, but Sean was now warning him to make haste.

Angus was just ready to make his entry when the

shout came from the freight car door. "Angus! What in the hell are you doing?"

Lydia May could feel him tense with recognition of the voice. He spun about just as Randy pushed Timothy to the side and jumped up into the car.

Angus didn't think; he reacted. The revolver was out of his waistband and fired pointblank as Randy started to lunge. There wasn't time for Randy's facial expression to change. The force of the blast lifted him from his feet and sailed him backwards out of the freight car door. The thud of his body on the gravel seemed louder than the gun's report.

"He's dead," the shaking Timothy Callahan whispered.

Benumbed, Sean and Patrick let loose their grasp on Lydia May. She stood silent and motionless. In that second she had the memory of Randy's voice, arguing, declaring his love, of his face, ardent, confident, handsome; and now she had witnessed his death.

She took a hesitant step, then made ready to run.

"Stop her!" Sean cried. He lunged but got only a torn piece of cloth for his efforts. Angus turned, but not in time. Patrick grabbed hold of an overhead pulley and sailed it along its track to the open door, with its lifting ropes dangling. The pulley itself went past Lydia May's head just as she prepared to jump down to the ground, but its motion caused the ropes to swing back, encircling her neck in mid-flight. Her body began to fall. Before she could reach up and free herself she was jerked back by the ropes. There was a horrible cracking noise when they stretched taut. She hung, her head at a crazy tilt, her feet just a few inches off the ground.

Such silence filled the freight yard that Timothy could hear his own heartbeat drumming in his ears.

Instantly he knew what they must do. Randy's pants were undone and he was left to appear as if he had been trying to rape the girl. The gun was dropped at Lydia May's feet to suggest she had fired the fatal shot and then hanged herself. The train was due to leave for San Francisco shortly and they would be on it. They didn't think that Charles Crocker would come looking for them to pay them the second half of their money.

As the train whistle announced its departure, Randy's lips moved and he moaned slightly. His head rolled to the side and his eyelids fluttered open. For a second he stared into Lydia May's sightless eyes. His eyelids closed for a second and then opened wide again. His will to live vanished.

18

Within a two-day span eight funerals took place in Sacramento. Most of the speculations as to the cause of the deaths were inaccurate.

On the wired instructions of Alicia Porter, her son was to be buried where he died. Somewhere in Wyoming Robert Porter was so shattered with grief that not even Crazy May could give him comfort.

Liberty could not bring herself to attend the services for Randy. She blamed herself for having exposed him, driving him insane and thus bringing his death.

A Methodist minister and his wife, alone, buried Randolph Porter.

An Irish priest had no problem filling his church for certain other funerals. Three times in a single day it was filled to capacity, and three times his sermon included a bitter attack on the Central Pacific and its reckless use of human life. Dion Saroyan, who had been killed in the fight with the Chinese, had been a good engineer and Catholic. Seamus O'Toole, another so killed, had been a good fireman and a Christmas and Easter church attender.

Father Murphy knew little about the Callahan brothers. He conducted a combined mass for them.

"Who, but God," he told his parishioners, "can know why these four lads chose that moment in time to seek a ride to San Francisco? But God was not responsible for the derailment of that train, I say! The blood of these four lads rests on the heads of those who put greed and avarice ahead of human safety."

Although the words were hurled down at the man in the front pew, Charles Crocker-ignored them. He did not blame himself for the Callahans' deaths any more than he blamed himself for the deaths of Randy and Lydia May. He loathed Catholic priests and he thought this one had missed the point. God had indeed taken their lives, as Crocker saw it—in vengeance for the lives they had taken.

Nor did he feel remorse the next day in attending the services for Lydia May.

Selena had overruled Nazareth on his request for a private service. She mourned, and in her mourning accepted the fact of Liberty O'Lee's presence at the funeral. The loss of a daughter was too grave to cause a scene over the past.

Nevertheless Selena felt her daughter would still be alive if Liberty had not acted against Randy Porter. She also felt Liberty had entered too deeply into the private life of her family, and could not quite forgive her for this. Liberty may have avenged the death of her husband, but Selena, in a mind now twisted by grief, felt that she had all the time in the world to avenge the death of her daughter.

Alone in his room that night, Nazareth Tedder pondered his sorrow. He had not wished to be with anyone after the burial. Lady Pamela would, he knew, immediately seek diversion. Selena would suffer her grief without seeing she could have prevented it years before. He would suffer alone with his own guilt. He had been the one who first had voiced the truth and later accused Randy. He was deeply sorry that he had not been strong enough to give Randy and Lydia May the life they had wanted together. He blamed himself and couldn't believe what the official report said. He couldn't believe that Randy was a rapist. He couldn't believe his daughter would shoot Randy. No, something was horribly wrong here. No, he would never believe it of either of them.

Against the dark curtain of his mind he saw what he must do. He would resign from the Central Pacific in the morning and devote his time and money to learning the truth.

Oliver Ames hired the Pinkertons to get the truth for him. He learned a little more of Randy's involvement with Silas Seymour in the death of Dan O'Lee. He also learned of Durant's spurious letter. The letter helped him blackmail Durant off the board of directors and get himself elected president. But he found that he couldn't get rid of Durant as vice-president because he unfortunately, knew where too many skeletons were buried.

But neither Tedder or Ames were able to obtain any evidence that would account for the deaths of Randy or Lydia May in an incontrovertible fashion. Selena and Nazareth so argued the matter that he finally moved out and took up residence with his father, an event which neither pleased nor displeased Howard Tedder. Howard had his own way of keeping his heart from breaking; he poured his time and energy into the snowshed construction.

The incident left Liberty spiritless for a time. When Ames, through Loung Li, offered her bonds at forty and fifty percent discount, she bought them with little enthusiasm. When the Associates organized the San

Francisco Bay Railroad, buying out the ferry and steamship lines, she bought that new stock with similar indifference. At one point, the San Francisco Music Guild requested a donation for the building of a new opera house and went away elated with her pledge of $50,000. Lady Pamela with her friends then threatened to boycott the Guild, which subsequently found itself forced to decline Liberty's generosity. To all such matters Liberty only shrugged.

She did continue to read her newspapers, and she would play with her children, wishing they were older and could communicate with her. All along she knew what was bothering her, even though she did not admit it to herself: she sorely missed the company of Kai Soong.

Before its Christmas recess, Congress declared that Promontory Point in Utah would be the junction point for the Pacific railroads. Liberty didn't even bother to look the place up on the map.

All who did, however, found Promontory Point to be little more than a desert plateau on the California Trail route around the north end of the Great Salt Lake. Even to those with a lively interest, it hardly seemed to matter. The fact was that on Christmas Day, the Central Pacific's easternmost railhead at Verde California, Nevada, was five hundred fifty-seven miles from Promontory Point; and the Casement work train, at the foot of Evans Pass, was the same distance to its other side.

The Central Pacific was snowbound. The Sierra blizzards were as devastating as they had been in 1867. Bull Crocker was forced to turn over thousands of coolies to Howard Tedder for the building of thirty-seven miles of snowsheds.

The Union Pacific's winter at Cheyenne brought blizzards, gunfights, hanging by the vigilantes and martial law.

Both railroads seemed to be mirroring Liberty's lethargy.

To bolster her spirits, Ta Soong returned Wang Wu to Sacramento as Liberty's houseboy; and one of the first happy duties the latter was able to perform was to announce the Christmas-visit arrival of Howard Tedder.

Old Howard was halfway into the room before Liberty realized someone was walking behind him. Grinning broadly, Howard stepped aside—and there was Nathan. Alarm was mixed with Liberty's joy in seeing him.

"Nathan," she whispered. "Oh, Nathan, you promised your mother!"

"Promised?" the boy said testily. "What can she do? Send me to bed without my supper? That's not a bad idea, seeing as how tonight is her annual boring dinner party."

"But, Nathan," Liberty said with gentle insistence, "I don't wish any more trouble with her."

"It was my idea, Liberty," Howard said, "and I shall take the responsibility for bringing him."

Liberty suddenly realized that Nathan was now as tall as his grandfather. Ever since he had begun his schooling in San Francisco she had had only fleeting glimpses of him. He was no longer a carrot-topped little imp, but an imposingly handsome young man of seventeen. She stood still, soaking in all the newness about him; then all at once she was against him, clutching at the fur lapels of his coat.

"Nat," she whispered. "Oh, Merry Christmas, Nat . . ."

Nathan bent down and kissed her.

"Merry Christmas, Aunt Libby."

"Come," she said warmly, "there are hot toddies on the hearth."

The talk fell very easily into Howard's work on the snow-sheds. Nathan Tedder said little. Each time he glanced at Liberty, an aching void formed in his middle and expanded and contracted with his breathing.

Why couldn't she have been my mother? he asked himself. Here was a woman who had always been warm and loving; she would let him speak his thoughts without fear of reprimand. If he grew a little too ribald, she would laughingly put him in his place, whereas his mother would have sent him from the room and silently punish him for days.

As she was bidding them goodbye she said suddenly: "Nat, you look so funny! What's the matter?"

"It's something that I learned in San Francisco. May I come back and discuss it with you this evening?"

"You may, if your mother will unchain you."

Nathan was back by nine, bubbling with an inner excitement he knew he could share only with Liberty.

"As you know," he began, "I've been staying with Gramma Lady in San Francisco. A few days ago I was reading in the alcove off her library when she got an unannounced visitor. They didn't know that I was there, but I could see them plainly. Aunt Libby, I've never seen such a painted old hag in my life, and her language was almost as thick as her lip rouge. Well, it was no handout she sought, but quite a hefty sum. You should have heard Gramma Lady tear into her. They sounded like two alley cats. Then the blackmail threat came. You won't believe what she threatened to expose."

"Please, Nathan," Liberty said suddenly, fiercely, "I don't wish to hear any more."

He was surprised, when he looked at her, to see that she was crying.

"You know, don't you?"

"Yes, Nat," she whispered. "I'm sorry, for your sake. It's true, though."

"Don't be sorry for my sake," he laughed. "I think it is horribly delicious to find out such a thing about the two of them."

She sat quite still, smiling at him through her tears. "I thought the same once also, Nathan, but it's best to let their past lie unspoken."

"You can do that, when it was you that the woman was going to expose them to?"

Liberty laughed lightly. "It wouldn't have done her much good, would it?"

"I don't understand!" he said bitterly. "They can say all the evil things in the world about you and you won't strike back with this knowledge."

"Oh, Nat, honey, it really wouldn't hurt them, but it would hurt you and Howard and Nazareth."

He leaned forward suddenly and kissed her full on the lips.

"That's to say thank you and also because I've wanted to do that for ever so long."

"I'll take that as a compliment," she stammered in surprise. "Now, I think you had better be good and go!"

"I'm not good," Nathan declared, wagging his red head. "I have terrible thoughts about you. I don't aim to go. I mean to stay here with you—where I belong. One moment I wish I were your son and the next your lover."

Liberty got up quickly from the settee, her brain fighting for the right words to say. She marched to the fireplace, her hair hanging loose about her shoulders and her eyes big with wonderment.

"Let me kiss you again," Nat murmured.

Perhaps, Liberty reflected, if I humor him, if I talk to him gently . . .

"If I kiss you," she whispered, "will you go?"

"Sure," Nathan said with youthful craftiness, "sure I will."

Liberty went to him, rising on tiptoe, her green eyes closing. Her arms stole upward about his neck, and her lips caressed his, warmly and tenderly. Nathan kissed her very gently. Liberty felt the master of the situation. I can manage him, she thought. She brought her hands to his face and cradled it, lingering over the caress.

It was then that she knew she had been wrong. Nathan's youthful gentleness vanished. His mouth clung to hers fiercely, fighting for possession, and his big hands, about her waist, were hoops of steel. Liberty tried to push him away. He merely tightened his grip. Vainly she hammered at his shoulders with her fists. Slowly, inexorably, she was being bent backward.

"I've been with no other," Nat whispered urgently. "Be my teacher."

Suddenly, he lowered his face to her breasts. Liberty trembled, sensing his erection, feeling it pressed hard against her groin. She took him by the hand and led him slowly to the stairs. She felt almost incestuous in what she was about to do. That she was even considering it amazed her and gave her a curious thrill. All of her loneliness seemed to be evaporating. She would do this; she would. Why shouldn't she?

The morning was gray and crisp as Nathan let himself into the Tedder mansion, but for him it was like a spring day. He felt liberated, joyous, his feet barely touching the ground. He was met by a tirade that quickly brought him back to earth.

"What is the meaning of this?" Selena declared hotly, storming out of the parlor still clad in her dinner gown. "I had to send for your father to look for you. Where have you been all night?"

Nathan grinned sheepishly at his mother and father. But there was more Tedder in him than Buttle-Jones and he saw no reason to lie.

"With Liberty O'Lee."

Selena began to shake with rage. "I need not ask what you have been doing all night long," she said accusingly. "But I shall not blame you. Oh, no, it's your grandfather and father I shall blame and hate for their continued friendship with that—that vulgar creature. You shall go to your room. You are never to see that whore of a woman again!"

There was, as Howard Tedder often said, a red imp inside his grandson. It reared up now, brazen and angry.

"And if I don't?"

"You'll regret it and so shall she," Selena said quietly. Turning, she started for the stairs.

Nathan said coolly, "A whore, mother dear, is someone who sells it, like you once did. Liberty gave it to me for free!"

Selena turned, her mouth dropping open foolishly, staring at the slim and handsome figure of her son as if she were seeing him for the first time. She leaned forward, looking into his face. "Damn that bitch for telling you such a lie!" she said bitingly. "How could you believe such a thing about your own mother?"

"She didn't tell me. I heard it from an old hag trying to blackmail Gramma Lady."

Selena sank against the railing, her face ashen, her

mouth working to shape words that never came out.

"You lie!" she finally bellowed, then her voice broke. "Nazareth . . . beat the truth out of him! Tell him it's not so. . . . Tell him, Naz. For the love of God, tell him!"

Gloomily, Nazareth shook his head.

"You'd have me lie to save your pride?" he said. "No, I believe he heard what he says he did, but pray he has enough family respect to forget it."

"Damn you . . ." Selena whispered. "Damn you to hell!"

"You did that the day you came back into my life, Selena!" Nazareth said cruelly. "You are just too self-centered to see that you are getting back some of what you have been dishing out for years." Then he took his hat and coat from the hall tree and walked to the door.

"Where are you going?" she screamed. "I still want Nathan reprimanded."

Turning, he looked at his son in disgust and pity. He did not condone Nathan's having an affair with Liberty—or with any woman. His son, he repeated in his brain. That had been the bargain—for him to give up Lydia May, Selena had to give him another child. He would not have Nathan ruined as Lydia May had been ruined.

"Nathan," he said sternly, "get your bags packed. I'll take you to San Francisco today to get your things out of your grandmother's house. On the first available boat I am sending you east to school."

"Dear God, Naz! I'll be alone if . . ."

Nazareth bent his head back a little, his thin lips smiling.

"That is precisely what I want, Selena! You see, we made a bargain. You made me suffer too long and hurt me far too much. I will not have you or your spiteful mother do the same with *my son!*"

Selena looked at him grimly.

"Nathan is going nowhere," she said.

"Nathan," Nazareth said heavily, "you can forget the packing. Come, we are leaving this moment."

Then he spun on his heel and marched through the door.

Nathan stood still for a moment. He had never disobeyed his father in his life. Nor had he ever before realized how little love he had received from his mother. He looked up into her stricken face and was amazed at how much she had aged in the last several minutes. But he could feel no pity.

"Mother," he murmured, "I think father is right. I have always wanted to go to school in the east."

Selena turned her back on him. She stiffened suddenly, hearing his feet cross the hall, and then the sound of the door softly closing.

She stood for a while, waiting his return. Then, slowly pulling herself up the stairs, her mind began to plot. She would make Nazareth rue this day. She would divorce him for desertion and gain custody of Nathan. She had lost a battle, but not the war.

At about the same moment Liberty sat pondering a message from Loung Li she had just transcribed. That the message had been dictated by Oliver Ames was obvious to her, though it might not have been to anyone else. Reluctantly, she took from her desk the monthly shipping schedule out of San Francisco. The S.S. *Newark* was scheduled to depart the next morning. After a few moments of thought she wired Ta Soong to get her reservations, then called in Wang Wu.

"I must make a trip back east, Wang Wu, but I don't wish it known. If anyone should ask, you will say that I am on business in San Francisco and refer everything to Ta Soong. He will know what to do. Now, let's go see to some packing. I want to catch that first train out in the morning."

Elsewhere, Nazareth did not want to wait for the next morning's supply train. He wanted Nathan away from Sacramento before Selena started bellowing, before he had to start making explanations to his father, and before the boy could make contact with Liberty. Keeping Nathan in tow, he went to his construction company office, emptied his safe of ready cash, wrote a couple of letters of introduction and hustled Nathan off to catch the noon steamboat to San Francisco.

"I will make your excuses for you," he said, before Nathan could speak. "This evening, when you land, check on the first available ship out. It may seem like a great sum of money I've entrusted to you, but be frugal—second class should be adequate. I shall wire the Metropolitan in New York to reserve you like accommodations there. You should be arriving by the time the schools reopen and you will be informed of what arrangements I have been able to make for you. Good voyage, son."

"Father," Nathan said grimly, "don't hate me for what I've done."

"Hate you," Nazareth said, softening. "I could never hate you, my boy. I was just about your age when I first experimented with life. It was a grave mistake. I—we—have never discussed this before. I just don't want you making the same mistake. What I am saying is that what transpires between two people should be their concern only. I do not condone what you did any more than I condone the manner in which you childishly boasted about whom you had been with. A gentleman, no matter his age, would have protected the lady's reputation. I am unsure why Mrs. O'Lee did it, nor do I desire to delve into the subject any further."

"Thank you, father." Nathan sighed gratefully. "I shall remember this discussion."

A week later, sick of his confined second-class quarters, he recalled the discussion very well. He was flabbergasted to find Liberty on the same vessel. He kept as their concern only the knowledge that he shared a first-class cabin for the remainder of the voyage.

Oliver Ames was in a bargaining mood. He needed Liberty to place stock bought on margin with certain political parties to gain support for the Union Pacific. He could not promise her Silas Seymour's head on a golden platter; on the other hand, now that Grant had defeated Horatio Seymour for the presidency, Silas was no longer that important to him.

If Nathan had stirred up some of Liberty's old spirit, being back in the middle of a political and business battle did the rest. She was so successful that a dividend of eighty per cent was declared on her stock, which she immediately reinvested. Moreover, she arrived back in San Francisco in April with a present from the George Pullman Company that was the immediate envy of Leland Stanford.

Arrogantly, Stanford wired Pullman: Was lavishly decorated car recently delivered here meant as present for president of Central Pacific?

Hardly! was the one-word reply.

Stanford remained arrogant even when the Associates had to seek Liberty's help in a mysterious guerrilla war that had broken out between the Union Pacific and Central Pacific forces.

"It's mainly a racial confrontation between the Irish

and Chinese," Stanford insisted. "We can handle it ourselves."

"Oh, Leland," Bull Crocker scoffed, "a tenth of the CP's crew, mainly foremen, are also Irish. When those damn UP men lay their blasts too far to the right, it's not only Chinese, it's them and horses and wheelbarrows and picks that blow up."

"I maintain the Mormons are behind all this trouble," Collis Huntington declared. "To keep work contracts for their own people they fought like hell to keep the Chinese coming from the west and the hell-on wheels rowdies coming in from the east."

"Ain't that way no more, Collis," Crocker advised sadly. "The grading crews are only a hundred feet apart. The Irish bombard the Chinese with rocks and frozen clods of earth, so the Chinese roll boulders down on their right-of-way. At night comes the gunshots, explosions and slit throats. No. Because there are hundreds of thousands of government subsidy dollars to be gained with every mile of track laid, I say someone with the UP is giving the orders."

Liberty could believe that but held her silence. They had not listened to her before. Why should they now?

"How could you be so close and not be joining?" she asked.

"Because the UP grading crews are not following Congress's order. We're on a direct line with Promontory Point and they're running north. If we keep laying track at the rate we've been going we'll be to the Point by May first."

Stanford scoffed. "Are you taking into consideration the delay these blasts and killings are costing us?"

"Yes," Crocker replied. "This meeting will bear fruit if Mrs. O'Lee can make Ames see the damage the war is costing him as well."

Liberty was sure that Oliver Ames was being purposely kept in the dark. She wired him a detailed report and he went into a rage. He immediately wired General Dodge for an explanation of the UP's failure to run toward Promontory Point. He was wired back: Durant's orders. Crews also unhappy over non-payment of back wages.

Ames wired Dodge back to disregard Durant and change the line back towards Promontory Point. Then he wired Durant that he wanted him and Seymour to cease the "unnecessary" warfare. The message was delivered to Robert Porter, who smiled and instantly burned it. He did not expect to see Durant for some little time. For at that moment, as Porter well knew, Durant's train was creaking up Bear River Divide. It would soon be under attack. Some would call the attack a kidnap attempt; some would reason that it came in response to Durant's refusal to hand over back pay. But Robert Porter would see it as sweet revenge against an old enemy.

One thing Porter did not know was that Durant was a million in arrears to Brigham Young's Mormons; to stall them, he had agreed to turn his eyes the other way and let them rid their land of whores, harlots and gamblers.

The explosions started seconds after Porter burned Ames's wire. Porter, stooping to the level of the window ledges, scuttled to the vestibule of the office car and peered out. Three tent saloons were in smoldering shambles, with several Irishmen buried alive.

The camp had gone mad. Hundreds of men were running about, firing rifles and pistols in the air. Porter cowered for an instant, then stepped out to the platform and barked at the nearest man, "What's going on?"

"War, man! Ole Crazy May's been running her girls up track to service the chinks and the boys don't like it. Everybody knows that all chinks got the sickness. She was warned, but must have got some of her chink friends to blow up her rivals. We'll find those yellow bastards and then go up track and kill a few more."

"You'll do no such thing," Porter roared. He jumped down and pushed his way through the surging crowd to get to Crazy May's tents and wagons.

The Mormon workmen had been planting the rumor about the Chinese for days. Maybelle had laughed it off, telling Carter Hoyt that the "men earn their money like horses and then act like asses."

That night they acted like berserk apes. Those without guns grabbed up what was at hand—spades, crowbars, spikes, picks, even splintered sections of rail. They practically destroyed Crazy May's. Men who may have worked side by side were now enemies. A man who had lain with one of the girls the night before now bashed at her skull without remembrance. Carter Hoyt sat stupidly grinning at the poker table; suddenly, bullets pierced his cards and plowed into his chest and stomach.

It was a night of total mayhem and carnage of vast proportions. Estimates of the dead and wounded ran into the thousands.

Robert Porter found Maybelle badly beaten next to her bed. Stunned, he sat down and cradled her into his arms. She blinked, unsure at first at who was comforting her, then smiled thinly.

"Robert," she said, "tonight I have seen the real savages of this new world. I should have died with the Indians. We are killing and driving from this land a gentle people we have taught to be savages because we are basically savage. A hundred years from now men won't even want your iron horse and rails. It will go like the buffalo, like the Indians, like the gold out of the ground. They won't be missed until it is too late . . ." She was silent for a long moment. Then her voice was fainter. "Pocket . . . best this way . . ."

And she was gone. He knew what he would find in her pocket. He had come near destroying it. It was a wire from Liberty O'Lee asking Maybelle to meet her when the two lines joined so that she could learn more of her past. It had been too stark a reminder to Robert Porter that the life he had found with Maybelle would be coming to an end. Now that worry had been taken from him.

Through blurry eyes he saw a pair of hob-nailed boots plant themselves firmly in front of him. He looked up into the grief-stricken face of Terrible Terry O'Bannon. Each man had been the other's rival for Maybelle's favors; now, out of respect for her, they joined in a moment of silence.

"Will you help me bury her properly?" Robert sobbed.

"Aye, that I'll be doing. And then what, Mr. Porter?"

"You'll order every tent owner, barkeep, prostitute and gambler to be gone by dawn or I'll kill everyone of them personally."

19

The west was to be joined with the rest of the union by ribbons of iron. Someone who wanted the meeting of the Central Pacific and Union Pacific to be strictly a California celebration suggested that the last spike driven be made of California gold. But which railroad would supply the spike? Even after the race was over, this question remained—a vestige of the fierce competition between them.

When the Governor Stanford Special shrilled out of Sacramento station the morning of May sixth, Leland Stanford's drawing-room car held a wide assortment of golden spikes and silver-plated sledgehammers in satin-lined cases. Stanford had ordered his entire private car redecorated to rival the private Pullman car of Liberty O'Lee.

May eighth was to be a day of jubilation throughout the United States, the biggest since Lee had surrendered to Grant at Appomattox. Most people could barely grasp the fact that a double strand of iron rails now stretched from coast to coast.

America waited . . . and waited . . . and waited.

"This is reprehensible," Stanford stormed. "Where

are the Union Pacific people? Where is General Dodge?"

For once the Casement brothers decided to let Robert Porter be a spokesman.

"A slight delay, governor," Porter stammered. "A bit of track in Weber Canyon was washed out by a flood and a bridge was weakened. The trains from the east will arrive as soon as the repairs are made."

The explanation for the delay seemed reasonable enough. The Central Pacific train had arrived in a drizzle that soon pattered into a downpour and alternated with fog and high winds for thirty-six hours. But it was too late to call off the celebration plans in Sacramento, so Stanford did not bother to send back a wire notifying Crocker that things would be held up for a while.

A second excursion and supply train arrived from Reno. Despite the rain, the erection of fourteen gaily decorated tent saloons, was begun.

Robert Porter complained about them to Mark Hopkins. Hopkins replied:

"I sympathize with the problems you've had with such establishments, sir, but the tents are here for the purpose of the celebration and I must remind you that they sit on Central Pacific property."

Porter, angered, turned the festivities for that evening over to the Casements, who set up a champagne banquet in a UP diner and sent over a procession of curtained carriages to bring the Stanford party aboard. To the chagrin of Leland Stanford, Liberty O'Lee was the most honored among the dignitaries. Stanford, as usual, had a few hostile things to say. After dinner, for example, he declared that the subsidies given the Central Pacific by the government had been more of a hindrance than a help.

Dan Casement, who knew not a mile of track could have been laid without the government dole, growled a reply.

"Mr. President," he said, "if government money has been such a big detriment to the building of your road, I move you, sir, that you return it to the government with your compliments."

An outraged Stanford returned to his car.

"Gentlemen," Liberty said soothingly, "if we are still detained tomorrow evening I would be honored by your joining me in my car for dinner."

"Thank you, ma'am," Jack Casement said, "and we can accept your invitation right now. The Durant train won't roll until the tenth."

In actual fact it was vanity that had kept Thomas Durant in his palatial car at Devil's Gate. General Dodge had resolved the so-called guerrilla war on May fifth. Most, if not all of the trouble, had been initiated by workers frustrated in their demands for back pay. These workers had then attempted to kidnap Durant. When this attempt had failed, they—not a "flood"—had ripped up track in Weber Canyon. Dodge had made peace by going over Durant's head and personally guaranteeing all the back wages due.

Durant had been infuriated by the general's refusal to consult him before acting. "You'll pay for this Dodge!"

"Listen, you, nothing would please me more than to get you out of my bloody hair. Go on across and take the work train down to Promontory Point. You can even have my sleeping car if you want it.

"Just get your ass moving."

"Oh, no you don't," Durant ranted. "I see your game. You want me ridiculed. I'm not going in any damn boxcar. No! I *am* the Union Pacific and shall ride in state."

"You're a crock of shit," Dodge muttered, as he walked away.

Dodge could not understand why Oliver Ames himself had not come to represent the line. Only Thomas Durant knew that. The man's ego was such that he had blackmailed Ames into staying away by threatening to have the secretary of the treasury personally investigate the "sales" of Crédit Mobilier stock to congressmen. Ames had quickly announced his decision not to go to Utah.

Liberty's dinner party was lavishly successful. The Pullman car itself, with its mahogany paneling, red plush furniture, velvet drapes, crystal candle sconces and teakwood tables, drew considerable attention, and the fact that Poong Soo and Wang Wu could serve fifty excellent meals out of its cubicle kitchen swelled the response to amazement. A question uppermost in many minds was where did Liberty sleep. She was happy to demonstrate. Several ceiling panels hid noiseless pulleys that could lower curtained double beds. If need be, she could accommodate a dozen or more overnight guests.

Two dinner guests brought Liberty both joy and consternation. One was a surprise guest.

An hour before her affair was to begin the Chinese work camp, a discreet two miles to the west, erupted with such noise that a new fray with the Irish workers was feared. The turmoil was caused by the arrival of a one-car train, however. It rode slowly through the Chinese camp while tong agents threw from its windows thousands of red-paper-wrapped coins. That mission accomplished, the train chugged in and came to a stop behind the Governor Stanford Special.

The single car was decorated with the flags of both the Ch'ing Dynasty and the House of Soong. Tong agents poured from it, their arms laden with brightly wrapped gifts for the dignitaries. Then Kai Soong emerged. He stepped to the ground, looked about, then started toward Stanford's car. Liberty saw him from her Pullman and her heart beat faster. Mark Hopkins recognized him and shouted for Stanford to come out of his car onto its platform.

Stanford stood there in his shirtsleeves and arrogantly waited for Kai Soong to walk the whole way alone.

Kai Soong bowed deeply to both men.

"Honorable sirs, stormy seas delayed our arrival from China for your ceremonies. Still, in the name of Emperor P'u Yi, I bring gifts to honor this great occasion."

"It isn't until tomorrow," Stanford said curtly and went back inside his car.

Mark Hopkins was highly embarrassed. The president of the United States had not seen fit to send an official representative, but the emperor of China had.

"I am happy, Kai Soong, that our delay here has made it possible for you to share in our celebration. Your emperor does us honor. What we have accomplished is in great measure due to the fidelity and industry of his people."

Kai Soong kowtowed. Hopkins's brief words would be the only recognition given the Chinese for their part in building the railroad.

"And now," Hopkins went on, "five cars up I think you will find an old friend."

Liberty felt reborn. She was almost sorry she had to go ahead with the dinner party, because she would have loved to spend the time alone with Kai Soong. Still, he was there, and she was able to speak to him occasionally, even though Robert Porter dominated a good deal of her attention in a somewhat maudlin manner. Porter had already told her about Maybelle's death. Tastelessly, he repeated the story, as if he were getting a certain vicarious thrill out of shocking Liberty with its details.

When at last alone with Kai Soong Liberty sighed: "I'm glad now that Howard Tedder didn't come out for the ceremony, Kai Soong. I wouldn't have wanted him to hear how Maybelle lived and died. I had hopes of reuniting them, but now . . ." She shrugged.

"Yes, it is best this way, Chu-chee," Kai Soong said. There was a worried note in his voice. "It must also be put from your mind. Let her rest in peace and Howard's memory of her as a little girl stay as it was."

"I suppose you're right. But Lord, Porter almost ruined the party for me."

Kai Soong smiled. "I shall wash him from your mind with words of great joy. Ta Soong met my boat with an offering of a thousand tea-cakes. The House of Soong is blessed with a grandson. My son has given me the honor of announcing this to you and to say that the baby's name shall be recorded in the family records as Kai Ku Soong—blessed grandson of the house."

"Oh, Kai," she cried, "I am so happy for you."

"Your happiness gives me happiness, Chu-chee."

He was silent a long moment. Each wanted the other desperately, but each was too timid to say so.

"Will you stay?" Liberty finally whispered.

"Not this night, Chu-chee," and again his voice held a troubled note. He took her hand and kissed it gently. "I wish you a glorious sleep and successful day tomorrow."

Just knowing that he was there afforded her a glorious sleep.

* * *

The day dawned flawless. By mid-morning the tent saloons were doing a good business in rotgut whisky, while elsewhere, in their special trains, the nabobs sipped champagne. Excitement stirred as smoke was seen on the horizon, but it proved to be only an excursion train from Salt Lake City, loaded with sightseers looking, in part, for the free lunch the Central Pacific had offered. By mid-afternoon most everyone was well-fed, quite high or drunk, and very bored with waiting. A thirty-foot gap in front of the flag-draped Governor Stanford was prepared for a ceremony that was taking ages to begin. Telegraph instruments chattered with impatient inquiries from all over the east and mid-west.

Finally, late in the day, more smoke was seen on the horizon, and this time the Union Pacific special did wheeze in—slowly, as if it were quite on time. As it began to disgorge its dignitaries, they were soundly booed.

Durant had a splitting headache. He didn't mind telling anyone who would listen that it was Dodge who should be booed and not himself. Immediately, then insistently, he demanded to know why the ceremony wasn't moving faster now that he had arrived.

"What's the delay now?"

"They're trying to get everyone out of the saloons."

"What's the delay now?"

"They can't agree on which of the golden spikes to use."

"What's the delay now?"

"A bunch of pettiness over whether a Mormon elder should get to say a prayer too."

Kai Soong questioned the delay too. He asked Liberty about it.

"That's the delay," Liberty said, pointing to where Stanford and Hopkins were testily debating a point with Durant and Seymour. "It's disgusting. Leland started it by declaring that he would drive the final spike as president of the Central Pacific. Durant said, oh, no, he wouldn't, whereupon Hopkins pointed out first that Stanford was the highest official present, Durant being merely the *vice*-president of the Union Pacific, and then that they were the first to be incorporated and began construction earlier.

"So then, Seymour claimed that the UP road was much longer and more important to the national destiny. Oh, Lord, I hate that man so much I had to walk away or forget that I was a lady and spit in his face."

"You have reason to hate and fear him," Kai Soong said darkly.

Before Liberty could comment Mark Hopkins came bustling by.

"What is it now, Mark?" she asked.

"Durant is positively refusing to help with the connection. He told us we could do what we like, but there would be no joint celebration. Leland wants me to get the spikes so that we can go ahead."

"Damn them," Liberty stormed. She gathered up her skirts and marched over to the arguing men like an avenging schoolteacher.

"The country waits while you two make asses out of us all."

"Madam," Silas Seymour put in acidly, "the matter hardly concerns you."

"Shut up," she snapped. She glared him down until he cowered. "You are a dead man, Seymour—it is only a question of time before the courts bury you and your filth." She drew a deep breath to control her quivering rage, then turned more quietly to Stanford and Durant. "If you two are not driving in those spikes together within five minutes, the reporters here are going to start hearing how each of these lines has been financially operated."

Twenty minutes later a bystander asked a familiar question: "What's the delay now?"

Someone answered him:

"Damn preacher! Old goat is reciting most of the history of the country since the pilgrims landed. Hell, we could have had another drink."

People drifted away. As it was, only about thirty saw Stanford swing a hammer at the spike, miss, grunt and hand the sledge to Durant. Durant, grimacing against his headache, swung and also missed.

The process was too wearying for Terrible Terry O'Bannon. He grabbed the sledge and came down smartly on the spike. The soft metal went into the ground and flattened out. O'Bannon put his big foot over it and raised the sledge as a signal the job had been done.

Bedlam now broke forth from all six hundred people milling about. In the thankful din they set up—at last, it was over—few saw Terrible Terry remove the gold, replace it with a real spike and thus actually unite the lines.

The engineers blew their whistles and inched their locomotives forward until their cowcatchers symbolically touched. Then, from the speaker's platform, Stanford asked for silence. Having been denied the right to orate before, he was not about to miss the opportunity now.

Liberty could not bear this final ritual; it was pompous and promised to be interminable. She returned to her Pullman car, hot and tired and disgusted. At the rate Stanford's speech was going Kai Soong would never be able to present the emperor's gifts and she saw that as a great insult.

The car was cool and she let down one of the beds

to rest for just a moment. She would live to see Seymour hanged; of that she had no doubt. Now her mind was awhirl with all of the people who should have been here sharing in this day of celebration but were not.

In San Francisco, Ta Soong looked at his newborn son and recalled the first Chinese he had taken to work on the railroad. He was thankful that his son would never have to endure a like undertaking.

In Sacramento Bull Crocker drank a silent toast to himself. He would let Leland Stanford have the glory. He was satisfied and proud that he had helped bring about the realization of Crazy Judah's impossible dream.

Howard Tedder did not indulge his pride at having designed the snowsheds. He was too busy drawing up plans for the home he had been commissioned to build in San Francisco as a surprise present for Liberty from the House of Soong. He greatly approved of the location Ta Soong had been able to purchase on Nob Hill. It towered above and looked down on the mansion of Lady Pamela.

Nazareth Tedder, in the next room, sat and gazed with pride at the report he had from Nathan's school The boy was making brilliant marks.

Across town, Selena sat cursing the day the railroad was started.

In New York City, Collis Huntington put down his pen as the gun salute in the street below began. His eyes were misty; he snorted and turned back to the account books. Now the real test was coming. To make the railroad profitable without government subsidy loans.

At his country estate Oliver Ames offered his brother

Oakes a drink. His toast was a true measure of his feelings for that day. "Goodbye, Thomas Durant. You are no longer of use to me!"

In Greenfield, Massachusetts, a woman rocked in the parlor of a white house. All day she had sat looking at the spire of St. James Church, at the same time waiting for the whistles to blow from the Boston & Maine roundhouse. The whistles blew. Anna Judah's hands trembled as she put on her hat and shawl and began to walk to her husband's grave. She looked at the church clock and saw that it was three p.m. On that day twenty-two years before, also at about three p.m., she and Ted Judah had been married. Whatever meaning the completion of the railroad held for others, it was, to Anna Judah, a fitting anniversary present.

Following the railroad boom came . . .

THE LAND RUSHERS

THE LAND RUSHERS is the seventh book in the series THE MAKING OF AMERICA and chronologically follows THE BUILDERS.

THE LAND RUSHERS came in hordes when the U.S. Government threw open the hitherto protected Indian lands in Oklahoma Territory. There were the "Boomers" and the "Sooners"; there were homesteaders, cattlemen, outlaws, card sharks, dancehall girls, dudes and debutantes. All of them, the good and the bad, were caught up in a raging land-fever, ready to run roughshod over anything that stood in their way. Often, the victim was the Indian.

Fighting the tide were a dedicated few such as Miranda Woodrowe and her part-Indian husband, Grand, who became a martyr in the cause of Indian rights. Miranda herself, searching for the secret of her birth, found herself swept away by a strange and perverse passion in that wild and turbulent time.

Seventh in the series
A DELL BOOK ON SALE NOW

BE SURE TO READ

HEARTS DIVIDED

HEARTS DIVIDED is the fifth in the new series, THE MAKING OF AMERICA. Many of the absorbing characters from THE FORTY-NINERS reappear in this romantic saga of the war that set lover against lover.

Danny O'Lee, the young prospector of THE FORTY-NINERS goes in search of his missing brother, and becomes deeply involved in the raging Civil War, and with a mysterious girl who may have been his brother's lover, and with a beautiful black abolitionist.

Finally, after many hair-raising adventures, Dan O'Lee finds his beloved brother—fighting on the other side—at the bloody Battle of Shiloh, a turning point in the little-known Civil War in the West.

There, a hero is born, a villain is unmasked and a love is renewed, while the Union finds a general in an obscure, cigar-smoking, whisky-drinking sphinx of a man named U.S. Grant. Here is another compelling novel in the acclaimed series, THE MAKING OF AMERICA.

A DELL BOOK ON SALE NOW

THIRD IN
THE MAKING OF AMERICA
SERIES:

THE CONESTOGA PEOPLE

Filled with hope, they headed Westward into unknown danger with Barry Fitzpatrick at the fore. It was the largest wagon train ever to leave Independence, and it was in trouble before it had traveled ten miles Westward. Among the diverse people aboard the Conestoga wagons were: a cold-blooded murderer, a 14-year-old wanton, an aristocratic lady with a stolen treasure, a mulatto with a secret white lover—and one wily and powerful man who swore the wagons would never get through.

In this novel, recreating the drama of the great Westward trek, we meet historic figures such as John C. Fremont, the famed explorer, his wise and beautiful wife Jessie Benton Fremont, and Jim Bridger, the legendary frontiersman. In vivid detail, we experience the saga of a turbulent journey toward a rendezvous with destiny.

THE CONESTOGA PEOPLE continues the epic of the great Westward thrust begun in THE WILDERNESS SEEKERS and THE MOUNTAIN BREED.

A DELL BOOK ON SALE NOW